T0374221

USURPER

Other titles by Aaron T. Brownell

Reflection

Contention; a Sara Grey Tale

The Long Path

Progression; a Sara Grey Tale

Shadow of the Fall

The Sons of Sava; A Kristin Hughes Adventure

The Black Map

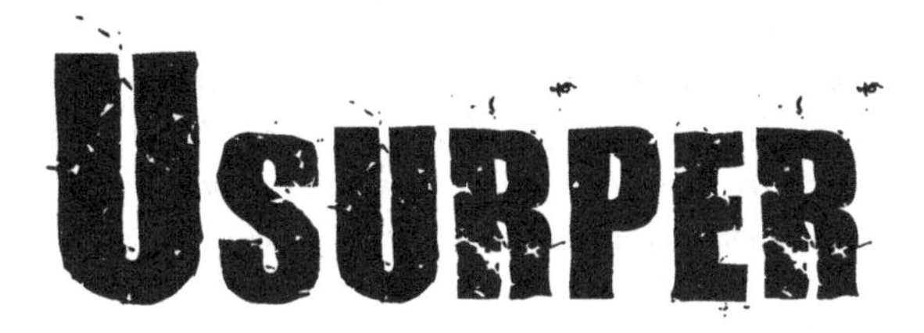

BOOK ONE IN THE BARREN SANDS SAGA

AARON T. BROWNELL

iUniverse®

USURPER
BOOK ONE IN THE BARREN SANDS SAGA

iUniverse books may be ordered through booksellers or by contacting:

iUniverse
1663 Liberty Drive
Bloomington, IN 47403
www.iuniverse.com
844-349-9409

ISBN: 978-1-6632-6311-7 (sc)
ISBN: 978-1-6632-6312-4 (e)

Library of Congress Control Number: 2024910105

Print information available on the last page.

iUniverse rev. date: 07/18/2024

Thank You:
Jeff, thanks for the hard work.

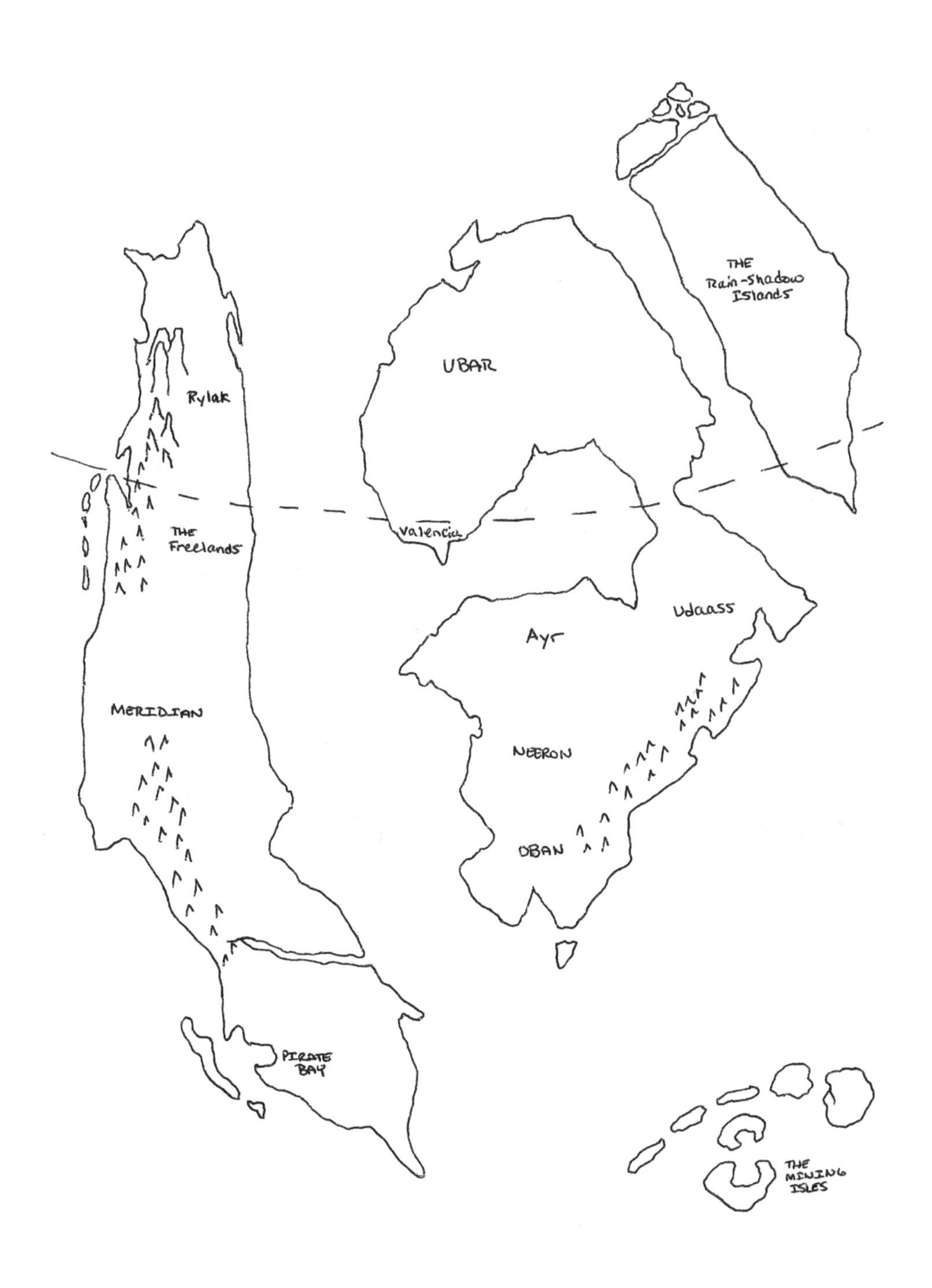
THE
Rain-Shadow
Islands
UBAR
Rylak
THE
Freelands
Valencia
Udaass
Ayr
MERIDIAN
NEERON
OBAN
PIRATE
BAY
THE
MINING
ISLES

Time, time, and half a time beyond the next dawn, a black tide sweeps the land. Only thaumaturgy intertwined can rebury a long dead house.

Darius
The Second Book of Prophesies
Number 47

Chapter One

Looking down through a break in the trees at the secluded stone and timber cabin situated in a grass-lined clearing, the waxing moon gave just enough illumination for the practiced eyes to gauge that it was inhabited. A night owl alarmed from a tree to the west of the observation point, only adding to the mystery of the scene.

"One man in the cabin?"

Quinn put a beefy hand under his chiseled chin and pondered the building.

"That's what I said, one man. About six feet tall and a touch over fourteen stone. We've fought way bigger men than that."

Bernard leaned against a tree just behind and down from the low rise that Quinn was laying on, secluded in the shadows.

"The last time that you were sure it was only one man, I got knifed in the kidney."

Bernard shook his head and looked at his friend as if he were a naive peasant girl. From his position in the shadows, Quinn didn't notice.

"Okay, fine, I lied. There are truly eight sound men of arms in the building. Sadly, if we attempt to bring them all in, the bounty sheet will still only pay us for one of them. So, in reality, there's only one of concern."

"So, there are other people in the building?"

"I don't know. Everyone that we talked with along the way said that the man traveled alone. You were there for all these conversations too. Besides, there's not a lot of movement or noise down there."

Quinn scratched at the stubble on his chin. He needed a shave, and a bath. It had been days since they had been anywhere near civilization.

"True. It does seem quiet enough. Let's get this done and head to town so we can get paid."

"I like the sound of that!"

Rotating up onto his knees, Quinn picked up the massive longbow that was his natural weapon of choice and leaned it against a tree already supporting his quiver of heavy-shafted arrows. Bringing his arm back in a fluid motion, he gripped the handle of a large battle axe and squeezed it tightly. The sinew of his fingers and palm groaned momentarily as he sunk his grip into the weapon's wooden shaft.

Without as much as a second alarm from the owl, the massive mercenary moved from the kneeling position to that of being under motion. Stepping sure and sound, never removing his eye from the work ahead of him, he traveled the dark edge of the tree line until he closed in on the nearest edge of the cabin. As he closed in on the structure it became clear that his friend's intelligence of the event was correct. No sound or movement came from the building that would give away multiple people.

Quinn's trained eye scanned every inch of his surroundings. Nothing out of the ordinary could be sensed around the small, woodsman's cabin. With eyes well-adjusted to the moonlight, he could tell the tracks around the door were only enough for one man. The smell of the chimney smoke lingered alone in the clear night air. No smells of killed game, which would be required for a number of men, were to be found. This was a one-man operation.

The briefest shift in shadows made Quinn reorient his vision to one side. The subtle movement in the darkness around him told him that Bernard had made his way through to the rear of the cabin. Quinn paused for a count of six to allow Bernard enough time to acquire a place that he liked.

At the ending of the count, and sensing that everything was right in the world, Quinn took two quick strides to the solid wooden door on the cabin's front and pulled back the battle axe. Looking at the door a second time as he planted his strike foot, Quinn paused in dropping the full power of the weapon. The door was thick, probably oak or beech. Built to keep the forest bears from coming inside. If capable of such a thing, it would probably just laugh at the first couple blows from the battle axe.

Deciding on a change in plans, he relaxed. Pulling one hand from the battle axe, Quinn reached out for the door clasp. As he had expected, the clasp slid sideways without resistance. People, even those on the run, seldom secured doors behind them this deep into the woods. In the deep of the woods, it was all mercenaries, rouges, and scoundrels avoiding one crown or another. There were some good folk about, but they mostly stayed to the main roads, where it was safer.

Being right-handed, Quinn closed his left eye. He wanted to maintain some night vision; in case a chase became necessary. Readying the battle axe a second time, he pushed the door open and stepped inside. By the hearth, a man could be seen hunched over a small fire. Equal amounts of smoke and light were escaping from the chimney and fouling the small cabin's interior. The man, startled by the presence of an intruder, secured his grip on a hand-and-a-half sword propped against the hearth stones. Looking back, he took in the image of a man filling the entire doorway, holding a black-bladed battle axe at the ready. The rouge's practiced eye could tell that the man in the doorway knew his business.

Springing to his feet with the vigor of a much younger man, the sword came slicing through the air in an overhand arc, from the high guard position. Quinn closed with a step and blocked the blow from underneath with the top edge of the battle axe's curved blade. With the man now close, Quinn could tell that a touch over fourteen stone was a bit on the light side. His opponent was a solid, heavily built man. No matter. Bernard had been right about one thing; he had squared off against much bigger men than this one.

Quinn snapped his head forward with a quick and controlled motion, pounding his forehead into the other man's nose. A crack of bone preceded a fountain of blood. The man staggered back a step or two, allowing room for Quinn to finish the job. Flipping his battle axe around in his hand, he swung the weapon up much like one would swing a hunk of log, slamming the heavy end into the man's head. Just as expected from the blow, the man hit the floor of the small cabin like a large sack of cabbages. Quinn looked down at the immobile object and wondered if he might have hit him a little bit too hard. In the end, it didn't matter. A body was as good as a person for collecting on a bounty sheet.

"I think you broke him?"

Quinn turned to see Bernard in the doorway, swords at the ready.

"He wasn't much of a challenge. Since you didn't have to do anything, make sure we're still alone. And then bind him, just for good measure."

Bernard slid the two short swords that were his go-to weapons up and over his left shoulder and into the dual scabbard that held them.

"It's not my fault the cabin has no back door. What do you want to do if he turns out to be beyond repair?"

"Run him through. He was going to end up in the next place sooner or later anyway. I'm going back to get my bow."

"Sounds good to me."

Quinn made his way back through the woods to where he had placed his large longbow with no more noise than he had made coming out of it. It was typical of less-ethical men to wait for an advantage before coming to the assistance of a so-called comrade. They would wait until fighting favored them. Quinn had seen it too many times to count. He wasn't in the least forgiving when it came to dealing with that sort.

Retrieving his longbow and quiver of arrows, he paused in the darkness and sensed his surroundings. Even the owl had gone away from this place. It was silent as the grave. The dead silence seemed appropriate considering the circumstances. He snatched up Bernard's leather bag and moved on quietly to the spot just off the main path where they had secured their horses. Looking and listening before entering the opening where the horses were tied, he was happy to see that they were still where they had been left. Usually, unguarded horses didn't stay around very long.

Wandering back to the little wood and stone cabin, Quinn took a moment to consider the way life had unfolded for him. He enjoyed the adventure of being a wandering mercenary for hire. Chasing down thieves and bandits paid handsomely. Still, it did lack any kind of permanence. Oh well, he had Bernard for that. His friend was the good sort, and a boon companion.

Quinn usually never thought on such things. Maybe it was the darkness of the woods? It had been a long day; it must just be the darkness in the woods. He didn't know much about the specific area they were in. The woods could be haunted? Maybe they had some type of spell placed over them? Since the thick forest by the sea was a main travel way between the great sand kingdom of Ubar and Ayr's capital city of Kanash, it seemed unlikely. Still, there was something strange about the place. It was a good thing that they weren't staying there long.

Tying the horses up outside the little cabin, Quinn reentered to find Bernard lounging by the fire and their prize rolled up in some old vegetable sacks.

"Run though?" Quinn asked, looking down at an obvious corpse.

"Yup."

"Memento Mori."

"Yup."

"It'll be light soon. We can take him into Gryazi and drop him with the local alderman. Or, I guess, we could run north to that town by the sea."

"I'm for Gryazi. Bigger town. More chance of finding work or reward."

Quinn rolled his eyes at the comment. It seemed that they always had something to do. And it wasn't like he was unfed.

"You look around?"

"Nope. This isn't the type of place that's stocked with food. There is a rabbit on the spit though. Tasty rabbit. I left you some."

Quinn grunted in response. He walked over to the hearth and yanked a leg off the rabbit carcass. Gnawing on the leg, he looked about the inside of the small building. Bernard was right. Nobody was leaving anything here for later. He looked in some baskets, plus under both a bench and makeshift bed. Nothing. Turning back toward the hearth, he noticed a small leather pack. It wasn't theirs. Must have come in with the dead man. Snatching up the pack, Quinn began to go through it. He pulled out a knife that he tossed to Bernard. There was a half-eaten loaf of some dark-colored bread that he tossed to Bernard as well. Bernard snifted at it and then tossed it into the fire.

Then, from the bottom of the otherwise empty bag, he pulled out a metal tube. It was maybe two inches round, and a foot long. One end of the tube was secured with a screw-on cap. The cap held the seal from the Great Temple of Drakchi. Quinn had seen the seal before. Under the seal was another seal, which he had not seen before, and writing that looked to be one of the old languages. Quinn could instantly sense that whatever had landed the man on a bounty sheet was in this tube. Unscrewing the cap, Quinn turned the tube over into his free hand.

There was a pause, then a rolled-up piece of paper slid out. The paper was old, as old as the tube. It was the type of paper which men of the last age used to make mechanical drawings on. Unrolling the paper, he stared at the image.

"What is it?" Bernard asked, looking over his shoulder.

"I'm not sure."

A six-sided object was represented on the parchment in true form, with uniform-sized holes equally spaced around its face. Round, cylindrical objects were circling around the center object, as if being directed toward the individual holes they were associated with. It was hard to tell from the picture what the six-sided device was for. Quinn ran his fingers along the edge of the paper and could tell that it had been ripped from a larger document.

"Maybe it's one of those new cannons people talk about?"

Bernard was speculating, as usual. Quinn stared at the image. Something deep down in his subconscious told him that he had seen this image before. Once, long ago, when he was too young to understand such things. He didn't know what it was, but he was sure that it being with this man was trouble.

Rolling the document up, he pushed it back into the metal tube and secured the cap. Quinn slid the tube into his quiver of arrows and shuffled the arrows so they looked natural again.

"It's almost daylight. I say we be on our way to Gryazi. Let's not mention this tube to anyone, for the time being."

Bernard nodded his head in agreement. His big friend was many things, but a worrier wasn't one of them. If he felt there was need for concern, then there was need for concern.

The two men threw the corpse of their bounty over Bernard's horse and put out the fire in the hearth. Light was just breaking out into the world as they came back to the main road leading south toward the small city of Gryazi. A man in a cart made his way by them on the road. He looked at the two sternly as he passed.

"He seems friendly."

"It's probably the dead man that's got him concerned," Quinn said without fanfare.

"Probably so."

Traffic on the road was light, and the two moved along quietly. They remained unbothered all the way out of the woods and onto the grassy valley that held the city. Two different patrols stopped them while crossing the open grasslands, inquiring about their business. Bernard produced the flyer for the men each time and explained that they were headed to the alderman's office. Both patrols let them pass. Both patrols lingered behind and watched them as they moved along. Quinn had wanted to ask why there were patrols in the area around the city but knew better than to ask too many questions in unfamiliar lands.

Riding into the city, they found it full of people. The streets and shops, back alleys and courtyards all teemed with life. Quinn had temporarily forgotten about the pressure of city life. He ran a hand through his thick blond hair, to get it out of his eyes, and sighed. His eyes scanned the crowds for trouble as they moved along. There was always trouble in the cities.

Tying up the horses in front of the building that they were headed for, they found both the alderman and the captain of the city guard to be in their offices. The two mercenaries made their way inside and sat their weapons on a side table by the armory guard, as was customary.

The armory guard looked down at the green ivy inlay on the heavy longbow and then up at Quinn.

"A gilded weapon. You with the Watchtower?"

Quinn looked down at his weapon and considered that he should probably get a cover for it.

"No. Not anymore."

"You a deserter?"

Quinn looked at the man in a way that made him instantly back down.

"No."

"Alright mister, I'm just asking questions that need asking. That's all."

Quinn was about to set the man straight when the captain of the city guard appeared and did it for him. Quinn and Bernard were shown into a side room, and the captain closed the door behind them.

"So, you found yourselves a dead man? Where did you find him?"

The captain seemed to be the jovial type, which was always nice.

"We came upon him in a small, woodman's cabin between here and the small town up by the sea. We followed him there, after talking to some folks we met on the road."

Bernard produced the bounty sheet that stated the dead man was wanted by someone important and handed it over to the captain. The captain read the whole flyer carefully, and then sat it down on his desk.

"It all seems legitimate enough. I think we must pay two of these a week lately."

"Where would you like us to put him?"

Bernard smiled a smile that said it was all just business.

"Out behind this building, you'll find a man that handles the dead. Tell him that I directed you there, and he'll take care of the body. Just a curiosity, why did you kill him? Did he resist?"

Quinn shrugged beefy shoulders.

"I only hit him twice. I don't think he had much fight in him."

"I guess not. The bounty sheet says that he was a thief and had something that needed to be returned. You find anything?"

Quinn shrugged again.

"The man is as he fell. If he is carrying something, then it's still on him. He did have a bag. A small leather one. It had a knife in it and a chunk of nasty bread. The loaf and the bag went into the hearth."

Bernard pointed over towards the table of weapons behind the door.

"The knife's on the table. Maybe that's what they're talking about in the flyer. You can have it if you want."

The captain thought for a moment.

"That's probably not a bad idea. If we end up needing to send something back to whoever issued the bounty sheet, then at least we'll have something to send them. Tell you what, go deliver the body. When you come back, I'll have your coin assembled."

"You wouldn't happen to know of a good public house in the city for afterward, would you?"

Bernard's smile was big and spoke of ale. The captain smiled back.

"Several."

Chapter Two

"The Ox and Plow?"

Bernard looked up at the wooden sign hung above the door to the public house which the captain of the guard had pointed them toward. The faded picture of an ox charging across a farmer's field with plow in tow still possessed enough life to let travelers know where they were entering, but just. His expression turned to suspicion.

"What?"

"I don't know. It sounds kind of rural."

Quinn dismissed the momentary notion to punch his friend in the side of the head. Granted, Gryazi wasn't the capital, but it also wasn't exactly the sticks.

"Considering we're next to the city gate leading to the south, it's on the cusp of being rural. Maybe whoever owns it was once a farmer?"

"See," Bernard said, happy that Quinn was agreeing with him.

"Still, it's an ale and a meal. Maybe even a bath and a bed."

"Maybe even a maiden."

Quinn slapped Bernard on the back and Bernard rocked forward onto his toes.

"See, that's the spirit."

The two men stepped across the dirt street and into the entryway of the building. With the opening of the door the sights, smells, and sounds of a half-full tavern washed over them. The smell of ale-soaked wood made Quinn smile.

Closing the door behind them, Quinn gave the establishment a good, solid look over. Everyone within view looked to be the usual sort found in a public house. They seemed mostly locals, which is what the guard captain had told them. The man behind the tavern bar came out from behind the long wooden-top slab and approached. Both Bernard and Quinn smiled with a neutral smile, and Bernard greeted the man as he got to them. The man was large and looked used to wading into the middle of rough situations. They both presumed he was the owner.

"Eating, drinking, or something else?"

The big man had a jovial sound in his voice.

"Definitely food and drink, please."

Bernard answered with equal jovialness.

"What type?"

"The local's fine, just make the cups as big as you can."

The man looked at Bernard and smiled.

"Those are the only kind we have. There's a table over by the hearth that you gentlemen can take your ease at."

The man pointed to a medium-sized wooden table with benches, on the right-hand side of a large stone hearth. Quinn nodded and stepped off toward the table. Bernard smiled at the man and handed him a full-weight gold coin from the local mint.

"That should get us started."

"Yes sir, it should indeed."

Quinn propped the longbow and his battle axe up in the corner of the room, directly behind where he was seated, and sat down with his back to the wall. It was his normal setting when in such places. It wasn't that he was paranoid. It was just that he liked to observe what was going on around him. Bernard tossed his big leather bag on the floor next to Quinn's weapons and plopped down on the opposing bench.

His friend had no more than settled in when a young woman appeared with metal drinking mugs the size of small pitchers. Quinn smiled and nodded respectfully to the woman as she sat the drinks down. Bernard thanked her for her trouble. She smiled shyly and skittered off back the way she had arrived.

"Ah, the absolute best part of this whole day."

Bernard took a large gulp and stretched a kink out of his back.

"Q, you didn't happen to notice if the young lovely had a ring in her lip, did you?"

Quinn smiled down into his ale glass. If his friend was one thing, it was consistent.

"She's probably old enough for the trade, but no, I didn't see one. I'm willing to bet that she's more likely the owner's daughter."

"Oh well, she seemed pretty enough to be a doxy."

"I wouldn't worry. The way you dropped the owner the coin, I'm sure one will be along shortly."

"Ah, city living."

The young girl reappeared and laid an assortment of bread and meat on the table. Quinn thanked her, and she smiled broadly before disappearing again.

It had been a long while since the two of them had been flush with coin. It had been even longer since they had come across a proper meal. Tonight was going to be enjoyed. Neither of them had any idea what tomorrow was going to bring. The unknown in it all made the adventures worthwhile. They both needed the adventure in it, which was why they got on as well as they did. It also helped them to carry on when times were lean, because something would be right around the corner.

Quinn had met Bernard several years back in a public house not so different from the one they were currently in. Bernard had crossed the wrong side of some local men and was receiving the beating of his life for it. Quinn had watched it all with passing interest, until it became clear that the group had no plans on stopping the beating. He waded in and put a blunt end to it all. He bandaged up his new acquaintance, expecting nothing more than a good story about some dumbfounded idea that had gone wrong. Instead, he gained a traveling companion.

It turned out that the two men together were the right fit. Where Quinn was a natural fighter and good with combat tactics, Bernard was crafty and soft-handed. Quinn was a military man, and Bernard was a burglar. Quinn carried a longbow and a battle axe, where Bernard carried short swords and a lock pick set. They were both good thinkers. Bernard was the natural talker of the two, which was fine with Quinn.

Quinn pulled off his hooded cloak, a staple of the Watchtower Guild uniform, and placed it atop Bernard's bag. Rolling his shoulders backward and forward, he flexed his whole upper body to get the knots out of it.

"Are we staying here or moving on?"

Bernard considered the question a moment.

"We should be in good shape for the next couple weeks. No reason not to stay and have a warm bed for the night."

"Good. I'm going to have a long, hot soak in a tub while you're handling your business with the doxies."

Bernard laughed heartedly.

"That sounds like a fantastic idea."

Bernard continued talking about something, but Quinn was no longer listening. His attention had been pulled to the front door. A group of men had come in who were even more out of place than they were. From their style of dress and the dark skin, they appeared to be Northerners. That wasn't strange, as people came south from the desert lands to both trade and travel. These men looked the traveling type.

The appearance of the one in the center of the throng said that he was important, maybe royalty? The man standing next to him was obviously his manservant. The others were guards. The large scimitars that they carried definitely gave them away as Northerners.

The public house owner pointed the group toward a large table on the opposite side of the hearth, and they began walking over. Quinn rolled his eyes, moving them from the group of men to Bernard, and Bernard instantly stopped talking. Bernard knew that Quinn's look said something was up.

The men stopped and shuffled to take up seats around the adjacent table. The important man took up a seat with his back toward the hearth, the same as Quinn had done. His manservant took up a seat on the same side of the table. The guards took up the remainder. Their initial conversation was conducted in the northern tongue and was the same as every other group of travelers. They were happy to be inside and sitting down. Bernard could tell without pause that they were the talking type.

"Greetings, travelers," Bernard offered up in a friendly tone. "What brings you down from the desert?"

The manservant made to speak, but the important man put a hand on his wrist to stop him. He knew that public houses were open to all, and as such had their own rules and customs. The king, in a public house, was equally as important as the farmer from the fields. Everyone was the same under the same roof. That was one of the good things that had come along with the current age.

"Marhoben, and greetings to you," the important man said smiling. "I am Kamal Nazari, of Ubar. These men are with me as I travel. How do you find this establishment?"

Bernard smiled pleasantly and started to continue, but Quinn cut him off.

"Crown Prince Nazari? It's nice to meet you and your company. I've heard that El Hataan is a beautiful city."

"It is. A true oasis in the middle of the desert."

"What has your troop moving through Ayr?"

The prince looked at Quinn curiously.

"I would have assumed that everyone from the area would know the answer to that question."

Bernard looked over at Quinn curiously as well. He hardly ever spoke with strangers. The young tavern girl reappeared from the edges, as a wraith sent to calm the mood. She spread a green and white gingham cloth over the prince's table and ran a fast hand over it to smooth it. A boy appeared behind her and began spreading out mugs of ale. A great goblet-styled pitcher of water was also placed on the table. Everyone paused as the two went about their work. When finished, the prince continued.

"I am on my way to Kanash, for the marriage of the king."

Bernard made a face.

"That explains all of the patrols we ran into. It's extra protection for those traveling to the wedding."

Both Quinn and the prince nodded in agreement.

"We're not actually from Ayr, sire. We just happened to stop here tonight, same as you."

Bernard was back in front of the conversation, so Quinn bowed out. The girl reappeared with an armload of small chickens and some loaves of bread. The food was scattered about the table before she was off again. Bernard was about to continue, but the girl came back with a medium-sized wheel of cheese for the prince, and fresh ale for Bernard and Quinn. As the girl placed the drink on their table, Quinn nodded in appreciation and thanked her properly. The girl smiled shyly and skittered off toward the kitchen. Bernard paid his friend no attention, but the interchange struck the prince as interestingly out of place for a pair of local travelers.

"So, where would two travelers be from, if not from Ayr?"

The question was casual enough, but definitely direct.

"My friend here is a Westlander," Bernard said, thumbing over at Quinn. "I am actually a Kraeten, though these days the world is our home."

The prince smiled while pulling a leg off the nearest chicken. It was a good, non-evasive, but meaningless answer.

"Currently, we're engaged as wandering mercenaries. We also tend to the random bounty sheet recovery, which is the business bringing us to Gryazi this night."

"So, blades for hire?" the prince said with equal parts amusement and suspicion.

"When the work suits us, yes. It's a free-spirited life."

The prince smiled broadly.

"I would agree that it is. The freedom to do as one chooses isn't given to most people."

Bernard gave the prince a politically neutral expression.

"I wouldn't say that it isn't given. It's more that most people don't act on the opportunities when they present themselves."

The manservant made a face that said people shouldn't argue with the prince. The prince, for his part, considered Bernard's statement for a moment.

"I agree with you, Bernard. Most people don't see opportunities when they appear."

"So, you said that you were here to collect a bounty sheet. Do you see it being a dangerous endeavor?"

The manservant was well-spoken but carried a more pronounced accent than the prince. Bernard laughed and then made a gesture with his hands.

"That work is all done, as they say. We finished the task today. We are, currently, in-between employments."

"You said you were traveling to Kanash for the wedding? Why didn't you stop into the house of the count? Certainly, they would have offered you more-comfortable accommodations than what you find here."

Quinn wiped the ale from his chin and smiled at the prince politely.

"We did, actually. Prince Jan Nosov, the Count of Gryazi, is the king's brother. He has already departed for the capital. So here we are, as they say."

"Bad timing," Bernard said with a laugh.

"Or, good timing, depending upon how you look at it. Besides, with kings, queens, and regents from all parts of the known world traveling these same routes to the capital, I'm sure that I'm not the only man of means staying in a public house this night."

Quinn began to make a face but neutralized it. The prince, however, noticed it well enough.

"Representatives from all the kingdoms, you say?"

"Yes, both rulers and regents from every kingdom in the known lands have been invited. It's rumored that King Gerald has even invited the Master of Drakchi, and the High Sorceress herself to the affair.

Quinn stayed quiet a moment, but the prince could tell that he was unhappy with what he was hearing.

"Rosalyn, you say?"

The prince and Bernard both looked at Quinn with curiosity. Not many people in the known lands called the High Sorceress of Maiden's Tower and Queen of the Freelands Folk by her given name. Well, not if they wanted to live a long life.

"You know the High Sorceress, Master Quinn?"

The manservant, whose name turned out to be Saleh, asked with open inquisitiveness. Quinn looked at him with a distant look, and a deep smile.

"I met her once, years ago."

"It has been said that, when she was young, she was the most beautiful woman in all of the known lands."

Quinn's deep smile turned distant.

"That would be an accurate statement. So, she's coming to Kanash?"

"The rumor is that she was invited," the prince answered. "If everyone who has been invited shows up, it will be the greatest gathering of power in the land during this age."

"This age has lasted this long because the powerful tend not to gather," Quinn responded with a distant quietness.

The prince inspected them both again, attempting to lighten the mood.

"You two seem the good sort. And, as you say, you're in-between employments, so you should join our company for the evening. We can exchange stories of our adventures. Two world travelers such as yourselves will have had many adventures, I'm sure."

Quinn nodded stoically, and Bernard laughed deeply.

"We've had numerous adventures," Bernard said, still laughing. "We would be honored to share your table, Prince Nazari."

Chapter Three

Quinn sat with his back against the outside of the public house and watched the majestic yellow and orange colors of the morning sun play across the field outside the nearby gate. The bench he sat on wasn't the most comfortable thing he had ever come across, but it offered a good vantage point to the grasslands beyond the city gate. The morning air was warm and carried a light scent of evergreen. He was presently clean and had even managed to wash his clothes during the bath. Sitting there, life was as good as he needed it to be.

Some carts came and went. Men were headed out to work the fields. *The honest life of an honest man,* he thought as a man ambled by with his cart. *It must be a simpler life.* Quinn considered his thoughts for a moment. It wasn't that his life was dishonest, it just wasn't farmers-in-the-fields honest. Oh well, he liked the one that he had, and since he only got one life, it was just fine. He had had to make many hard choices to get this life. His father had told him many times when he was young that life was a series of hard choices. His father had been right.

The door to the public house opened and the owner stepped out with a bucket of slop for his pigs penned up out back. Quinn nodded at the man, and he responded with a smile and warm greeting. Even the owner of the public house seemed happy with his lot in life. *He, too, seems the good sort,* Quinn thought, watching the man disappear behind the side of the building. Quinn could just tell about people. He had always been a quick and accurate judge of men and women. It was a skill that had both served him well and kept him alive. His father had been the same way, though he used his gift in different ways.

The door opened again. Quinn didn't look over to see, as he figured it was the public house owner with another bucket of slop for his hogs.

"Morning."

Bernard looked rested, clean, and happy. Quinn could tell that his day was getting better by the minute. At least he didn't have to smell Bernard as they rode.

"Good morning. You look pleased with yourself."

"That bath idea that you had yesterday was just the ticket, old chum."

Bernard had read the term *old chum* in a volume one day, and now used it as Quinn's unofficial moniker.

"You do look clean."

"It's amazing how much scrubbing gets done when there are four hands doing the scrubbing."

They both laughed. Bernard walked over and handed Quinn a glass full of water. Sitting on the flat wooden bench, next to his friend, he ripped a round loaf of bread in two and handed over half.

"Here's to another good day above ground."

Quinn bit off about a third of his offering and began chewing. The bread was still warm.

"Are we square with the owner?" came out in garbled pieces as he chewed.

"What?" Bernard looked over at him funny as he finished chewing.

"You heard me."

Bernard smiled back in jest.

"Yup, we're all paid up. We can wander off whenever we choose."

Quinn took another bite.

"That's good."

The two sat and finished off their breakfast in a kind of quiet satisfaction. Each of them had known many days which had started off with nothing to eat, so now they enjoyed all the ones that didn't. Bernard finished his water and sat the cup on the ground next to the bench.

"So, what do you think? Where to next?"

Quinn shrugged.

"I don't exactly know. According to you, we have no need to work for a couple weeks, if we live quietly."

Bernard smirked, as he knew that the "quietly" part of the comment was pointed at him.

"So?"

"So, I was thinking that we might make our way south, toward Neeron."

Bernard nodded an acknowledgement. The city Fatezh was just inside the border of Neeron. The city had an old, and well-respected, temple. It dated to the previous age and held many important historic volumes.

"You feel like doing a little reading?"

"Yes, I do. It's been a while since anything useful went into my brain."

Bernard leaned his back against the wall and turned his head, that he might lower his voice to a secretive level.

"And research that piece of parchment?"

Quinn nodded slowly.

"And that, too."

"It's good with me, old chum. Trading the woodlands of the north for the grasslands of the south is a sound move. Pretty women down Neeron way."

Quinn threw the water down his throat in one large gulp.

"Is that all that you think about?"

"Well ..."

Bernard was about to expound on his point when he was interrupted by the public house door opening.

"Gentlemen, good morning to you both."

Quinn stood as Bernard spun his head fully around to see the Crown Prince of Ubar stride out the door into the morning sunlight.

"Good morning, your highness."

The prince nodded respectfully to the two men as they said hello, and then stretched to take a kink out of his frame.

"It appears to be a good day for traveling. This is certainly a good omen."

"It's a fine morning, your highness. You should be blessed with a fine journey."

The prince smiled broadly.

"And what of the two of you?"

Bernard smiled happily enough but kept his tone a little lower in stature than that of the prince. The rules of everyone being equal inside the public house only applied to inside the building. Out on the street, their new friend from last night was The Crown Prince of Ubar, and needed to be addressed as such.

"It looks like we'll be headed south, sire, toward the Temple of Fatezh."

An almost imperceptible smile crossed over the prince's expression as Bernard spoke. Bernard missed it, but Quinn didn't.

"I hear that the temple is well-respected. Do you plan to find work there?"

Bernard suppressed a laugh.

"Where we are both quite literate, we're definitely not scholarly men. No, it's more of an educational sojourn, sire."

"So, men of means then?"

Both men laughed this time. The prince followed suit, as it was meant to be a jest.

"We're okay for a while, if Bernard doesn't consume too much ale. Something will come along after that," Quinn said respectfully.

"It always does," Bernard added.

The prince smiled broadly and pulled his robe a little tighter over his shoulders. Both men could tell that the prince was built for the heat of the desert, not the cooler temperatures of the plains.

"I bet that it does, gentlemen. I bet that it does. Since you are in-between services, might I suggest that you travel west toward Kanash with my group? I am told that there is a road along that path which leads south. You could head south once you reach there."

The two looked at each other. Bernard seemed to think it was a fine idea. Quinn shrugged.

"That's a most generous offer, sire."

The prince made a gesture with his hands, as if to say that it was quite fine.

"The two of you proved to be good company last evening. I think you'd probably also make fine traveling companions. Plus, two more seasoned swords in our group over the next days will always be welcome."

Bernard smiled and nodded.

"We're pleased to be included in your company, sire."

"It's settled then. Do you require mounts?"

Bernard looked over at Quinn.

"Do we? Where are the horses?"

Quinn smirked at his friend.

"They're out back, tied up next to the hogs."

"Oh, that's good."

Bernard turned back to the prince, who was now surrounded by the remainder of his company.

"We possess mounts, your highness."

The prince laughed.

"I can tell that I'm going to enjoy this part of my trip."

The group collected itself in front of the public house and headed toward the gate. Moving out of the city, the farming fields around Gryazi were already bustling with activity. The men that Quinn had watched pass by were now hard at work. The sun, for its part, had managed to rise up higher in the sky, making the bright morning hot. The sunlight warmth pleased the prince greatly, and he kept his path out in the wide-open to absorb as much of it as possible.

The prince's men formed a loose ring about him, offering some resistance on all sides. The prince, his manservant, and his two new traveling companions rode in the middle of the ring. The random conversations of the public house slowly gave way over the journey's days and nights to a conversation about the countryside they were passing through. Prince Nazari was interested in the plains of the Middle Lands and the way things were done by the people there. He asked many questions as they rode. Bernard answered each of the questions enthusiastically. Half because he seemed excited to be traveling in such company, and half because he was the talkative one. Quinn was always happier being stoic. Some days he didn't talk at all, all day long. He would just respond by shrugging his shoulders or making hand gestures. Bernard was the natural talker, which suited him fine.

The road that the group had chosen to travel ran a straight path alongside a steel rail. A great engineering structure from the previous age, sections of it had survived all across the many different kingdoms of the land. Pairs of endless steel rails, atop wooden beams, rested in a river of small uniform stones. No one knew exactly what it was or how it had worked, but it was an undeniable sign that the men of the previous age were supreme builders.

Quinn watched it lay there as they rode. He had read volumes from before the calamity which had ended the previous age of men. The men had been an ambitious and industrious lot. They had constructed many wonderful things. Bits and pieces of that lost age could be found in every corner of the lands. But in the end, it was all for not. All of the knowledge that was required to make any of it work had been lost with the men that had built it. Now it was just a constant reminder of a potentially better time. Better, maybe, but long-dead now.

They came upon a point where a roadway crossed over the great steel snake, and Prince Nazari noticed Quinn's distraction with the object. The prince asked about it, which fired up Bernard. He explained the genius of the mechanical age before and some of the things which had been left behind on the land. The prince listened in rapt fascination as Bernard described the different ideas people had come up with to explain what the steel snake might be used for.

"So, Bernard, along with being a swordsman, you're also a mechanic? A man of many talents."

The jab made Quinn smirk.

"No, sire, I don't belong to the Guild. I find honest work to be lost on me."

Everyone laughed and then began to move along again. *Truer words about Bernard had never been spoken,* Quinn thought, as he pulled his mind away from the past and back to the countryside that they were presently in.

The prince shifted the gait of his horse and angled over so that he was between Bernard and Quinn. Neither man bothered to adjust course, as the four interior men had been weaving in and out of each other's paths as they rode, changing and exchanging conversations as they went.

"Quinn, my new friend, explain your cloak to me."

Quinn looked back at his cloak from the Watchtower, which he had wrapped around his great longbow before strapping it all to his saddle. He made a face and then smiled as he turned toward the prince.

"It's a cloak from the Watchtower garrison at Kalduhr. The marking around the hood denotes its wearer as having the rank of sergeant."

The prince nodded as Quinn spoke.

"I thought it was a Watchtower cloak. They are known throughout the entire land. Even to the north in my country, in the great dune sea, the Watchtower has an outpost."

"The Southern Sands Watchtower. I've been there."

The prince looked over at Quinn suspiciously, and then relaxed back into a smile.

"You have traveled to my country?"

"Yes, sire, when I was young. I was sent to learn at the Great Citadel on the Rain-Shadow Islands. My journey took me through the southern edge of your country."

Quinn instantly wasn't sure why he had just said so much. It was just going to lead to more questions that he didn't want to answer.

"You studied at the Watchtower Citadel, my friend? Many great men would envy the chance to have their sons do such a thing. But you said before that you are a sword for hire?"

"I am."

"I have always been under the impression that the Watchtower was a life's pursuit, not mere employment."

The statement was a true one. The standard contract for entry into the ranks of the Watchtower was twenty years. The Watchtower was neutral and needed its men and women to stay long enough to lose their sense of being from one place or another. Once in the ranks of the Watchtower, they were brothers and sisters of the Watchtower.

Quinn knew that that was true. He also knew that there were different loopholes in that system.

"It normally is a calling, yes."

"So, you were in the Watchtower long enough to make sergeant, and then left. Deserter?"

Quinn's head rotated around slowly until he was staring at the crown prince.

"I was released from their service, after a particular engagement."

The prince smiled in a way that said he was sorry for testing Quinn's limits.

"I am sorry, my friend. I had no intention of questioning your honor."

Quinn shrugged, as if to say it was forgotten now, and the two rode on in silence for a time. Finally, after deciding it had been an acceptable interval, the prince picked the conversation up again.

"Quinn, tell me of your longbow? We also have such weapons in the desert, but they are of a different design from yours."

"Its name is Fell-Crest, and it's a yew stave hewn shaft, with a human sinew string."

The prince looked surprised.

A named weapon? You're truly a man of many surprises."

"It was named after being used to fall the king of Crest's Edge in the Battle of the Southlands. That was in year 83 of this age. It was the battle that caused the solidification of the Kingdom of Meridian. It's a good weapon."

"How did you come to possess it?'

The prince had shifted to a point of genuine curiosity, so Quinn decided to indulge him.

"It was given to me by its previous owner, when I joined the Watchtower."

"And the ivy vining on the shaft? Was that part of the naming ceremony?"

Quinn made a face that said he'd rather not talk about it but continued on anyway.

"The ivy cresting means that it was also gilded by the Watchtower.

It happened after it was used in battle to save and safeguard troops in peril. The battle which I alluded to earlier."

The Crown Prince of Ubar looked at Quinn and nodded respectfully.

"So, an ex-Watchtower sergeant, with a named weapon, who has done heroic deeds in the throes of battle? I'm surprised that you're not in the employ of a king."

Quinn looked out into the middle-distance ahead of them and sighed.

"I choose not to be. I'm not one for doing things that I find to not make sense to me."

The prince looked straight-on back at Quinn, his dark eyes alive with fire.

"I know exactly what you mean, my friend."

The four continued on. Bernard and the manservant, Saleh, carried on a spirited conversation regarding the many differences between the deserts and the grasslands. Bernard was fascinated by the many different ways that Saleh explained the desert sands, and the ways that they behaved.

The company crested a small rise and looked down on the pronounced tee in the road which would lead some men south and some men east. A median height stone marker stood adjacent to the outline of the differing roads and demarked the intersection in the routes. Prince Nazari took in the road marker and looked over at Saleh, making a motion with his hand. Saleh instantly moved on, the ring of guards following along with him. The prince, Quinn, and Bernard stayed fast.

"So, my friends, this seems to be where we part ways. I am wondering if you might entertain a little light work, seeing how you are in-between employments?"

Quinn and Bernard looked at each other, and then back at the prince. The prince shifted to look to Quinn.

"You chose not to be employed by kings, but how about a prince? I wanted to travel with you along this road so I might gauge what type of men you truly are. Fortunately, it turns out that you're the right sort for me. Trustworthy, I think."

"What do you have in mind?" Quinn said, dropping all of the formalities.

"Since you're already headed south, and you say that you know the area around the Watchtower of Kalduhr, I would like you to travel to a small natural inlet to the north of the Watchtower."

Quinn nodded.

"There's two inlets to the north of Kalduhr, arranged in a small twin-bowl affair, but deep enough for ships to port."

The prince smiled at Quinn and pulled a sealed parchment from his saddle bag.

"I'd like you to place this parchment in the hands of a man named Silas Kahn."

Quinn made a face. Bernard stayed neutral.

"Blue Bill Montgomery."

This time, the prince made a face.

"You know him?"

"He's captain of *The Seamus*. And the leader of Pirate Bay, if there is such a person."

The prince nodded to Quinn respectfully a second time. He reached into his pack and pulled out a pouch of gold, three or four times the size of the one they had been given for the bounty.

"Ride fast and hard. He will be anchored there in six days' time. Place the parchment directly into his hands and give him my regards. That's all. Work done. Then you can enjoy your time at the temple."

Bernard collected both the document and the gold.

"We'd be pleased to be at your service, sire."

"Be quiet about your task and guard your backs. I bid you well, my friends. It is my greatest wish that we meet again one day. I thought when leaving home that I was going to have to send my guards south, but providence has provided me with the two of you. Be safe, gentlemen."

The Crown Prince of Ubar jammed a foot into the ribs of his horse and the beast shot off toward the remainder of his company. Bernard and Quinn turned south and rode on.

Chapter Four

Kanji wandered slowly down the main market street in Kanash and marveled at the great display of goods available. As he walked, he pondered the idea that the people here had no real idea how well they lived. True, life in the cities of the plain wasn't as glamorous as it could be. There was always crime and graft at every corner. Hustlers looked to take advantage of the wide-eyed strangers who passed their way. There was some poverty, crime, and disease in every place. Still, the people here were all fed and had fresh water to drink. They were protected from the elements and basically safe. They were much better off than man was meant to be.

Kanji paused in an open square and looked up at the great meeting hall which consumed most of one end. Huge wooden double doors on each side of the building's centerline gave entrance to a monument of stone and glass. Flat sheets of light stone covered its roof. A spire anchored each corner of its front. A high-rising spire of two different geometries sat on the right side, and a massive bell tower spire twice its size sat on the left. Once the eye was drawn skyward, stone gargoyles could be seen staring back down to earth, spouting out the rain shed from the roof.

Kanji knew that the great meeting hall was a survivor from the previous age, when men of great ability produced the impossible. Now, it was a status symbol of a great nation-state. He had no doubt that going inside would produce even more splendor for the eye. Ancient paintings, and the ornate tombs of powerful men, would accompany the real prize – huge walls of colored glass. He knew that the dull glass he was looking at on the outside was simply a weather covering for the treasures inside. Inside would be spectacular windows of multi-colored glass telling the stories of a bygone age. Pulling his eyes back down to earth, he turned and meandered down a wide, side alley which led to a larger open area beyond the meeting hall.

Coming to the first stall in the square, he stopped to inspect its offerings. The man at the stall was selling different types of clothes and garments. Kanji inspected the display and smiled at the man's prosperity. The man at the stall took in Kanji's measure with practiced objectivity and smiled back.

"Master. It is good to see a teacher out at the market. Is there something in particular that I might help you with?"

Kanji adjusted the red cloth head wrap that marked him as a Master so it showed a bit more of his face to the merchant, and smiled politely.

"Good morning, sir. I was just taking in the sights and smells of the market here. You seem to be doing well for yourself in this place?"

The man nodded and smiled with satisfaction that someone else had noticed his success.

"Yes, Master. I'm surely making my way. I started with a small wooden box for a table, outside the walls of the castle, when I was just a lad. Now I'm here in the square, with in-demand items for sale."

Kanji nodded respectfully.

"Perseverance is a thing that makes people better. Have a good day, sir. I wish you great success."

The merchant thanked him kindly, and he moved off deeper into the crowd about the square. Meandering along through the mass of people out buying this and that, he said hello to different individuals as they passed. Everyone responded to him in a happy tone. The great fortress city of Kanash, Capital of the Kingdom of Ayr, had a contented population.

Noticing an older woman out of the corner of his eye, he oriented himself toward a baker's stand and wandered closer. The baker had placed a stack of loaves into a small basket for the woman. The basket was well-worn, and Kanji guessed that it belonged to the old woman. The woman held a pile of various styled small coins in her hand and was attempting to make the purchase. Seeing Kanji, the old woman exhaled a sigh of relief and cast off an obvious sense of concern.

"Master, sir. Could you help me please?"

Kanji nodded respectfully to them both and flipped his red cloth head wrap down onto his shoulders that they might see him fully. Stepping closer, he smiled a calming smile.

"Good morning to you both. How might I be able to help you today, madam?"

The old woman smiled broadly at being referred to as madam.

"I'm not good with my numbers, and I'm not sure how many of these coins to use for these loaves of bread."

Kanji extended his hand, and the lady gave him the stack of coins. He inspected the different coins, from the different kingdoms, and removed four of the nine she had presented. He handed the four he had selected to the baker and returned the rest. The baker smiled politely and dropped the coins into his small wooden cash box. The old woman thanked Kanji several times before retrieving her basket from the bench. The two men watched as she hustled off through the crowd in the square.

"Mrs. Tamber. She's the widow that runs the lost children's home. She gets donations to help cover the cost of things, and always worries that people will question her about how she spends it. She's a good person, but she worries a great deal. You showing up put her mind at ease."

Kanji smiled at the man and then pulled his red head cloth back up over his head.

"Does she buy from you often?"

"Every third day, for as long as I can remember."

The baker shrugged his shoulders. It was the way that the world was. Kanji nodded to the baker, as if in agreement, and meandered off toward the other side of the market area. At a small table, Kanji spotted a woman sitting. She sat with purpose, a small cup the only thing in front of her on the table. Her posture was not the purposeful orientation of nobility, but the purposeful orientation of someone who was constantly assessing the world around her. A long, dark, hooded cloak hid all but the smallest of her features. The wispy edges of strawberry blonde hair could be seen extending from under the bottom of the hood's opening. That was all that anyone in the land needed to identify her as a sorceress.

Kanji knew that if someone could look in under the hood, they would see a face that was smooth and soft, yet just beginning to show the faintest signs of age. Blue eyes surrounded by black rings, set above pale lips, all wrapped in the lightest shade of long red hair. Her countenance was one of infinite inquisitiveness, tinged with a strong hint of melancholy. Kanji had been wondering where she had wandered off to.

Striding up to where she was seated, he paused and smiled at the Sorceress from the Great Temple of Drakchi.

"So, Enella, how do you find the fortress capital city of Kanash?"

Kanji's tone was inquisitive, as any master's tone was when presenting a question. Enella smiled softly under the protection of her hood.

"The wine in this place is very good. You?"

Kanji laughed out loud. Enella lifted her head so that he could see her smile.

"The people here are prosperous and happy. That's a good sign of a good leader. What do you say that we go and make our introductions?"

Enella stood. Kanji stepped in and moved her chair for her as she did so. She thanked him for the gesture and the two turned in the direction of the fortress's great house. The table girl, who had been keeping her distance from the sorceress, waited till they were in the crowd before walking over to collect the empty cup.

Strolling up to the guards at the main entrance to the great house, Kanji extended a folded parchment with the royal seal of Ayr broken loose from one side. A seemingly content guard inspected the invitation for a moment, and then inquired as to their names and titles. The guard had seen a pile of the parchments already and knew what questions were required. Handing the parchment back to Kanji, the guard requested that they follow. The armored man led the two newcomers through the wide halls of the great house straight to the throne room for the king of Ayr. Pausing before the throne room guards, the doorman made a gesture with his hands that the others understood.

"Guests of the king."

The throne room guards nodded and pivoted to open the large wooden doors.

"It's getting pretty busy in there," one of the throne room guards added as they passed.

Stepping into the vast, ornate, reception room, Kanji and Enella took in a sea of finely dressed people from across the court. A large group of counts, countesses, regents, and princes stood on either side of an open receiving aisle which led across the room to the dais, where King Gerald sat. Seeing the red cloth head cover of a master and the strawberry blonde hair of his escort, King Gerald stood and spread his arms wide in welcome.

The throne room guard following slightly behind them paused and oriented himself in the proper stature for the introduction.

"Your highness, Head Master Kanji Chen, from the Great Temple of Drakchi, and Sorceress of the Temple, Enella."

The two newcomers bowed toward their host, and then returned to their previous form.

"Master Chen, you honor my wedding with your presence. And Enella, what a wonderful surprise to have the resident Sorceress for the Great Temple here as well. You are both greatly welcomed."

"You honor us with your invitation, my lord."

"Did you just arrive, right now?"

King Gerald of Ayr, all but six-foot-two-inches tall and some sixteen stone, seemed genuinely interested in having a conversation. His blue eyes, set between a full head of brown hair and a thick beard, twinkled as he spoke.

"We came with the dawn sun, my lord. The journey across the water and through the Kingdom of Udaass was pleasant, as were the eastern plains of your great country."

"Here all morning? And what is your opinion of Kanash, Master Chen?"

The teacher made a conciliatory face.

"Your city is well-maintained. Its buildings are grand and well-kept. The people are fed and clothed, and by observation, appear to be prosperous. It would seem that your rule is approved of by the people."

The king laughed heartedly at the master's conservative response.

"We do our best to be good stewards of the masses, as is our calling."

Kanji Chen nodded to the king.

"Very true, my lord. Very true."

"And Enella, how are you finding our city?"

Enella drew a small breath and slid the hood of her cloak off of her head. A large mass of mildly curly strawberry blonde hair tumbled out onto her shoulders. Her pale blue eyes set in dark shadows radiated strength and bore straight into the king's depths. Though for all of her natural strength and beauty on display, her voice was subdued and modest.

"I have similar opinions to Master Chen. Your city is filled with friendly souls, which speaks well of you."

King Gerald smiled with some effort. The hold she held over him was without question. Enella lowered her gaze, and the king's natural enthusiasm returned.

"I'm glad to hear that. And your journey here, was it pleasant?"

"Yes, my lord. I enjoyed the beauty of your large plains. Full fields of wheat that were fed by the sun and stream."

"I'm very glad to hear that."

The herald of the hall reappeared in the doorway with another figure for presentation as Gerald was readying to switch the conversation back to Master Chen. He looked past the two to the herald, and then back to them.

"It seems that we have more guests to welcome. I am truly honored by your presence and bid you both a luxurious stay in Kanash."

Enella flipped the cloak hood back up over her head. The ladies of the court instantly began to gossip in low tones. Both Enella and Kanji bowed and turned to exit back the way they had come.

"You might try being more civil. Maybe a little less penetrative gazing into the royalty."

Enella made no physical response to Kanji's jab.

"I was civil. His heart is true and good. He's a fine-enough ruler."

Kanji smirked and looked toward the end of the great hall to take in the appearance of Master Jonah, the master of Kanash. A well-dressed man of eastern complexion and dark hair, his beard just starting to transition to a salty grey. Even from the distance still left between them, Kanji could conclude two things: The bulky man's dark eyes took in everything around them; The man was observant. And he wore his red head wrap down around his shoulders, like a scarf. He liked the trappings of status that his position at court brought him.

"I wondered where he was," Kanji whispered to Enella as they made their way toward him.

At an acceptable distance, Master Jonah strode forward and extended a firm hand. Kanji took it and shook with equal resistance.

"Master Chen, Sorceress Enella, it is an honor to have you both in Kanash."

Enella patted Kanji on the shoulder, nodded to Jonah, and then continued along out the door of the hall.

"Is she tired from your travels?"

Kanji Chen shrugged in a neutral fashion.

"Don't know. She's been in a mood all day. Now, let's walk and you can tell me all about the city and your time here."

Jonah pointed toward a set of stairs to one side of the throne room which led up to a second-level viewing area. Kanji followed Jonah, stopping along the way to say hello to several people in the court as they passed. Jonah led them up and then out a side door to a walkway leading out onto a great covered balcony. From the balcony, Kanji could see the entire courtyard of the great house, as well as a fair piece of the city. It was a kingly view.

"So, your time here has been good?"

Master Jonah inhaled the sweet air from the flowers below the balcony and smiled.

"It has been a great blessing, Master Chen. King Gerald is a good king. He has a deep caring for his subjects. The kingdom of Ayr is prosperous. They do a large trading business with both Udaass and

Neeron. It brings in wealth that the king has used to invest in his people."

Kanji nodded and considered Jonah's wording for a moment.

"Invest in his people? How so?"

Jonah made a look that said he was being tested, which he knew that he was. But part of being a master was to amass knowledge.

"He imports goods that they need and controls the cost, so that the prices stay where the people can afford to buy the goods. He spends a great deal of money on finding and training mechanics. That way he can learn about the ruins of old which are scattered about the kingdom. He has hired many City People to keep the clean water moving in and waste moving out of the cities of the kingdom. They keep Kanash quite clean. He has produced a good place for his subjects to live. He does this in every city, not just the capital."

Kanji had studied the City People Guild and the Mechanic Guild at some length over the years. They had made strides, the mechanics, to learn the old systems in an attempt to bring life to them again. He and Enella had stopped along the way to speak with some Ayr mechanics investigating and working on the great steel snake to the east. They had proved an intelligent and inquisitive bunch.

As for the City People, they were as well respected as any guild in all of the lands. They were the men and women who moved and maintained the waste and water. They kept the sewage traps around the city emptied, and the flowing water clean and fresh. They were as much the engine that drove the city as the commerce below them in the large square.

Kanji smiled and sat on one of the benches along the wall.

"Tell me, Jonah, what have you learned since you came to live here?'

Jonah smiled broadly as he looked out over the city. Sitting on a cushioned bench across from Master Chen, he broke into the start of a large synopsis of his time in Ayr. It was going to be large, but Kanji could also tell that it was going to be calculated. That was the way with some people.

Chapter Five

Rosalyn leaned back against a large grey rock in the midst of the green grassland and let the midday sun shower down on her. She knew that she couldn't stay long in the bright sunlight, since its energy would burn her naturally pale skin, but she loved to feel the forces of nature acting on her. Radiantly red hair that reached the small of her back tumbled down over her shoulders covering most of her exposed skin. That level of cover would be good enough for a moment or two.

Rosalyn tugged at the end of a precisely knotted ribbon, unleashing the knot. As the ribbon slid from one eyelet to the next, she could feel the corseted section of her green silk dress loosen. The sensation brought her instant joy. She didn't understand why she wore such clothing, other than it was the style of the day.

Being naturally petite and thin, at only five-foot-seven-inches tall, and a modest eight-and-a-quarter stone, her small breasts didn't require the stability of a corset top. She looked down at the wild mass of red Celtic hair flittering all about and thought that if anything about her needed taming, it was that. The thought made her smile. Her sensation of happiness echoed out into the nature surrounding her, causing the birds to sing sweeter and the sun to shine brighter. A bird of several colors flew down from a nearby tree and landed on the large grey rock. It chirped several times, as if to say hello, and then sprang back into flight.

Rosalyn thought about the bird. Did it know how lucky it was that it could fly? To soar above the ground? To see the world as no one else could see it? She understood that nature had forced the bird to make sacrifices so that it could fly. The bird had no arms or hands. It had small spindly legs to cut its weight. Its whole body was built to fly. Still, that all seemed a fair trade.

After considering the state of the bird, which had circled the open field several times and then headed off for somewhere else, she considered herself. She was no different from the bird. Nature had made choices when she was born, giving her the ability of sorcery. It had somehow chosen to give her abilities, whereas it had chosen to give almost every other girl none. It hadn't been a conscious choice with her input involved. It was just the way she was made, like the bird.

Closing her eyes and thinking about the sky momentarily, Rosalyn's body lifted slowly off the dirt of the ground. She rose into the air several feet, until she could lower her legs to the upright position. Continuing to climb skyward, she rose slowly until her toes were a good ten feet free from the earth. Rosalyn stretched her arms out fully to each side as if to invite the sun to shine brighter. Smiling, she began to slowly rotate in a clockwise direction. Looking out over the large grassy field, she could now see all the way to its edges, and even down into the trees growing by the nearby stream. A new view of the world. In some small way, the same as her friend the bird.

Settling back down onto the ground, her feet slipped back into the green grass. As her body took up its own weight, the jeweled crown on her head shifted slightly to one side. She shifted it back to its proper place and smiled to herself. The heavy ring of beaten gold topped by four decorative lilies, on its four stationary points, each inlaid with green jewels, had obviously been made for some king from the previous age. It now served to symbolize the leader of the Freelands Folk. Leadership wasn't a position that she had in any way wanted. Much like the light of a new day, it was something that had just come to her.

When Rosalyn was a child, the King of Meridian had taken her into his care. She had been raised in the palace, with his own children. Her youth had been a happy time. She had been a princess by position.

But, once her natural abilities began to manifest themselves, she was sent north by her new father, the king. She had come to the Freelands so that she might be taught the ways of the sorceress by the teachers of Maiden's Tower. Those days had passed long ago. Now, fully grown, and seasoned, she was considered to be the most-powerful sorceress in all of the known lands. With her formidable abilities, she had been pushed into being the High Sorceress of Maiden's Tower. She would teach the newcomers how to handle their natural gifts. Her position as High Sorceress had inevitably brought on the crown. The Freelands Folk wanted someone that was wise and formidable to speak for them. She had taken on the role reluctantly. It was a position that she had no desire to obtain. She knew too well how power corrupted people. She knew how it twisted the way that they thought and acted. She had been given power over earth and object at birth, having people put more upon her seemed unnecessary.

Rosalyn thought about Bianca, her sister in every way but blood. She was the oldest daughter of the king who had plucked her off the streets and given her a home. She hadn't spoken with Queen Bianca of Meridian in several seasons now. Rosalyn hoped that she was well. Closing her eyes, Rosalyn focused on Bianca's face. She could feel that the queen was well. As she focused on Bianca's image in her mind, she could feel her smile. The queen of Meridian had felt her touch from far away and obviously appreciated the gesture. *Ahh, things had been simpler when they were children,* she thought as she released the image from her mind.

Deciding that she had probably been out in the sun for long enough, Rosalyn waved her hand toward the big yellow orb in the sky and began to wander toward the trees growing by the stream. The giant yellow ball pulsed slightly, as if to say goodbye, and went back to energizing the world.

Stepping into the shade of the thick grove, she could feel the warmth of the sun deep in her skin. Maybe she really had stayed out in the field a little too long? Nonsense, the sun did what the sun did. It was the world. It was good.

Setting down by the edge of the stream, Rosalyn flattened out the water with the passing of her hand through the air, so that it might act like a mirror. Looking into the mirror, Rosalyn saw an image of herself and Bianca when they had just become women. Rosalyn noticed that she had looked so much younger back then. Considered to be the most beautiful woman in all the lands during her youth, time and the throes of power had softened her features. It had also made her spirit a little melancholy.

Bianca's sister and brother came running into view as the image moved on the water. The group played and laughed, content not to understand the choices they would one day have to make.

Rosalyn let the image go, and the water returned to its rippled surface. Those times had passed, and they were never coming back. She knew that dwelling on the past only limited the present.

Rosalyn considered the image a second time. It had made itself manifest in her brain for a reason. She knew that the deep inside of the brain always knows what one should do. If people listened to themselves, they would know their path. The problem with the world was that almost no one listened. She hadn't really thought about her neighbor to the south for some time. Maybe it was time to go and see her sister? That thought instantly made her smile. That was it. The smile was the sign which led to the choice.

Rosalyn flattened out the water a second time and cast her eye out over all of the Freelands Folk. The farmers were in the fields and the miners were up inside the hills. Everything her gaze fell upon looked quiet and peaceful. Turning her eye toward the school, all of the girls seemed captured by their studies. The teachers of the tower had things well in hand. Yes, it was well in all of the Freelands. It was a good time for a journey. She could disappear for a day or two and no one would notice. Rosalyn smiled again, as the image in the stream shimmered out of view.

The High Sorceress stood still and listened to the language of nature. All was calm in the world. A raccoon could be heard up the stream cleaning a small clam in the water. Several different types of birds in various directions were chirping and singing. The day was as carefree as it could rightly be expected to be.

Rosalyn reflected on the present state of the land. She, and all of her people, knew that peaceful seasons didn't last long. They were always undone by doubt and trouble. Always. She sensed trouble in the spirits. She didn't know from what direction it would come, but it would come. Maybe that was why she was thinking of going south? Meridian and the Freelands Folk had been neighbors ever since the Freelands had broken off from the kingdom. The truce had always been a peaceable one. The trade in goods and ideas was prosperous for both sides. No, if the trouble she sensed in the ether really was coming, then it wouldn't be coming from the south.

If not the south, then the north? The only thing in the western wastelands to the north was the holy mountain of the Lone Oracle. He was the keeper of the dead and the harnesser of the dark sorcery. There was also the abandoned city of Rylak, otherwise known as the Kingdom of Bleached Bones. It had been the place chosen to stack all the dead at the end of the last age. Dying was the natural fate of all beings that grow to be too many, whether they be deer or human. No, the Oracle had no need to raise an army of dead men. Trouble wasn't coming from the north either.

Rosalyn walked down the stream, so as not to disturb the raccoon's lunch. She came upon a reasonably deep pool in the stream and stopped. She inspected the spot. It seemed a perfectly suitable place from which to exit.

Collecting her hair into a mass, Rosalyn turned it several times to form a loose mane, and laid it over her left shoulder. Closing her eyes to focus on a place, she murmured low in an ancient tongue and the water became as still as glass. The light breeze stalled until the air was at a full stop. The mood of the land stilled completely. Rosalyn stepped slowly into the glass still water with small and deliberate steps. She allowed each foot to gain purchase before proceeding to the next step. One step at a time she moved deliberately and continuously into the water until the tips of her crown disappeared below the surface. The whole of the place retained its utter stillness for several seconds, then as with the snap of fingers, returned back to its original active ways.

Far to the south of the little stream, in the gardens of the great castle of Meridian City, the waters of the central fountain became as smooth as glass. A pair of women standing near the fountain became concerned and stepped away. Slowly, as if in slow motion, golden tips of lily broke the surface as a queen's crown rose smoothly into the air. The image continued until Rosalyn stepped up onto the marble edge and then down, out of the fountain's pool. As the toe of her left foot broke contact with the water's surface, the water in the fountain returned to its normal state. Rosalyn, looking every bit like a drowned house cat, waved a hand up and down her body expelling the water until she was as dry as at the start. Stepping barefoot away from the small pool of water she had created, the younger of the two watching women gasped at the open use of sorcery. Rosalyn looked over at the woman and smiled politely.

"Is the queen in residence?"

The older of the two women answered as the younger was still somewhat shell-shocked.

"Yes, High Sorceress. She's in the castle."

"Thank you, ladies."

Rosalyn smiled and nodded politely. She stepped off on her way, perfectly oriented to her childhood home. Making her way out of the gardens, she moved for the doors that led through the hallways of the back parts of the castle. Listening to the life inside the building, she could tell that Bianca was in her throne room, so Rosalyn slowly made her way in that direction. She walked without sound. No one inside the great stronghold of Meridian knew that she had arrived. She had always liked to arrive in places quietly. It was always better for her.

Stepping through a door on the right-hand side of the throne room, Rosalyn took in an interesting sight. The queen, and three of her guards, were playing a game called *Toss the Bag.* One tossed a bag of hard peas down the length of the throne room floor in an attempt to make it land on one of the kingdom's great seals which were inlaid into the floor at either end of the receiving space. They had made up the game as children to pass time during the long winter months. All four of the current participants appeared to be enjoying themselves greatly. A young, fit guard tossed the bag, and it slid straight to the middle of the seal at the far end of the room. Everyone cheered his success.

"That was a good shot."

Heads snapped around as Rosalyn spoke, making her intrusion into the space. The guards scrambled for weapons as Bianca literally jumped for joy and ran to where Rosalyn was standing. Bianca wrapped her arms solidly around Rosalyn and squeezed. Rosalyn returned the favor, though without the vigor of her host. Loosening the squeeze, but not letting go, Bianca, Queen of Meridian, and head of the Great House of Rhodes, smiled lovingly at her sister in everything but birth.

"My beautiful sister. It's been entirely too long since you've come to visit. You look well. Tell me that you're well?"

Bianca released her hold and stepped back to take in a full view of Rosalyn. Rosalyn smiled softly and placed a hand on Bianca's cheek.

"I am fine. And you? Are you well? You look as lovely as when we were children."

Bianca laughed.

"I'm in great spirits. But we all know that you were the true beauty of the land when we were coming of age."

Rosalyn smiled softly a second time. She was unaccustomed to people flattering her. Most everyone was mildly fearful of her and just gave her space to pass.

"You're too kind, sister. But if there's a greater beauty in your kingdom, I know not who it could be."

Bianca laughed happily a second time.

"You always were a politician. Come, let's sit and talk. I've missed you so."

The pixie blonde queen, of the same height as Rosalyn and only a half-stone heavier, walked to some benches that sat on one side of the throne. Her bright blue eyes twinkled as she looked at Rosalyn, the same way they had when they both were girls.

Rosalyn watched the queen of Meridian move across the floor. Where Rosalyn's corseted bottes was a restriction to her movements, Bianca's corset shaped her upper body and gave her naturally slim figure the curves of a more well-endowed woman. All of her features were smooth and elegant. Though only some three years younger than

Rosalyn, Bianca still looked fresh-faced and lovely. Rosalyn wasn't sure why, but somehow, she suddenly felt older.

"Now, my lovely sister, from one queen to another, what's brought you south from the Freelands? Not that it isn't a complete joy just to see you."

Chapter Six

Rosalyn shifted her dress about to get comfortable on the bench. Bianca watched her every move in attempting to glean some bit of useful information, some reason why she had come. After a fashion, it seemed that the High Sorceress was ready to converse.

"I know they mean well, but might you dismiss your guard? They are all fierce fighters, for sure, but I promise you that you're completely safe."

Bianca smiled so wide that it was almost in jest.

"There are no safer hands to be placed in than those of the High Sorceress."

Rosalyn made a small, passing expression that escaped Bianca. Rosalyn knew all too well that her power had limits, even if the people of the land thought otherwise.

"Guards, could you please leave us be. I would like to converse with my sister quietly."

Seeming almost relieved to be dismissed from the duty, the three guards filed out of the throne room wordlessly. The large wooden doors closed behind them, leaving the two women alone.

"I honestly can't say how happy I am that you came to visit."

"Thank you, Bean. I do miss everyone, but it seems that the needs of the land never go away."

Bianca's eyes twinkled at the use of her childhood nickname.

"And those of the great house of magic as well, I would imagine."

"Very true."

"I know exactly what you mean. Meridian is a safe and prosperous kingdom, but it requires constant attention."

"Your people are fed, and happy, and loved. Not so much can be said of other kingdoms in the lands."

"True, but still ..."

"Well, one thing is for certain: The stress of rule hasn't affected you greatly. You really do look as lovely as when we were girls. You don't have one worry line that I can see."

"Oh, I have them. I just keep them hidden behind the long hair."

Bianca's long blonde hair hung in long loose curls and framed her face elegantly.

"Hmm, a power that I haven't yet mastered."

Both women laughed happily.

"Alright, spill. What brings you south?"

"A sense of trouble, but not from the north or the south."

Bianca inspected her adopted sister's expression intently for several seconds before making a face.

"You're probably just sensing all of the turmoil caused by so many crowns moving about at one time. I wouldn't worry too much."

Rosalyn made a face.

"You think it's that simple?"

Bianca stood and walked to her throne chair. Pausing, she retrieved a small cream-colored parchment from a side table and turned to walk back to where Rosalyn was seated. Bianca waved the parchment around in the air, like it was supernatural.

"The great wedding of our age, or so it states. King Gerald thinks a lot of himself. He's invited every house in the known lands to the thing."

Rosalyn held her hand out in front of her. Snapping her fingers, a similar parchment appeared between her fingers.

"I know, Bean. It's supposed to be quite the affair."

Bianca's eyes turned quizzical at the sight of the second invitation.

"He invited the queen of the Freelands Folk? High Sorceress or no, he really is pulling out all the stops, isn't he?"

Rosalyn smiled softly. Bianca had meant the words differently than they had come out.

"It would seem that he wants the whole world to witness his special day."

"So it would seem." Bianca's image shifted from her usual neutral political expression back to her girlish one. "Are you going? We can travel together! Oh, please say that you're going."

Rosalyn looked at Bianca quizzically.

"So, you're going? I would have thought that you would have already left for such a journey. It will take you some weeks to get to Kanash."

Bianca shrugged.

"It was planned that we leave tomorrow. A nice ride to the coast, and a sail across the Central Sea, to the Kingdom of Ayr."

"We?"

"Catherine wants to come with me. She's never seen a royal wedding. Secretly, I think she hopes she can meet a nice prince. Don't blame her, this whole peninsula's a little short of available princes."

Both women laughed. Catherine, the youngest of the Rhodes sisters, was the quiet and soft-spoken princess. Somewhat continuously melancholy since her childhood, she was also the best educated of them.

"A young prince would be good for her, and for you, too, I think."

Bianca presented her shocked face.

"Oh, and you're still chaste?"

Rosalyn smiled.

"Bean, I'm not from a great house. I'm not a princess. I can have sex as freely as I choose to."

Bianca shrugged.

"Fair enough, trollop."

Both women laughed girlishly.

"Still, tomorrow?"

Bianca made a face that said Rosalyn should have known better than to ask the question.

"You know me, I'm always late for things."

Rosalyn chuckled. She literally couldn't stop herself from doing so.

"You've been late for everything, ever since we were girls. If I remember correctly, you were late for your own coronation."

Bianca made a face that said, yup. That's me. I'm late girl.

"So, tell me that you'll come with us. Having you along would definitely make Margarette happier."

Margarette Rhodes, the middle princess in the Rhodes family, was leader of Meridian's army and the Countess of Warrington. By far the moodiest of the Rhodes sisters, she was very much all-business. Her general disposition was one which presented a slight scowl.

"So, Margarette's staying here?"

"She has no appetite for court galas and princess dresses. To be honest, I'm not entirely sure that she cares about princes, either. Besides, it would take a saintly one to deal with her on a daily basis. They'd end up crossing swords."

Rosalyn stayed neutral.

"So, she hasn't changed since last we spoke?"

Bianca laughed so loudly that it echoed in the hall.

"Nope! Not one bit."

Rosalyn stood and paced about slightly.

"Just out of curiosity, who gets the chair when you're gone?"

Bianca spun around and looked at Rosalyn as if she'd just been slapped. The expression lasted only a second or two before disappearing. The queen knew that her adopted sister had many qualities, but spitefulness wasn't one of them. The High Sorceress was an enigma to everyone, save Bianca Rhodes.

"Well, I'd like to think that my children would squabble over it. Hopefully, there's a boy in the mix. Kings are better at ruling countries than queens, I think. If children aren't meant to be, Catherine is best suited for the job. She's smart *and* kind. Plus, she's younger than the rest of us. Why?"

Rosalyn shrugged as she paced.

"No reason. I didn't mean to make you sad. I was just curious if you'd ever stopped to think about it."

Bianca let a small shadow slide across her features.

"Oh, I think about it upon occasion. It's one of the things that monarchs can't escape thinking about – the line of succession."

Rosalyn made a conciliatory gesture but didn't speak. She felt Bianca wasn't exactly finished.

"Some days I wish I was just a princess. If Alexander had assumed the throne, I'd just be a princess. It seems an impossible dream, these days."

The clouded expression passed over Rosalyn's face this time.

"I'm sorry. That wasn't right of me."

"It's fine, Bean. The past is the past."

"So it is. Now, what about you, Queen of the Freelands Folk?"

Rosalyn gave back a questioning look.

"I was asked to be queen. When I am no more, the people will find someone else to do the job. Maybe they will decide to have no queen at all."

Bianca made a face.

"Democracy? What a quaint idea. Nevertheless, will you travel with us to the wedding?"

"Tell me what you know about the situation in Ayr, and of this wedding."

Bianca plopped down in her throne chair and hung her crown on one of the chair's rear legs with a practiced ease.

"Things in Ayr are quiet enough. They have had several good crops in successive seasons. Their stores are full. Their dealings with Neeron to the south, and Udaass to the east, both have been on good terms. They don't do much cross-border trade with their neighbors to the north in Ubar, that's all one way, but they have also never really traveled into the sand sea much."

Rosalyn nodded as she spoke, taking in each word used and assessing it for meaning.

"King Gerald seems to be on good terms with all of his counts and regents. He's a mostly happy sort of fellow, from what I understand. Which basically rings true. I met him right after my coronation. He was pretty sure and full of himself back then."

Rosalyn nodded some more as she made a slow pace around the throne room's receiving floor.

"And the wife?"

"What am I, your spy? You can easily look into the mist and see all of this for yourself."

Rosalyn turned to Bianca and shrugged.

"You always have the good dirt about what's going on."

"Can't blame a girl for having an extensive spy network, can you?"

Rosalyn shrugged again.

"No. No you cannot."

"Anastasia Savin, five-foot-nine-inches tall, and just a smidge under ten-and-a-half-stone. Reported to be endowed with an ample bosom. Long black hair and brown eyes. Supposedly she's possessed of the Roman heritage from the last age, or it's said to at least show in her features."

Rosalyn looked up at Bianca.

"So, big chest and striking features? I hear the men like that sort of thing."

Bianca looked down at her petite frame.

"Me too."

"Go on."

"She comes from an aristocratic family in the city of Fatezh, located on the Ayr-Neeron border. The family is of no renown. Rumors say that, at the start of the age, they were a princely family, but they got displaced along the way. They do have some money, but no influence to speak of."

"The start of the age was almost three-hundred-years ago. That's a long time for a family to linger in anonymity, without just fading to dust."

"True. It's said that she wormed her way into the king's sight, and then slowly cast a spell over him. She's rumored by pretty much the whole court of Ayr to be a manipulative bitch."

The statement made Rosalyn smirk.

"Aren't we all?"

"I'm not. I'm loved by all, thank you very much."

Both women laughed.

"Yes, you are, sister. Yes, you are."

Bianca was readying a retort when one of the large wooden doors to the throne room swung open. Both queens refocused their attention on the intrusion, as Princess Catherine came running in across the receiving floor. She ran straight to Rosalyn and hugged her tightly, just as her sister had done previously. Rosalyn looked up at Bianca and smiled.

"I knew she was coming from the front door."

"Rosalyn, you've come to visit! It's so good to see you! I thought that it was you. The pendant has been going crazy for a good forty-five minutes. I figured someone important was here."

Catherine stepped back a step, so that Rosalyn could see. The ELLAWYN pendant, a gift of protection that Rosalyn had bestowed upon Catherine at her sixteenth birthday, hung on the end of its chain and pulsed with power. Rosalyn laid a hand gently on the pendant and let the built-up power dissipate into the room.

"It probably charged itself when the portal opened. That, or there's another sorceress in the city."

Rosalyn became very still for five or six seconds.

"It doesn't feel like there's another nearby."

"It's so good to see you, sister! Have you come to wish us a safe voyage?"

Rosalyn looked up at Bianca, who had a huge smile on her face.

"I've been trying to convince her to join us."

Catherine beamed with delight.

"Oh, please do! It's been too long since you came to visit. Please join us! Please!"

The hazel eyes of the five-foot-seven-inch, seven-and-a-half-stone, blonde-haired princess sparkled with glee. Bianca had seldom seen Catherine's eyes sparkle in recent years. Rosalyn could feel that in the queen's countenance and smiled softly at her little sister.

"Fine. You've won me over. I'll go to the wedding with you."

Catherine bounced up and down on dirty bare feet. A look most uncommon for a princess.

"Besides, with so many young princes in the city, someone is going to have to look after your virtue."

Bianca laughed as Catherine hugged Rosalyn tightly a second time. It appeared as if she was going to a wedding.

Chapter Seven

Bernard stood on the unexposed edge of a small clearing across a wide expanse of open ground from the town of Roadstead and surveyed the situation at hand. It all looked quiet enough. The whole town looked pretty sleepy from a distance. And it probably was mostly that. It was what happened in the side streets and alleys of such places that really gave them their reputations.

Bernard could see people coming and going out on the main road. They all looked the regular sort, men with wagons of things, and women with bundles and baskets of produce. Frankly, it looked like any other port town they had ever been to. Bernard would have been happy to proceed along as natural, but his burly friend was being more cautious. Quinn had been acting strange ever since they had come across the dead man's metal tube. *It was most-definitely the tube causing the behavior,* Bernard thought as he surveyed the scene. *Quinn wasn't scared of any man or any situation. Quinn had killed more men than anyone Bernard had ever heard of.*

"Looks quiet enough to me. What does your nose say?"

Bernard turned to look at his friend. Quinn shrugged stoically.

"We've got time on our side. Let's wait until the cover of night. I have a pretty good idea where he'll be spending his evenings."

"Works for me."

Bernard squatted down and took up a position next to a large tree. He watched the people come and go for some time before a nap overtook him. The day was warm and the breeze coming out from under the canopy of the trees was cool. Just the right conditions for such things.

Quinn kicked Bernard's boot as the sun dipped behind the buildings of Roadstead and headed for its spot out to the west beyond the sea. Bernard yawned and cracked his neck to straighten it out.

The two men collected the handful of things lying about and mounted horses for the ride into town. Moving along the edge of the wood line, they intersected the main town road and turned toward the water. The road was straight and deeply grooved from the many loaded carts that had traveled it over the centuries.

Like many sections of roadway scattered throughout the land, it was a much older construction made from little bitty pebbles in a mixture of a packed black tar-like substance. The mixture had been pressed flat by some great force. Whatever it was, it had been laid down by the men of the previous age. They were a collection of builders far superior to the ones in the current age. Their roadway, though centuries old, still functioned as intended. Some of the pieces that Bernard and Quinn had seen were still black in color and possessed the faint remnants of painted lines on them. This road section, out in the bright sunlight and heavily used, had faded to a slate grey color.

As they approached the edge of the buildings which defined the outer edges of Roadstead, men could be seen in the road ahead. Quinn's practiced eye knew that they were those of the Watchtower Guild several miles to the south. The imposing Watchtower of Kalduhr stood overlooking both the sea and the grain fields of Neeron. A guild designed to keep the peace across the land, the Watchtower Guild had watchtowers and garrison posts stationed in all prominent locations around the lands. It was said that there was even a Watchtower garrison to the south across the sea, in the great mining isles.

The men currently standing in the road ahead of the two must have been sent to keep peace in town. That told Quinn that the peace wasn't as peaceful as usual. Quinn considered that for a horse stride or two and decided that it didn't really matter. They had taken the prince's coin.

They were now going to go wherever they needed to go. Personal karma was definitely more important than a little violence.

Bernard and Quinn rode slowly up to where the Watchtower men were standing and brought their mounts to a slow and methodical stop. The more senior man looked them over and rolled his palm down onto the grip of his sword as he took in Quinn's Watchtower cloak.

"State your names and your business here in Roadstead this night."

The younger man took in the edge of the senior man's voice and reached to grip his sword as well.

With the practiced moves of one who wore a cloak daily, Quinn slid his hands up and over the hood, pulling it free from his head. He smiled at the guard standing in the roadway as if it were any other day in the world. The senior man took in Quinn's features and began to laugh. The younger man's eyes darted around not understanding what was transpiring.

"Quinn, is that you? Truly?"

Quinn smiled again and let the man laugh for a bit.

"Tomas, my old friend. It is good to see you alive."

Tomas Sanzz, Watchtower sergeant, relaxed his posture completely and smiled broadly.

"The Mighty Quinn. I keep hearing rumors of your exploits. What brings you to Roadstead?"

"We need to see a man about a boat."

The younger man took the statement as troublesome, but Tomas just laughed.

"Will you be heading to Kalduhr when you're done with your boat business?"

Quinn considered the question for a moment. They had good food at the Watchtower fortress of Kalduhr.

"Is Brittaney Fyr still the captain of the watch?"

"Yup, and she still dislikes you."

Quinn made a face.

"I think not."

"Well, nevertheless, you stay alive my friend."

The senior man stepped from the road and pulled the younger

man out of their way. Quinn nodded in response as the horses began to step off.

"Always good to see a familiar face."

Tomas laughed loudly and waved. Bernard and Quinn turned the corner around a nearby building and disappeared.

"It's always nice how you get us through the roadblocks so smoothly."

Quinn just nodded at Bernard's comment and kept moving forward.

"Okay, Mighty Quinn, where do you suppose we're actually headed to?"

Quinn looked over at his friend, who seemed quite pleased with himself, and scowled.

"Down by the main port docks there will be a public house called the Crossed Keys. If Blue Bill's ship is in port, and he's not on it, that is where he will be."

Quinn spoke with a tone that suggested he'd been in the place before, so Bernard didn't question further. Each of them had undertaken many private adventures prior to becoming friends. Bernard had as many hidden bits of knowledge as his sturdy friend did.

The two men made their way quietly across Roadstead, all but unnoticed by the masses. They pulled up and dismounted at a small livery next to an obviously seedy drinking hole and tendered their mounts to the old man in charge. Bernard flipped the man a coin and asked if they could be watered and fed, as they wouldn't be too long next door. The farrier smiled and nodded, happy to be paid in advance for a change.

Stepping into the doorway of the public house Bernard could instantly tell that this was the type of place where he could enjoy himself. The noise coming from the large main gathering room was loud and raucous. Quinn made another face and followed his friend through the door.

Stepping all the way inside, the keeper of the bar walked over to that end of the long slab of lumber and smiled at the two.

"Good evening, gentlemen. We're pretty full tonight, but there's surely an open seat somewhere."

"Just two ales, and an inquiry."

The barman looked at the big, cloaked figure with suspicion.

"We're looking for Blue Bill Montgomery. Is he in this evening?"

The barman looked out over the sea of pirates, cutthroats, and dock workers in the main room.

"Why?"

"We would be pleased to converse with him," Bernard said, picking up a cup of the ale.

The barman scratched his chin stubble.

"Just talking?"

"Just talking," Bernard said pleasantly through a mouthful of beer.

"He's upstairs. Room number three."

"Thank you, good sir."

Bernard and Quinn stepped off in the direction of the stairs that led to the upper level. Most of the men and women in the public house watched suspiciously as they made their way up the stairs to the open, wrap around walkway. They moved straight to door number three and Quinn wrapped three solid times. The door opened to a weathered, salty face.

"What do you want?"

Bernard smiled at the grizzly old sailor.

"Looking for Blue Bill."

"The question still stands."

The second query came from farther back in the room, and made the old doorman move out of the way. The man moving was a sign to Quinn and Bernard that a flying object may be headed their way soon. They stepped inside anyway. Quinn slid his cloak hood down again and took a good hard look at the man that was now speaking. Tall, at maybe six-foot-two or three, and a solid fourteen-and-a-half stone. Long, thick dark hair and matching dark eyes, with enough scars to be a pirate king, though his face was unmarked and deeply tanned.

"We have some business to discuss with you. Private business."

Bernard spoke directly, but in a relaxed and reassuring manner.

"About?"

"About private matters."

Quinn made his statement with slightly more directness.

The pirate king sat and thought for a moment.

"Fine. Everybody out."

There was no protesting from the pirate inner circle. All the men and women simply got up and left the room. The three men sat quietly long enough to make sure that everyone had moved on from the door outside. Even though a captain's word was final, it paid to be prudent.

Deciding it was good enough, Blue Bill reached out and grabbed up a huge pitcher of ale from off the table. He refilled his glass and then pointed the pitcher toward Bernard, who accepted it.

"So, what's this business that you wish to speak of? Did I sink some ship or raid some port owned by your employer?"

Bernard laughed mildly.

"Not that I know of."

The pirate smiled broadly.

"I know, I killed someone, and their people are paying you to get revenge? Trust me when I say that won't be easily accomplished."

Bernard shook his head.

"As far as we know, that's not it either."

Blue Bill smiled even broader than before.

"I owe someone money?"

"Nope," Quinn said directly.

The pirate quit smiling and looked at Quinn directly.

"Have we met before? There's something about you that I find familiar."

Quinn made a quizzical face, as if he wasn't sure of the answer.

"No, Silas Kahn, I don't believe we have ever met before," Quinn said, using the pirate captain's given name. "However, we are here tonight to deliver a message to you from Crown Prince Nazari of Ubar."

Quinn shifted his gaze to Bernard, who removed a rolled parchment stamped with the waxed seal of Ubar. Bernard handed it over to the pirate.

Silas Kahn turned the parchment over in his hands several times, before stopping to take in the seal thoroughly. It was unmistakably the seal of the northern desert kingdom, and it was unbothered. Just above the seal was the silver ring around the parchment which denoted a royal correspondence. Silas Kahn slid the parchment into the top of his boot and returned his attention to his guests.

"How did the two of you come to be in the service of Ubar?"

"We were riding with the prince through the western lands of Ayr. And, since we were headed in this general direction, he asked that we do him a service by delivering that message to you."

Bernard's response was calm and composed, like one of the defenders in the law courts.

"And how did you come to be riding with the prince?"

"We met in a public house in Gryazi, after dealing with a bounty sheet."

Silas Kahn was a good judge of men. You didn't get to where he was if you weren't. And he believed the story he was being told.

"And you two are?"

"My name is Bernard, and my gruff friend here is Quinn." Bernard poked a finger in Quinn's direction. "We're your basic wandering mercenary types."

Blue Bill's eyes twinkled with delight.

"You're more than that. I've heard tales of the two of you. Yes, your exploits are the best gossip in the public houses of many places."

Bernard made a gesture with his hands that said it was nice to be spoken well of.

"We're equal opportunity employment."

Silas Kahn laughed heartedly.

"So am I, my friends."

Bernard laughed with the pirate. Quinn stayed stoic. Bernard reached out for the pitcher to refill his ale glass as Blue Bill reached down toward the floor to retrieve a half-full bottle of rum. He snatched out the cork and took a drink. Handing it over to Bernard, he also drank. Bernard handed it off to Quinn who, to both men's surprise, consumed a good mouthful.

Silas Kahn rubbed a scar on his forearm. The scar had a blue tint to it, from the way in which it had healed. It had been the one which everyone assumed had given him the name Blue Bill. Truthfully, the original Blue Bill had died in a sea battle some fifty years before Silas

Kahn had even been born. The next man in line to be pirate king had simply assumed the name because it struck fear into the hearts of those traveling the seas. Silas had inherited it from him, so to speak, when the last pirate king died. Now, he was the third Blue Bill Montgomery to pirate the seas. The rumors that he was beyond killing had made his ship all but unsinkable, and his men the scourge of anyone he set them against. Everyone in the room knew that he was just a man. But gossip had a way of making men more than what they were. Same as the gossip about Bernard and Quinn.

"So, you said that he paid you to deliver a message? That job seems done. What now?"

"Now, we'll move on to whatever comes next."

Silas smiled.

"You're both smart and sturdy. Ever consider sailing?"

Foamy ale came shooting out of Bernard's nose as Silas finished speaking. The sight made the pirate laugh.

"I don't think I'm up for the life of a pirate."

"It's pretty much the same life you lead now. We just do it on a boat."

Quinn smiled as the other two laughed. It seemed a true statement.

"Thanks for the offer, but we'll pass."

Blue Bill Montgomery, pirate king and scourge of the known seas, simply shrugged his shoulders in defeat, before handing the rum bottle back to Quinn a second time.

Chapter Eight

The herald entered the throne room of the castle and announced the arrival of King Lorimere of Neeron, with Queen Vivian. King Gerald came quickly to his feet as his longtime neighbor entered. The man that made his way very slowly, and deliberately, up the middle of the floor showed his age more than when the two had last met. The blue-grey fuzz around the crown of a balding head and the many wrinkles made him look frail. Still, his five-foot-ten-inch frame was straight up and toned. Walking along beside him was Queen Vivian Lorimere – a young woman with a happy disposition and long auburn hair. The fresh-faced beauty could have easily been mistaken for the king's granddaughter. It had been told that the two had met when the king made his way to the city of Fatezh to conduct business with her father, Count Peter Burdin. The king was introduced to the young lady while out on a ride and fell completely and utterly under her spell. When she was officially deemed of proper age, she traveled to the capital and became queen.

Anistasia Savin took in the juxtaposition of the two opposites and maintained a neutral expression. She stood respectfully, and smiled politely, as she took her place next to King Gerald. At five-foot-nine-inches tall, she was only light rays shorter than her husband to be. The little more than ten stone that she weighed was naturally spread along her frame. Her long black hair was worn straight and loose down her back, so as not to hide her more than ample breasts. The satin dress she wore had been cut and sown to accent all of her features and gave her a better-than-everyone-else look. The look was lost on King Gerald. It was not, however, lost on King Jasper Lorimere or Queen Vivian.

"King Jasper," King Gerald said smiling with wide open arms, "and Queen Vivian. I'm so honored to receive you."

The king and queen nodded respectfully to their host.

"It was our honor, King Gerald, to receive your invitation. Your new queen will obviously be the beauty of the kingdom, no doubt."

Anistasia Savin smiled modestly and curtsied as expected.

"You're too kind, sire."

Jasper Lorimere looked over at Vivian, who just rolled her eyes as if to say, *don't use me for help now.*

Everyone laughed at the comeback, though Jasper and Anistasia's laughter was slightly subdued. The herald reappeared in the doorway and Gerald stepped down off of the dais to shake Jasper's hand.

"The best rooms in the castle are yours. Rest after your trip and we'll talk a little border business later in the day."

Jasper Lorimere shook Gerald's hand firmly. Releasing his grip, the king and queen of Neeron stepped off to one side of the floor with others in the court to make room for the King and Queen of Oban.

Marko de Santi, six-foot-two-inches of unquestioned royalty, strode into the throne room with a gait that hid his fifty-years of life. A solid gold crown sat squarely on a full head of grey hair, framing a purposeful face and a full and thick grey beard. Light metal plate bearing the crest of his house sat over mail and had no limiting effect on his movement.

Gliding gracefully along beside him, almost as if to present the visual difference between power and authority, was Valentina de Santi, the undisputed real power in the throne room. The Queen of Oban, a true regal lady from the great house of Rhodes, was modest and wise. Her brilliant blue eyes saw all that happened in her midst and offset the fine grey strands that were just starting to infiltrate her naturally brown-black hair.

Being the established elder of a great house, aunt to queens and cousin to kings, Queen Valentina was the most powerfully connected woman in all the lands. Everyone in the throne room became quiet as she made her way across the floor to the dais of King Gerald and his soon-to-be queen, knowing the power that a single word from her lips could command.

King and Queen de Santi pulled to a stop before the King of Ayr and nodded respectfully. Gerald accepted the gesture between peers with a smile and then nodded respectfully to Queen Valentina. She returned the gesture as an acknowledgement of position and smiled properly.

Gerald threw out his hand and Marko grasped it in a handshake that would have had the same impact if it were a clash between mountain bears. Both men shook. Neither man flinched. Character was maintained.

"Marko, it's good to see you!"

"How long has it been? Since the duels at Graycott, I think?"

"I think you're right. Too long indeed. Those were good duels."

"Agreed. We both fought well and made our kingdoms proud."

"That we did."

Gerald turned his gaze to the queen.

"Queen Valentina. We are honored by your presence at this occasion, majesty."

The queen smiled politely.

"It is you who honor us with your invitation. It would be uncalled for to refuse such an affair or to not be able to travel through your beautiful kingdom."

A small wave of relief moved over the crowd in the throne room as the Queen of Oban responded positively in an upbeat tone.

Gerald smiled and shifted slightly, as if to redirect attention to the woman standing quietly on the dais.

"King and Queen de Santi of Oban, I would like to present Anistasia Savin, my soon-to-be wife and Queen of Ayr."

Marko de Santi looked up at her and nodded in approval. Valentina remained neutral, though she made a small gesture as if to respond positively. Anistasia smiled politely and curtsied as expected. Following the curtsy, she stepped down to take a place next to King Gerald.

"Your kingdom pales in comparison to the beauty of your bride, Gerald."

Anistasia smiled in a modest fashion, as did Gerald.

"I agree with my wife, my friend. She'll make you many fine children. Your days are about to be much more house than state, I think."

The men laughed along with most of the crowd that was in attendance. The women did not. There was always great demand on the wife of a royal to produce children. The world was still a hard place and a ruler needed multiple children to make sure that one survived to continue the name.

Gerald took in the look of his guests and made a calculated decision.

"You both must be tired from your long journey?"

"The trip was lovely, but of some distance, yes."

"In that case, I won't keep you from resting. There is a banquet tonight, to celebrate all who have come. I hope you will be able to attend."

Queen Valentina nodded gracefully.

"That sounds lovely. I look forward to your celebration, King Gerald."

Gerald nodded. Anistasia curtsied. Marko shrugged. Valentina de Santi turned and glided back out of the throne room.

Gerald expelled a large breath of air. Inhaling again, he looked over at his bride-to-be.

"Well, that went better than expected. She's not known for being a good traveler."

"She seemed very sure of her place in the land."

"She is."

Anistasia was about to comment when the herald appeared in the door and made a flourishing gesture with his hand. Gerald, seeing it was a count and not another king, stepped back to the dais. He was taking a seat as the herald announced the arrival of Count Luca Perin, Regent of Lugo.

King Gerald was just situating himself when Luca Perin came to the mark on the floor and stopped to bow in acknowledgement of the crown.

"Greetings, Count Perin. I'm glad to see that you could make the journey."

"As the others who have come before me, I'm honored by your invitation, and that you would think of us in Lugo."

The five-foot-eight-inch mid-aged count spoke with a slight bit of hesitation that underlaid his non-royal blood. One of the many regents that became count not by birth but by deed, he always found it a political minefield to speak in court, especially someone else's court. Still, the seasoned and battle-tested warrior turned ruler carried himself with the surety of a military man. His short brown hair and beard showed none of the stress that battle brought, though his face showed the years. His blue eyes had a knowing look about them.

Where the kings and queens of the lands came with a retinue and guard detachment, most of the counts and countesses came alone or with their spouses. As such, one of Luca Perin's hands rested casually on the hilt of his mid-length, two-handed sword while he spoke. Gerald took no offense in it. It was the natural stance of a man who was under arms.

In the rear of the throne room assembled with the group of guards that lined the rear of the great gallery area and both of the long walls down the sides, Stas Bok stood taking in the scene. He shrugged to shift the metal plate armor covering his shoulders to a better position. Deciding that it was better, he continued to look about aimlessly. The captain of the city guard, and leader of Ayr's army in the field, Bok had seen the show before.

At five-foot-ten-inches tall and a stout sixteen stone, the powerfully built Stas Bok was a lifelong servant of the crown. He had started adult life as a foot soldier and moved through the ranks until he landed on top of the pile, as captain of the city guard. His helmet hid a full head of grey hair, but not the thick bushy beard or bushy eyebrows. The beard and eyebrows helped to hide the numerous wrinkles and scars that life had given him. Being almost at the age of retirement for military men, he was happy to just stand in the back and watch things unfold these days.

Standing next to Bok, the captain of the Kaltan Watchtower scanned the crowd with a lazy consistency. Gerald had requested assistance from the Watchtower, considering the vast amount of royalty he was accommodating in the capital for the wedding. As with every request he had made of them, the Watchtower was happy to assist. The Watchtower Guild was always happy to mediate such affairs to keep the peace high and the crime low. It was also a good chance to show their good deeds. This allowed them to continue receiving the ever-required funding that the royalty provided the peacekeeping group.

"How much longer do you think they are going to receive guests, Stas?"

The big captain of the guard shrugged his shoulders and his metal plate armor rattled quietly.

"I don't know. About an hour or so, I should think. The better part of the day has passed, so it can't go on much longer."

"Good. I'm hungry."

Stas Bok chuckled, and his bushy beard became animated.

"Me too, my friend, me too."

The herald reappeared in the open doorway with another couple to announce, and the two men responsible for the security of the capital went back to watching the crowd.

Chapter Nine

Anistasia Savin lounged in the king's upper courtyard, sitting just inside the shadow of a large tree. The continuous meeting and greeting earlier was exhausting and seemed pointless to her. They had all showed up for the wedding. That was great. But really, it was unimportant. The wedding would happen with or without all of them. She was going to marry Gerald and become queen of Ayr. No one that showed up was required for that to happen. It was only a day or two from reality now.

She had invested too much time and energy in the pursuit of her king. She had worked hard to make sure that she caught his eye and pleased his sight. And she had worked harder to please him once she had finally been captured in his gaze. Yes, she had worked very hard to become a queen, and she was going to become a queen.

A light breeze whistled its way through the courtyard and shifted the silk of her dress around. Anistasia looked down at the garment. Gold and crimson were good colors. Soon they would be the colors of royalty.

Truthfully, the dress didn't help her mood any. The bodice was loose, allowing her breasts to present themselves properly. She much preferred a corset. That kept them in place and was frankly a little easier on her back. Whatever. Looking and being pleasing was the price of a crown, and Anistasia was happy to pay it.

The young queen of Neeron wandered into the courtyard. She looked pleasantly content with her life, and her geriatric king. Anistasia scoffed under her breath. Granted, she, too, was whoring herself out just to get a crown, but not to the point that this girl had. From the queen's fresh face, she wondered if the old king had ever used her. It seemed unlikely. Anistasia took in her features a second time. She really was beautiful. It was no wonder she managed to get ahead.

Queen Vivian Lorimere noticed Anistasia by the tree and turned in her direction. Anistasia smiled politely as the young queen approached.

"Good afternoon, Anistasia."

Anistasia smiled properly and stood from her lounge chair to present herself. Vivian waved a hand, as if to tell her not to bother.

"Oh, don't bother with all that. You're going to be a queen yourself very soon."

Anistasia thanked her and sat back down.

"Would you like for me to have a servant fetch another chair, ma'am?"

Vivian Lorimere blushed slightly at the use of the moniker. She had never really gotten used to their use.

"Vivian, please. And no thank you. I'm just out taking in the views of your beautiful city. You must be pleased in catching such a worthy prize?"

Anistasia smiled. The young queen had hit the nail right on its head.

"Yes, the city is lovely."

The queen of Neeron nodded in response and then thanked her for her hospitality.

"Are you sure you won't take a chair, Vivian?"

"No, I'm just going to look about while my husband rests. Enjoy your quiet time. A royal wedding can be a stressful thing to endure."

Anistasia agreed in a demur fashion and watched as the young queen wandered off toward the short wall that looked down on the inside area of the large walled city. As the young queen walked out of Anistasia's view, another person walked into it. A man stood in shadow by a hedge near the fortress end of the short wall, all but completely hidden to courtyard view.

Anistasia stood and stretched. Adjusting her dress, she strolled casually to a point one or two steps away from where the man was standing in the shadows.

"It's good to see that you've returned. Do you have what I asked for?"

Shadowman took a step out into the light and handed over a small pouch, about a foot long, with a weighted object inside. Anistasia's dark eyes twinkled with pleasure as she opened the pouch. Sticking her hand in to retrieve the object, her twinkle turned to a smoldering fire.

"What the hell is this?"

Shadowman looked at her with a perplexed expression.

"It's a knife."

Anistasia slowly began to boil.

"I can tell that it's a knife. Why are you giving it to me?"

Shadowman continued to look perplexed.

"You asked me to retrieve the objects that were turned in with the body when the bounty was collected. That was the only object that was turned in with the body."

Anistasia turned and looked at Shadowman directly.

"The only thing?"

"Yes, my lady. The captain of the city guard said that the two men who turned in the bounty only left that knife with it. He said that was it."

Anistasia pondered the statement for a moment. Shadowman began to get concerned.

"The two men that handed over the body, what happened to them?"

"The word around Gryazi was that they made acquaintances with an Ubari prince at a public house. The prince is apparently headed here for your wedding. They left the city as part of his company."

"So, they're here in Kanash somewhere?"

"As near as I have been able to determine, no. They must have parted ways on the road between here and there."

Anistasia pondered again.

"Find them. They will be in possession of a metal cylinder about this long." Anistasia made a gesture with her hands. "I want that metal tube and what's inside it. Don't come back without it. I don't care what happens to the men."

Shadowman looked at her with a neutral expression that implied he really didn't care for the task, but would probably do it. Anistasia fumed.

"Do you understand what I want from you?"

Shadowman nodded.

"Good. Go do it."

Anistasia drummed her fingers on the top of the short wall as Shadowman disappeared back the way he had come. The man could be annoying, but he was very good at what he did. He would find what she wanted, sooner or later.

Looking down into the outer courtyard which led off toward the gardens, Anistasia watched the mix of people come and go. It seemed that the lower courtyard was quite the busy place, full of wedding guests and servants. Stopping her gaze on a table by a huge shade tree, she watched two men sitting. One, she was sure, was Prince Jan Nosov, the Count of Gryazi. Gerald's younger brother was tall and handsome, still having the fresh face of youth, though fully a man. Everyone seemed to like him. Most likely because of his pleasant disposition.

From her vantage point she couldn't tell exactly who the other man was. He was tall, and powerfully built. The other man was obviously older, since he appeared to be somewhat balding. He wore a thick leather covering; she was guessing over mail armor. *He must have been hot sitting out in the sun as he was,* Anistasia thought, wandering back to her own shade tree.

"So, Peter, I saw your daughter this afternoon. The Queen of Neeron. I was in the throne room when they presented themselves."

Count Peter Burdin, Regent of Fatezh, smiled in that way that approving fathers do. At six-foot two-inches-tall, and a good fourteen and a half stone, Jan was wondering why his daughter wasn't built like a milk maid. Burdin's heavy blond beard and brown eyes, however, presented the look of a man who was not to be messed with. Jan decided not to judge.

"Yes, she's a good girl. She'll grow into a good queen, I think."

Jan Nosov nodded and smiled. As all knew, Neeron was a happy kingdom. Everyone had their level of want fulfilled.

"So, what about you?"

Jan looked across the table with inquisitiveness.

"What do you mean, what about me? Gryazi has been getting along just fine since I became count.

Peter Burdin smiled and rubbed his beard.

"I mean, Prince, and next-in-line for the throne – until now. What about you and a place under the crown? Gerald getting married complicates your life, no?"

The Count of Fatezh and the Prince of Ayr had been friends for some time, controlling lands which bordered each other. Jan knew that his friend was just provoking an argument to lighten the mood of the day.

"Complicate? It certainly doesn't help."

Both men laughed. A pair of regents from somewhere in the kingdom paused and introduced themselves to the prince. He thanked them kindly, and then they moved along, as most regents did.

"She comes from down your way. What do you know about her? My brother doesn't talk much about how they met. More just about how they spend their nights.

Jan made a face that made Peter Burdin laugh heartedly.

"Don't begrudge a man his pleasures, Jan. Running a kingdom is a stressful business."

Jan smiled and tilted his head until his neck cracked.

"Oh, I don't. I just find it all curious."

Peter Burdin shrugged.

"These things usually are. Her parents actually live in Fatezh. They're aristocrats of some variety. The rumor is that the family was once in the royal line, but they fell out of power."

Jan made a knowing face.

"Well, that explains how she could worm her way into court."

"It appears as though she did a proper job of that."

Both men laughed.

"If she ends up getting pregnant, old boy, that will push you out of the game as well."

Jan nodded.

"I've thought that same thing more than once."

"Yup, if she pushes one out, boy or girl, you're gonna want to start sleeping with a knife under your pillow."

Jan made a face that suggested Peter should come back to reality.

"I'm just saying the obvious."

Jan Nosov made a hand gesture that said, "whatever." It made Peter Burdin chuckle.

"What I say is obvious, Count Burdin, is that it's proper time to go find ourselves an ale."

"Or some stout wine," Peter countered, as he stood up and stretched.

"Come on, I know the way to the cask cellar."

The big count smiled at the prince.

"I bet you do."

Chapter Ten

Queen Bianca Rhodes looked around the carriage at her two traveling companions and then back out of the window and onto the quiet rolling landscape of western Ayr. Large tracts of gently swaying crop fields interlaced with woods and streams gave the look of prosperity to the kingdom. Her gaze glanced around at the entourage of guards that were escorting them. The guards seemed to hold the same opinion of the place that she did. Where she could assess that the crop fields of Ayr weren't any more prosperous than those of her country, Meridian did have more mountain ranges to contend with. Still, the grass was quite green over here.

As Catherine sat looking wide-eyed at everything passing by, and Rosalyn sat stoic, eyes closed in contemplation, Bianca looked into the middle distance and thought. The journey from Meridian to Ayr had been a smooth one. Rosalyn had expedited things in her subtle way to make the trip across Meridian less than the required two weeks it normally would have taken. The passage east across the great Central Sea had been smooth as well, with the help of a continuous wind that the sailors couldn't quite explain.

Bianca's group had taken up all the berths on the vessel she had rented. The captain was glad to have such honored guests onboard his ship, and Catherine had taken advantage by asking an endless series of questions. Their landing near the Watchtower of Aul Torum had been easy, and the Watchtower greeting was also welcome. She and Rosalyn had discussed the state of the guild on this new continent with the local commander before setting off in their carriage. The commander had told them of some other royals who had passed just days prior, and that they should make Kanash in plenty of time for the wedding. Bianca had left them a small chest of silver for their hospitality and then headed east.

Now, that same capital city was in sight of them. The towers of the fortress had been visible on the horizon for a good half-hour. Princess Catherine had been staring at it, willing it to come closer. She was excited by the spectacle. It was obvious that she was the only one in the carriage which held that opinion. Bianca could tell that Rosalyn, like herself, was happy to attend, yet also apprehensive.

"Rosalyn, please. Can you speed up the carriage? Or make the distance not so far?"

Catherine obviously wanted to get to their destination. Rosalyn opened her eyes and took in the view of the countryside around them. She turned her view back into the carriage and smiled at Catherine contentedly.

"Sorry, but no. One should not change the world. The journey will take the time that it takes."

Catherine pouted.

"Are you sure? You did it before, making the wind blow."

Rosalyn smiled.

"Quiet."

Catherine went back to staring at the great fortress city in the distance. Rosalyn considered the request for a moment. Did they need to move faster at this point? Probably not. They were making fine time; there was no reason to rush. As she had attempted to teach so many of her students at Maiden's Tower, rushing into the use of magic created many more problems than it tended to solve. She herself had learned that lesson the hard way.

Still, since all was currently quiet in the lands, she spoke to the horses and their pace increased. Catherine felt the Ellawyn Stone she wore on the chain around her neck warm and knew that Rosalyn had used her sorcery. Sensing the increase in the speed of the carriage, she smiled out at the landscape.

The remainder of the trip was without issue and the carriage pulled onto the main ramp of Kanash castle with good sun still left in the day. The castle fortress had been constructed on a natural rise along a smooth bend in the river. A wide entry ramp ascended along the sidewall out of the old city, on the opposite side of the rise from the river, and into the main castle gates. Bianca's personal guard shifted into file, ahead and behind the carriage, and her captain rode forward several strides to converse with the sentries manning the gate. A large sentry dressed in ceremonial armor hopped onto a mount and escorted them through the interior of the fortress, past the ancient meeting hall with its twin spires, through the market area and into the lower courtyard for the private residence of the king. A good half-dozen other carriages could been seen evenly spaced around the outer edge of the open gathering area. Apparently, they weren't the only ones taking their time to get here.

The three ladies disembarked their carriage and stretched, in a perfectly ladylike fashion. Princess Catherine looked up and took in the multi-story keep which served as both the castle and the western defensive side to the fortress. Where Meridian's castle was ornate, this castle was sturdy and purpose-built. It struck her as both splendid and menacing.

"Well, let's get this over with. I'm hungry."

Bianca's statement was much more man-in-charge than it was delicate queen from the western lands. Rosalyn smiled at her.

"I agree."

The threesome, escorted by Bianca's captain and three local men at arms, made their way to the main entrance. Bianca and Rosalyn produced their finely lettered invitations and the lead guard on the door nodded respectfully. The guard did his best to take in Rosalyn's long red hair without acting like he was staring at her. Unlike other special women he had encountered, she wore her hair long and out in the open for all to see. It made all of the guards in the area apprehensive, just like it was meant to do.

They were led down wide hallways to the entrance for the throne room. The heavy wooden slabs which usually blocked the opening were open, as if someone had just been escorted in before them. The three paused and waited quietly. Catherine spun her head around, looking wide-eyed at everything she could see. The trip was a grand adventure in an otherwise static life, and she wasn't going to miss one thing or detail while it lasted.

An interior ceremonial guard acting as herald for the throne room entrance returned and collected the invitations, so he knew whose name to announce. He inquired about Catherine's status, as she was not specifically mentioned on Bianca's invitation, and turned to head back inside. As the three women stepped into the massive, completely full, and lavishly decorated throne room, and began their slow walk across the polished floor to the dais where King Gerald waited, the room fell from its usual hum into one of complete silence. Several hushed murmurs echoed up from the edges of the crowd, but everyone held their pause as the women glided past. Bianca looked down at her silk slippers and smiled.

"It's always nice to be upstaged by your sister. Reminds me of when we were girls."

Rosalyn glanced in Bianca's direction with a stoic look.

"Trust me. I'd be happy to let you soak up all of the fanfare, just as I did when we really were girls."

Catherine didn't hear any of the exchange. She was busy taking in all of the faces of all of the people in the throne room. It looked to her as though there were people from every land. There were many different styles of dress and colors of skin. She thought about the stories the pirates of the western coast had told her. She had always thought that they were made up stories, but now they all seemed to pale by comparison.

Rosalyn and Bianca hit their mark on the floor and paused. Bianca put out a hand to stall Catherine's forward motion, and her little sister skittered to a stop as well. Not trying to conceal her smile, she reoriented her gaze toward Gerald.

The king stood alone on his dais. There were two chairs, but only one royal. Bianca assumed that Gerald's would-be queen must have retired for the day. She could count all the days she had wanted to retire early in her own court. Still, rulers ruled. The lone recipient already told her something about their hosts.

Gerald was smiling broadly. His blue eyes twinkled above his thick beard. He looked at Rosalyn as if he were trying to formulate a greeting that would be acceptable to her. The silence pressed on for four or five good ticks before Catherine, new to the conduct of foreign courts, leaned in toward the king slightly.

"Say hello."

She said it just loud enough for the four of them to hear, but several others in the front of the crowd picked it up as well, and a second round of murmuring spread over the vast room. Bianca and Rosalyn both looked over at Catherine in a semi-shocked manner. Gerald began to laugh loudly and happily.

"Oh, my dear. I can already tell that we are going to get along famously."

The mood broke. The ceremonial guard and herald pursed his lips and announced the arrival of Queen Rosalyn, Queen of the Freelands Folk, Queen Bianca Rhodes, Queen of the Kingdom of Meridian, and her sister, Princess Catherine Rhodes.

The herald departed. Gerald bowed to the three ladies. All three women curtsied properly and then waited for the king of Ayr to speak.

"It is my great honor to have the High Sorceress of Maidens Tower herself under my roof, as it also is to have the royalty of Meridian."

"The honor is ours, King Gerald. Your invitation that we partake in your great day was most appreciated."

Rosalyn spoke with the fluid grace of a queen, and the clear tone of an unchallenged ruler. She held the most real, usable power of any ruler in all of the lands, and everyone knew it. There was a slight pause before Gerald decided to proceed.

"Your journey? I trust you found it unburdensome?"

The three women looked at each other with different types of smiles. Bianca decided that she would field this one.

"It was, King Gerald. The passage across the Central Sea was calm, and travel through your lands was most enjoyable. You have a prosperous and happy kingdom. My little sister has found it all to be an adventure."

Catherine blushed slightly, in a demur manner, which instantly made her the attention of every prince in the room. Gerald smiled in a way that made Rosalyn sense he had finally calmed.

"Ah, to be young. I remember when I first went out into the world. It was all wondrous. So big that I didn't think there was any way one could begin to see it all. Sadly, the affairs of state took over my life soon after."

Rosalyn and Bianca nodded in understanding.

"That's the way of the world, or of royalty, at least. The demands of one's time come early and are never few."

Where Rosalyn held the room with power, Bianca held it with diplomatic savvy. Her words rang in Gerald's ear as true as any he had ever heard.

"Very true, Bianca. Very true indeed."

The herald reappeared in the far doorway and his fancy dress caught the King's eye.

"I am honored by your acceptance of my invitation, great queens. I trust that we can find some time to converse before you're forced to return home again?"

Both Rosalyn and Bianca agreed. Trade across the sea was a matter of concern for all three kingdoms.

The three curtsied properly and turned to make their way back out of the mob scene in the throne room. Along the outer wall, a pair of men followed their movement, turning around the end of the throng to meet them by the entrance door. A regent of some variety pressed through the space between the two groups, allowing the women to exit the throne room. The larger of the two men stepped into the mid-point in the hallway and cleared his throat, causing all three women to pause.

Turning with the others and instantly assessing the man as non-threatening, Rosalyn looked past him to his associate. He seemed as though he was from the desert lands to the north of Ayr. Bianca and Catherine fixed their gazes on the first of the men. The man wore loose-fitting clothes covered by a magnificent vest and fine robes. Atop his dark, sunbaked face he wore a cloth head wrap, held tight by a large jewel. His dark eyes held no malice, but to the opposite, a look of hopeful opportunity. Bianca took in his measure and figured that they were about the same age.

"Pardon me please, fine ladies. My name is Kamal Nazari. I am Crown Prince to the kingdom of Ubar. I, too, am honored to greet my neighbors to the west of the great sea."

The prince had no more than gotten his name out when the two queens in the group flashed him with a look of recognition. The lone princess in the group was more enthralled by a mysterious stranger from the desert.

"Price Nazari, we are very pleased to make your acquaintance as well."

Bianca and Rosalyn nodded as Catherine spoke. The prince looked at the princess and smiled warmly. Not in a vain or lecherous way, but with hospitality and curiosity.

"It would be my great wish that we might dine together tonight, so that we might also discuss better trade relations between our three kingdoms."

Catherine's eyes screamed yes, so the other two didn't argue.

"That sounds lovely. Currently, we will be going to rest. We will look to collect you at the local dining hour," Bianca said, matter-of-factly.

The prince placed a hand over his heart and bowed slightly. The three ladies turned and continued on down the hallway.

Chapter Eleven

Bernard and Quinn made their way quietly down the closed-in street toward the southern end of Fatezh, orienting themselves in the general direction of the temple. The city of Fatezh had taken on a gritty and dangerous nature since the last time they had passed through it. They were hoping to avoid any new entanglements that might come with that change in prominence.

Each man, in his own way, was a natural at avoiding trouble. For some reason that no one could rightly explain, together they drew out trouble like metal to a magnetic stone. It was crazy how they continued to find problems in the nicest of settings.

Quinn was bone sure that this day would be no different from the rest. He could sense that his friend Bernard didn't care one way or the other. He never did. Bernard was happy, independent of the setting or situation. Okay, he didn't like getting rained on, but who really did? No, he was just one of those insufferably happy people.

The two turned a corner onto another closed-in street. They were about halfway along it when a man walking behind them in the sparsely filled street made the same exact turn. They continued on their way without breaking stride, maintaining their natural gait. Turning another corner at the end of the street, they stepped into a small square. The top of the temple could be seen over the buildings on the square's opposite side.

Bernard and Quinn continued on across the square to a spot where a man was setting up a stall. He appeared to be selling loaves of bread, and the loaves smelled fresh. Quinn paused and smiled at the seller. The man following them was joined by another foul-looking sort and the two made their way slowly around the square's outside edge, stopping to linger by a rain barrel. Another man stepped into the square and turned to the opposing side from the first two.

Quinn purchased a loaf of the fresh bread and a jug of water that looked to be drinkable. He could tell that the man was happy to have business so early in the day. The man thanked them both as they stepped off toward the temple. The seller pocketed his new coins and went back to looking as if he was broke.

Stepping into the next street, Quinn found a closed-in path, much the same as the last couple they had traveled through. Picking up pace, they moved to a pair of doorways on either side of the little street and blended into their openings. They had no more than done so when the two lingering men stepped into the mouth of the street. They took in the empty section and instantly began running, assuming that Bernard and Quinn had done the same. In haste, they ran right past the doorways that Bernard and his beefy friend had chosen for concealment. Letting them pass, Bernard stepped back into the street and whistled. The two running men skidded to a stop and spun around. Sadly for them, they spun around several seconds too late. Bernard speared the first man in the face with the sword in his right hand and removed the other man's head at the shoulders with the sword in his left hand.

The third man had no more than made it completely into the opening of the street when Quinn launched his large flat boot blade in the man's direction, sinking it deep into the last man's throat. Quinn walked casually to where the last man lay gurgling in his own blood. He attempted to gurgle some words as Quinn yanked the blade free of the man's neck. Quinn wiped the blood off on the dead man's tunic and slid the weapon back into the top of his boot.

"Wrong street, shithead."

Reaching down to grab a wad of cloth, Quinn unceremoniously tossed the corpse out of the street's opening. Looking back at the baker man, he shrugged. The seller shrugged back and continued on with his business. Quinn turned and headed to where Bernard was standing. He, too, had already cleaned his blades and returned them to their scabbards.

"Three dead before breakfast. We're ahead of schedule."

The lack of concern in Bernard's voice for the corpses made him wonder if anything really fazed his friend.

"They needed killing. Now, let's be on our way."

The two friends made the remainder of the trip to the temple unbothered. Stepping out of the street and into an open area surrounding the temple, it was obvious to see why the place had such a reputation. The building had to be a solid three stories tall, completely made from cut stone. It had glass windows on each of the floors, and they were all intact. With its outer columns and porches, it was massive.

Obviously built in the previous age, the building had lasted out the apocalypse and stayed on to teach new men about old ways. It was truly an impressive structure, and the worthy centerpiece of any city.

"Now there's something you don't see every day."

Bernard nodded his head as he spoke, taking in the building. Quinn couldn't argue with him, even though they had both seen the building several times over the years.

"I agree. It looks as though the downturn in the city hasn't affected the temple. That's a good sign."

"Let's go say hello."

Bernard and Quinn made their way around in a counterclockwise direction until they came upon the side with the main entrance. Several members of the city guard stood at the temple's entrance. Quinn sighed and kept walking.

They approached the guards in a direct manner, presenting the image of two men who were going into the building. At a proper distance, they both raised their hands, palms out, in the universal sign of surrender. The lead guard raised a hand for them to halt when he decided that they were at a fine talking distance.

"What brings you two to the temple this day?"

"We'd like to speak with the master of the temple. We're in search of knowledge."

Bernard had a pleasant tone, and his smile made the guards less on-edge than Quinn's large mass and neutral expression did.

"What kind of knowledge? You two look better-suited for brawling than you do for letters and volumes."

"Most days, good sir, that's an accurate statement. But today, it's volumes over swords."

The lead guard scratched at his chin whiskers and thought about Bernard's words. The talking one seemed likeable enough, and his friend could probably take them all at once if it came to fighting.

"The master is a busy man. Try not to consume his time."

The men guarding the entrance parted, allowing Bernard and Quinn to pass. Bernard thanked them warmly as they stepped off for the large stone steps leading up to the main entrance doors.

Passing through a door that rotated around them in a circle allowing entry and exit, Bernard and Quinn found themselves in a large opened gathering area. Wide staircases on both sides fed in from wide walkways on upper floors to a great central staircase leading into the middle of the gathering area. It was like something out of a castle. Definitely the work of men with vision and a sense for scale. At the base of the great staircase, a sophist stood patiently, an unassuming look on her face. Quinn took in the red piece of cloth on the woman's dress denoting her as an apprentice to the temple. Bernard was still absorbing the scene when Quinn stepped to the woman in a nonthreatening manner and smiled politely.

"Good day, mistress sophist. A wish that good health be upon you this day."

It was obvious from the sophist's pause that she was not ready for the large, weapon-bound man in front of her to be both well-mannered and well-spoken, still she made no outward show of surprise.

"Greetings, good sir. What brings you and your companion to the temple this day?"

Quinn pointed at his quiver of arrows and then gave the sophist an open-palmed gesture which implied that he meant her no ill intent. She nodded respectfully. Quinn removed his quiver from off of his shoulder and retrieved the metal tube from inside.

"I would like to speak with the master of the temple regarding the contents of this tube."

Quinn rotated his hand so that the sophist could take in the temple seal on the tube's cap. The woman gave a curious expression, and then pointed an open hand toward the stairs. She turned to follow her hand gesture and the two men trailed along behind her.

The three made their way to the second floor and off into a sea of high shelves which filled the entire floor. Shelf units, some ten or twelve feet high, with at least eight individual shelves per unit, completely filled the entire space in uniform rows, turning the floor's space into a great maze. Every shelf in every section they passed by was completely filled with volumes. The volumes were of every shape and size. The wealth of knowledge that they must contain was staggering to contemplate.

The sophist walked quietly on the carpeted floor, but with purpose, as she made her way directly to a large open area next to a bank of high windows. Light streamed through the windows and onto a series of tables positioned to catch the best of the light. An older man stood before one of them, inspecting an opened volume. A large red cloth covered his head and disguised his features to the group, but it was still easy to tell that he was in deep contemplation.

The sophist cleared her throat, and the master of the temple pulled himself from his work. Turning to face them, he smiled contently.

"Master, these gentlemen would like to converse with you."

The older man assessed both their measure and the metal tube in Quinn's hand quickly.

"Thank you, Mildred, for showing them the way up."

Mildred nodded to each man, and then turned and headed back off the way that she had come.

"Good morning to you. I am the master of this temple. Call me, Samual. How may I help you this day?"

Quinn rotated the tube so that it was cap end up and handed it over to Samual.

"We removed this from a thief with a bounty sheet on his name. He was found up in the forest lands north of Gryazi, in the kingdom of Ayr."

Samual inspected the tube and its multiple seals, the outermost one being that of the Great Temple in Drakchi.

"Go on," Samual said in a calm and fatherly way.

"We have two requests. The tube contains a section of a larger document. We are hoping that you might be able to help us understand it."

Samual made a face that implied that was exactly what his job was and extended his hand to accept the metal tube.

Removing the cap, Samual slid the rolled-up paper free of the tube and smoothed it out flat on the nearby tabletop. He stood for several seconds taking in the quality of the drawing. The six-sided object with its equally spaced holes about its face was a very good rendering. He inspected the round cylindrical objects seemingly meant to be inserted into the holes and used as keys. Moving from the drawing, Samual inspected the script on the edge of the paper, where it had been torn free from whatever used to house it. When finally satisfied, he looked back up at Quinn with a neutral expression.

"I've seen something like this before. In a volume, I think. But it was a long time ago and I can't place it clearly. Can you tell us what it might be?"

Quinn spoke calmly and with clarity, though he admitted he could not place the image. It was interesting to Samual that he knew it at all, considering men of his profession weren't given to being men of letters. His statement implied an education, which made Samual curious.

"I don't believe we have any volumes with this specific thing in them, but I think I have something else that might answer your query."

Samual turned from the table as to walk back into the maze of stacks. Quinn scooped up the drawing and tube, as Bernard turned to follow. The master of the temple led them up to the next floor, and over to a room which he unlocked with a large flat key. Stepping in, they could see that the room was full of more moderately sized shelves, and a countless number of volumes. Moving across the room, they paused at a door on the far side and the master unlocked that door with a different key.

This room was different from the remainder of the temple in that it was taken up with a series of waist high cabinets, each one being approximately four-foot by six-foot and containing more than a dozen drawers each. Samual made a show of thinking and then opened a drawer in the third cabinet. He removed a large collection of drawings secured along one edge by a flat metal bracket and sat them on the flat top of the cabinet.

Samual thumbed about a third of the way into the stack and flipped it open, revealing a complete drawing of the six-sided object. It was set into the middle of a large door of some type, and obviously serviced as a lock. The several long rods visible in Quinn's drawing could now be understood to be a set of six keys. One rod for each hole. There was a large amount of precisely spaced text down one side of the drawing sheet. Quinn was just getting ready to start reading when Samual decided to help him out.

"What you gentlemen are looking at is the schematic for the safe door, which secures the great stronghold room, under the city of Rylak."

"Shit," Bernard and Quinn said in unison.

"That's one appropriate response, I guess. The stronghold room is said to possess a power capable of controlling the entire world."

"Shit," came out a second time.

"Six keys are needed to unlock the lock to the stronghold's vault door. The six keys are the six scepters which were granted to the six houses which started this age."

"Why six scepters?" Bernard asked, realizing it was the first words he had uttered in the temple that weren't an expletive. Samual assumed it a reasonable question and continued.

"It is said that whatever this great power is, it is the thing that helped to end the last great age. It was deemed that it could never be used a second time, so it was secured, as opposed to being destroyed. Men are like that. It was locked away with the bones of the dead and the keys were scattered across the lands. At the time it was thought that no one would be strong enough to conquer all six of the newly formed kingdoms, so they wouldn't have to worry about the keys ever being collected into one group again. Or that's the folklore. It was all centuries ago."

"So, each king has a scepter, and all six scepters are needed to open the lock? But there are eight kingdoms in the land."

"Technically, there's about ten. Places like the Rain-Shadow Islands, The Mining Isles, and the Pirate Lands aren't considered real kingdoms by most. And the Freelands Folk are no longer actually people to Meridian. The map has changed over the centuries."

"So, only the original six kingdoms have scepters which are also keys?"

Samual looked over at him and nodded.

"The whole affair was chronicled in the third volume of histories, by Joshua the Scribe. Sadly, we don't possess a copy of the histories. The only complete and known set is located in the Great Temple in Drakchi, which is where your piece of paper came from."

"Why would anyone actually want to open the stronghold room in Rylak?"

Samual made a conciliatory expression in response to Bernard's question.

"Power. Why do most men do any of the things that they do?"

"A more reasonable question. Why didn't they steal your drawing, as opposed to robbing the great temple? This is a much easier place to get in and out of unseen."

Samual smiled.

"That is an excellent question. Probably because very few people know that these drawings exist, while many people know that the great temple has a copy of the histories of Joshua."

"Well, we're certainly not going to tell anyone," Quinn added with a calm surety.

"That is comforting to know," Samual replied politely.

Quinn studied the drawing set for several moments, trying to fix the whole thing in his mind. Samual waited patiently and let him think.

"You have been most kind to us, Master Samual. If it's acceptable to you, we would like to stay the day. I would like to spend some time reading."

Samual considered the request for but a moment and then nodded his head approvingly.

"We are always happy to have people come to the temple. You may inquire with Mildred for any volumes that require finding. She will be happy to assist you. Now, what was your second request?"

Quinn smiled.

"We would be happy if the tube and its contents saw its way back to the great temple. Would you be able to assist us with that?"

Both Samual and Bernard looked at Quinn quizzically.

"That's its rightful place. That's where it should be. I've already made the journey to the Rain-Shadow Islands once. I have no desire to repeat it."

Samual nodded politely.

"We would be more than happy to honor your request."

Chapter Twelve

The sun broke full and hot over the interior of the Kanash fortress. It was the first time in living memory that all of the defensive gates had been closed and manned. There were even guards posted by the tunnel steps leading down into the Dragon's Den cave which exited by the river. Though no dragon had been seen in Ayr during the entire age, it was hoped that one would return one day.

The massive grass courtyard that occupied the majority of the fortress's western side, from the great meeting hall to the entrance stair for the Dragon's Den, had been transformed into an outdoor banquet hall fit for the most royal of royalty. King Gerald had invited so many royals to the wedding that not a third of them would fit into the meeting hall, if it had been used. The open grassy courtyard was the only area in the fortress large enough to host the event.

The whole arrangement had been designed by the planners in a semi-circular fashion. Tables closest to the front held the royalty. Tables behind those held the counts and regents. At the focal point of all this was a large, raised table to host the king and his new bride, along with an entourage of court staff and functionaries.

The planners decided to do the whole affair in a single spot, as no one could work out the proper succession of moving the various kings and queens from one place to another without provoking one to offense. The guests had been shown to their individual sections as they had arrived. Numerous minglings and collections of individuals naturally appeared as all waited for the event to begin. There was some jostling of position, as several people shifted about to get closer to others they wished to converse with.

Circling around the outside of the whole spectacle was a thorough layer of the king's guard. Enveloped around them was another layer of protection offered up by the Watchtower. It had taken the whole garrison from the Watchtower of Kaltan, and some more from Aul Torum to accomplish the job.

Bianca and Catherine entered the fray about midway through the arrivals train. Catherine was all but overwhelmed by the pageantry of the scene playing out in front of them. Bianca did her best to keep her younger sister grounded. The High Sorceress came along slightly later, parting the crowd like a breaking wave when she walked in. The opening her presence carved in the sea of people was filled by the king and queen of Oban, who pushed it even wider open.

Upon arriving on the spot, Bianca and Catherine curtsied properly as they greeted Queen Valentina. Ceremony completed, each one hugged their aunt affectionately, and spoke happily. Rosalyn gave the queen a curtsy but abstained from the hugging. Queen Valentina took her hand instead and held it warmly.

The collection of monarchs discussed trade and pirates. Princess Catherine scanned the crowd, cautiously attempting to find the charming prince they had dined with the previous evening. Rosalyn noticed but said nothing.

The guest train continued uninterrupted for some time, with the grassy lawn swelling with guests. At the tolling of ten strikes from the meeting hall's bell, everyone situated themselves and the event began.

A procession of individuals, led by the king, queen and the caretaker of the meeting hall, entered the grass lawn from the base of the southwestern tower and made their way over to the raised table from behind, affording all a grand view of them. Each person moved to their required position behind their chair and stood, looking in toward the two center seats. King Gerald and Anistasia Savin took up their station and waved warmly to the gathered crowd. The caretaker of the meeting hall stepped in, and with a wave of the hand, everyone grew quiet.

The elder man spoke of Gerald's youth and his assumption of the throne from his father. He went on to speak of his peaceful and contented reign over the Kingdom of Ayr. Turning slightly, he oriented himself toward Anistasia. The caretaker spoke of her upbringing in Neeron and her royal bloodline. He continued on to talk about how she had captured the affections of the king from their very first meeting. That had been more than a full year back.

The caretaker collected their hands together, and using an old ceremonial cloth from the meeting hall, wrapped it around their hands to bind them together. Nodding to the couple, Gerald leaned in and kissed Anistasia softly. Anistasia reciprocated, closing her eyes and keeping her lips against Gerald's long enough to pass by etiquette and move on toward the outer edge of passion.

Turning to address the gathered assembly, the caretaker stated that with their witness to this act and from this day forward the two would be one. The king's wife would now and always be known as Anistasia Nosov, wife of Gerald. The caretaker bowed to the assembly and then to the king, as he stepped out and off the raised platform. Loud cheers and calls that lasted a solid five minutes broke out after the pronouncement. King Gerald finally had to put his hands up in defense to quiet the assembly.

Taking the moment, the king thanked everyone for attending the wedding, and expressed his profound gladness of so many people being able to share in the day with Anistasia and himself. The remarks elicited another round of cheers and calls from the entire gathering.

The ale was being poured and the meat was being brought around when Bianca elbowed her little sister in the ribs. Catherine looked over, exhibiting her shocked face. Bianca had seldom done such things since becoming queen.

"See that one seated to the right of the king? The sturdy one with the short brown hair? That's Prince Jan. He's the king's brother. He's also still unmarried."

Catherine inspected him momentarily. Yes, he was definitely handsome and strong.

"And?"

"I'm just saying that he'd make a fine husband. And a good alliance for Meridian."

Catherine blushed.

"Bianca, stop."

"What? He's a good catch."

Rosalyn leaned in slightly.

"He's the Count of Gryazi. A girl could do a lot worse than that."

Catherine turned her head to look past her sister toward the high sorceress.

"You too?"

"We're just trying to help, dear."

Catherine inspected him again and blushed again. The thought of being taken by him was appealing.

"He is handsome."

"But," Bianca countered, knowing the way that her sister used pauses as stopping points.

"But I like that crown prince that we met. The one from the desert lands. He's also unmarried, and he's dashing. He's probably not interested in a plain princess like me, though."

Bianca stifled a laugh that made the other people seated at their table look over. She made a show of taking a drink of wine, and all went back to normal.

"Oh, my little sister. All of the men here, and half of the women, know that you're available. And all of them want to get their hands on you."

Rosalyn nodded emphatically, adding her concurrence.

Catherine blushed again.

"Women too? You think that?"

Bianca and Rosalyn nodded in unison.

"Well, I don't know anything about anything like that. However, I'm going to find that crown prince. What was his name?"

"Kamal Nazari," Bianca and Rosalyn said in unison. This time loud enough to collect stares from the others at the table a second time. Rosalyn waved it off, as if to say that she would speak at whatever volume level she chose. Everyone went back to their own conversation.

"Yes. I'm going to find Prince Nazari, just as soon as we are allowed to get up."

Bianca smiled at her little sister, as if to say that she was still a touch naïve. Bianca considered the whole exchange for a quick second, instantly finding Catherine's naiveté a little odd. For the amount of time that she spent in the company of pirates, she should be better versed in the ways of the world. Maybe it was just the setting and the day?

"Catherine, you're a princess from the Great House of Rhodes. You can get up whenever you desire to, no matter the crowd."

Catherine looked at Bianca and Rosalyn in semi-disbelief, and then over to her aunt, Valentina. Valentina hadn't been specifically eavesdropping on the girls' conversation, but she had been close enough to take in what was being said. The Queen of Oban nodded authoritatively to her niece.

Catherine began to shuffle in her chair. Bianca reached out and placed a hand on hers, making her pause.

"You can do it, but that doesn't imply that you should do it. Princesses are also polite and getting up in the middle of such an event to converse would be seen as impolite."

Catherine nodded in understanding.

"Later then."

Bianca and Rosalyn laughed full-on this time, making everyone turn in their direction for a third time. Fortunately, the servants were coming round with the wine, pulling the guests' focus from the distraction being caused by the girls.

King Gerald noticed the laughter echoing up over the sounds of the general conversation and the boasting that was going on about the gathering. He leaned over to his brother Jan and smiled.

"See those two, Jan? The Rhodes sisters?"

Jan nodded his head as he was taking a drink of ale.

"They rule over the Kingdom of Meridian and are nieces to the Queen of Oban."

Jan glanced down at the two blonde beauties seated next to the high sorceress.

"I know that, brother."

"I'm just saying that, if you could get your hands on one of them, it would be a grand prize indeed."

Jan Nosov was about ready to unleash a witty comeback on his brother when the caretaker of the great meeting hall reappeared, bringing with him an all-consuming silence.

The Caretaker of the Great Meeting Hall of Kanash thanked everyone for attending the wedding interval and asked for their patience as things were adjusted for the coronation ceremony. With the wave of a hand, he bid the wedding party to rise and step from the stage.

As if on cue, thirty sturdy men appeared from one side of the lawn. They filed in forming a row along the front and rear of the raised platform. With a single, practiced heave, the raised platform top was lifted free and marched off to the opposite side of the grass. The crowd watched the seating area float away as another twenty men carried in a replacement top. This new section contained the two throne chairs from the castle's throne room. A group followed behind the chairs, placing thick purple carpets all about the assembly to make it look as if it were still inside.

The king and his new wife took their seats on the raised dais as the remainder of the wedding party gathered around it in a tight circle. The caretaker scanned the crowd, and deciding that everything was acceptable, waved his hand with a flourish.

Buglers and trumpeters appeared on the surround of the ramparts for the entire circumference of the grassy area and began to blow a processional march. With the beginning of the music, a line of young boys and girls entered, each one carrying an object of royal importance on a purple silk pillow.

The caretaker picked up a thick purple robe from the first child. Turning to face Anistasia, she stood and then bent down to one knee, adjusting her dress as she did so. The caretaker draped the robe over her shoulders, speaking a collection of statements regarding her new station in the kingdom as he did so.

The next child in line brought with her a magnificent gold and jeweled crown. The caretaker placed the crown on Anistasia's head, saying some more words about her new title. With each of his statements, he spoke in the old language of the country, giving the whole ceremony a deeply arcane feeling.

The third child held a wood, stone, and jeweled scepter. It was centuries old. And though antique, solid and sturdy in its countenance. The caretaker picked up the instrument of rule and placed it in the new queen's hands, stating that all could see her legitimacy to rule of the land.

Offering some further sentiments in the old tongue, the caretaker finally bid her to sit and take her place next to the king. Turning around to the assembled committee, the Caretaker of the Great Meeting Hall of Kanash announced the coronation of Queen Anistasia of Kanash, Queen to the Kingdom of Ayr, and rightful ruler of the lands.

The entirety of the assembled royalty stood in a smooth wave and bowed or curtsied in acknowledgement of the new monarch. The trumpets and bugles on the ramparts blew loudly, announcing to everyone in the kingdom not allowed inside the fortress that a queen was now in residence.

Rosalyn kept a fixed eye on young Jan Nosov as the whole affair unfolded. The brother of the king conducted himself through the whole of the extravagant procession with a fixed neutrality. There was nothing he could do about it, so he wasted no energy on it. Rosalyn considered him smarter than the rest gathered around the dais.

Jugglers and tumblers came into the scene, leading an army of wine bearers. They were followed by another army of servants possessed to remove the tables and chairs, making ample room for the festivities to come.

Catherine clutched Bianca's arm.

"Come. Come with me, so I can track down the desert prince."

The Queen of Meridian looked at her little sister, as if to say that her decorum was slipping, and then smiled.

"I need to do queen things and talk a little politics with some other kings and queens. Take Rosalyn with you. She won't let your virtue get lost in the crowd."

Catherine produced her blushed face and then her shocked face. Rosalyn looked over with a curious expression.

"I had planned on doing a little politicking of my own. Donations to the tower aren't what they used to be. But I guess that it can wait long enough to find you a prince."

Catherine smiled broadly and clutched Rosalyn's arm, as if to drag her away immediately. As they separated, Bianca headed directly for the old king of Neeron, and his young queen. Neeron was one of Meridian's principal trading partners. Bianca wanted to discuss the continued stability of those arrangements.

As Catherine and Rosalyn waded into the crowd, Enella, Sorceress of the Great Temple of Drakchi, crossed their path purposefully.

"High Sorceress, I wanted to pause and say that it is good to see you once more."

Rosalyn smiled broadly and reached out gently placing a hand on Enella's cheek.

"It warms my heart to see you. You look well. Say that you're well?"

"I am. You also look in a good spirit."

"I am, mostly."

Enella smiled softly, understanding the natural melancholy that knowledge and power produced. Enella noticed Catherine's expression out of the corner of her eye, mostly because of the spike in glow from the ELLAWYN pendant.

"Where are my manners? Enella, Sorceress of the Great Temple of Drakchi, I would like to introduce you to Princess Catherine Rhodes, from the Great House of Rhodes in Meridian, my most-loved little sister."

Enella curtsied to the princess as Catherine bowed appropriately to the sorceress.

"It is an honor to meet you, Princess. How many would like to be able to say that they are sisters with the most powerful woman in all the lands?"

Catherine smiled politely.

"Yes. I'm also the sister to the High Sorceress of Maiden's Tower."

Enella made a face that said she didn't get the joke, as Rosalyn did everything she could do to not laugh out loud.

"Nevertheless, it's nice to meet you, Princess. I do wish you well."

Enella could feel the magical energy that the two sorceresses were emanating now pulsing from the ELLAWYN pendent. Rosalyn laid a gentle hand on the pendant hanging outside of Catherine's dress and allowed about half of the stored energy to dissipate into the surrounding atmosphere. Enella smiled softly.

"That is a powerful protection, Princess. Your sister must care for you deeply to bond you with such a thing. I hope that it offers you all of the protection that it is meant to, throughout all of your journeys in life. One never knows where the roads of life may lead."

Catherine smiled softly.

"Thank you. You are very kind, Sorceress. Hopefully, tonight, life's road leads me to a prince."

Both of the sorceresses laughed, understanding the immediacy of youth. Catherine didn't get the joke but decided to let it pass. Rosalyn and Enella embraced, wishing each other a pleasant journey through life and a happy spirit. Other people stopped by to chat as Enella stepped away. Catherine scanned the crowd for the mysterious desert prince as a band of players began to play.

Chapter Thirteen

The sun was setting on the temple in Fatezh as Quinn sat down a volume on ancient politics titled *The Prince* and looked about the reading area for his weapons and his companion. As expected, Bernard was lounging in a heavily padded chair located next to their stack of weapons. He also possessed a volume, except his volume was resting on his chest and his eyes were closed. *Oh well,* Quinn thought, *one of us has to be on-guard in this town. Might as well be Bernard.*

Quinn whistled low and Bernard's eyes snapped open.

"Yeah?"

"Almost dark outside."

Bernard adjusted his gaze to one of the windows.

"Yup."

Quinn closed the volume he had been reading and sat it on a small holding table next to his chair.

"What do you think?"

"Public house?"

Quinn smiled, knowing what his answer was going to be.

"Public house."

Both men stood. Bernard sat his volume gently on top of Quinn's and began collecting weapons. Mildred appeared on the edge of the reading area so quietly that neither of the acutely aware men noticed her presence.

"Finished? Are there any other volumes that you would like to consider?"

Both men whipped around, startled by the unexpected voice. Their reaction didn't faze Mildred's calm demeanor in the slightest.

"Mildred, you're quiet like a cat."

Bernard smiled at her and then returned to collecting weapons.

"So I'm told, Mr. Bernard."

"We're done, I think," Quinn stated politely. "We've taken up too much of your time already. We do thank you for all of your assistance throughout the day."

"You are too kind, Mr. Quinn. It's always a pleasure to have people that are respectful of the temple. Are you leaving now?"

"Yes, ma'am. You wouldn't happen to know of a good public house nearby?"

Mildred made an expression that showed she was actually considering the question.

"Three blocks straight south, Mr. Quinn, you'll find an establishment called The Palace Gate. I think you'll find it friendly enough."

Master Samual appeared from a space behind Mildred as his voice flowed through the opening between two stacks of shelves.

"Three blocks south. We can't screw that up. Thank you, Master Samual. And you, Mildred. You have both been very hospitable."

Samual nodded, and Mildred glided off from the direction that she had originally appeared. Bernard and Quinn adjusted their things about their body in preparation to be going, and Samual waited patiently to escort them out. Once ready, the three walked quietly through the second-floor stacks and down the wide stairs to the large open gathering area inside the main doors.

Quinn pulled on his Watchtower cloak and flipped the hood up over his head. Bernard, spying a collection box by the office's door, walked over and dropped three full-weight gold coins into the slot in its top. Master Samual placed a hand over his heart and bowed slightly, saying thank you for the gift. Returning to form, he inspected Quinn's cloak.

"Yours?"

"Yes."

"A sergeant in the Watch?"

"Former."

"Interesting."

Samual paused a moment after to consider Quinn's statement.

"Black mark or collection clause?"

Quinn looked around the open area, not really wanting to answer the question.

"The second one."

"Interesting indeed."

Samual was about to ask a further probing question when Bernard came walking back over to where they were standing. Quinn could see that he possessed a look of unwanted sobriety.

"The Palace Gate, you say? Sounds fancy."

"It's adequate, I would say. There isn't much left in this place that I would consider fancy."

All three men shrugged. It was the way of such things.

"I'm pointing you toward the south, because I think you might want to keep going that way?"

Quinn took in Samual's serious countenance and nodded.

"Go on."

"Moving through the Kingdom of Neeron, in a southwest direction, and continuing into the Kingdom of Oban, you'll eventually come to a crossroads town called Orba."

Bernard nodded.

"Yes, I know of it."

Samual smiled politely.

"I've heard that there might be a man there who might be able to help you with the knowledge you seek. To further your quest, as it were. He's a collector, of sorts. They call him Raphael, most of the time."

Quinn nodded slowly, followed by Bernard.

"It's rumored that he was once in possession of a complete collection of the histories. If you are fortunate, he may still be."

Quinn smiled politely.

"Thank you, Master Samual. We greatly appreciate all of the kindness that you've shown us this day."

Master Samual extended a hand and Quinn did the same, both men clasping at the forearm. Quinn released his grip, finally noticing the brand on Samual's forearm. Master Samual shrugged, and let his robe fall back down over top of it.

"When I was young, I had a sense for an adventurous life. But as youth tends to do, it led me down the wrong road. I took the first way out of the Watch."

Quinn paused, thinking about some of the roads that youth had taken him down, and then nodded respectfully.

"Times change, as do people. I, for one, certainly hold you in high regard."

Master Samual put his hand on his heart a second time. Deciding that the talking was over, Quinn looked over at Bernard, nodded a final time and strode for the door. Bernard turned to follow at a somewhat more leisurely pace.

Three full streets south to the step, the two men came to the public house which the master of the temple had mentioned. Calling inside, they found a pleasantly full tavern area and some available rooms upstairs. Deciding not to make a scene, they opted for a single room with two sturdy beds. Bernard gave the barman a coin and he gave them a wooden room number with a metal key attached.

Quinn collected the key from the barman, and swords and such from his friend. Stepping off, he headed for the stairs. Bernard collected a pair of full tankards and headed for a free table where he could take in both the stairs and the better part of the crowd. He was just settling in nicely when Quinn reappeared, trudging down the stairs. He plopped down with his back to the wall and collected the full tankard.

"This place have food?"

Bernard made a skeptical face.

"I'm betting so, but if the food is as good as the ale, do we want it?"

Quinn took a drink, consuming about half of the large pewter handled container.

"I see your point. Might be better to just wait."

Bernard looked about the place. It seemed quiet enough for a rough and ready place like Fatezh.

"That business at the temple, on the way out. What was that all about?"

Quinn had slowly been developing a mood since they left the temple. He wasn't normally the moody type. His countenance was normally more neutral, with a tendency toward violence.

"It was nothing. Just some passing remarks between two old Watchtower troops."

Bernard took a drink and looked at Quinn, trying to decide if this conversation was worth setting him off.

"So, that's what the brand was? On his forearm?"

Quinn nodded, staying basically neutral.

"You get one if you break your contract and leave the service."

Bernard was readying his next question when he realized that the expression on Quinn's face meant he was done talking about it.

"Well, at least we have a roof over our heads tonight. Maybe there's some work in this town?"

Quinn finished off the large mug of ale and sat the empty down in front of Bernard.

"If there is, then it's not the kind we want. We should have moved straight on out of the city."

Bernard stood, collecting the tankards.

"For the Goddess of Good Luck, Quinn, stop brooding. We'll be on our way soon enough."

Quinn looked at his oldest friend in the world skeptically.

"You shouldn't tempt the Goddess of Good Luck, Bernard."

Bernard shrugged and turned in the direction of the barman.

"Have you seen our life? That's what we do, old chum. Every day."

On the opposite side of the tavern, deep in the shadows of the overhanging upper floor, Shadowman sat at a table with two burly locals. He had given each man a solid gold coin and enough ale to make them agreeable to his needs. They were expendable. The city was full of such men.

"See the man walking over to the barman? Short blond hair and about eleven and a half stone?"

Both locals nodded in unison.

"Go kill him, and then be ready to kill his friend."

Both men stood and skulked over to the middle of the tavern floor, intercepting Bernard about halfway back from the bar.

"Hey you!" The bigger of the two men grunted at Bernard, being close enough for Bernard to smell his foul breath.

Bernard paused and sized up the opposition.

"Yes?"

"I don't like the look of you, boy. I'm going to put a knife in your belly and split you open from noodle to neck."

The big man brandished a dragger with a thoroughly rusty blade and held it up for Bernard to see. Bernard, deciding not to wait for another foul-smelling and witless comeback, flexed at the elbow, as if preparing to pull his swords, and then sighed heavily. He didn't have his swords.

Reassessing the situation before bad breath guy could stab him, he jerked both hands up quickly splashing the big man in the face with ale. The man cursed and began shaking his head to get the stinging ale out of his eyes. Swinging his left hand in a roundhouse, with everything he could quickly muster, Bernard slammed the knife man in the temple with the side of a thick pewter tankard. The big man grunted as blood flew from the fresh gash that the blow had created.

Bernard ducked to dodge an incoming fist from the second man, and pivoting on one foot, kicked him squarely in the kneecap. The second man collapsed in a scream of pain.

Bernard refocused his attention on the big knife man, who was just starting to get his dim wits back. Deciding to stay offensive, Bernard slammed the man's face with a series of punches, finishing the flurry with a bone-crunching shot to the throat. The big knife man collapsed to the floor, unable to breathe from the blood he was gargling, allowing Bernard to return his attention to kneecap guy.

Kneecap was about halfway up on shaky feet when Bernard squared up on him. He drew back his fighting hand, the mashed-up tankard still clinched in the other one, and prepared a second round of destructive punches. Pulling the trigger on a volley, he had to yank his punch as he watched the man collapse in front of him, a thick spray of blood shooting from the back of his skull. Bernard looked down at the floor, taking in the hilt of Quinn's boot knife protruding from the man's head.

Bernard reached down and yanked it free, a jet of blood and grey matter coming out with the blade. Turning slightly, Bernard shoved the blade deep into the big knife man's chest, helping him dispense with the last of his life.

With both men dead, the thick mass of people which had gathered around the scene began to disperse. Quinn stood and walked over to retrieve his boot knife. Bernard collected the dead man's dagger and rifled through both men's pockets for anything of use. The quick search produced nothing but two newly minted, full-weight, gold coins from the royal mint of Ayr. Bernard shrugged. It was the way of such men, in such places. Nothing of note, except despair.

Bernard stood and walked over to the barman, who was possessed of a mild scowl. He looked back at the two corpses in the middle of the tavern floor, and then back at the barman. The man did have a point. Smiling, he sat the dented-up tankard on the bar top, followed by the dagger and the two gold coins.

"Sorry about the mess, sir. It was unintended. Any chance I can get our empty ales changed out for fresh ones? Oh. You can keep all that, for the mess we made."

The barman smiled and scooped up the coins before they drew too much attention from the crowd. He handed over fresh ale and put the dagger under the bar with a half-dozen others he had picked up off the floor.

Bernard sat the full ale glasses down in front of Quinn and looked at him quizzically. He now seemed even moodier than before. Bernard wasn't sure why. It wasn't like this was the first time they'd killed a couple of nobodies in a bar fight.

"You could have helped sooner."

Quinn picked up one of the ale mugs.

"You were doing fine on your own. Besides, I was watching their employer sneak around the outside of the scene and up the stairs."

Bernard sat.

"And?"

"And he popped the lock and slid into our room while everyone was watching your little altercation."

Bernard took a drink.

"Think he's still in there? Maybe I should have kept the dagger?"

Quinn looked up at the door to their room.

"He didn't come back out. I'm betting that he made his way out a window and onto a nearby rooftop."

Bernard seemed curious.

"Why?"

"Because, unless I miss my guess, he was Shadowman."

Bernard made a face of unmasked skepticism.

"Oh, please. There is no Shadowman. It's a story. He's just a thief, looking to make an easy mark without being seen."

Quinn shook his head.

"I disagree. Besides, I think we should be on our way, while we can still use the darkness for cover. We're stacking up too many bodies in this place."

Bernard took a large gulp of ale.

"Now that, I do agree with. Let's get out of here."

Chapter Fourteen

King Gerald Nosov of Ayr sat on his throne with an insuppressible smile under his thick, dark brown beard. His new wife, Anistasia Nosov, first queen of Ayr in two full generations, sat next to him with a similar expression. The two had been feasting and celebrating continuously since the Caretaker of the Great Meeting Hall had wed them. The whole extended capital city had been taking part in the merriment. It had been a monumentally joyous occasion.

Now, with the mood slowly dissipating for everyone save Gerald, it was time to return to the affairs of state. He could feel that all of the crowns and honored guests were thinking a similar thing. One didn't want to be out of their kingdom for too long, for fear that problems would arise. Nobody wanted to return to that.

The kings and queens were the first to announce their goodbyes. King Marco and his queen had left for Oban that morning. King Kamber of the Mining Isles was also on his own way south to find a ship. King Diego de Paz from Udaass had also come and bid the wedded couple a fine farewell.

Master of the Great Temple of Drakchi, Kanji Chan, and their sorceress, Enella, had also made the exit. They had been followed by a whole host of counts and countesses that were scattering back out across the continent. It had truly been the greatest single gathering of power and wealth in the entire age.

Gerald looked over at his new queen while he considered the

extended cost of the whole affair. The massive outlay of coin that had been required, and still would be required to cover the cost, would put a good dent in the national coffers. The outpouring of coin from the assembled nobility was also a huge sum. Gerald took in the content and satisfied expression of his new wife and knew that it was all money well spent. His was going to be the grandest kingdom of the age. What it cost to make it so was a cheap price to pay. Besides, it was a dent, not a hole. There was still plenty of coin left with which to conduct affairs, and much to spare after that.

The herald of the hall appeared and pulled jolly King Gerald back to the here and now. Both King Lorimere of Neeron and his sweet young queen, followed by the Crown Prince of Ubar, came into the hall to address the royal couple. As protocol dictated, King Lorimere went first, while the prince waited patiently. Gerald and Jasper talked trade for several minutes, and the tensions that had arisen near the border north of Graycott over output from Neeron's mines in the mountains there. The delegates from Ayr, Neeron, and Udaass had been smoothing out the tensions for some days, and all was about to be resolved. The discussion between kings was a keep the faith solidarity between old friends' type of conversation. Both men circled around the conversation with the candor of men who had been in such conversations many times in the past.

King Jasper and Queen Vivian finally departed, allowing Crown Prince Kamal Nazari of Ubar to approach the throne. The prince thanked the king for his gracious hospitality, and the kindly and gracious nature of his kingdom. The two men also talked trade for several minutes, as Ayr was a large exporter of foodstuffs to the northern desert kingdom just across the inland sea. The two neighboring kingdoms had always gotten on well. King Gerald assured the prince that he could carry back news to his father, the king, that it would continue uninterrupted during his reign.

Crown Prince Nazari extended King Gerald the customary departing gestures of his people and stepped off to exit the throne room. Walking out of the throne room, the prince considered the last number of days. He and his entourage had collected many wonderful stories and had partaken in some good adventures during these travels out of the country. Now, upon the edge of his return journey, he was sure that more adventures lay ahead. Pausing to look through a stone-cased window down onto the central market square, he considered his two new friends. He wondered if the man named Quinn, and his companion Bernard, had made it to the port as he had requested them to. Had they found the pirates, as he planned that they would? The prince felt in his bones that they had. He was a good judge of men. He was sure that both Quinn and Bernard were the kind who saw things through to the end. He had instantly liked them both, right from the first meeting. They had sound character.

Kamal Nazari continued on through the hallways and corridors of the castle for the fortress of Kanash with the ease of a welcomed guest. He was feeling confident that his men had already made their way to the stables and found their mounts. It was time to be on the road. He needed to go find a man with a ship having black sails.

Stepping out into the open lower courtyard entrance to the great house, he saw several sets of mounted riders and carriages collected for other departing nobles. A quick scan produced the group of men and horses he was looking for. He turned toward them and continued walking. It was time to go.

The prince had covered about a third of the distance to his men when he heard the word "Akeem" rise up over top of the noise in the courtyard. Recognizing his name, he paused and scanned the crowd for the voice which had produced it. It was a young and sweet-sounding voice. It took him but seconds to locate the beautiful blonde features of Princess Catherine Rhodes of Meridian. She was standing next to a carriage waving her arm with enthusiasm. The high sorceress and her sister, the queen, stood a couple steps to one side. The queen had a look of amusement on her face, which the high sorceress lacked. Crown Prince Kamal "Akeem" Nazari turned on his heels and purposefully strode in the direction of the ladies.

Princess Catherine marched forward, closing the distance that Akeem needed to cover. She smiled at him with a radiance that suggested to him that she didn't do it often. No, if he had to bet his coins, he would say she was the melancholy sort. Not depressed or downtrodden, but sad in some unexplainable way. Whether that was actually true or not, it certainly wasn't the current state of things. Akeem paused an appropriate distance from the princess and bowed slightly with a smile and a flourish.

"Princess Catherine. It is most pleasant to see you again before we all depart for our separate kingdoms. Your wit and beauty are things seldom found in this world. I plan to tell many stories about them when I am finally back in Ubar."

Akeem kept his tone light and princely. He wasn't taking any chances on offending her sister, the High Sorceress of Maiden's Tower and Queen of the Freelands Folk, for any reason. To his relief, Catherine blushed, as all young princesses do, and the two queens standing behind her laughed out loud. They were obviously worldlier than their young charge.

"If he's going to talk to you like that in public, then you need to keep him, Catherine."

Queen Bianca Rhodes was still laughing as she spoke. She turned toward Rosalyn and smiled boldly.

"Good men are hard to come by."

"As are princes," Rosalyn added with a rare genuine public smile.

Akeem nodded respectfully to the two powerful women and made a gesture with his hand that suggested he and Catherine should move back closer to the carriage.

"I would like to think, with some amount of mild humility, that I am both of those things."

Rosalyn looked at him as if she was looking straight into the deepest part of his being and judging him upon its merit. It lasted only seconds, and then the high sorceress nodded her head slightly as if to agree with his statement. Catherine and Bianca watched the mystical shakedown with spectator enthusiasm and waited for the outcome. With the head nod they both smiled broadly.

"My sister is protective of me," Catherine said matter-of-factly.

"Both of her sisters are," Bianca added holding a light tone. "Even if you're a queen, you can still be used by men."

"That's very true, majesty. In the great pursuit of rule, all things are sought out and used for their value, people included."

Rosalyn's eyes narrowed like a hawk staring down at a rabbit.

"That sounds like the opening statement in an agenda, prince."

Akeem wasn't sure if he hadn't just mistakenly crossed a bridge or not.

"It wasn't intended as such, majesty. I was simply agreeing with Queen Rhodes."

Akeem looked at the ground and then at Princess Catherine, who was still beaming, and made a conciliatory expression.

"I confess, I've never had to address two queens at the same time before. I am guessing there's some type of protocol between Meridian and The Freelands Folk as to who comes first or what title is used. I apologize for not knowing that custom."

Bianca laughed so genuinely that Akeem wasn't sure if he hadn't just made things worse for himself.

"Prince Nazari, you're doing just fine standing your ground, despite the numbers in opposition. You should definitely travel to Meridian one day, so you might learn about our customs firsthand."

Akeem smiled and let out a breath.

"I would like that very much. Ubar does a fine trade with both Meridian and The Freelands Folk. I would like to see that our trade relationship continues on for both co … I mean all countries."

Rosalyn smiled and nodded, respecting his catch of the slip. There were still places in the world that saw The Freelands as some type of Meridian territory, and not its own state. It was okay, their coin all spent the same to her people.

"Well, until that day, we wish you safe travels."

Bianca smiled politely, wrapping up the conversation.

"Thank you, majesty. It should be quite fine. My company travels southwest, toward the port of Roadstead."

Catherine's eyes got as big as carriage wheels.

"That's the same place we're traveling to. You should ride with us."

Catherine turned to look at Bianca, sisterly pleading in her eyes.

Rosalyn was obviously suspicious, but Bianca wasn't going to crush Catherine's hopes. Well, not this day anyway.

"Prince Nazari, it would be nice to speak at a more leisurely pace about our trade relations with your kingdom. If you're heading in the same direction as we are, it would seem a fine time to do so."

"It would be an honor to do so, majesty, as long as our presence with your group isn't seen as an imposition."

Catherine slid an arm through Akeem's and smiled radiantly.

"It's not. It's really, really not."

Bianca smiled and pointed Rosalyn toward the carriage door before she could protest.

Chapter Fifteen

Queen Anistasia Nosov walked casually around the private terrace of her new residence, taking in the bright morning sunshine and pleasant breeze. The last of the wedding guests had departed for whatever part of the globe they had originally come from. Her husband, King Gerald, was out discussing whatever needed discussing. The affairs of the kingdom on this day most likely revolved around paying for the wedding. It really had been a lavish affair. No doubt it probably cost a small ransom in coin.

As she slowly paced, she considered another thought. There really had been a great amount of deal-making going on over the course of the last days. The king and all of the other leaders had taken the opportunity to discuss all sorts of business partnerships and trade deals. He was probably out solidifying whatever side deal he had made over the last days. She imagined that all the other leaders were doing the same.

Anistasia, newly minted queen of Ayr, stopped and considered that for a larger moment. She really needed to integrate herself into these discussions. It would be good to know what inter-kingdom deals were in-place between Ayr and the surrounding lands. This would tell her much about any leverage or weakness the other kingdoms possessed. Her husband was well known for being a man who wouldn't strong-arm his subjects or neighbors. He was well-liked and much respected for this trait. Anistasia wasn't her husband. She had no issues with using collusion or leverage to get what she wanted. After all, that was how she had become queen. She had slowly wormed her way from the bottom of the aristocratic ladder to the throne room of Ayr by any means necessary. She had managed to gain and control more real power than any member of her family in over two centuries. She hadn't gotten here by worrying about what other people thought of her, or by letting others make her decisions.

Anistasia paused and reached up to remove the crown from her head. She loved the weight of it, and the way that it felt sitting on her head. It was the universal sign of power. Turning it around in her hands several times before placing it back on her head, she knew that she needed to start inserting herself into things. The real question was how to start.

Anistasia adjusted her crown slightly, so it sat properly. She would need to start slow. Pick the points where people would be willing to hear her ideas. The problem with that is that there really weren't any easy opportunities available to her in Ayr.

Ayr had been a one-man monarchy for over a century. It was well-designed to function in that fashion. A system of counts and regents handled the daily business of the land. They, in turn, answered to the regent of the royal house or the king. She knew that everyone on the regent's council and the regent of the royal house distrusted or openly disliked her. Most all of the king's court did as well. The Ayr court was a suspicious lot for sure.

Still, the regent's council was the right place to start. They had open meetings and decision-making power. She wanted to get inside that circle of influence.

Even with the great distances she had managed to cover, she was still on the outside of the powerful looking in. The queen of Ayr was a new position in the government of the kingdom. It was becoming obvious to her as she pondered that it was largely thought by the regents to be a ceremonial one. She was a sovereign, in equal measure to her husband, but without any power. The power of the kingdom still resided with the king, followed by the regents, and then the prince. Gerald's younger brother, Prince Jan Nosov, Count of Gryazi, had more real power than she did as queen. He could become a formidable opponent when it came to capturing power in the kingdom.

Anistasia paused her pacing and let the light breeze washing over the terrace distract her thoughts. The palace inside the Fortress of Kanash was a fine place to spend one's life. Opulent and well-staffed, it was as comfortable as a fortress could be made to be. The breeze lifted the scent of the trees up and carried it to her across the manicured lawns. It was the pause that Anistasia needed to reframe her thinking.

Power? What was power, really? There were only two kinds of real power in all of the lands. When you boiled it all down to the bones, only two kinds survived. There was political power. That was what she had been considering. Political power was the type that people gave you when they perceived you to be in a more advantageous position than themselves. Most all disputes created and resolved by men over the millennia were of the political power sort. Whoever had more money or land or whatever got to make the rules. This style was entrenched in this kingdom, and that would probably never really change. As long as there were collections of people, some would always have more than others. And those with more would decide for the rest.

The breeze lifted up the fragrance of some flowers and made Anistasia smile. She was used to thinking in terms of political power. It was the way that the game of power was usually played. But to be honest, there was a second type of power in the lands. It was the power of raw, naked force. The type of power that came from the tip of the spear and that point of a sword. In truth, the spilling of blood had gotten every king his kingdom. It had also been the way that each of them had really kept it. It was much more well-known to the lands at the dawn of the age, when things were being fashioned out of the last apocalypse. It was how the land had been shaped, and then reshaped.

Anistasia Nosov was many things. One of those things was a student of history. The faults of those that came before her were great lessons to be learned without the actual consequences that the originators had suffered through. At the end of the last age, the world had swum through a sea of blood. At the start of the current age, it had been the same. Now, in the time of settled borders and established families, the use of force was no longer of the archer and infantry type. It had become the political type.

Anistasia considered the size of the army Ayr possessed. Her new kingdom was one of the kingdoms which still kept a good-sized standing army. The army of Ayr, along with the armies of Oban and Meridian, were now looked on as the stabilizing forces for the world. The three powers that kept the boundary lines fixed.

Of course, this produced a situation where other kingdoms now had smaller armies. This made those kingdoms weaker in her eyes. You could either defend yourself or you couldn't. Political power had to be backed up by something real. To her, that something was steel. Still, the political area was where she needed to start. She needed to set her sights there.

Anistasia was about to resume her pacing when a servant of the house appeared in her side vision. She paused and turned to face the servant; a congenial smile temporarily stuck upon her face.

"Pardon the interruption, majesty, but you have a guest."

The queen stayed neutral. She had received about a half-dozen guests since the royal exodus had finished. They all had been various city aristocrats, all of them offering one favor or another. This one would surely be no different.

"Thank you. I'll receive whoever came to visit out here."

The servant nodded and spun around to retreat. Anistasia was alone once more for the briefest of moments. The door the servant had used to exit opened again and an old man with short grey hair stepped out into the sunlight of the terrace. He was of moderate height, and thin. He wore a dark-colored robe with long sleeves over dark-colored trousers. The outfit gave him a northern appearance, despite his moderately pale skin tone. Queen Anistasia smiled genuinely and closed the distance to embrace him. The older man accepted the embrace, before bowing dutifully.

"My queen, it is good to see you well."

"Grgur, my old and trusted friend. Tell me you're well?"

"I am, my queen."

Anistasia turned and Grgur followed. They walked slowly out into the middle of the terrace. There was always someone watching and listening in the castle. It paid to be discreet and out of earshot.

Grgur inspected the opulence of the terrace as they walked, taking in the large trees, blossoming flowers, and manicured grassy lawn. Accepting it as a place made for a queen, he nodded his head approvingly. The gesture made Anistasia smile.

Deciding that they were in a good area, out of hearing distance from the information gatherers, Anistasia paused. Grgur stopped at an appropriate and acceptable distance from the queen and placed his hands behind his back. It was his normal stance.

"I hear that your wedding was the event of the age. A thing not to be outdone for a hundred years or more."

Grgur smiled warmly.

"It was quite the spectacle, even by your standards."

Grgur nodded.

"And you even managed to get yourself coroneted. Your plan is moving along nicely, my queen."

Anistasia smiled and nodded for the watchers in the shadows, giving the appearance of two people having a perfectly ordinary conversation. She glanced over to a large oak tree to their left.

"Yes, great things have small beginnings. I'm several steps down a long road. But now I have you here to assist me."

Grgur contemplated the tree for a few seconds.

"How well established are you? May I begin my work?"

The queen looked at some red flowers which were blooming by the rock wall. She didn't know what kind of flowers they were, but they looked appropriate for their location. She had never been much of a botanist.

"No. I think not yet. I need to insert myself a little farther into the affairs of state first."

Grgur nodded stoically.

"A sound move, my queen."

The queen nodded stoically.

"Do you know when the others are arriving?"

Grgur looked out onto the fortress below and thought.

"Some are here now. Others are on the way. Everyone you require should be at home in the city by week's end, or, I should think, by the new moon at latest."

"The new moon is good timing. Have them ready, but don't act. I sense timing will be important to my endeavors."

Grgur nodded.

"As you wish, it shall be."

The statement was sound, but with the slightest hint of subjugation to it. That little hint warmed Anistasia's blood. She smiled contentedly.

"You're a good friend, Grgur. I'm glad to have you here."

Grgur nodded stoically, sensing that the conversation had run its course.

"Yes, my queen."

The queen nodded and Grgur bowed in response.

"I'll send word when the time is right."

"Be well, majesty."

Grgur stepped back, turned, and strolled off at a moderately slow pace, continuing to take in the manicured lawns. Anistasia continued looking at the fortress interior, returning her thoughts back to her original issues.

Chapter Sixteen

Bernard and Quinn had walked along the king's road south of Karacase with a light heart and little worry. The Kingdom of Neeron, though having rougher sections like Fatezh, was a gentle and good-natured land. Old King Jasper Lorimere was a good and well-liked ruler. His young queen, Vivian, daughter of the Count of Fatezh, was universally loved by all. It was a place of skilled labor, hard workers, and happy spirits.

The Kingdom of Neeron, much like its large neighbor to the north, was predominantly a land of open fields broken by thick forests. Their main difference was Neeron's mountain chain which ran along its eastern border, separating the plains from the southern seacoast. The king, like his father before him, had invested heavily in finding and opening mines in the mountains to claim the rich mineral deposits. Now a great exporter of minerals and gemstones, Neeron was a rich and prosperous place.

The two adventurers had passed several road patrols as they moved south. The patrols were out to keep peace along the roadways and provide a general sense of security in the kingdom. The patrols, officially a piece of Neeron's undersized army, were a good-natured lot to interact with. They covered the vast interior of the country not looked after by the Watchtower. The patrols hadn't bothered either man, just paused their travel to see what their business was.

This travel south and east had been better than most. Now, as they came up to Neeron's southern border that led them into the kingdom of Oban, it seemed that it was going to continue on that way. Bernard and Quinn crossed the border without incident, nor hardly a question placed to them. They stepped off and continued on their way toward the city of Orba.

The border city of Orba had started life as a small mining town. It was the place everyone stopped with collected ore or gems to sell them for supplies to keep going up into the mountain mines of Oban. With only the foothills of the mountain range inside the border of Oban, the growth for Orba to become a large city never materialized. The well-adjusted place was now maybe half the size of normal cities out on the plain, yet just as prosperous. Walking into the city, it was easy to tell that the city had held its own. The clean streets were made of stone and Old Realm materials. The multistory buildings were of good repair. Sets of City People could be seen out moving from building to building, collecting the waste from the traps and providing water for the casks at the front doors. Neither Bernard nor Quinn had ever seen City People in cities the size of Orba. The industrious Public Workers Guild was second in social status only to the Mechanics Guild, and were usually found out in the bigger cities. They moved the waste out and the fresh water in. They kept the streets clean and the air fresh. They made a society function and were highly valued positions in that society. Their presence in the city definitely impressed.

Bernard and Quinn wandered three or four blocks into the urban center of the city before coming upon a medium-sized public square. Half a dozen stalls were set up selling the necessities of the day. A number of shops circled the square, consuming the ground floor of most buildings. The spaces that weren't businesses seemed to possess public houses, and all of them seemed to be open for business. Quinn pointed to some outdoor seating at a nearby public house and Bernard moved to it without conversation. They had no more than dropped their things and sat down when a young boy appeared with a welcome smile on his face. Quinn took the boy as a good omen.

"Good morning. You look like you're from out of town. Most men don't carry heavy arms here."

The boy's mood was jovial. It made Bernard smile.

"You figured us out fast. We'll need to make more of an effort."

The boy laughed.

"It probably won't help."

This time both Bernard and Quinn laughed. The kid was right. They stuck out everywhere they went.

"What's your name boy?"

The boy looked at Quinn and smiled.

"Robert, but most people call me boy."

Quinn smirked.

"Well, Bob, I'm Quinn. This ugly specimen over here is Bernard. You wouldn't happen to work here, would you?"

Robert smiled broadly.

"Bob? I like that. Yes, sir, I work here. Quinn and Bernard, you say? Like from the stories people tell? Wow, never thought I'd meet famous people when I woke up today."

Bernard laughed. Quinn rolled his eyes, as if to say, *Oh, great, we're famous now.*

"Excellent," Bernard said, assuming that Quinn was close to using up his word count for the day. "How about you fetch us up a little bread and meat? Some water would be greatly appreciated as well."

Robert nodded his head as Bernard spoke.

"No ale?"

"It's a little early in the day for ale, but I like the way you think, Bob."

Bob nodded and turned to leave.

"Be right back."

Bernard shuffled a little to settle himself into the heavy outside chairs that Quinn had pointed out.

"I like this place."

"Yup, it's quite nice. Probably on the expensive side?"

Bernard thought about the statement for a second.

"Probably right. Oh well, we'll be fine. Only gonna be here a couple days, at best."

Quinn ran his hands through his long blond hair, stretched until something within his skeleton popped, and then started scratching his scalp.

"How are we doing for coin, by the way?"

Bernard thought, visualizing their coffers in his mind.

"By our normal standards, excellent. We still have a bit of the bounty sheet coin left, and all of what the prince gave us. We should be good for a while, no matter what we do."

"That's nice."

Bob appeared with a loaf of round bread, a big slab of cheese, and a pair of small game hens just off the roasting spit. A staple in almost every public house in all the lands, the hens smelled fresh and well cooked. Bob laid down the plates and bowls on a table next to where they were sitting and turned to head back the way he had come.

"You think there's any work in a town like this?"

Bernard watched Quinn yank a leg from one of the hens as he spoke.

"Probably, there's work everywhere these days, though it does seem a pretty fancy place."

Quinn sucked the meat free from the leg bone before tossing it into an empty bowl.

"Probably pays well then?"

Bernard nodded, grabbing the other hen before Quinn could attack it.

"You're probably right. You getting the itch to kill someone? I mean, it's been a couple days."

Quinn smiled, keeping his mouth closed so the hen couldn't escape.

"No, I'm good. Just no reason to turn down work, if it pays well."

"Agreed. But we're here to do something else. Or are we done with that?"

Bernard was talking but Quinn wasn't listening. He was looking across the square at a young woman who was handing out bread to some old people who looked down on their luck. She was young, maybe nineteen or so, and of adequate height for a woman. Quinn was guessing, from across the square, that she was maybe five-foot-eight-inches and a slim eight-and-a-half stone. And though she used a thin, white linen dress and wrap to cover here snow-white skin and blazing red hair, it was obvious to his trained eye that she was endowed with sorcery.

The girl turned once to glimpse at the newcomers sitting outside the public house and her eyes locked with Quinn's. Shockingly bright blue eyes the size of small saucers conveyed a person somewhat more sad than happy. Quinn could sense that her breath paused for the shortest interval as she inspected him. A second in time which could have been an hour.

The girl returned to her task, and when finished, moved on out of the square. Quinn was curious. Curious in a way he had never been curious before.

"Q?"

Bernard said it loud enough to pull him back from wherever he had wandered off to.

"What."

Bernard exhaled.

"I thought we were here to do something else."

Quinn blinked a couple times to get it together, trying to remember the conversation they had been having before.

"We're definitely here to do something else. I meant afterward. You know, before we go back to the everyday."

Bernard looked at his friend quizzically.

"Go back to the everyday? What in the depth of the abyss does that mean? Drink some water. I think you're getting the sun sickness, and it's not even hot out here."

Quinn looked at the large water pitcher on the table. Bob had come and gone in the time he'd been looking across the square. How'd he miss that?

"Water sounds good."

Quinn reached out and retrieved the pitcher, dumping about half of it in a wooden drinking cup. Sliding the pitcher over to Bernard, he palmed the loaf of bread as he pulled his hand back. He snapped it in two and pushed Bernard's share in his direction.

The bread and hen put up little resistance. Quinn virtually inhaled his portion of it. Washing it down with the mug of water, he rolled his shoulders back and stretched. He was still hungry. It must have been all the walking. Normally, he could go a few days without a good meal, but walking long distances always made him hungry. He was happy that they had ended up someplace with good food. Seeing how Bernard was still working on his hen, Quinn reached out and snagged the chunk of cheese Bob had brought out. He waved it in the air to get Bernard's attention.

"You want any?"

Bernard chewed a couple times and then shook his head.

"No, I'm good."

Quinn shoved a large portion of the cheese into his mouth and bit off about a third of it. He was in mid-munch when Bob reappeared from inside.

"Questions for you, Bob. You seem the type that's in the know, as it were."

Bernard smiled at the young lad and automatically brought him over to their side.

"Yes, sir. I tend to see everything that happens around me, if that's what you mean?"

Bernard smiled again. He had thought as much.

"That's good. I'm curious if you've ever heard of a man named Raphael? He would be older than us. He probably has a bookstore or some type of shop here in the city."

Bob thought for a moment or two, a series of odd expressions moving across his face as he contemplated.

"You mean the collector? His name was Raphael or something close to it. He had a lot of books."

"Had?" Bernard said, not shifting from his generally congenial disposition.

"Don't know that he's around anymore. Haven't heard of anyone seeking him in months now."

Bernard looked over at Quinn. Quinn shrugged his shoulders as if to say, *oh well.*

"Any idea where he might have got off to?"

Bob worked through another series of facial gestures.

"Hold on a minute."

Bob turned and disappeared into the public house. Bernard yanked a stray piece of meat off his hen and stuffed it in his mouth before speaking.

"This one might be a dead end."

Quinn made an expression that said things were about going to plan for them.

"Or it might be designed to look that way. You know, to throw off the people that aren't serious."

"Good point."

Bob reappeared.

"Man inside says that Raphael hasn't been seen around here in near on a year now."

Bob seemed pleased to be helpful, so Bernard kept going.

"That's sad. Say, you wouldn't happen to know where his shop was located when he was here, would you?"

Bob beamed, obviously knowing the answer to the question.

"Sure. If you go that way," Bob pointed in the same direction the redhead had disappeared into, "say, for five sections, you'll come to another square, maybe half the size of this one. He had a shop in the far corner building, I think on one of the upper floors."

Bernard nodded his head.

"That sounds like we can't get lost getting there."

"Nope. It's pretty straight along. In the other off corner, there's a street-level shop. He used to sit there in the afternoons and drink tea, I think. Might want to check with the shopkeeper. He might know something more."

"That sounds like a great idea. Tell you what, could you get us another pitcher and tell us what we owe?"

Bob snatched up the pitcher and trotted off back inside. Quinn had completed eating the chunk of cheese by the time Bob returned.

"Man inside said that two regular weight coins should cover the food."

Bernard handed over two regular weight silver coins to Bob, who smiled and thanked them. Pausing slightly, Bernard pulled out a thin gold coin and handed it over as well.

"That's for the information."

Bob produced a broad smile.

"Wow, thanks mister!"

Bernard smirked and nodded while Quinn divided up the water between the two wooden mugs.

"Happy to help, Bob."

"Before you rush off, can you answer another question?"

Bob and Bernard looked at Quinn, who was shoving all of the water from the mug into his mouth.

"Sure."

"You have a sorceress in this city. Young, pretty, big blue eyes. What's her story?"

Bob produced another broad smile. He knew this answer too.

"Gweneth. She's come to Orba, say three or four years ago. She's nice, and really pretty. She spends her days helping the old folks and the ones down on their luck. Not sure if she has a mister, or anything like that. She's always alone when I see her."

Quinn nodded and disappeared into thought for a moment.

"Thanks, Bob. You've been a big help."

Bob nodded at both men and turned to head back inside.

"If you stay in the city, come back for dinner," Bob said over his shoulder.

Bernard laughed.

"I like that kid."

Chapter Seventeen

Jerimaih had made good progress since departing the temple in Fatezh. The sophist-turned-courier left Fatezh on a sturdy steed and rode almost non-stop to a way station town along the border road. After some refreshment for his mount, he continued on to the town of Ishim.

In Ishim, Jerimaih settled into a public house and proceeded to rest both himself and his horse. It was this pause in motion, as short as it may seem to be in a journey of weeks, which would seal his fate. It allowed others to close the gap.

Leaving out of Ishim on the northern road, he followed the ancient steel lines that snaked across the land. He found comfort in the old navigational aid. Knowing from his reading that the steel snake ran, unbroken, from Ishim to the border town of Neya, on the border of Ayr and Udaass, Jerimaih relaxed his pace and enjoyed the views that the countryside provided. His whole trip had been without calamity, and it seemed that it was going to continue that way. There was time to enjoy the view which the great wheat fields of eastern Ayr provided. Golden fields that stretched as far as the eye could see.

Jerimaih stopped at a spot where the great steel snake crossed over a small river and took a break in the shade that the construction's bridge provided. A cool breeze ran down the river and pulled the heat out of the day. The courier refilled his water bottle and let his horse drink from the ample supply in the river.

Being up on the border of Udaass meant that his journey was almost half over. All that was left was to travel across Udaass and onto the port south of the Southern Sands Watchtower. There he would book passage on a ship crossing the Eastern Strait to the Rain-Shadow Islands. Once in the islands, he could make the trip over to the Great Temple of Drakchi by joining one of the caravans.

Jerimaih was excited about this last leg. He had never been to the great temple, nor had he seen the desert. To ride the desert expanse as part of a caravan would be the experience of a lifetime. He could only imagine the stories he would be able to tell upon his return. Maybe, if he told them well-enough, they might let him write them down too. He decided that if the masters allowed such an indulgence, he would keep it factual. He was a sophist. The acquisition of knowledge was his life's pursuit. To acquire, collect, and pass-on knowledge was his task. To learn that which could be learned in the span of one's life and make that knowledge available to those who came after. That was his charge, and his life. He would do it with dignity.

Jerimaih remounted his horse and made his way back onto the road leading to Neya as a stranger came along, moving in the same direction. The stranger was nondescript in almost every sense. Even his horse, medium build, and weight, and medium brown in color, wasn't worth mentioning in his story without a certain level of embellishment.

The man rode up and adjusted his horse's gait so that his speed matched that of Jerimaih. He spoke with no accent that allowed the sophist to place his kingdom of beginning. He sounded as if he was almost from nowhere at all, which was just nonsense. Everyone in the land was from somewhere.

Jerimaih engaged the man in conversation, explaining to him that he was a courier for the temple in Fatezh and he was on his way to the Great Temple in Drakchi. It was an exciting trip to be taking. The man asked questions of the general variety; How long had he been at the temple, what was his focus of learning, and others like that. Jerimaih answered each of the questions without reservation, not wanting to seem better or more important than the man now traveling alongside him. The other man nodded in a semi-interested way as the courier talked.

The two continued on in this fashion for a league at the slower pace of travel required by the ongoing conversation. The horses shuffled along as the two spoke. The pair broke a small rise in the roadway that blocked the long running view to the rear and showed a sharp bend immediately ahead. They continued until they were just off its back side. Liking the location, the nondescript man slid a flat blade out of a sheath on his belt and stabbed the young courier several times in his side, making sure that he thoroughly punctured the kidney and the liver.

Jerimaih cried out after the first blow, but to no avail. Several more thrusts landed in the same general area, creating searing pain. He fell from his horse to the roadway with a thud. The nondescript man stopped his horse and dismounted slowly. He stepped over to where Jerimaih lay, whirling his knife around in his hand with a practiced ease, like a butcher, before bending slightly to efficiently slice open Jerimaih's throat. The throat cutting was directly followed by a single stab to the chest, punching a hole in his pounding heart. Jerimaih died quickly and efficiently.

Shadowman stepped over to the dead boy's mount, which was waiting patiently by its fallen rider. He wiped the blood off his blade and replaced it in the sheath. Reaching out, he pulled the courier's bag off of the rear of the saddle. The leather bag contained a book, a small knife, some uneaten bread, a water gourd, and a metal tube. Shadowman removed the metal tube and dropped the remainder in the road. Inspecting the seals on the tube's cap, he opened the tube and checked the contents inside. As expected, the rolled-up parchment was still inside. Shadowman replaced the cap and slid the tube into a pocket in his coat. The coat was kind of an annoyance but had been necessary to conceal his leather armor from the young courier. It had been a convincing ploy.

The assassin had been on the hunt for the courier for some time. After going through the two bounty hunters' room at the public house in Fatezh, he had come to the conclusion that they had deposited the tube at the temple. It had taken only a bit of investigation to find out that the local temple was returning the item to the Great Temple in the

Rain-Shadow Islands. Since the route from the temple was an obvious one, he just needed to catch up with the courier and relieve him of his cargo. Shadowman had found this to be easier than expected, with the young courier slowing to rest along the way.

Finding the right person on the road was of no real concern, since all sophists dressed alike. He picked him out at a distance and just waited for the opportunity to present itself. Which it had.

Still alone on the road with the corpse, Shadowman took hold of the extra horse and led it over to his own. Mounting his horse, he turned and began back the way that he had come. The dead courier was left lying in the middle of the roadway, looking the same as many a poor soul who had found misfortune in the midst of their travels.

Chapter Eighteen

Bernard followed young Bob's instruction across the square and into the long section that ran for three street lengths to the next open area of the city. Quinn wandered along behind him, half taking in the surroundings for potential problems and half thinking about the red-haired girl. There was just something about her. A kindred spirit, maybe? He didn't know. Philosophy wasn't his calling in life, action and adventure were.

Bernard paused at the first crossing street and inspected the hanging storefront signs denoting everything from butchers, to bakers, to clothes makers. Orba seemed a well-to-do city. It was also possible that they were just in the good end of town. Bernard considered that option. That had certainly happened to them on past occasions. Though they both had been men of writing and learning in different times, they were generally more comfortable in the seedier end of the city these days. They understood the motivations of people in the seedy end. Those motivations usually aligned with their own. Quinn caught up and gave both sections of the cross street a good glancing once over.

"This place is fancy."

Quinn nodded.

"Hope they have a less-fancy end."

Quinn nodded in response and smiled, coming back to the here-and-now of the situation.

"They all have a seedy end."

Bernard gave his friend a wry smile.

"Fact."

The two continued on, taking in the scenery as it unfolded before them. The next two sections of street, along with their side street sections, looked the same as the first one had. Well-to-do shops for people of taste. All of it clean and neat, all things considered, a prosperous place.

Stepping into the second square, the painting they had been walking through began to age. The square was clean and maintained as before, but older. One could begin to feel the city here. The small change instantly put the two at ease. Bernard walked to one side, taking a walking path around the storefronts and building entrances of the square's perimeter. Quinn walked out into the square's center and scanned the upper levels of the buildings. People came and went from side streets and shop doors, none paying the two newcomers any great amount of attention. Bernard walked happily around two sides, coming to the corner that Bob had told them about. Quinn continued on the diagonal, a sneaking suspicion rising in his gut that they were being watched from somewhere.

The two paused outside a well-worn shop door. The shingle hanging overtop the door said *Alonzo, Fines and Geldstein, Collectors.* Just as Bob had mentioned, it looked vacated. Bernard tried the door. It was locked. He looked over at Quinn.

"What do you think? Let ourselves in and take a quick peek?"

Quinn looked around the square at all the people coming and going.

"Probably better not."

Bernard nodded and looked up at the sign again.

"I thought we were looking for one guy. Master only gave us one name, right?"

Quinn nodded slowly, looking at the storefront next to where they were standing. The shingle over the door presented the image of a general goods shop. He tilted his head toward the shingle and stepped off in that direction. Pausing at the door, he looked over at Bernard and grinned.

"You're the people person."

Bernard inflated his chest in a self-important way.

"Yup. That's me."

Quinn stood outside and waited, trying not to look imposing to the good people passing by. Two different sets of shopping ladies passed him by as he waited. He nodded to them politely and produced a gentlemanly greeting for each. The women were momentarily concerned by the image of the imposing, weapon carrying man on the street in their path. They became pleasantly relieved that he possessed manners above his obvious station in life. Quinn paid them no never mind as he worked to quiet his mind so he could address the sensation that he was being observed.

To Quinn's well-honed senses, he didn't get the impression that whoever was watching them was suspicious of them. It was more a sense of curiosity. Or maybe intrigue. He lazily scanned the entire area, not getting any good sense of where the sensation was coming from. He was sure that whatever the sensation was, it was real. His gut told him it was real. His gut had kept the two of them out of countless scrapes over the years. It also helped him when he needed to make tough choices. A lot of men that they ran afoul of just needed killing. The sense helped him make quick, rational decisions about such things.

Bernard came out of the shop with an expression that said the information he just got was a mixed bag. Bernard took up a spot, leaning on the wall next to Quinn, and shrugged.

"Well, this is going to turn into a wild goose chase."

"How so?"

Bernard waited for a man and woman to pass by, nodding politely with Quinn as they did so.

"Apparently, Raphael is the Alonzo in Alonzo, Fines and Geldstein. He is also the only one in the shop, or he was the only one in the shop. The nice lady in this shop said that he was an extremely odd guy."

Quinn looked into the middle ground of the square and sighed.

"Great. So, he's bat shit."

"Exactly. He's also gone."

"Where?"

"She didn't know. Apparently, he just packed up and moved out a couple months ago. Pretty much what our boy Bob told us. Sounds like the man that owns the building just hasn't re-rented the space yet."

"Two questions."

"Go."

"Where would a crazy collector go with all of his treasures? And what would make him want to pack up and leave?"

Bernard looked around the square. It was as respectable a square as the next one was.

"I would say, no idea, and he's crazy."

"Hmm."

"There's no accounting for what crazy people do."

"Agreed."

Quinn looked to the corner of the square opposite from where they were leaning against the wall. A well-appointed public house sign hung above a corner building door. Several sets of chairs sat on the walking path out front of the place. Quinn shifted his mouth from side to side.

"You feel like staying the night?"

Bernard looked about and then at the public house.

"Sure."

"That place looks too nice for the likes of us. I'm betting they have a few bounty sheets on the wall. And I want to sit and do a little thinking drinking."

Bernard smiled and pushed off the wall they were leaning against, the uniform red rocks mortared together with cement leaving creases in his arm.

"I like the way you're talking, old chum."

Quinn pushed himself off the wall as well.

"Thought you might."

Quinn spent his afternoon hours sitting in a semi-secluded section of the establishment with his feet up on a sturdy wooden table. The barmaid wandered by his spot at a set interval to check on his desires. To Quinn's mind they seemed to be off on some type of scavenger hunt for information about something which was really probably nothing. He was beginning to come to the conclusion that, whatever they, or he, thought they hoped to find at the end of the path, it was probably nothing. In the grand scheme of life, few things really mattered.

Why did he care that the man in the woods had a stolen tube from the great temple? Why did he care that the parchment inside looked to be a lock and keys to some long-lost fancy vault from the last age? Why couldn't he shake the idea that it all mattered somehow? Not just a concern, but really mattered. If it really did matter, why weren't the kingdoms handling their own affairs? What was the point of all this consuming his time?

Quinn wiped the hair out of his face and dumped the contents of the whiskey glass down his throat in one solid go. The whiskey in Orba was good. The prices weren't good, but the whiskey was. He looked over at Bernard. His friend had come in, dumped his things in the room they had acquired, and then waded straight into the middle of the bar's crowd. He was still set in the middle of the crowd at the bar. From Quinn's vantage point, it appeared as though Bernard was regaling some men at the bar next to him with a story about some adventure they had undertaken. Quinn smiled. Apparently, they were famous. Or, famous according to Bob. At least Bernard was making friends here. Bernard was definitely the talker of the two. He had what Quinn's mother called the gift of gab. That suited Quinn just fine. Bernard was smart, well-spoken, and of keen intellect. He could smooth information out of most men with little effort. That left Quinn to stand around and look imposing. Looking imposing, and then being imposing, that was his job. Bernard needed no help. He was good in a scrap. Truthfully, they were equals when it came to the killing. Maybe that was why they got on so well.

Quinn glanced over at the window next to him and realized that the sun was all but down. He had spent the entire afternoon thinking about whatever it was that they were doing and had come up with no good conclusions. He wasn't hungry and he had drunk his fill. So maybe a good, long, sleep would help with whatever was going on. He stood and stretched, listening to his body crack and pop into place.

The barmaid came over, smiled politely, and waited for instruction. Quinn nodded to her respectfully and pointed over at Bernard.

"See the fellow up there at the bar? The one telling the stories?"

"Yes, sir."

"He'll have coin for all of this." Quinn waved his hand at the table. "Tell him that I said to make sure that he tips you properly."

The barmaid smiled and blushed at the same time.

"Yes, sir."

Quinn stepped off to the stairs that led up to the half-dozen rooms above the public gathering space. He took the steps two at a stride, since they were close together, making the second-floor landing with a final bound. He walked to a room in the middle of the hallway on the left-hand side and opened the door. Stepping inside, he closed the door, closed his eyes, and inhaled deeply. Expelling a lungful of air and about half of his exasperation with it, Quinn flexed his shoulder back and forth to loosen a couple of knots. Sleep would be good. A nice bed and deep sleep.

A knock emanated through the wooden door behind him. It was neither soft nor loud. Which meant that it was neither Bernard nor a member of the local companionship. Quinn made a face. There was no one in this city that should be looking for him. Reaching down, he slid the long flat blade out of his boot and rolled it back in his palm so that the spine was against his forearm. Sliding the door open enough to attack, if necessary, he inspected his visitor. It was definitely not who he was expecting.

Opening the door fully, he took in the fresh-faced features of the young red-haired sorceress. He watched as her eyes transitioned from an opaque black to the radiant blue he had seen earlier in the day. Up close, what he had earlier thought to be a light tan was now, in fact, a sea of freckles. She was captivating. Or, her ethereal draw was captivating, Quinn couldn't be sure which.

"Are you going to invite me into your room?"

Quinn blinked and realized that he had been staring at the young sorceress with an agape expression. He wiped the long strands of blond hair from his face and put on a more-respectable expression.

"Pardon my rudeness, sorceress. Please, come in."

Quinn removed himself from the doorway and the young red-haired sorceress entered the room, almost gliding in.

"You move softly, sorceress."

She smiled at Quinn in a way that settled every last nerve in his being.

"Please, sir, call me Gweneth. I am daughter of Enella. And you are the notorious Quinn, friend to the one called Bernard, and owing to no man."

Quinn rolled the word notorious around in his head for a couple seconds as Gweneth took in his full measure. She instantly sensed that he was more than was first inspected earlier. Much, much more.

"I met your mother, once, when I was younger. She's a power to be respected. If you're of her blood, then I would imagine that you have that type of power as well."

Quinn kept his tone measured and respectful. Gweneth smiled a melancholy smile as he spoke. Quinn could feel that she was a person who was more sad than happy. He didn't know why it was so, but he could sense it.

"Quinn? A name that hides secrets. A man of adventure and learning. One not to be crossed, even if lightly. One who could be king by his own deeds if he chose to be. But one who chose a life on the road instead."

Gweneth slid a finger along the outside of his arm as she spoke. Her words were hypnotic. Quinn could sense that she was probing his mind. He blinked several times and shook off her charms. Inhaling, he smiled politely.

"We're all many things, Gweneth. You strike me as someone more sad than happy, which makes me sad."

The sorceress smiled another sweetly beautiful melancholy smile.

"You're right more than you know. But then again, choices made in life have to be lived with, don't they Watchtower sergeant?"

Quinn nodded. She was a good sorceress. Or she had taken in his cloak which was sitting on the bed.

"That they do. However, I suspect that any decisions you've made are fresh enough to be undone. You've only stepped into full age."

Gweneth blushed against her will. He had a nature that disarmed her.

"Sadly, some choices cannot be unchosen. They have to be lived with."

Quinn nodded stoically.

"I know exactly what you mean. Now, how may I be of service to you this evening?"

Gweneth slid another finger lightly down his muscular arm and considered the question for one or two seconds. Finally, she decided to get on with business.

"You've come to the city looking for a man named Raphael. You hoped that he might be in possession of a set of *The Histories*."

Quinn produced a suspect expression.

"Yes."

Gweneth smiled softly.

"I'm friends with your new friend, Robert. He tells me about people that I might find interesting. The second piece of information I gleaned from the ether."

"Go on."

"As you have determined, he has left the city."

"Yes."

"He departed for the port city of Asturias in the kingdom of Udaass. He traveled with a trading caravan which was headed that way."

Quinn hung on her every word, though he tried not to. It had been some time since he was engaged in conversation with a sorceress. It was obvious that some of the things he had learned along the way had gotten rusty without use.

"Is he still in that city?"

"Yes. He set up a shop in a small building near the main market street."

Quinn thought about it for a moment.

"Okay, why tell me? What's in it for you?"

Gweneth smiled a true smile, as if Quinn had finally asked a question worth answering.

"A great many things. I'm a guidepost on your journey. I've been placed in your way to keep your path headed in the right direction."

"Placed here?"

"We're all subject to the exterior forces of the world. Some of us understand this. Most don't."

"So, we're headed to Asturias then?"

"Soon, but not immediately."

Quinn gave the sorceress another quizzical look.

"Why?"

"There's something you need to do here first."

And there it was, Quinn thought, *the price he was going to pay for her visit.*

"And that would be?"

Gweneth waved her hand lazily in the air and a bounty sheet materialized from the ether. Continuing to move her hand slowly, the sheet hovered waiting on Quinn to grab it. Gweneth smiled and tilted her head to one side slightly.

"Make sure that you spend some time talking to him before you turn him over. You'll find the time well-spent. Now, I am going to depart. I very much already look forward to our next meeting."

Gweneth's radiant blue eyes transitioned into an opaque black and she shimmered out of existence inside a swirling black cloud right before Quinn's eyes. Once again, Quinn stood with mouth agape. He didn't even know that such a thing was possible.

Bernard stepped into the room and looked at his friend. Quinn was standing there holding a bounty sheet, with a stupid, open-mouthed look on his face.

"You okay? You sounded like you were talking to yourself."

Quinn shook his head to clear his mind and saw Bernard.

"What?"

"Are. You. Okay?"

"Yes. I'm good."

"Are you sure? Did they drop something in your whiskey?"

"I had a visitor."

Quinn handed over the bounty sheet. Bernard inspected the price on the bottom of the sheet and whistled.

"Well, whoever they are, I like their choices. This sheet is a solid payday."

It may be more than that, Quinn thought. The only thing he was sure about was that he wanted to see the Sorceress Gweneth again at any cost.

Chapter Nineteen

The vast majority of the trip had been spent at a leisurely pace. Akeem wasn't sure, but he assumed that it was just the pace at which women liked to travel. The two sets of guards had been split to maximize the level of protection available. Ubar riders rode ahead and behind, and the Meridian riders surrounded the travelers. Everyone agreed it was serious overdoing. Still, three heads of kingdoms and an added royal person seemed to warrant it. Everyone agreed that Rosalyn could do the job of all the men guarding them, but still.

The first long stretch of the journey was taken up by Akeem being accompanied on horseback by Princess Catherine. She seemed obviously young and impressionable. Her two guardians in the coach kept a fixed eye on her, not giving her any room to get into trouble. Akeem had no intention of letting any such thing transpire. As far as he could tell from their time together, she was young, beautiful, and presented herself as intelligent, if not experienced in the world at-large. She was just the sort of woman that Akeem had been searching for since he came of age.

All the kings of Ubar had been men of families. He was sure that his reign would be no different. A beautiful princess from a foreign land would make the start of a good family. It was an interesting idea but fleeting. There were more important matters to contend with during this ride than the folly of courting. Still, her company was purpose-built for just that very thing.

A second long stretch of the journey had been passed with Akeem joining the two queens in the carriage. The discussions of trade and the collective ideas exchanged between Ubar and the two prosperous lands to the west consumed a large stretch of road. Akeem found both of the women to be solid negotiators. They were sure of what they wanted from the discussions and didn't back down from coming away with what was fair and equal. The crown prince quickly developed a hearty respect for them both. They were good rulers who looked after their people. It was completely commendable.

The High Sorceress was the head negotiator, but stated that she would have to confer with her people before agreeing to any lasting deals. After all, the Freelands Folk were just that, free. They were a loose collective at best. Akeem was aware of the steps needed to conduct business with the Freelands Folk and was unconcerned by the wait. It was really no different than waiting for couriers with dispatches to come and go.

The slim and elegant blonde-haired beauty to her side was a different affair entirely. Happy and jovial in tone, Queen Bianca Rhodes spoke with absolute authority. She made no bones about what she wanted and what she was willing to pay for it. She was a ruler. She ruled her kingdom's affairs completely. Akeem respected her stance, and her ability to walk a negotiation into her favor. She didn't even consider conceding.

There was something about this woman, Akeem thought. *She had an internal strength. A power that was born, not made.* She reminded him of someone else he had met. He couldn't put a finger on who, as he met a lot of people. Still, she had a quality.

Business was interrupted once by a call into a roadside public house. The ladies rested and ate while Akeem checked on the animals and talked with the men. He liked the solid professionalism of the Meridian guards the queen had brought along with her. They seemed to instantly get on with his own guards. It appeared that military men were the same, no matter the land that they came from.

After the proper interval had passed, the group continued their trek southwest once more. The traveling days had started as sunny and bright, but had transitioned to cloudy and rainy as they approached the coast. A storm was blowing up out in the Central Sea and heading in toward land. It made them all wonder if they were heading to sea when they got to Roadstead, or if they were going to become temporary residents. Rosalyn reminded the questioners that nature moved in cycles which weren't meant to be tampered with. The coming storm would pass when it passed.

Riding into the seaside port town by the main road, it became obvious that the cycle Rosalyn was referring to was just getting good and started. It didn't look like anything, or anyone would be putting to sea. Oh well, that was what a good public house was for.

Akeem rode to the head of the column and addressed the Watchtower troops stationed at the perimeter of the town. The Watchtower sergeant-in-charge acknowledged the presence of the three sovereigns and explained that they might be more content waiting out the storm at the Watchtower on Kalduhr Tor. The crown prince thanked them for their hospitality and explained that they had all had a long journey down from Kanash. If appropriate accommodations could be found for the queens and the princess, they would happily stay in Roadstead. The Watchtower sergeant pointed them toward a private house in the nicer part of the town and wished them safe travels. He dispatched three of his own men to lead them into town, and to make sure it all stayed quiet. With so many people gathered up due to the storm, it was hard to tell when trouble would appear.

The private house the group had been led to turned out to be big and comfortable. It was owned and run by a lady of the town who happily took in the royalty on her doorstep. A large sitting room in the front of the house had windows that looked down on the port. Ships could be seen tied up tight to every available pier. Both Catherine and Bianca took in the outline of a large black galleon tied up to the central pier, her many gunports all closed tight to the weather. The women did their best to appear uninterested. Akeem took in the same ship, a somewhat more content expression escaping his features. Rosalyn sat in a high-backed chair instead of taking in the rain-soaked view at the window. She could feel the movement of people in both the house and the town around it.

Catherine turned and spoke with Bianca in a low tone. Akeem was standing too far away to hear the exchange, but it was obvious from her expression that she didn't like whatever Catherine was saying. The High Sorceress closed her eyes and said nothing, though Akeem noticed that the pendant which Catherine wore warmed with a subtle red glow, like the light shown through a ruby. He had no idea what was going on and he certainly wasn't going to get involved to find out.

The owner of the house showed the retinue of guards to a set of rooms in the house where they might find rest. A handful stayed vigilant to the task and stationed themselves at the various doorways. The ladies were shown to comfortable upstairs rooms. Akeem was shown an upstairs room as well, though he returned downstairs to the sitting room to continue inspecting the town. The mass of the storm which came to life out on the Central Sea was all but on land now. It covered the town and its port in a thick blackness that was only momentarily broken by brilliant streaks of luminous lightning. The lightshow was promptly followed by large claps of thunder that shook the very air around them. Akeem was used to the huge storms that the desert produced, and the lightning shows that came with them, but this storm from the sea was new to him. It was menacing, as though it had a mind of its own. If he were home, he would assume that the jinn were displeased.

Deciding that the house was sufficiently quiet, and the ladies were contented, Crown Prince Kamal "Akeem" Nazari collected himself and stepped to the door. Greeted by his manservant, Saleh, he smiled.

"It's time to go."

The other man nodded and looked out through the leaded window in the thick door.

"Could be better weather, sire."

Akeem gave him an expression that said we live with what we are given in this world. Saleh nodded stoically.

The two men stole through the door into the storm, Akeem gripping the door guard on the shoulder in a brotherly way. The man nodded but stayed on station as the two men disappeared into the blackness of the night.

The walk from the private house to the docks was quick and straightforward. The compact size of Roadstead made travel a fast affair. It only took two inquiries to find the public house where all the pirates were holed up at. It turned out to be in the middle of the docks, right in front of the pier that held the giant black galleon. It was secured tightly for the brunt of the storm to come. It sat alongside a section of pier that was left over from the previous age. A long straight monolith of manufactured grey stone, the old pier was an ample anchor for the big ship. The two men turned from the sight and entered the front door of the public house, finding the ale-soaked tavern area absolutely bursting with humanity. It was obvious to Akeem that the number of the mass considered to be locals was slim. He inquired as to the whereabouts of the pirate captain Blue Bill Montgomery and was pointed up the stairs by the barman, who was holding out two fingers.

Akeem and Saleh made their way to the stairs wondering how they were ever going to get out of such a place alive if things went badly. The army of ale-soaked hard men between them and the stairs let them pass by unbothered. It was obvious from their differences that the strangers were high-born men, or at least one of them was, and high-born men only came to such places when they needed hard men.

Two men stood outside of room number two, milling about in the hallway. One man carried a cutlass in a leather scabbard – a weapon a touch too large for the confines of the hallway. The other man possessed a small axe, a wholly more appropriate weapon. Saleh stated to the men that they were here to discuss business with the pirate captain. Cutlass man rubbed his chin and inspected them with a hard stare. Deciding they seemed okay, he pounded twice on the door. A yell came from the other side, which made him open the door and wave his hand. Akeem entered the room followed by Saleh.

Pirate captain, and scourge of the high seas, Blue Bill Montgomery sat in a thickly padded leather chair with his feet up on a small wooden box. Akeem estimated that the six-foot-two pirate probably came in at around fifteen stone. A frame of heavy, solid muscle, with long, black hair and menacing brown eyes. His skin was so deeply tanned from a life at sea that Akeem could have been excused for mistaking him as a man of the desert.

The pirate sat with an air that showed complete authority. He was the one in charge in the room. The blonde-haired whore on his lap possessed a similar expression. Her steel lip ring was dull, suggesting that she plied her trade mainly in the salty air around the docks. Akeem casually took in the half-dozen other pirates and whores in the room, all of the steel lip ring variety, and shook his outer robe once with a sharp snap to shed the rainwater from its surface.

"Captain Montgomery, I presume two men approached you earlier and made you aware that we were coming this way. I do apologize for keeping you in port this long."

A light went on in Montgomery's eye and he slapped the whore to get her off his lap. Coming to his full height, he extended a hand to Akeem and smiled.

"Crown Prince Nazari, it's a pleasure to meet you. Don't get much call to converse with the royalty of Ubar."

Akeem nodded respectfully. Saleh looked unimpressed with the pirate's tone. Akeem took his tone as a good sign.

"I understand. We are a touch outside your normal work area."

Montgomery laughed deeply, the smile on his face softening slightly.

"I found your message very interesting, as I did the men who delivered it."

Akeem nodded.

"I was unable to present it myself, so I sent them along to make contact with you. I assume that they came and went unharmed?"

The smile turned to a smirk.

"They were the type who would surely give better than they received. Still, yes, they left unbothered. I actually tried to hire them on. Sadly, they weren't the sailing type."

Akeem smirked this time.

"I would certainly think them the dry land type."

"Agreed."

"Now, to business. I would like to secure your participation in a deal, as the notice stated."

Blue Bill nodded in a very non-committal way.

"Yes. Your note laid out what you wanted from the arrangement well enough. It was a little short, however, on what we might get in return."

Akeem nodded and smiled wryly. The negotiations had begun.

"It seems that point is a position of barter?"

"True enough it is. What are you offering?"

"Two leagues north of the Doha Port, straight along the coast, there's a deep-water inlet. A small trading town without a name that I'm aware of is set around it on two sides. I offer you, and your comrades, safe harbor, to use as you see fit, for a span of time that we two agree is commensurate with what I'm asking you to cover."

Every pirate in the room snapped their head around to take in Akeem's completely serious expression. Saleh did the same. The offer was ludicrously one-sided in favor of the pirates. Bill Blue stared at him, thinking that the prince was having fun with him.

"You serious?"

"Completely. As long as you deliver on your end, I will deliver on mine."

Montgomery scratched his chin as a show of thinking. There had to be a catch. Nobody willingly surrendered a port to pirates without first defending it valiantly. A knock came to the door. Blue Bill scowled.

"NOT NOW!"

The door opened anyway. Someone outside was going to get Bill's rapier in their middle when this was over.

There was a pause in the action as a small-framed figure stepped into the room with both an air of mystery and the movement of absolute authority. Blue Bill Montgomery looked into the delicate features of a face cast in the shadow of a rain-soaked cloak hood. Akeem watched the pirate's expression soften and then snap back to its original position.

"EVERYONE OUT! Prince, you stay," Blue Bill commanded, snapping a finger at the Ubar ruler.

The room emptied without question or comment. Akeem turned slightly to take in the outline of a young woman. The door closed and several seconds passed in absolute silence before Princess Catherine slid her hood back onto her shoulders. Blue Bill's countenance changed completely, giving way to the princess's obvious command of the room.

"Your Royal Highness. I was unaware that you were in the town. Do you travel with the queen?"

Catherine stepped in to close the distance and laid a hand gently on the pirate's face. Akeem and Saleh stood motionless in a mild state of shock.

"Silas, my old friend. I'm happy to see you well. Though, from what I noticed, you could make better choices in your whores."

Silas Khan, the third pirate captain to be given the moniker of Blue Bill Montgomery, tilted his head in slight chastisement over the whore.

"She's merely a passing fancy, highness."

Catherine smiled and punched the pirate in his thick chest in a mocking way.

"I'm gonna bet that you spend a fair amount of time passing your fancy."

Silas scowled. Catherine smiled, knowing she had gotten the better of him, and turned to face Akeem.

"Prince Nazari, you keep interesting friends."

Akeem and Saleh both stared at her. This couldn't be the same woman they had traveled with earlier on the road. Not at all.

Silas broke the awkward silence.

"Two questions."

Catherine nodded.

"How did you know I was here? And do you know this man?"

Catherine looked at Akeem and smiled as though she was smiling at a lover.

"I caught full view of *The Seamus.* Even with her black sails collected and her gunports closed, the bleak and breaking lightning made her look a true harbinger of mayhem. And, where *The Seamus* is, so are you."

Silas nodded. It was a true statement. The ship was his real home.

"As for your guest here, he is Crown Prince Kamal "Akeem" Nazari, heir to the house and lands of the Kingdom of Ubar."

Catherine touched the prince in a way that made Silas understood he was somehow important to her.

"Is he as good as his word?"

Catherine turned back to Silas Khan and shrugged casually.

"I can confirm that the prince is who he says he is. As for the dealings between men, I have no comment. Personally, I trust him fully, for he has done nothing to make me question his chivalry. Unlike you."

Silas scowled openly and then began laughing. Catherine caught the look of Akeem's concern out of the corner of her eye and turned slightly.

"Relax Akeem, the pirate captain here has never been anything but kind to me. Though I confess that mostly it's the kindness someone shows to a puppy – or someone's younger sibling."

Akeem made a face that stated he didn't understand.

"He's not actually interested in princesses. I'm just someone he has to placate. His aim is, and has always been, my sister."

Silas Khan made a face which suggested that, if Catherine was a man, she would be dead where she stood.

"I'm offended by your use of the word placate. We have always been honest with one another, highness."

Catherine made a conciliatory expression.

"True, Silas. That was unkind. Forgive me, please?"

"You need never ask for forgiveness, highness."

Catherine smiled warmly.

"You're a good man, Silas Khan, independent of your profession, lifestyle, and reputation."

The pirate captain laughed heartedly.

"Probably true, but enough about me." He looked past Catherine to Akeem. "Prince, you have an arrangement. My ship will be departing on the first good tide following the storm."

Akeem stepped forward and the two men shook hands solidly.

"I'm glad to hear it. My manservant, Saleh, will be making the passage with you to negotiate in my stead."

Catherine tilted her head slightly.

"Are you heading toward Pirate Bay?"

Silas shook his head.

"No, highness. It's business travel. Do you and the queen require safe passage to the continent? I can arrange such."

"Queens, plural. Our sister, the High Sorceress, is traveling with us."

Akeem noticed a look of concern cross the pirate's face. Part of the reason that Ubar was out of the pirate's normal travel path was that its southern lands lay directly east across the sea from The Freelands Folk. One did not cross the High Sorceress without repercussions. Two adventurous souls had tried in the past. Both of them had met with bad ends.

"If they require passage, we will grant it unbothered."

"Thank you, Silas. I'll pass along your offer to them. It's always good to see you well. Now, I'll let you two men get back to your manly dealings. I sense that you're still working things out."

Catherine pulled the hood of her cloak back up over her head and turned for the door.

Chapter Twenty

Master Jonah walked across the open lower courtyard of the king's residence with the appearance of a man who didn't have a care in the world. For everyone who came into contact with him, in and around the Kingdom of Ayr, that appearance seemed true. An outwardly happy man who possessed the trust of the king. A Master who sat with the wise men of the land and who could discuss engineering with the Grand Master of the Mechanics Guild. A trusted teacher of the aristocratic youth. In every way a man who held the world in the palm of his hand.

Jonah waved to the exterior guard and entered the fortress residence without objection. He said hello to the staff as he passed them in the wide halls of the residence. All who worked there were honored that such a man would know their names and greet them. Jonah stopped and inspected a flower cutting which one of the young girls had placed on a hallway table. He asked the girl if she knew the variety of flower she had placed in the vase. The girl responded that she didn't. The flowers had been delivered by the flower seller in the city, the same as every other day. She had simply arranged them, though she said that she hadn't seen any like them around Kanash. Master Jonah laughed and explained to the young girl with a happy smile that the flowers weren't from Kanash. They had been delivered from the Kingdom of Neeron, the queen's home kingdom, to make her feel more at ease in her new kingdom. The girl inspected them a second time, and then exclaimed to Master Jonah that she would make sure the flowers looked their best for the queen. Jonah told her that she was already doing an excellent job, which made the girl beam with delight. He nodded and turned to enter the throne room.

Jonah pushed through the heavy double doors of the throne room and paused to make sure that they closed completely once again. Inspecting the room as he walked across it, he found it holding a single occupant. Queen Anistasia Nosov sat contently on her throne, wrapped in an elegant burgundy gown, the crown of power floating above her majestic features. Master Jonah smiled and gave her a half-bow, the look of which was almost conspiratorial.

"Good morning, Master Jonah. You're on the cusp of being late."

Jonah smiled and put up a hand as if to say, *wait for it.* Mere seconds passed before the large brass bells housed in the meeting hall spire began to ring out at the top of the hour.

"Right on time."

The queen smiled.

"So it would seem."

Master Jonah took another look around the throne room to assure himself that they were actually alone.

"Are you ready to start your grand undertaking?"

The queen nodded with a full and unequivocal nod.

"Yes, I am. You sound like you have a plan rolling around in your head?"

Jonah looked up at her crown, the gold and jewels sparkling as if lit by an unknown light.

"First step on such journeys is always the hardest to take. You've already taken that."

The queen nodded, if for no other reason than to keep him talking.

"The next step, though somewhat more delicate, isn't nearly as difficult."

"Agreed," the queen said in a monotone voice. "I'm thinking that next step involves visiting the Regent's Council. You?"

Jonah smiled at his leader.

"My thoughts exactly. They don't really like or trust you, but they do bow to power."

The queen made a neutral expression.

"So it would seem. I assume you have a way into the council, Master? You've been in-place here long enough."

Master Jonah bristled slightly. It had been some time since anyone had talked down to him.

"Yes, majesty. We will start slowly. I'm an accustomed face at the council meetings. I will smooth your way in through the door. If you give them leave to talk and then listen carefully, they will tell you all that you want to know."

The queen shook her head with a smirk.

"So, be demur and know your place is your plan? I already figured that out on my own."

Jonah began to make a face and then concealed it.

"That wasn't what I meant, majesty. I simply mean that if you present yourself as curious, but clueless, the regents will talk in your company without worry. Subterfuge is always a useful tool."

"Relax, Master Jonah. I came to the same conclusion myself some time ago. I agree with your approach. Besides, there's always someone in the room at such events that no one is paying attention to, it might as well be me."

"We will make that person you, majesty."

The queen smiled.

"Yes, we will."

Master Jonah smiled a sinister smile.

"We'll use their knowledge against them."

Queen Anistasia stood and smoothed her gown. Stepping down from the raised dais, she waved a hand toward the doors.

"Let's be on our way."

The two walked from the throne room, Master Jonah a full step behind the queen, as was protocol. They made their way peacefully enough through the residence and out into the main lower courtyard. Crossing to the inner gate, they continued out into the market square that separated the fortified castle residence from the back of Kanash's

Grand Meeting Hall. The queen engaged several people along the way in an outwardly attempt to seem gracious. The common folk of the market area were excited to be in the presence of the queen.

It took longer than Jonah had planned to cross through the open market square and maneuver around the side of the meeting hall to the huge front doors. They arrived just as the half-hour bells rang out. A pair of aristocrats associated with southern trade came up to the doors at a brisk pace but halted and bowed at the sight of the queen. Smiling, the queen nodded her head respectfully and waved them on by. They continued into the hall, now animated in conversation at the queen's presence.

Master Jonah stepped into the opulent meeting hall, all of its side nooks, columns and tombs bathed in the light of towering stained glass, and acted as herald for the entrance of the queen. Queen Anistasia Nosov, freshly minted monarch of the kingdom, walked in delicately and took up a quiet seat in the area where the king usually sat. All of the counts and regents in attendance were intrigued by the presence of the queen. That was with the exception of the regent from the royal house who oversaw the council meetings. Lead Regent Makal Rymer, an old and suspicious man who had migrated north from the mountain lands of Udaass to gradually take on the voice of the king, was openly suspect of her presence.

The caretaker of the Meeting Hall came over to where the queen sat and expressed his happiness that she would come to the meeting hall. The queen thanked him and expressed her great appreciation at the glorious way he had handled the wedding. The caretaker bowed humbly and stated that it was the least that he could do for her majesty. The queen thanked him once more as he stepped off into the shadows to let the Regents Council meeting begin.

Makal Rymer walked to the front of the assembly and stepped behind the speaking stand. He laid out a set of papers, as though they were individual points of discussion, and then pivoted slightly toward the queen.

"It would appear that the council is greeted this day with the presence of her majesty. If it pleases her majesty, we might start by discussing whatever topics she brings to us before continuing on with the more mundane affairs of the kingdom."

Several of the counts in attendance laughed. The Regents Council meetings were widely known as long-winded and boring affairs.

"I come to you fine people this day with no specific interest or topic, Regent Rymer. I am simply interested in learning about the affairs of the kingdom and how things work here in Ayr."

The obviously suspicious Makal Rymer looked out over the gathered council members. All of the crowd seemed content to have her attend.

"So, your majesty would like to learn about the running of the kingdom?"

The queen smiled in the most submissive and ladylike fashion that Master Jonah had ever seen. It had the intended effect.

"If I understand the concerns of Ayr, I can better help the people of the land. Please, Lead Regent Rymer, be about your business now. I promise not to be a bother to the fine people gathered here today."

Seeing no possible way out of the situation, Makal Rymer swallowed back some bile and oriented himself toward the regents. Queen Anistasia adjusted her seat and readied herself for the show.

As had been expected, the Regents Council meeting was a long, dry, and thoroughly monotone undertaking. Different counts and regents stood and regaled the gathering with tales of one problem or another affecting their individual town, county, or region. The individual tales were all followed by long-winded discussions that ranged from chastising dissertations of mismanagement to uproarious arguments regarding policy and procedure. The queen watched it all unfold passively, making mental notes as to who the real leaders and power brokers in the room were.

One of the counts, in the midst of a fairly contentious discussion, had asked what the queen's position on a particular subject was. The queen had quietly differed her voice to Master Jonah, stating that she was too new in such a setting to make judgements regarding such situations. Her comments won the rounded approval of almost everyone in the hall. Master Jonah had made a quick statement in favor of the speaking count, and everything moved on.

It was nearly the middle of the afternoon when all topics requiring voice had been heard. The gathered collection of counts, aldermen, vice regents and regents filed from the meeting hall as Queen Anistasia stood and walked quietly toward the inner row of ornate tombs which lined the semi-circular space behind the elevated speaking area. As the lead regent and Master Jonah stepped outside to converse, Anistasia paused before a magnificent marble sarcophagus. The carved likeness of the occupant, a powerful man in armor with a sword, lay atop the lid of the bone box below. A flowing script in some dead language covered two sides of the sarcophagus, no doubt detailing the man's many great deeds. The craftsmanship of the entire piece was absolutely exquisite, and Anistasia marveled at the mastery of the previous age.

The caretaker walked up quietly and paused a step away from where the queen was standing.

"It is a magnificent piece of art, is it not?"

The queen nodded emphatically.

"Who was he?"

"One of the great statesmen from the previous age. It seems he was highly revered in his day."

"So it would seem. It's obvious he held real power."

The caretaker of the Great Meeting Hall nodded respectfully.

"True. He must have been a knowledgeable man, because knowledge is power."

The queen turned to face the caretaker directly, taking in his tone.

"And say that I wanted to gain knowledge?"

The caretaker smiled deceptively.

"That would be easy, as long as you know where to look for it. Do you read, majesty?"

"Yes."

"In that case, one might look to the volumes in the Meeting Hall Archives stored below our feet. They hold the discussions and decisions of all the business conducted at the Regents Councils."

The queen smiled warmly.

"And how might one go about accessing the archives reading room?"

"Her majesty is a ruler of Ayr. The reading room is always open to the rulers of Ayr. I imagine that you'll find it full of all kinds of useful information."

The caretaker of the Great Meeting Hall bowed slightly and walked off quietly in the direction from which he had approached. Anistasia Nosov turned back to the dead man's tomb and considered the excellence of the stonework. She would need to find herself a stone mason who could produce works of this nature.

Chapter Twenty-One

Anistasia poured over the entirety of two shelves worth of volumes before finding something useful. The great men of the Regents Council were a long-winded bunch of bureaucrats. It seemed to her that all they did was discuss and philosophize about their problems. There was little practical decision making going on in the meeting hall. In reality, that was the second thing that she had learned down in the subterranean vaults that housed the archives of the Great Meeting Hall of Kanash. The first thing that she learned was that for all of its show, the Regents Council wasn't actually needed for anything. That bit of information would be supremely useful when the time came.

Anistasia had gone back some eight years in time reading about the affairs of the Great Kingdom of Ayr. It had become her daily ritual. She would rise with the king and take breakfast. She would lounge with him while he considered his day. Once her husband had departed the residence, she would leave behind him. She would take the walk through the market square beyond the castle residence and take in the respect of the common folk. A quartet of armed guards would accompany her, staying out of the way enough so as not to put off the locals of the market. All the guards were dressed in the colors of the House of Nosov, but they were her men. She had brought them along and quietly inserted them into place. The same way she had placed some people into the army and found appropriate housing for her man Grgur. She had found him a place where he could be most useful.

Things had quietly come together quite nicely for her. And now, sitting in the bowels of the meeting hall surrounded by volumes, she had found another piece for the huge puzzle she was constructing. She had known for some time that one of the six things she desired most resided in the Court of Ubar, situated inside the desert city fortress of El Hataan. She also knew that no army had crossed the great sand seas of Ubar and survived the crossing. The natural defenses of the desert were formidable and the warriors of Ubar were fierce. Anistasia had held the feeling for some time that she would need to soften the kingdom up a little if she was ultimately to achieve her desired ends. In the dry and annoyingly long-winded volumes of the archive she thought she might have found a way to do some of that softening.

Eight years back from her current year the king of Ubar had made a trade deal with the king of Ayr and the Great Bank from the Mining Isles. Ubar had secured significantly higher volumes of grains and food crops to carry them through a prolonged drought brought on by the ill temperament of the desert from the Kingdom of Ayr. The trade deal was secured with a loan from the Great Bank of the Mining Isles. The huge payment of gold from the bank had allowed Ayr to conduct many needed civil activities which bettered the lives of the peasant population. The remainder of the coin had bolstered the king's coffers. In all the meetings since then, there had been no mention of a reversing trade deal or Ubar paying down the loan. If the kingdom was in debt to the Great Bank, they were weak to financial pressure from the outside. That bit of information provided an opportunity that could be exploited.

Anistasia moved on to look at her own kingdom's finances. Those books had been a little harder to get a look at. But with her new friend, the caretaker of the Great Meeting Hall, the doors slowly opened without noticed resistance. Her husband had inquired once about all of her studying. She had explained that she was trying to learn all about her new home so that she too might become a beloved champion of the people. Her story seemed to placate the king, because he didn't ask her to stop. To the contrary, he seemed rather pleased with the idea.

As Anistasia had expected, the Kingdom of Ayr sat on a rock-solid financial footing. It possessed no outstanding debt of any kind. It held secure two-way trade deals with Neeron, Udaass, and Oban. It had a one-way trade deal with Ubar as well, where they bought grains and food stuff from Ayr with minerals and salts mined from the desert. All of the trade deals produced a surplus of capital. The king's treasure room held a vast reserve that was large enough to carry the kingdom through any unforeseen calamity. The Kingdom of Ayr was as sound as a kingdom could be financially. She had known as much from her many days sitting with the king at court, but it was good to confirm it with accurate records.

Ayr's economic status allowed it large political pressure. That pressure could be brought to bear by Anistasia on the Great Bank if utilized properly. The right amount of persuasion might get the bank to call in Ubar's loans. With the loans called in, Ubar would be weak to outside pressure. Then, maybe, timing would allow an opportunity for Ayr, or the queen, to advance on El Hataan. Maybe the stress of it all might just be enough to send Ubar's king, an old and decrepit man, off into the next place. That would surely help her cause. Still, at the end of the day, no outside army had ever crossed the desert sands and lived to return home again. Or that was the narrative laid down in all of the volumes.

The queen began to ponder. Had any army actually tried to take El Hataan during the current age? No time sprung to mind in her head. This question had lead Anistasia back to the archives. She had dropped some full-weight gold coins into the stone receiving bowl inside the entrance door each time she came to visit the meeting hall. Her guards would wait outside or inside the entrance to the meeting area as the caretaker escorted her down to the archives room. The large ring of keys he carried, purchased by the gold coins in the receiving bowl, allowed her access to the knowledge of the kingdom.

Anistasia had sat there at one point and considered the thick volume that sat on the table before her. What would her life be if she hadn't learned how to read and write? If she didn't know her letters, she would have had no way to learn the things that really gave power. When she was a girl, she had hated the mistress who had come to teach her. The old hag had been a strict and overbearing woman. Anistasia had resisted the lessons as best as she could. But as with all things, some of it had managed to stick. When she learned as a young woman what she could actually do with that little bit which had stuck, she embraced learning with an unmatched ferocity. Her limited ability to read and write quickly transformed themselves into a fluid command of both. And with that fluid command she had been able to put her family back on the map, amass a small fortune, and work her way all the way into the court of Ayr. Now, she was queen of the land. A notion unknown or unthought of by the young girl who had resisted her mistress.

That old hag had taught her one solid lesson while they were together. That was the usefulness of discipline and punishment. Anistasia learned by example that punishment was a practical weapon. Through the following years she had used both the need for discipline and the application of punishment with great effect. After all, disloyalty could not be tolerated. Not in her endeavors.

The long turn through the histories had told her what she thought they would. No army in the current age had ever tried to take Ubar by force. It seemed that the great defensive sand sea of the desert had never actually been properly tested. Maybe all of the stories were just that, stories. If so, they were very effective ones. Still, it did open up possibilities. Maybe someone really could take the kingdom by force. Anistasia had always assumed that it would come down to trickery in the north, but maybe not. She was hoping not. Force of arms always had a better outcome when it came to subjugating people. It was a good thought for a future day.

Sitting under her sitting tree in the upper terrace overlooking the market square, Anistasia smiled to herself. No one was going to see what she had coming for this world, nor would they be able to stop it from happening. It was time for action. The world had been quiet long enough. It was time for mayhem to consume things.

Anistasia stood and smoothed out the wrinkles in her dress. Turning toward the doors, she walked casually toward the residence. Her private guard, all of them milling around the perimeter of the terrace, stiffened and adjusted to follow her. The two in her general direction preceded her inside. Anistasia made her way to her chamber and took up a seat at her writing desk. After situating herself properly, she looked up at the closest guard.

"Do me a service and go find my personal messenger, please."

The man snapped his heals in affirmation and stepped backward to turn. Anistasia picked up her pen and dipped the business end in a small jar of black ink sitting on the corner of the table. Sliding the wetted end across a new piece of parchment, the queen of Ayr laid down about a dozen lines of text. She signed it with her name and station before waving it in the air several times to set the ink. With complete confidence, Anistasia rolled up the correspondence and slid it inside a small silver collar. The silver collar designated the correspondence as one coming from a royal house.

Sitting the parchment and the pen down on the desk, she retrieved a rectangular block of wax and held it to the nearby candle flame. One or two seconds passed before a large dollop of hot wax dripped off the block onto the rolled parchment, sealing the middle of the exposed edge down to itself. Anistasia pressed her signet ring into the hot wax, marking it with her official seal. She had no more than finished putting the finishing touches on it when the guard returned with the messenger. Anistasia nodded to them both and then handled the freshly penned document to the currier.

"Deliver this to the Mining Isles. Put it squarely in the hands of King Kamber himself."

The messenger, a completely unassuming individual, nodded once and bowed slightly.

"Yes, majesty. I will see it there."

The queen smiled and the messenger exited the room with purpose. Anistasia turned her head to look out the open doors onto a large private balcony. The midday sun streamed in with thick yellow beams of power. She watched the light dance small dust particles in the air for a moment, trying to decide if the beams of light were an omen or just the sign of a beautiful day. Turning back toward the guard, she smiled, deciding on the latter.

"Please have the girl outside fetch me up a pitcher of wine and bring it to me out on the balcony. You lot can relax. I think I'm going to be in for the afternoon."

"Yes, majesty," came from all four men in unison, as they turned to exit the room.

The girl with the wine found the queen on her balcony, happily soaking in the midday sun. The girl filled a large, elegant glass and handed it to the queen submissively. Stepping back as the queen received the glass, the girl waited patiently for the next commandment. Anistasia took in the image of the young girl, or young woman, head bowed in submission to her obvious better, and smiled. *It was the way the world was meant to be,* Anistasia thought while tasting the wine. *The weak yielding to the strong.*

Anistasia wondered if the girl had learned anything of the world yet. Did she know the power her body possessed over weaker people? Had she ever used that power? From the girl's submissive stance, she was betting not. Maybe she would teach her the power of her body on one of these warm afternoons. The wine girl was certainly pretty enough. It might be an enjoyable way to pass a sunny afternoon. Anistasia considered the many times she had used her own body to get what she wanted from life. A number of men and women had been occupants in her private chambers over the years. Each one of those liaisons had served its intended purpose, including the one that had led to her wedding night.

"That will be all. Thank you for bringing me the wine."

The girl curtsied and promptly disappeared from view. Anistasia sighed. When she had taken full control over this world, she would live life any way she chose to. She would wield absolute power, absolutely. After all, that was what the treasure in the vault promised. Absolute power. The power to control and command every person in the lands.

It had been decided at the conclusion of the Great War, which brought low the previous age, that such a power could never be used. Anistasia had decided otherwise. After all, no weapon ever built by the hands of man had ever gone unused. No matter the type of weapon or the age it was made in, they all got used eventually. Anistasia would be the one to use this weapon. She would open the vault located at the end of the world, retrieve the weapon sleeping inside, and unleash it on the world. The thought of absolute power made her warm all over, or maybe it was the sunshine and the wine? *No,* she thought, *it was definitely the thought of her end goal.*

Chapter Twenty-Two

The carriage made its way up the central road through the middle of Warrington with ease. The Queen's Guard rode ahead of the carriage and a group of Watchtower soldiers from the Great Watchtower of Thorne, located at the group's coastal arrival port, brought up the rear. People on both sides of the roadway waved to the queen and Princess Catherine as they passed. Both ladies called back to the crowd with well-wishes. The day was bright and Bianca Rhodes thought that she could vaguely hear the sound of birds singing in the distance. The age-old black flat road surface allowed the carriage to roll along without a bump as the royal assemblage made its way slowly by, waving and well-wishing the fine people of Warrington. At the end of the long straight procession way lined with shops and tall sturdy buildings on both sides, they finally came to the house of the regent. A large stone affair with a thick wall and portcullis, the residence of the countess was really a small castle set inside a city, set inside the plentiful wheat fields and crop-filled plains of Meridian.

The lead guard stepped quick on his mount to the entry gate and everyone parted to let the queen's entourage pass into the residence entry unbothered. The driver of the carriage, an old man who had been in the family's employ since Bianca's father's time on the throne, gave the carriage a wide swing on the stone cobbles of the entry drive and aligned it with the waiting Countess of Warrington.

Bianca looked out at Princess Margerette Rhodes, Countess of

Warrington, Commander of the Armies of Meridian, potential next-in-line for the throne, and observed her sour expression. Bianca turned to Catherine and smiled a sad, tired smile.

"It seems that sister's in a foul mood."

Catherine gave a conciliatory look and shrugged slightly.

"I don't remember a time that she hasn't been."

"True. Does seem to be a constancy about it."

Bianca looked back at her sister standing before the carriage. Built like the rest of the Rhodes women, Margerette Rhodes stood a pleasing five-foot-eight-inches tall and was a hair's breadth over nine stone. Those traits and a long mane of blonde hair was where things parted ways. A warrior, used to standing her ground against men who were larger and stronger, she was thin but almost completely muscle. Her muscle was trim and shaped in a fine feminine wrapper. She had collected her fair number of scars over the years, though none were visible to the casual eye. What was currently observable was a pair of ice-blue eyes and a sour disposition.

Bianca Rhodes stepped from her carriage and waved to the riders from the Watchtower.

"Thank you for your company. I'm sure that we'll be fine from here."

The lead rider waved back a salute and the Watchtower soldiers circled back out of the central gate, disappearing from view. Bianca turned to look at her guard.

"We'll be some time, so take your rest. But we're not staying, so no public houses."

All of the guards laughed, acknowledging the command. Bianca put her hand on the old driver's leg and smiled softly.

"We'll only be a couple of hours and then it's off for home. Rest, old friend."

The old driver thanked her, calling her Princess Bianca in his remarks, as he had consistently done since she was old enough to ride in the carriage. She smiled warmly and turned to her middle sister.

"You really felt it necessary to travel in this region with an armed escort?"

Bianca took in Margerette's tone and sighed a second time.

"It's my kingdom. I'll do what I want in it."

"Majesty."

Princess Margerette Rhodes offered no bow or curtsy, but turned on heeled boots and strode back into her residence. Bianca looked at Catherine and sighed another sigh.

"Yup. In a sour mood for sure."

Queen Bianca Rhodes and Princess Catherine Rhodes walked casually into the regent's residence and made their way to a well-lit temple at the end of the first hallway. The two ladies took up station in heavily padded leather chairs that faced the overflowing stacks and settled themselves. The head housekeeper appeared, almost as if on cue, and curtsied proper like.

"Your majesty. Princess Catherine. The countess will be happy to receive you in the banquet hall."

Bianca smiled a huge smile at Catherine.

"Wow. We really must have caught her on a bad day?"

The housekeeper snickered, unable to stop herself from doing so. Catherine laughed to make her feel better about the slip. Bianca smiled at her, as if to say, it's all fine.

"Lady housekeeper, might you be as good as to fetch something cool for me and my sister here. We've been long on our journey. Oh, and if you could relay to the countess that the queen of Meridian would be happy to receive her in the temple, that would be smashing."

The housekeeper smiled broadly.

"Right away, majesty."

The housekeeper had no more than disappeared from view when a massive grey beast of a dog came crashing through the semi-opened doors of the temple. The big grey bull mastiff made two bounds, completely crossing the temple floor, and half-lunged, plopping his great big head and ribcage in Catherine's lap. Catherine expelled a full chest of air as the dog compressed her lungs flat. He looked up at Catherine through hooded eyes and slapped her with a thick wet tongue, dragging it across her face and off of her chin. Catherine laughed and began scrubbing the dog's smooth fur.

"Buster, you goofy beast! I've missed you boy."

Bianca shook her head at her little sister.

"That thing's almost as big as you are. You're lucky you weren't hurt."

Catherine laughed and continued to scrub the dog's fur with her hand.

"He's a good doggie!"

Bianca was going to make another comment when the door opened all the way.

"Buster. Get down."

Catherine looked past the dog's big head at her sister Margerette and continued petting the happy animal.

"He can stay if he wants."

"Buster. Now."

The big beast of a dog pushed himself off of Catherine, landing on four solid paws. Looking over at his master, he lowered his head as if to signify that he knew he was in trouble and trotted back out of the room. Margerette followed him with her eyes and then turned back to look at Catherine, who was attempting to straighten out her wrinkled dress.

"He could have ruined your dress, or hurt you, by doing that."

Catherine made a face.

"He just wanted some love. You should spend more time with him."

"I spend more than enough time with him as it is. Now, what brings you two to my door? Not that it's not always pleasant to see you both."

"We're headed back to Meridian City, from our trip to Ayr."

Catherine's voice still held the excitement of an adventure.

"Yes. The wedding of the ages."

Bianca rubbed a spot between her eyebrows, as if to try and stave off a headache.

"Peggy! We've been traveling for several days in bad weather and on foul seas. Needless to say, I'm in a mood. So, whatever has your knickers all twisted up, put it in a drawer somewhere because I don't care. You understand?"

Margerette Rhodes was about to let go a verbal retort when the housekeeper reappeared with a pitcher of wine and a tray of sweet cakes.

She placed it on a side table situated between the queen and Princess Catherine, curtsied, and exited the brewing storm. Margerette let her be about her tasks unbothered and slowly decompressed.

"You win. How was the wedding?"

"I had a nice conversation with Aunt Valene. She sends her best. I was also able to handle some trade issues at the affair. All in all, probably not a complete waste of time."

"Was Aunt Valene well?"

"She seemed tip top for a lady of her age. Her husband Marco is as boisterous as ever."

"Good to hear that she's well. By the way, where's the other member of your party?"

Bianca and Catherine looked at each other.

"Rosalyn," Margerette said in monotone.

"She decided to go north on her own. I think she could sense your mood."

"You allowed the Queen of the Freelands Folk to travel unescorted in your kingdom?"

Bianca made a face.

"She's the High Sorceress of Maiden's Tower, Peggy. She's been able to take care of herself since we were all little girls."

Margerette Rhodes poured a glass of wine and sighed into it.

"Yes. She's the special sister."

Catherine decided to pour salt in an obviously opened wound.

"You're a Princess of the House of Rhodes. You could effortlessly be Queen Margerette, of somewhere, if you were remotely adventurous. Everyone knows that you've wanted that golden crown ever since you were little."

Margerette began to fume and shake slightly.

"Adventurous? Yes. We all saw how well that worked out for our brother, didn't we?"

The mention of their brother in the negative made Catherine visibly hostile.

"Alexander had the courage to live his life as he chose. You won't speak of him like that."

Bianca looked over and put a gentle hand on Catherine's arm. The room was quickly descending into chaos.

"Both of you, stop! Life has played out as it was meant to play out, and it will continue to do so. We aren't here for another family holiday conversation. We're here for business. Now, both of you, act like it."

Bianca didn't want to think about being queen only because her older brother, and rightful heir to the throne, decided to turn it down. And since he was never heard from again, the throne was hers, and the rule that went with it.

"Fine," Catherine said quietly.

"Okay," Margerette countered, at about the same volume.

"I had several minutes to talk with the new queen while Rosalyn was out finding a handsome prince to converse with Catherine."

Margerette looked at Catherine quizzically.

"His name is Akeem, and he comes from the deserts of Ubar."

Margerette made another face. "And how was our new royal?"

"She seems nice enough, still, at the same time ..."

"Yes?"

"I get that crawling suspicion under my skin that she can't be trusted very far."

Margerette Rhodes nodded at her older sister in a sure and concise manner.

"I would say that your intuition is spot on."

Margerette had stopped calling her sister Bianca the day that she had placed the crown of Meridian upon her head. No one was sure why.

"Tell me. What have your ferrets ferreted out?"

The Kingdom of Meridian had a well-established network of spies stretched to all corners of the land. Their spies, lovingly referred to as ferrets for their ability to sniff things out, saw and heard all that was of consequence. The network answered to Margerette Rhodes, head spy master of the land.

"Many, many interesting things. Starting with the fact that all of the regents in Ayr, and a large number of the counts and countesses, think the same as you do."

Bianca finally had her sister talking and didn't want her to pause.

"Go on."

"Well, it seems that our new queen wormed her way into court and had every intention of doing so specifically to gain the favor of the king."

Bianca nodded.

"No one in Ayr court spends too much time in a room with her, save their Master, a ladder-climbing man named Jonah."

"I met him. He seemed quite nice, and well-spoken," Catherine said, trying to be helpful.

"What of Jonah?"

"He's been a staple of the Ayr court for some time now. Educated to Master at the Great Temple of Drakchi, Ayr is his first real royal seating."

"And this Anistasia Nosov, Queen of Ayr?"

"Anistasia Savin, the nobody daughter of some old, broke and powerless aristocratic family from Neeron. She appears to be a hard-knocks kind of girl. She made her way up the ladder of influence through a series of events fueled by manipulation, misdirection, random killings, and nicely placed sexual favors."

Catherine made a face that Margerette wasn't going to let pass.

"A woman's body is a potent weapon, if used properly. Your pirate friends know this all too well."

"Hey!"

Bianca put up a hand before Catherine popped her cork, and both of her sisters spiraled into chaos again. Bianca pointed to Margerette.

"Keep going."

"There are a series of things that may seem unrelated, but taken collectively, may spell trouble."

"Go."

"There was a bounty sheet for a thief put out. That thief was apprehended in the northern part of Ayr and turned into the magistrate of Gryazi. The pair that did the apprehending traveled to Roadstead to meet with Blue Bill Montgomery before proceeding on to the Temple of Fatezh."

"Big man with a bow and axe, and a smaller one with a pair of matching short swords."

Both sisters turned to look at Catherine.

"Yes," Margerette said quizzically. "How do you know that?"

"They delivered a sealed massage from Prince Akeem to Silas Khan. The two had a meeting the night we landed in Roadstead during the storm."

"What kind of meeting?"

"The business kind. They were coming to some type of arrangement; I'm guessing between the pirates and Ubar. Akeem sent his manservant on with the pirates, to wherever they were headed after the storm, to barter in the prince's stead."

Bianca smiled at Catherine and nodded, then looked over back to Margerette.

"Okay, keep talking."

"While in Fatezh, they gave the Master of the temple a metal cylinder with a parchment stolen from the Great Temple of Drakchi."

"So?"

"So, that cylinder was promptly sent via courier back to the Rain-Shadow Isles. It only made it as far as the near side of Udaass. The courier was killed, and the cylinder was reacquired."

"Reacquired by who?"

"Good question. The people of the countryside tell rumors that the courier was killed by Shadowman. They say the marks are there, or the lack of them."

"Shadowman is a myth," Bianca said emphatically.

"Says you. The ferrets say that the cylinder reappeared yesterday in the chamber of one Queen Anistasia Nosov of Ayr."

"Alright, I'll bite. What's in the cylinder?"

"Don't know exactly. A rolled-up parchment of some type. The bounty sheet men, who both interestingly seem to double as men of letters, spent a fair amount of time with the Temple Master looking over old, turn of the age, documents. Finding only part of the answer they wanted, they headed out."

"Headed to where?"

Margerette Rhodes downed a glass of wine and took up station in a chair facing her sisters.

"The two men headed southeast across Neeron. Supposedly they were heading for the mining town of Orba. I'm told that they went looking for a man who made his living in rare volumes and forgotten knowledge."

"Did they find him," Catherine asked in a curious tone.

"No. It seems that the man no longer plies his trade there."

"So, what happened next?"

"For the bounty men?"

"Yes," Bianca said in the same tone as Catherine.

"Nothing of note. They spent the night at a public house and picked up a new bounty sheet while they were there. I presume they went off tending to their trade."

"Well, that's an interesting story."

"Were the adventurers handsome?"

Margerette and Bianca looked at Catherine, who smiled and shrugged.

"In a roguish way, I guess. I didn't enquire."

"You always miss the fine details."

Bianca chuckled and Margerette frowned.

"Is that all the important bits," Bianca asked, smiling at Margerette.

"No. That was just kind of the buildup."

"Buildup to what?"

Bianca's tone was queenly this time.

"It seems that since Anistasia got her crown and her official sovereignty, she has been spending an excess amount of time at the meeting hall, swimming through the official archives of Ayr. Just after the cylinder returned to her grasp, she dispatched a messenger with an officially sealed and ringed correspondence."

"Saying what? Going where?"

"Don't know the contents, but the messenger headed due south. He's made it as far as the border of Oban and is still heading south."

Bianca rubbed her chin and then that spot between her eyebrows.

The headache was coming on after all. She turned and looked at Catherine.

"Catherine, please go tell the guard and the driver that we will be staying the night."

Princess Catherine stood without question and headed toward the door. Bianca fixed Margerette with a hard gaze.

"There's nothing south of Oban but open ocean. And Aunt Valene rules Oban."

Margerette Rhodes shook her head.

"Wrong. On the far end of the Halcyon Sea lie the Mining Isles, home to the City of Dyme and the Great Gold Bank."

Bianca sighed a deep sigh.

"Can we please trade out the wine for whiskey?"

Chapter Twenty-Three

Quinn sat in the corner of a small intersection where four random streets came together and blended into the shadowy corners of buildings. Bernard stood on the opposite corner dressed in old workers' garments and tried to look poor and tired.

They had cased the tiny Hamlet of Mullen, on the road leading south out of Orba, for the better part of half-a-day. The spot they eventually chose seemed to be the one which funneled the most townspeople through as they came and went about their business. They had given a woman a half-weight silver coin for pointing them in the right direction while out on the road. Now they needed to stay patient and see if the tip paid off.

Truth be told, it usually took one or two weeks to come across a solid lead for someone on a bounty sheet. The chase was as much an investigation as anything. They only had the better part of two days invested in this chase. They were well ahead of the curve. *That would make Bernard happy,* Quinn thought, sharing a rare smile with the darkness of his hiding place. Bernard liked things neat and tidy. "Chase the easy money, we're not working for the crown here," was one of his famous lines.

He was right, to a point, Quinn mused, watching the string of random people pass by from his shadowy post. They were working for themselves, and that work had always been good. But that wasn't the why of why they did things. You fought the fights that needed to be fought.

People ended up on bounty sheets for all manner of reasons. That being said, there were really only two types of bounty sheets. There were sheets where someone had committed a crime of some type, and then there were sheets with known criminals on them. Quinn liked the second kind, where Bernard gravitated toward the first. It was the criminals that were the good fight to Quinn. Removing them was a good deed done, if there was such a thing in their game. Frankly, there were beings in the world who just needed killing, and he was happy to accommodate.

A man moved by them in the crowd. He was an everyday man and unassuming, just like the one they were looking for, but it wasn't him. Quinn glanced over at Bernard, who had also taken the measure of the man. He didn't budge from his position. It was definitely not the one they were looking for.

Quinn's need to deliver a little justice, to kill those that just needed killing, was one of the things which had separated him from the Watchtower Guild. They were a mighty army. Each soul trained to fight as well as any soul on the planet. Sadly, for a guild with a calling to the fight, they did little of it. They stayed to peacekeeping. The evil men and women they encountered were simply handed off to whichever local constabulary they happened to be operating in. That type of act was pointless. The local courts of the land were overrun with work. The people they handed over did some small amount of time in crowded jails and were released. Or they escaped easily enough and found themselves on bounty sheets. To Quinn's deep-seated sense of right and wrong, the bounty sheet business was a much more meaningful profession than that of the Watchtower. He fought the fights that needed fighting. He killed people that needed killing. It was everyone's job to make the world a better place to live in. He did his part by separating the wheat from the chaff.

Quinn watched a young woman go by and thought about the sorceress named Gweneth. She was as beautiful a woman as he had ever seen in his time. And her melancholy drew him to her in a way that he couldn't explain, even to himself. He had known many beautiful women in his time. They were of all types and stations. One was even reported by many to be the most beautiful woman in the whole land. None had had any lasting anchor on him. They came and went like spring blossoms. He didn't consider them once they were gone. That wasn't the way his life was. After all, he could easily live to be one hundred or not see out the day. That was the random chance of the bounty sheet business. There was no reason to make attachments. He could tell that that line of reasoning, a solid guide for him throughout his life, wasn't going to work with Gweneth. And for once, he didn't want it to.

Strange girl, that Gweneth. Penetrating blue eyes. Lonely and suspicious blue eyes. He could see her eyes true when he closed his own and thought. A fresh face, full of youth and covered with freckles the way a summer field is dotted with clover. She was still in her youth, still holding on to being a girl, but definitely a woman, with a woman's body. And with her wild fiery red hair came power. She possessed levels of power that Quinn had never come across before. He didn't know that a sorceress could even travel as she had when she had left his room back at the public house. Quinn assumed that she inherited her power from her mother. One didn't get to the position of Sorceress for the Great Temple of Drakchi without being able to wield great power. Enella, her mother, was both powerful and kind. Quinn remembered that he could sense a kindness in Gweneth that was like her mother's. It was deep down by her essence, almost buried, but still there.

Strange girl. He couldn't shake her from his thoughts. He didn't want to shake her from his thoughts.

A man walked by in the crowd. An everyday and unassuming type of man. This time he looked like the one that they were looking for. Quinn shook the sorceress from his mind as he watched Bernard slowly turn and shuffle off in the same basic direction as their mark.

Bernard and the mark turned a corner in the near street and disappeared from view. If things went to their normal ends, Quinn had about three minutes to get to where he needed to be. He pushed himself out of his shadowy corner and proceeded at a slight trot to an adjacent street. This street was long and straight, with two other streets crossing through it to form intersections. Quinn worked his way to the second intersection and took up a good spot in one corner. If things went to plan, Bernard would corral the man onto the second side street and Quinn would snatch him up. This approach usually worked out quite well.

"Quinn!"

Quinn looked down the side street as the man and Bernard bolted through the opening at a dead run. Things had obviously not gone to plan.

Quinn took off at a full run moving down the street that paralleled Bernard's street. Fully full out, he pushed through the next intersection and continued on down the street. He had to dodge the biting end of a horse, jumping to one side as he slid around the beast. The man on the cart behind the horse yelled some type of profanity that was lost on Quinn as he sprinted away. Dodging a second cart, this one full of trash, he yelled an apology to the City Person pulling it along.

Making the next corner street, Quinn turned a hard and tight right-hand turn at full stride, cutting to intersect the two that should be coming at him from the other street. Hitting the point in space where the two different paths of the running men came together, Quinn thrust out an arm and snatched the bounty up by his throat. It took Quinn several strides to stop his own forward momentum, with the mark dangling from a clinched fist out in front of him. Quinn came to a stop, pinning the man to a building wall made of uniform red stones, and waited for Bernard to arrive. Bernard was an excellent orator, and a world class thief. He was also a master swordsman, but he was not fleet of foot. One might even say that he was a tad on the slow side. That was okay, because that was why Quinn was there.

Quinn looked at the bounty hanging from his extended arm as Bernard came jogging up gasping for air. He lowered the man to the ground and relaxed his grip enough so that the man could breathe comfortably.

"Definitely more of a thief than a fighter," Quinn said, inspecting the man passively.

"I'm not built for that. You hear to kill me, big man?"

Quinn considered the question for about two seconds.

"Not today. Bounty sheet aside, I just want to talk awhile."

"Bounty sheet aside?" Bernard said questioningly.

"Let's hear what the man has to say for himself. Gweneth said that he would have a tale to tell."

Bernard knew it wasn't good to take a stance counter to Quinn's once business had started.

"Okay, we talk. Let's do the talking."

The bounty, whose name turned out to be Willden, part-time conman and thief, looked at Quinn suspiciously. He knew the way of the streets better than the next man.

"You just want to talk? Then why did you chase me down?"

Bernard looked over at Willden incredulously.

"Because you ran, shithead."

There was a head nod of agreement.

"Fair enough. What about the throat clinch?"

He looked down at Quinn's arm which was still pinning him to the building wall.

"Right," Quinn said reflexively. "But understand, one shift to the left or right and you're a dead man."

Another nod of understanding.

"I'll keep me head as long as possible."

Quinn released his grip, shaking out his hand to get the blood flowing back into his fingers. He dropped his arm and attempted a stance which was a little less menacing. The sweat he had built up from running in the bright sunshine made his dark colored tunic sticky with perspiration.

"Tell us, what do you know about a metal tube with a rolled-up parchment inside it?"

Willden sighed deeply.

"Seal from the Great Temple in Drakchi on top of the cap? Fancy drawing inside?"

"That's the one," Bernard said.

"Do you know of a woman named Anistasia Savin, from the Kingdom of Neeron?"

Both men shook their heads to the negative.

"These days she goes by Anistasia Nosov, Queen of Ayr."

Quinn thought back to their ride with the prince, and the necessary side trip south.

"The royal wedding that just took place," Bernard continued.

"That's the one. See, before she became queen, she belonged to some forgotten aristocratic house in Neeron. Supposedly, at the turn of the age, they were a princely lot, but these days they rank somewhere about two shelves above the public house keepers. They still have some money, but no influence, and no power. Absolutely zero royal standing."

"So?" Bernard added, looking down at the price listed on the bounty sheet, and rethinking not taking a stance counter to Quinn's.

"That family station didn't sit with young Anistasia. She's the power-hungry type. So, she studied all of the histories, and ended up concocting a plan to get herself a shot at real power."

"Go on," Quinn added in monotone, before Bernard could complain/threaten Willden again.

"Well, she started small. The Alderman of Tilling, over Graycott way. Once she had him in her pocket, she moved up the food chain to the local Regent. She moved from Regents to Masters, until she found herself a foothold in the court of Ayr. There she set her sights firmly on the king."

"Why not stay in Neeron?"

"Because old man Lorimere already found himself a pretty young girl for a bride, in the form of Queen Vivian. Now she's a true jewel. The daughter of the Count of Fatezh. There was no space in Neeron's court for a power-hungry manipulator, but King Nosov was still single, which meant there was opportunity in Ayr. And Ayr has a standing army, where Neeron only has a defensive militia."

"So, she's ambitious. What does that have to do with Ayr's army, or the stolen tube for that matter?"

Bernard's face expressed annoyance. Willden shook his head like he didn't get the obvious.

"No, no, you're looking at it backwards. The tube is the reason for Ayr."

"How so?"

"Did you get a good look at the parchment?"

"Yes. It was a drawing of a key and lock mechanism. It was supposedly removed from one of the histories."

"Exactly. A set of keys that unlocks a lock, set into a vault door located at the end of the world. A vault said to possess a power capable of controlling the entire world. She needs the army in Ayr to take the keys that open the vault. That way, she can finally fulfill her lust for power. She wants to rule the world."

"Rule the whole world?" Bernard said, almost mockingly. "That's a task that couldn't be completed with ten armies the size of Ayr's."

"I disagree. One good army, which she now possesses, and a bunch of well-placed thieves, and one can obtain anything that there is to obtain."

Bernard considered some of the places that he had broken into over the years.

"Okay, fair enough. What does any of this have to do with you?"

"I stole the parchment from the Great Temple in Drakchi for her. I admit that I felt bad about having to rip it from the volume, but getting the entire volume past the temple guards wasn't possible. That kind of theft was out of the question. This was at the point in time when she had just inserted herself into the court of Ayr. She was a wily and manipulative thing and has only gotten better with age."

"Contract job?" Bernard asked curiously.

"Yes. A single pay job. Had I known that she was going to try and pay me with a sword through the belly, I would have declined the opportunity."

"Her, herself?" Quinn asked.

"No. She's way too cunning for that. The deal went through a middleman. A swordsman type, like you two."

"So, she's not to be trusted?"

"Not to be trusted is an understatement of monumental proportions. She lacks any sense of right and wrong whatsoever. She is completely and utterly untrustworthy. She will use any means available to get what she wants; be it money, sex, blood, bondage, or pain. The best thing that any sane person could do is kill her upon their first meeting. Otherwise, you're just going to become a cog in her machine."

Quinn considered the idea of killing a queen. He wasn't sure about that.

"She's bent on taking over the world, and she will burn it all to the ground before she sees herself fail. Mark my words."

Quinn and Bernard looked at each other and Quinn made a face that Bernard didn't like. He didn't like it at all.

"Now, I've told you what you wanted to know, what happens to me?"

The two exchanged another look. This one was much more middle of the road.

"Well, a bounty sheet is a bounty sheet," Bernard said to Willden without emotion.

"Does that sheet say dead or alive?"

Bernard inspected it again.

"Yes, it does …"

Before Bernard could finish his sentence, Willden slid a flat blade out of his pocket and stuck it into his own neck. The initial splash from the pumping artery sprayed across Quinn's chest, accenting his sweaty tunic. Willden sunk to his knees and then slumped to one side without uttering another word. Obviously dead to the trained eye, Bernard looked over at his equally irritated and shocked friend.

"Well, I didn't see that coming."

Quinn looked down at the spray of the man's blood on his tunic.

"Me either."

Chapter Twenty-Four

Queen Anistasia Nosov walked quietly through the fortress of Kanash, her guard circling around her to keep the vagrants at bay. She was in a reflective mood. It had been a long, hard climb up from obscurity to become the Queen of Ayr. Now, the only thing really standing in the way of her putting her master plan into action was her husband. The King of Ayr was a good man. He would certainly want no part in what was coming next. That was fine with Anistasia. She hadn't had any plans of letting him join in on her glory anyway.

Along the northern wall, well past the shops and open areas, the queen came to a building which comprised part of the heavy fortress wall. The lead guard stopped at an unmarked door and banged on the heavy weathered wood with a gantlet-covered fist. A small shuffling could be heard coming from the interior before the bolt was retracted and the door inched open.

Master Jonah looked out past the lead guard and smiled.

"Good morning, majesty. Please, enter."

The guard stayed motionless as the Master sidestepped him and addressed their sovereign. The guard was completely comfortable with the action at this point. He was betting that most of the well-to-do people in the city didn't even know what his name was.

The guard stepped to one side so that the queen could enter the room. As Anistasia expected beforehand, the room was a collection of tables, each containing a variety of glass vessels on small metal stands. Several distinct, yet foreign, smells could be sensed coming from separate areas in the space. At a table to one side, Grgur stood looking intently at a glass jar as he dropped liquid into it, one drop at a time. Three or four drops of the fluid and the liquid in the jar turned a solid light-blue color. Two more drops and it became clear again. Grgur swirled the liquid around inside the glass and smiled to himself. Setting down the dropper, he looked up from his concoction and noticed that other people had entered the room. He smiled at the queen this time, the lines on his weathered face clinching up around his eyes as he did so.

"My queen. Good morning to you. Are you well on this day?"

Anistasia smiled, unable to help herself. It was the way that Grgur was. She walked over and put a hand on his cheek.

"Yes, my old friend. I am well."

Anistasia turned around and nodded to the lead guard. Nodding back, he stepped from the room and closed the door behind him. The three were alone.

"First bit of business first," Anistasia said, addressing Grgur. "Are we ready to proceed?"

The old man nodded once.

"Yes."

The queen turned and looked at Jonah.

"Okay, where do we stand on the consolidation of power?"

Master Jonah rubbed his chin a moment before answering.

"The prince is in Gryazi, as one would expect. Or he was as of yesterday. He won't be an immediate problem, but he will need to be dealt with. He's definitely not as naive as his brother."

Anistasia smiled in a way that said Prince Jan Nosov was of little concern.

"I've dealt with countless men like the Count of Gryazi. He's of no real consequence."

Jonah gave a neutral expression.

"As far as the kingdom itself goes, the regents will fall in-line, eventually. The structure of things is too rigid for them to rebel outright. They only retain any form of power if the system continues, and they know that."

The queen considered the statement for several seconds.

"So, if they're shown a plausible path, they'll follow it. Even if they don't want to."

"Exactly."

"That's good to know."

The queen looked over at Grgur.

"Do we have a patsy ready to go, if need be?"

The Master and the old healer nodded one solid affirmative. Jonah did the talking.

"We have a disgruntled old man from Graycott, down in Neeron, all ready to take the fall. He thinks that Ayr unfairly taxes the crops they take in on trade. He's quite disillusioned with the rule of this kingdom and its trade practices. It seems that there are numerous small pockets of disillusioned people in that part of Neeron. You just need to observe closely to see them."

"Excellent."

Turning back to Master Jonah, she fixed him with a level gaze.

"The real question: Where does Stas Bok stand?"

Jonah made a face.

"That one could go either way. There are things to consider."

"What things?"

"Stas is not a young man. He's on the cusp of retirement. He may simply choose not to get involved. Next, he's a lifelong military man. He has complete control of Ayr's army. He may fall in line when commanded to do so. If he decided to fall in line, the military will go with him without questions."

Anistasia could sense that Jonah wasn't finished.

"Or?"

"Or he may object to your rule and stand against you. As I mentioned, he has complete control over your military."

"Will the military absorb a new leader, if he decides that he isn't inclined?"

"Highly doubtful. He trained almost all of the company captains himself. They are a uniquely loyal bunch."

Anistasia considered that for a moment.

"Okay, best guess. Which way does he go?"

Jonah scratched his chin in a stalling tactic.

"At the end of the day, I say he falls in line. At his core he's a military man. Those types take orders well."

"That choice would certainly uncomplicate things. If the opportunity presents itself, someone should explain the ramifications of opposition to him."

Jonah nodded slowly.

"Majesty."

Anistasia could feel that the Master still had thoughts rolling around inside his head.

"Go on."

Jonah paused briefly.

"The real unknown is what the Watchtower will do if we march south with the army."

Grgur looked over to the queen with some curiosity. He and Jonah had been having this very conversation the previous day.

"The Watchtower Guild is a peacekeeping force. I doubt that they want to stand against an entire army. Besides, even if they decide to do so, they aren't any great threat. The Watchtower Guild is a formidable force if it is collected together for battle. But they aren't collected together, are they? They're scattered across all the known lands, one company to a keep. A single company, no matter how well trained they are, won't slow us down any amount."

Grgur smiled at his glass vessels and put his head back down. Apparently, the queen had been giving some thought to the Watchtower as well. Jonah considered the remarks and couldn't see anything immediately wrong with the queen's assessment, so he said nothing.

"We'll need to make sure that the remainder of my men are properly placed so there aren't any problems with the transition."

Jonah smiled broadly.

"That has already come to pass. Your men and women are set in places that can stave off resistance, should any arise."

The queen nodded with a neutral expression.

"Good work. So, we can proceed?"

"Yes, majesty," came in unison from the pair of men.

The queen turned her attention back to the old healer.

"Grgur, my old friend, tell me a story."

Grgur quit the distraction of the glass jars to focus attention on his ruler. Smiling a slightly evil smile, he reached beneath the work counter and produced a small glass vial full of a clear liquid, maybe one good ounce in volume, sealed with a cork stopper. Setting the vial down gently on the queen's side of the worktable, he waved his hand over it slowly, as if enchanting it with some magical power.

"I give you the instrument of your triumph, my queen."

The queen looked at the obvious vial of poison and nodded respectfully to her healer and chemist.

"Do continue."

"This is what the sages of the previous age called hemlock. It's an especially effective paralytic poison."

Anistasia didn't understand the words, but she liked the sound of them. Grgur could see her loss of comprehension and continued.

"You mix it into his drink. I would suggest a glass of wine, prior to sleeping, so he will be laying down. The poison kills by numbing the muscles into inaction and then shutting down the breathing."

The queen smiled.

"So, he'll die in his sleep?"

Grgur made a conciliatory expression.

"Not exactly, ma'am. The poison shuts down the body, but it keeps the mind alert while it does its work. So, when the king finally suffocates, he'll know that it's happening."

Master Jonah made a shocked expression, where Anistasia's was somewhat closer to wonder.

"Interesting."

"It would not be a good way to die, all choices considered."

"I would say not," Master Jonah said, forgetting that he wasn't supposed to contradict his leadership. Anistasia turned and considered Jonah's expression.

"If it works as promised, I may need to keep another vial around for loose ends and such."

Grgur shrugged, as if to suggest that making it wasn't particularly difficult.

"I'm told that it has a slightly bitter taste, so you will want to hide it in something sweet."

The queen nodded that she understood.

"Oh, yes," he started as if suddenly remembering something important, "Don't get any of it on yourself. It will soak into your skin and have a similar effect."

"That's definitely good advice," Anistasia Nosov said as she picked up the vial from the counter.

"How long does it take?"

"If you use it all, the effects should be quite immediate. I would think that in less than one hour you'll get the desired effect."

Anistasia looked longingly at the vial as she slid it into the small silk pouch dangling from her right wrist.

"Power is never given; it is always taken."

Chapter Twenty-Five

The scream emanating from the royal couple's private chambers rocked its way through the entire fortress residence. It was such a displacement from the normal sounds of the residence that it took the staff a moment to respond.

Soon enough, as if motioned on by a higher power, everyone in the king's residence was moving toward the noise. The royal guard was the first through the door. They found a distraught queen clutching the king's body, wailing and crying as she attempted to shake the heavier man. King Gerald's large and imposing frame lay motionless in the bed. It was still. Much too still to be okay.

"Get the healer! Now!"

The scream from the queen to the guard at the head of the charge through the door went right past him and landed in the ears of the third man. Without words, the third man spun round and headed back the way that he had just come. Two or three more guards joined the first guard by the bed, along with a maid and a house servant boy. They circled around the bed taking in the sight. The queen barely noticed them. She listened to the king's body and rubbed his chest while she wailed in pain.

An old lady from the staff shuffled into the room and made her way to where the others stood. Taking in the image of the king, she turned an ashen color.

"Did you summon the healer?" she asked one of the guards in a loud and pronounced voice. The man stammered out a positive response.

The scene stayed the same for the next five minutes, as if it was locked in glass. It was broken by a pair of men careening through the open door. The lead man of the two was the third guard. He was followed steps behind by the king's healer, an old and wise man named Marcant. The two men pulled up alongside the others and took in the scene. Instantly, the old man assessed that the king was not still among the living. Drawing a solid breath, he grabbed the guard next to him by his breast plate and looked him in the eye.

"Get all of these people out of this room. Do not let them wander off anywhere. Not one word of this leaves here. Do you understand?"

The man nodded blankly.

"Do you understand, soldier," the healer asked while shaking the man's breast plate.

The guard snapped back to reality and acknowledged the healer. Commanding each man circled around the bed by name, he charged them to file back out of the room and assemble in the hallway. The guards collected the residential staff that had come into the bed chambers with them as they left the room. The ashen old lady stared at the healer while being pushed from the room. The healer took in the image of the queen and sighed heavily.

"Majesty, you need to stop."

The queen continued to hold the king's body and cry and shake.

"Majesty," The healer said firmly, reaching out to touch her on her shoulder. The physical touch seemed to have the desired effect, as the queen refocused her attention from the king to Marcant. She blinked several times, seemingly not even realizing that other people were still in the room with her.

"You have to let go of him now so I may look at him."

The old man's words were calm, yet stern and commanding. The queen reflexively followed the instructions, collecting up her sleeping gown as she slid to one side of the large bed.

The Queen of Ayr watched passively as the old healer went about his tasks. He checked the king's eyes, opening the lid of each one to look inside. The king's eyes were motionless. He leaned down to the king's face and listened for the sounds of mortality. None of the sounds seemed to be present. The old man pulled the king's lower lip down, followed by his jawbone, to open his mouth. Mouth agape, the healer inspected the inside of the mouth and smelled the lingering air for any foul smells. It didn't seem as if anything of note presented itself.

Putting his hand on the king's chest, Marcant hovered motionless next to the body and waited. No movement of the chest presented itself. The king's body was as still as a marble figure. Postulating for several seconds, the healer slid a small flat blade from his pocket and removed the protective cap over the blade.

"What are you doing," came from the queen in a shaky tone.

"Not to worry, ma'am. Sometimes, the body needs to be shocked back into existence. If he is alive, it will help. If he is dead, it won't hurt."

Somehow, the straightforward explanation penetrated the queen's distraught exterior, because she paused her questioning and nodded in understanding. Marcant rolled the king's near hand over so that it lay on the bed palm up. With a deft hand, the healer inserted the tip of the blade into the king's palm a full quarter of an inch. Extracting the blade, he inspected the scene. The king's body put up no resistance to the penetration whatsoever. A crimson tip was extracted from the palm, but no outpouring of blood followed, as would be expected from a cutting wound. The old man bowed his head over the dead king and spoke some words in a still voice which the queen didn't understand. Looking up at the queen, she could see moisture in the man's eyes.

"The king is dead."

The queen stared at the old healer, as if unable to comprehend what he was saying.

"What?"

"You husband, the king, is dead."

She blinked a couple times and then put her face in her hands and began to sob audibly.

"How? What? How?" came out from between tear-soaked fingers.

The healer stood and walked around the bed to where the distraught queen sat. Placing a gentle hand on her shoulder, he spoke in a soothing tone.

"I do not know how the king died, majesty. We will have him removed to my rooms, where he may be properly examined."

The queen looked up in confusion.

"Removed?"

The healer nodded slowly.

"Yes, majesty. We cannot leave the body here. It wouldn't be proper."

The queen nodded slowly. The healer called for the guards standing outside the door to come back in. Three of the men reappeared; all visibly shaken. They took in the distraught image of the queen, feeling all of the despair she radiated. The healer directed the men to collect the king's body and remove it to his rooms. The guards did as directed, delicately lifting the dead king's body from the bed.

As the men exited the room with their cargo, two maid women came in and stripped the bedding from the bed. The healer told the women to have the bedding delivered to his rooms as well. The women made no comment to the request but continued with their task. As the maid women exited the room, the old healer returned his attention to the queen. She seemed more composed in a room without her dead husband, but still fragile. The healer felt for her and the state she was in.

"Your grace?"

The queen blinked a couple times to focus.

"Yes," came out in a very common manner. The tone of normal folk.

"Tell me about what happened last night when you and the king retired for the day."

The queen thought for several long seconds. The healer could see her trying to pull memories up from a deep abyss and thought that maybe he shouldn't have asked such questions of her so quickly. Her pain was still fresh. Still, precious facts disappeared as the time passed. It was all best when it was fresh.

"We had a late meal and retired here as usual. The king had had a long day. He was obviously tired. We had some wine and sat on the balcony for a short time, then we retired to the bed."

The healer thought.

"How long did you spend on the balcony?"

The queen shrugged her shoulders, looking more like a person than a royal. *Grief does that to people,* Marcant thought.

"Maybe twenty or thirty minutes. We had a glass of wine. He told me about his day. We had a second glass of wine. After, we came in."

"And you went straight to bed?"

"Yes. The king went to sleep almost immediately. As I said, he had had a long day."

The healer thought for a moment.

"Did he seem to go very deeply to sleep?"

The queen made a confused face.

"Yes. He fell asleep almost as soon as he lay down. He usually does when he's worn down."

Marcant thought.

"The wine – who brought it to you?"

The queen made another confused face.

"We have wine here in the bedchamber most all of the time. It's over there, in the pitcher. Why?"

Marchant walked over and smelled the remainder of the wine. It smelled like wine.

"And the king's glass?"

Anistasia pointed to a small table by the bed. The old healer walked over and collected the cup sitting on it.

"How? Why? How?" the queen muttered under her breath, seemingly ready to slip back into deep despair. The old healer smiled at her in a calming way, as if he was trying to calm a small child. It had the desired effect.

"My initial guess is poison, majesty. Though, I don't know the type or origin of it."

"Who … would do such a thing?"

"I don't know that either, majesty."

"He was loved by all."

"I would say that's true, but still."

"Still what?" the queen asked quietly.

"But he is still dead, majesty."

The queen began to sob and put her face back into her hands. The old healer put a calming hand softly on her shoulder. This time, the effort didn't help. The queen's grief was consuming.

"I'll send for the Master. He can sit with you and help you with your pain."

The queen continued sobbing. The healer looked down at his remaining monarch producing a sad expression, and then quietly stepped from the room.

Chapter Twenty-Six

Bernard stood on the ramparts for the fortifications which separated the City of Asturias from its deep-water harbor and stared out through the stone crenellations at the bulk of the Udaass naval fleet moored in the expansive harbor. Taking in the sight, he ran an ungloved hand through his short blond hair and sighed audibly. Quinn heard the sigh from his seat several feet away and looked over at his friend.

Quinn wasn't as daunted by the sight of the fleet as Bernard obviously was. They had both seen such sights before in their travels. He knew that in these situations it was better to just be quiet as a thief, stick to the shadows, and be as unobtrusive as possible. Strangely, those were some of Bernard's better qualities, which made him wonder why his friend was really agitated.

In the truth of it, Bernard wasn't agitated by the fleet or the amassing of troops around the port city, but by his friend. Quinn had been quietly annoyed by something ever since the bounty sheet man stuck himself. Bernard knew his friend too well after so many days together. Quinn wasn't the type to be annoyed by things that transpired in the outside world. He had never been the kind to get embroiled in the affairs of kings and countries. Those very qualities were two of the reasons the two of them got on so well. Bernard couldn't figure out what was going on, but he'd had about enough of it.

"Q. What's going on with you these days?"

Quinn looked up at his friend's back. Bernard was still taking in the sight of the fleet.

"What do you mean?"

Bernard turned around so he could look Quinn straight in the face.

"Don't be a shithead. You know exactly what I mean. Not that you've ever been overly sociable, but ever since that old dude knifed himself you've been twisted up. Come on, we traveled here in half of our normal time. Like some great doom depended upon it. So, what gives?"

Quinn made a face. Bernard, his truest and maybe only friend in the world, was a masterful study of people. That was one of the things which made him a good thief. Quinn considered the question a moment longer.

"I'm thinking that it has to do with my time in the Watchtower."

Bernard took the response at face value. It made sense that a Watchtower sergeant would have a deep-seated sense of right and wrong.

"The idea of conspiracies and kingdoms going to war for more power than they need strikes me as the opposite of peace in the land."

Bernard absorbed Quinn's response and rolled it around his brain. The motto of the Watchtower Guild was: *To protect the lives of the many, and maintain peace throughout the land.* A war between kingdoms would certainly destroy any peace there was in the land, as well as kill more than a few.

"It's not intentional, B. I just think that whatever this is that we've stumbled into, we should see it through. Something about it all seems to be directing us this way."

Bernard smiled.

"Yes. First, it was an Ubari prince. Now, it's a girl with fiery red hair."

Quinn laughed, unable to stop himself. He shrugged a pair of beefy shoulders at Bernard.

"True. But they both ended up paying us well."

"That's the truth of it, too. We just finished off the coin from the bounty sheet up in Ayr. We haven't even broken into the coin from the prince, and this last fellow paid out in royal stamped gold. We could take the whole next season off if we chose to."

Quinn smiled at Bernard wryly.

"You wouldn't know what to do with an off-season."

Bernard laughed and then looked around to see who was nearby or might be listening in.

"Neither would you, old chum. Neither would you."

Quinn stood and bent backward until the motion produced an audible cracking sound. Moving his head from side to side on his neck, a long expletive sigh came out with a lungful of air. He reached out and picked up his mighty longbow wrapped in his Watchtower cloak and then looked up at Bernard.

"We've come all this way, what say we go talk to the man we came to find?"

Bernard nodded in agreement.

"Good. Prince, sexy sorceress, crazy dude. It's a full hand, isn't it?"

The two men made their way to the wide steps that made their way down off of the ramparts and out on to the city streets. Putting boots down on the streets of Asturias, the view of the fleet disappeared behind a defensive wall. In the opposite direction one could see the mountain tops on the landside hanging above the city like deep green spires. They disappeared behind buildings and then reappeared in open areas as the pair walked along. The more Quinn looked at the mountain tops, the more he thought not of natural beauty but of defenses.

"You know, think about this place for a moment, Bernard."

Bernard let a man pass by them on the street and then glanced over at Quinn.

"In what regard?"

Quinn stepped to the side so that a woman and her child might make their way down the street unbothered. The woman took in the sight of their arms and ushered her child off at a quickened pace.

"Well, Orba was a mining town. It wasn't the safest place in the lands to set up shop. Nor was Fatezh for that matter. Then, if you consider Graycott on the way here? It was another city set on the foothills of the mountains. It, too, also may be a little reckless of a place."

Bernard could tell from the way he was talking that he was heading somewhere, so he stayed quiet.

"Now, you have Asturias. A solid city, with city guards and good defenses. It's situated with water on three sides, and mountains on the fourth. The city is currently also full of military men. Defensively speaking, it's the best choice so far."

"So, you think he came here to feel safe?"

"Don't know. I just think it's a good place to hole up if you're worried about such things. Maybe he's not as crazy as you think he is?"

Bernard smirked as another man of arms passed them by. There were as many mercenaries as there were soldiers in the city, which helped the two blend in a little better.

"The shopkeeper back in Orba said he was a straight-up nut job. Talked to himself and the whole business."

Quinn shrugged.

"We've both been known to put up a disguise from time to time."

The two turned the corner of the street into a small, open area. In front of them was a shop tile hanging over a doorway. It read *Alonzo, Fines, and Geldstein. Collectors.* Bernard took in the sign, almost the same one as hung over the door back in Orba.

"I guess we'll find out soon enough."

Quinn waved a hand toward the door and Bernard stepped up to open it. Pulling the door free of its frame, a little bell hanging from a metal strap rang. The sound of the bell was neither loud nor soft and seemed quite appropriate for the entrance of a business. Both men stepped inside and let the door close behind them. The interior of the shop was exactly as Quinn had imagined it in his mind. A space completely composed of shelves and small tables, all of them chockablock with volumes, small statues, scrolls and the like. Though it didn't possess the musty smell of most temple stacks, one wouldn't be wrong in imagining that it did. There was the sight of dust particles hanging in the air and the faintest smell of honey. Quinn smiled, which worried Bernard a little.

An older, thin and grey-haired man came out from a back room stirring a small cup. *The source of the honey smell,* Quinn mused silently. The man looked up from his cup and took in his two new customers. He stopped stirring and frowned.

"I knew that this day would come. Didn't think it would be today."

Bernard looked at the old man quizzically, like he was crazy.

"We're looking for a man named Rapheal Alonzo. Is he here today?"

The man blew softly across the top of his cup.

"And what business might you two gentlemen have with Mr. Alonzo?"

"We understand from a trustworthy man that you might be in possession of a complete set of the histories by Joshua the Scribe."

Quinn's voice was honest and direct but not overpowering. The man gave them both a second looking over.

"So, you're not here to kill me?"

Quinn and Bernard looked at each other. Bernard made a face.

"Not today. We're just here to converse. You don't plan on stabbing yourself in the neck when we're done, do you?"

The proprietor of the shop made a face that suggested he was more curious than nervous, which made Bernard officially consider him crazy.

"I don't plan on doing any such thing, why?"

"Let's just say that such things have come to pass lately."

The man named Rapheal looked at Quinn deeply for a second that seemed like a minute. Where Rapheal was certain from the beginning of the talking phase that neither of the men in front of him was a simple sword for hire, he was now sure that their stories were deeper than he had first thought.

"Well, since you're not here to kill me and I'm not in the mood to do it to myself, please sit and we'll converse."

All three men took up seats around a small table covered by a mid-brown lace covering. A small stack of volumes held the covering in place and acted like a centerpiece. Rapheal sat his cup down and drew a breath.

"You said that you were interested in the histories?"

Bernard smiled and started.

"Yes. The Master of the Fatezh Temple pointed us in your direction. He said that you were once rumored to be in possession of a complete set of volumes. The only complete set outside the Great Temple at Drakchi."

"Interesting. Sadly, the set in the Great Temple isn't complete anymore. A thief removed a section of one of the volumes."

"Yes. We've seen the parchment, "Bernard said a bit quieter than before. "We had the Temple Master in Fatezh return it to Drakchi while we were there."

Rapheal Alonzo looked at them both so that he might fix their images in his mind's eye.

"So, you're the two that found the thief in the woods? I've heard stories about you two."

Quinn nodded.

"And you turned over the man, but not the parchment?"

Quinn nodded a second time.

"And you made your way to Fatezh, looking for answers?"

A third nod.

"It will sadden you to know that the parchment never made it back home again. The courier was killed in Udaass while on the road east and relieved of his charge."

Quinn and Bernard looked at each other in semi-disbelief.

"How," Bernard asked pointedly.

"By Shadowman, from what I hear."

Quinn looked at Bernard as if to say, *I told you!* Bernard looked back at Rapheal.

"Are you sure?"

"As sure as one can be about such things, why?"

"We had a run-in with Shadowman just after leaving the temple in Fatezh. He distracted the crowd in a public house and used the distraction to search the things in our room."

"Seems that he didn't find what he was looking for?"

"Apparently not."

Rapheal Alonzo thought for a moment while looking deeply into his tea and came to the decision that these two men were the sort to be trusted, all appearances to the contrary.

"I am going to assume that you had time to study the parchment in the tube. You speak as if you had."

"Yes. I made a good study of the parchment," Quinn said without hesitation.

"And what was on the parchment?"

The question was plain enough for the conversation that they were having, but Quinn knew that it was actually a quiz. He also knew Rapheal already knew the answer.

"It was a diagram of the lock and key mechanism for a great vault said to date from the end of the last age."

Rapheal Alonzo smiled broadly.

"That it is. Now, last quiz question: what's in the vault and where is it located?"

Quinn looked at Bernard, who simply shrugged, and then looked back at Rapheal.

"Something of great power, and I don't know exactly. That's why we're looking for the histories. There was conversation regarding Rylak, but we're guessing that there should be more information on the accompanying pages."

"And there definitely is. The third volume tells the tale of the great downfall which led to the closing of the last age. It also tells of how the power used to make the collapse happen was captured and entombed in a vault never to be reopened. That is the story that you are chasing after."

"Exactly," both men said in unison.

Rapheal made a conciliatory expression.

"Sadly, I can't help you."

They both stared at the old man in shock. The man seemed to be a great wealth of knowledge.

"Can't or won't," Quinn asked in a monotone voice.

"Can't. I'd be happy to, if I could. You two seem to be the good and steadfast sort. That's rare in this age."

"Why can't you?" Bernard asked in a somewhat more quizzical tone. The question made Rapheal smile.

"I have been in possession of a complete set of volumes of the histories on two different occasions. The first set was inherited to me when I was still young. I gave that set of volumes over to the Great Temple. It was that or have it stolen along the way. I was too young then to know how to guard such treasures. The second set came to me shortly after I really started my journey as a collector. That would be the set which the Temple Master in Fatezh spoke of. I held that set of volumes for several years before selling them in a royal sale."

There was a pause that cut the air in the room like a knife.

"Considering the Shadowman business, I would estimate that this last set of volumes may be the only complete set that is left to us."

Quinn and Bernard looked at each other. Both had faces varying between shock and awe. Quinn sighed a deep sigh that made Rapheal put on a sympathetic expression.

"Seeing how I ended up wounding you as opposed to helping you, would you like some tea? I have more in a pot in the other room."

Both Quinn and Bernard blinked several times.

"It's really quite good with some honey. The honey is fresh from the beekeeper."

Chapter Twenty-Seven

Anistasia sat in the day room of her private chambers and stared at the rocks making up the far wall of the room. It was a stack of different sized rocks which had all been put together to make a sturdy wall. The wall was hard and sound. The stack of rocks seemed to be a good representation for her plans. They were the same; a host of various sized events which had all come together to form the greatest takeover of the age. She was a stone mason of destiny if the wall analogy was taken to its conclusion.

Anistasia shifted in the heavy leather backed chair to find a little more comfort. The black dress and head covering that she wore signified to all in the land that she was in mourning. It was good that she should be. King Gerald, her husband and ruler of Ayr, well, old ruler of Ayr, had only been dead some days now. She needed to grieve. That was what widows did, they grieved. The only problem was that she didn't feel like grieving. She felt like starting the conquest. But still, she sat.

The truth of the thing was that it was all about timing. The country needed her to mourn, at least a little while, to feel good about the whole thing. If she simply charged ahead on day two, the whole of the country would be in outright revolt. She didn't need to deal with that on top of everything else that was to come. She needed the common folk to be passive and the army to be compliant. The first one just required a wee bit of time. Peasants were naturally a passive lot. They were the bottom of things and they understood that deep in their bones. The army was another matter to be dealt with. She would handle that situation later when the time was right.

A small knock came to the closed door of the day room pulling Anistasia from her thoughts. Coming out of her meditations, she paused to consider her late husband. He had been a good man, with a good heart. There had been love there, for a short time. It wasn't a good way to die, Grgr had said. Her husband really had been used for her cause. Oh well, so had countless others. He just happened to be the newest one added to the tally sheet.

"Come in," the queen of Ayr said in a subdued voice.

The door opened and Master Jonah and the head of her private guard stepped in, followed by Grgr. The threesome closed the door securely and bowed to their mourning queen. She nodded respectfully and sighed.

"It's you three. Good. I've had to shut myself in here to stop from being bothered by the household staff."

The lead guard made a small smile.

"That situation has been corrected, majesty."

The queen looked at the man with clear eyes. Things in the greater plan were still afoot. Her people were still out doing what they were supposed to be doing.

"Elaborate on that."

"We have posted a pair of guards at the door to your chambers, majesty. No one more will bother you during this time of reflection."

Anistasia smiled curtly. She had been expecting something more.

"Go on."

"Three individuals have been inserted into your domestic staff, majesty," Master Jonah continued, understanding her tone better than the guard had. "They will handle your personal interests inside the residence. A half-dozen others have found positions in the larger staff, caretakers, stable men, and the like. You have general control over the house, and by proxy the fortress."

"All of your personal guard are individuals who are loyal to you. The king's personal guard has been disbanded and their members returned to the ranks of either the Kanash defense force or the larger army," the guard added for effect.

The queen nodded, with a pleased expression this time. Things were indeed still moving along. She looked to Master Jonah.

"Has there been any obvious movement on the part of the army?"

Jonah considered the question a moment, reflecting on their previous discussion over the topic.

"As of now, no, majesty. Everything is quiet where the army is concerned. There is wild gossip traveling around the lands about our Neeron conspirator, which is obviously being taken up by the army troops, but they are still quiet."

"And Stas Bok?"

"He is currently handling his duties as the captain of the Kanash defenses."

"Do you think that he suspects anything?"

Jonah looked at the queen with a perplexed expression.

"Absolutely. He and his garrison have a good hold over this place. I'm sure that he knows someone didn't just sneak in under his watchful gaze without being discovered, majesty."

Anistasia made a face.

"And he is just riding it all out to see what happens?"

"More likely he's biding his time, my queen," Grgr added. "He's a well-seasoned warrior with deep loyalties throughout the ranks of the army. He's seen transitions play themselves out before, in other cities and kingdoms. He may just be waiting to see which way he should act."

"And the army with him?"

"Yes, my queen."

Anistasia drummed her fingers on the thick arm of the chair.

"So, we're really no further ahead on this front than we have been?"

"No, majesty" came from all three in unison.

Anistasia made a conciliatory expression and moved her head from side to side, as if to say that that sounded about right to her. The threesome before her waited for her to continue the conversation. When she did so, she was looking straight at Master Jonah again.

"Alright, we'll deal with that when the time comes. It will be what it's going to be. New topic. Lead Regent Makal Rymer. He's going to be a major complication for us."

Jonah nodded decisively.

"True, majesty. He is in a good position to cause complications and he really doesn't like you."

Anistasia made a face that said that was about par for the course inside the Ayr court.

"Then he goes."

"In which manner, my queen."

Grgr looked as though he was neither for nor against the idea. His neutrality made the queen pause.

"At this point, getting him out of power is probably an end in itself."

"Maybe, my queen, maybe not. He still has many friends about this land."

"I don't know if I would refer to them all as friends," Jonah countered. "Many of them are just bowing to his power as lead regent."

Everyone looked at Jonah quizzically. He was the one who had spent the most time with the regents.

"The regents, overall, are untrustworthy. They are all political people and politically motivated. Leaving him to his own devices will come back to haunt us later. If we are going to remove him from power, then we should remove him permanently. No loose ends. There will be short term panic, but only until a new lead regent is named."

The lead guard shook his head.

"Two royal house officials dying in such a short time isn't coincidence, it's conspiracy."

Grgr made a gesture with his hands.

"Then we make sure that it doesn't look unnatural. Just a situation of bad luck."

Anistasia liked what she was hearing.

"Go on."

"Several days a week Rymer takes a long walk down though the city to the house of the west gate captain. They were friends when they were boys and migrated up to Kanash together. He just needs to have some mishap befall him along the way one day. Maybe a runaway cart from a city person or other unforeseen and unexpected everyday event."

"Can that be arranged?"

"Yes," came from the lead guard in a sure tone. "I know several city people that are morally pliable and untrustworthy enough for such a task."

Anistasia nodded. Her queen-like grin from previous days returning as the men spoke.

"Make it happen."

The guard nodded respectfully.

"Next topic."

All three men readied themselves.

"Prince Jan."

"He is currently in Gryazi, majesty."

"He must go. I don't have unquestioned control over the kingdom until he has been removed."

The lead guard and Jonah looked at each other, as if they had spoken about this previously.

"Majesty, the prince may prove somewhat more problematic. Gryazi is a well-defended city."

"Does killing one man require a siege?"

Anistasia was having no backing up at this point in the plan.

"If we march on it in force, it will take a siege, yes majesty."

"So don't siege. Try being a little more conspiratorial. After all, isn't that what we're doing?"

"Yes, majesty," came from all three men.

"Well, one man to handle the prince, and a couple men to watch his back while he makes his way through the city. That can be done in-house."

The guard looked sure as he spoke. Anistasia knew that she could call on several different men that would be happy to kill for her.

"They can't look like troops," Jonah countered. "That whole city is probably on edge. They would need to look the everyday sort. Men out finding work or whatever. It is almost harvest season around Gryazi."

The guard nodded in understanding of what the master was saying.

"Don't worry, I have just that sort in mind. They won't be noticed."

Anistasia looked to the guard with a pleased expression.

"Make it happen, soon."

"Yes, majesty."

Anistasia thought through her list of mental notes. It seemed that they had covered all of the big topics for the moment.

"Let's circle back around to one thing. After Rymer has his tragic little accident, do we have anyone good that might replace him lined up?"

Master Jonah nodded.

"Yes, majesty. There are at least four in the main body that could easily step into his position, and all would be amenable to your agenda if it puts them in power."

The queen gave an affirmatory expression and a small nod of the head.

"On second thought, majesty, if you find it palatable, you might consider honoring the dead regent in some way. A statue in one of the squares or something like that. It would help distance any suspicion that might lead toward you."

Anistasia smiled broadly.

"That's definitely masterful thinking. We should do it."

Feeling like everything for the day had been discussed that needed discussing, Anistasia Nosov, Queen of Ayr, gave each of the men a look which asked if they had anything needing addressing. With no positive responses, she waved them to the door and returned to her contemplation of the stone wall on the opposite side of the room.

Chapter Twenty-Eight

Prince Jan Nosov paced back and forth across his great room in an agitated state. His two main regents and the captain of the city guard attempted to calm him down so he might think sensibly. They had been at it for about an hour with little evidence of success.

"How? How is it possible that some miscreant from nowhere Neeron can sneak into the palace and poison my brother?"

The pair of regents gave several noncommittal answers at little more than a whisper.

"Well?"

The prince stopped his pacing and looked at them pointedly.

"Well?"

"We don't know, sire."

The prince returned to pacing.

"That's right! You don't know. Do you know why that is? I'll tell you why that is. Because he didn't sneak in. He's a patsy."

Everyone looked at the prince skeptically.

"That self-serving, evil bitch that he married did him in."

The two regents snapped their heads in a shocked fashion to look at the prince. The captain of the guard stayed quiet momentarily. To him, the statement was the first thing that rang true since their meeting had begun.

"And if she did?"

The question from the captain was quiet, but direct and firm. Prince Jan stopped pacing again and turned to look at him.

"I'm going to ride to Kanash and stick a knife in her eye. Then I'm going to push until it comes out the back of her head."

The captain sighed and looked at his prince in a disapproving way.

"You need to stop thinking like a brother, or a count for that matter, and start thinking like a prince."

Jan gritted his teeth as the criticism washed over him. The regents waited for the rebuke to come, but there was none. The prince had always held the captain's words in high esteem. He was older and had seen much more of the world than Jan had. He was the only person in Ayr, save his dead brother, who talked to him as though they were equals, as opposed to sovereign.

"Go on."

"If the queen did kill the king, then that plan was put in motion long ago. She didn't think it up over breakfast tea. She intended on usurping power from the beginning."

"So," the prince said, in a slightly less-agitated manner.

"So, if she had a plan to get rid of the king, she has a plan to get rid of you, too. You don't kill a king and leave a prince alive and free. That thinking invites retaliation."

Prince Jan calmed fully and considered the idea. The captain had a solid point.

"Well then, we need to reassert power before there's a question about who the real leadership is."

The captain shook his head slowly. The depth of this danger hadn't fully sunk into the prince yet.

"No, we don't. The queen is the real leadership now. Your brother made her a sovereign in power after the coronation. She runs the country now. You're still in the number two position here. If a queen kills a king, it's a transition of power. If a prince kills a queen, it's treason."

"Treason? If she killed my brother, she committed treason against the crown."

The captain made a face that suggested he didn't agree.

"Maybe, maybe not. Nevertheless, she is the crown now."

The prince went back to pacing, this time much more deliberately.

"So, we need to unseat her?"

"I don't see that being easily done."

The regents swung their heads back and forth from prince to captain as the conversation went along. Both men were too scared to interject.

"Why not?"

"If she had a plan to kill the king, then she definitely had a plan for bringing the royal guard and the army under her thumb."

"Well, I'm not letting that two-faced bitch steal my country from me."

The captain of the guard sighed a second time and made a conciliatory face.

"Maybe, maybe not. Your main objective right now is staying alive. If you don't stay alive, all of this hot-blooded rambling is for naught."

Prince Jan blinked a couple times and looked at the captain quizzically.

"If she had the brass balls to kill your brother in his own bed, she's damned sure going to kill you."

The prince made a conciliatory face of his own.

"That's the first thing said in here that can't be argued."

The prince went back to pacing deliberately. More thinking as he paced than stomping about like before.

"If she has the army at her back, then Gryazi isn't safe. We can't stand out a siege of that magnitude."

The two spineless regents were agape. Neither the prince nor the captain paid them any attention. Politicians were all men of weak character and little moral compunction.

"I agree. Staying in Gryazi is a fool's errand. So is staying in Ayr, for that matter."

"The Watchtower could be safe ground. The Watchtower of Aul Torum is well-defended."

The captain made a motion with his head that suggested the young prince was gambling.

"The Watchtower is a sound idea, just not any of the ones in Ayr. They are too easy to be infiltrated by locals working on the queen's coin.

The Watchtower at Aul Torum is full of true and capable men, but it isn't safe enough."

The prince considered that for a moment.

"So, where would you suggest?"

The captain considered the return question for a moment.

"Either the Southern Sands Watchtower in Ubar or the Great Watchtower of Thorne in Meridian. You want a place where you and your opposition are both strangers in a strange land. That way you're better to see them coming at you."

The prince nodded.

"That's sound. The question becomes which direction to turn?"

The prince made a face to the captain that suggested the two regents couldn't be trusted with such information. The captain returned a small hand gesture with his hidden hand which said he agreed.

"Let's just get you on the road. We can discuss logistics later."

The prince turned his attention to the two regents.

"Gentlemen, I thank you for your council this day. Now, go be about your affairs."

The two men began to protest but the prince silenced them with a raise of his hand.

"No buts, be on your way. The city will need your steady hands soon enough."

The two men stood and shuffled out the door, both holding their robes to clear a path for their feet. The prince and captain waited for the door to close and the sound of them walking down the hallway to dissipate before continuing.

"You know they're going to betray you."

The prince nodded decisively.

"Of course they are. They're politicians, aren't they?"

The captain stood and stepped to where the prince was standing.

"You need to go with haste, sire."

The prince reached out and shook the old man's hand solidly.

"And you? Will you come with me?"

The captain shook his head.

"No, I'll stay my ground. I'm charged with the safekeeping of Gryazi and her lands. That I will do."

The prince nodded in appreciation. Noble men in troubled times were always a rare thing to find. It wasn't his place to question that.

"Well, thank you for all of your guidance. The wisdom of age is always more practical than the tenacity of youth."

The captain smiled at the prince in a fatherly way.

"You'll do fine, Jan. Stay low and blend in, like the dirt road travelers tend to do. Most of all, trust no one you meet. Everyone has an agenda, and very few of them are the same as yours."

The prince nodded in understanding.

"Now, get yourself changed into something less princely. I'll have a pair of good men see you out of the city and onto quiet roads. Head yourself north toward the sea. Once you cross the inland sea and set foot in Valencia, you can decide whether it will be east or west."

The captain turned and headed for the door. The prince began unbuttoning his tunic.

Chapter Twenty-Nine

Two dozen scribes sat in quaint three person rows stretched out across the floor of the throne room and scribbled as the queen spoke. Each of the scribes diligently taking down the words exactly as stated. People in the fortress had already died for questioning the queen's intentions and none of the scribbling scribes wanted to be added to the list.

Waiting for each scribe to finish their work, the queen rose and stepped down from the throne chair, moving to the nearest scribe. She held out her hand and the woman on the floor handed over the message which she had written. The queen read the message that she had just dictated and smiled broadly. It was note for note what the queen had said. The queen handed it back to the woman on the floor and returned to her throne chair. Adjusting herself adequately, she looked out at the group.

"Have more copies produced. When they are ready, have them sent to all of the great houses, as well as all of the counts, countesses and regents. Use the guest list from the wedding as your guide. Have them all sent today."

No one in the room questioned the order given or its timeline.

"Good. Now, be about your task."

The entire collection of scribes stood quickly and made their way out of the throne room without speaking. No one was going to say anything that ran counter to the queen.

Queen Anistasia Nosov, ruler of the Kingdom of Ayr, smiled to herself as the minions left. One good bit of business was concluded. The world should know that her husband, the late King of Ayr, had died, and that Neeron was at fault. This was the beginning. Looking over at the captain of her royal guard, she gave a serious look.

"Are the heads of the army assembled?"

The armored knight nodded respectfully.

"They are, majesty."

"Good. Show them in."

The sturdy wooden doors of the throne room opened and a large collection of hard, well-armored men and women strode in, some three dozen or more captains. They formed into a loose collection of rows naturally as they paused. The queen watched and waited as they got where they wanted to be.

"Leaders of the army. Make ready to travel. In a fortnight we march south to Neeron."

A series of shocked expressions worked through the group of senior soldiers. The queen waited it out, making note of which ones seemed counter to her ideas. To her surprise, the leader of Ayr's army – the large, imposing, and greying Stas Bok – didn't as much as stir one of his bushy eyebrows. He simply stood stoically waiting on the next sentence. Farther back in the collection, a junior archery captain had less restraint.

"Why are we mobilizing the army for one man? A half-dozen of my men can handle any such man, no matter where he is on the planet."

Murmurs rose behind the idea. Another one, a cavalry officer the queen assumed from his look, also had a dissenting opinion.

"Majesty, we need only summon Neeron to turn the man over for trial."

The queen looked the second man directly in the eye, as if to disagree. Turning her head slightly, she nodded to someone standing past the cavalry man, and then turned and nodded to another out past the archery captain. Two men wearing the queen's colors stepped quickly from the wall along the long axis of the throne room and stabbed the two captains with punch knives designed specifically for penetrating plate armor. The archery captain received three full-depth blows from the twelve-inch, four-sided, spiked blade. The cavalry captain received two. Both captains dropped directly to the stone floor of the throne room, quickly becoming islands in small lakes of blood.

"Would anyone else like to raise a dissenting opinion?" The queen's voice was clear and loud, her countenance direct. No one spoke.

"Good. Now make preparations to have the army assembled and marching south within two weeks."

No one spoke. The queen nodded.

"Good. That is all. Be about your business."

The doors to the throne room reopened and the collection of leaders, knights all, filed out. Stas Bok stood his ground and waited. The queen waited as well. She had assumed that this next part was coming from the beginning. When the doors closed a second time, Stas looked back at the two dead men lying on the pavers. Turning his head back to look directly at the queen, he made a face that suggested it was simply their time to die. The expression made the queen uneasy. The leader of her army didn't scare easily. That quality might be a problem for her later on.

"Majesty, I have two questions that require answering if the army is to be marching south."

The queen nodded, as if to suggest he continue.

"Are we headed for a border skirmish or a siege? Your tone earlier implied siege."

The queen looked at the leader of her army and smiled in a way that made Stas Bok uncomfortable.

"Does the idea of a siege against Neeron bother you, Captain Bok?"

The old man stayed calm like a mill pond at night. That made the queen curious.

"No, ma'am. The two types of battle require distinctly different levels of preparation. We need to make the army ready for the right type of combat."

The queen smiled. He was all-business. Maybe she had misjudged the old warrior?

"Definitely a siege. Now, the second?"

"If you have a timeline, which a fortnight from now currently puts us under a new moon, I'd be interested in that as well. It seems from your timing that you plan to use the darkness of night to your advantage. This implies that you have a rough battle plan. Or am I developing that for you?"

The queen smiled again. The old soldier was cagey.

"I have a rough idea, though I am keenly interested to know what you think would be a good combat strategy. Maybe, if you're as sound a military leader as I'm led to believe, I can just add ideas to your plans. Maybe that will sit better with your junior officers?"

Stas Bok nodded one time. Definitely.

"The army will be ready to march, on-time, as requested. I'll have a battle plan for you to hear three days from now, ma'am."

The queen smiled.

"Good. Make it happen."

The captain of Ayr's army nodded an affirmative response.

Stas Bok turned on solid heels and strode to the door in a manner that stated to all in the room he was unconcerned with any of the queen's guard lining the walls. Walking out, he didn't so much as tilt his head to check on a follower. He was a man of combat, unfazed by lesser men. The queen watched him stride off, not sure if she was going to end up killing him or trusting him completely.

With the big business of the day concluded, Anistasia waved her hand in the direction of her private guard, and they began filing out. She waited for them to leave and then stood. For a solid moment she just stood there, alone, in the emptiness of the throne room, thinking about what had transpired in the last hour or two. She made herself conscious to feel the weight of the crown on her head as she considered her steps. This, where she was right now, was real power. Real power, the kind that had to be taken, not given. Like the rulers of the lost ages, she had taken her power. And now she was on the cusp of going and taking even more. The feeling that it brought on was intoxicating. She hadn't planned on it feeling this way. She had assumed that it would feel cold and foreign when utilized, but real power felt warm and comforting. Many of the stories about war and conquest began to swirl around inside her head. Those stories made more sense to her now. They possessed new meaning. The use of real power was like a drug. Realizing this, Anistasia decided that she was going to dive into the deep end of the lake and swim around in this new aphrodisiac.

The queen shook all of the thoughts from her mind. She was just at the beginning of her long road. There were many miles to go before she could pause and relax in the power's embrace. For now, she needed to keep a level head.

Anistasia stepped down from the dais and walked to the door obscured behind the pair of throne chairs and a thick tapestry. Moving through the door into a small antechamber, she took in the presence of Shadowman sitting in a comfortable chair, a metal tube sitting on a table next to him. The queen smiled broadly, two rows of perfect white teeth showing through full lips.

"You are perfectly timed. I was wondering how you were getting on."

Shadowman stayed stoic in his demeanor.

"All things in their time, my liege. Your cylinder, and contents, as requested."

The queen walked over and picked up the metal tube, taking in the different seals on its cap.

"And the ones carrying it?"

"The courier is dead, as requested."

"And the others?"

There was a pronounced pause in the conversation that made Anistasia shift her vision from the tube to the assassin.

"And the others?"

"What about them? You asked for the return of the cylinder, and you didn't care what happened to the ones carrying it. That obligation has been satisfied in full."

The queen thought. She couldn't remember the exact phrasing she had used before, and she certainly wasn't going to tell someone like Shadowman that he was wrong. Well, unless she was absolutely sure that he was wrong.

"Okay," The queen said, changing tack. "The original thief and the courier are both dead?"

Shadowman nodded.

"So, that leaves two bounty men and whoever dispatched the courier alive."

"The courier was dispatched from the temple in the city of Fatezh."

The queen walked over to a sturdy standing cabinet and paused to retrieve a small ring of keys hidden in a pocket sewn into her dress. She slowly flipped them over, one by one, until she came to the one she was looking for. Sliding it into the lock on the cabinet door, she rotated the key to release the clasp. The cabinet, full of private journals and maps, also possessed some coin. It had been used by her late husband to grease the skids with royal messengers and diplomats. Anistasia removed a coin holder containing two full rows of full-weight stamped royal gold coins and walked them over to the table. Shadowman took in the sum as she sat it down next to the tube, a small fortune to the average man.

"New request. Eliminate anyone that has seen the contents of the inside of that tube since the time the thief stole it from me. Specifically, to include the Temple Master and the bounty men."

Shadowman made a face, as if he was considering this option against other work he might have planned. Anistasia had dealt with the assassin enough to know that if he said no, she had little chance of changing his answer to a yes. Trying would certainly lose any favor she had gained over the years.

"As you wish, my liege. Would you like their deaths to be quiet or to send a message?"

The queen exhaled a breath she didn't know she had been holding and considered the question for a second.

"Whatever you feel is appropriate is fine. I just want all of this tied off. No loose ends. I don't need any dissenting opinions coming along, if you know what I mean?"

The assassin nodded stoically but said nothing.

The queen smiled at the nod and walked back to lock the cabinet. Shadowman stood and collected the two sleeves of coins.

"Excellent. Safe travels then. The timeframe isn't dire, but sooner would probably be better."

Anistasia Nosov, Queen of Ayr, stepped from the room without bothering to wait for a response. There was no need; the assassin had already disappeared back into the shadows.

Chapter Thirty

Anistasia stood on the shadowed side of the observation tower taking in the views of the countryside. From the high tower on the south end of the fortification she could see both the sprawling fields to the south of Kanash, and river to the west which snaked its way by the foot of the outcropping the fortress was anchored on. She had seen pictures in the archives of the fortress during the last age. Then, it sat in the middle of a large city, more a spectacle than a castle. Looking out over the grassy fields and wooden village huts within her field of view she could hardly imagine its previous life.

Two floors below her outlook, Anistasia could hear metal-covered boots impacting thick wooden steps and knew that her guard was climbing his way up to her. She inhaled deeply, taking in the scent of wheat mixed with water and pines. She could almost smell it now. She could almost smell the blood and the mud and the stink of rot that was about to sweep its way over the quiet fields below. She was so close now.

A guard's helmet broke the barrier where the stairway came up through the floor, and the sensation was gone. *It would return soon enough,* she thought.

The guard made his way completely up onto the top floor that was the observation deck of the tower, and was followed by a large man. The man had the appearance of someone very used to hard work. The guard stepped to one side so the queen could fully take in the man's countenance. She appraised him for a second, attempting to calculate how the next conversation was going to play out, and then smiled mildly.

"You are the Grandmaster of the Mechanics Guild?"

The man nodded strongly once.

"I am, majesty. The name's Adam."

The queen's smile softened. She liked a man who was sure of himself. After all, the Mechanic's Guild was not an entity to be taken lightly. They were the most respected and strongest of all the guilds. One didn't climb to the top of such an organization without being sure of himself.

The queen turned her gaze to the guard.

"You can leave us. We have matters to discuss."

Without a word, the guard turned and began his trudge of many steps back down the tower stairwell. *He definitely wasn't sure of himself,* Anistasia thought, watching the guard's helmet disappear through the opening in the floor. *He needed to be replaced by someone who was.*

Returning to the here and now, Anistasia looked from the floor opening back up at Adam. Having his full attention, she waved her hand out toward the south and turned to look that way. The Grandmaster of the Mechanics Guild stepped over to the railing with her, leaving ample space between the two of them. He was no stranger to royalty or their strange ways.

"Tell me Adam, what do you see when you look out over the land?"

Adam took in the view. The wheat fields were ripe and almost ready to signal the beginning of harvest season.

"Prosperity, ma'am."

Powerful, and a politician, the queen thought. *An interesting combination, for sure.*

"Don't be coy."

The queen pointed to a section of the great steel snake which slithered through the countryside heading southeast toward Ishim. One of three such snakes that made their way out away from Kanash for various distances. The mechanic took in the section of snake the queen pointed at, its two thick steel rails sitting atop squared logs, all floating on a small river of smashed stones. Technology and engineering left over from an age gone by. The physical remains of a dead civilization, same as the castle fortress that they were standing in.

"Hmm, the great snake. Or one piece of one of them anyway."

The queen nodded.

"Yes, the great snake. Tell me Grandmaster, what do you think that it really is? Or better put, was?"

Adam stayed quiet a good moment, considering his response. Either she knew the answer and was testing him, or she didn't, in which case he could say whatever he chose. Considering recent events in Kanash, he decided on the first thought.

"It is the remains of a transportation system. An engine, of sorts, rode on the steel rails and pulled or pushed carts that carried goods. The timber keeps the rails square and properly separated, and the bed of stones acts as a cushion. It allows the rail/timber combination to flex under the weight of the machine as it passes over it."

The queen smiled genuinely.

"Exactly right, Adam. Exactly right. Tell me, have you ever seen one of these engines?"

Adam turned his head just enough to get all of her expression in his peripheral vision.

"I have, ma'am. There are remains of one sitting in a small pond of steel rails just outside of Lugo. We looked at it for some time several years ago."

"And your thoughts?"

"It appeared to be powered by some large contraption that ran on a fluid of some type. We couldn't figure out how to make it work, so we left it there. It was too heavy to move with a hundred oxen."

The queen smiled again. She liked Adam. He was matter of fact about things.

"I like your choice of words. Contraption. It seems fitting. I know the contraption that you speak of. I looked at it too, several years ago. Tell me, would you be interested in making a second attempt of sorts?"

Adam turned and looked at the queen, face-on. She seemed as serious as anyone he had come across.

"Take a second look at that one? If you wish, but it will probably be for naught. We know nothing about how the last age used fluids to make power."

The queen smiled, wryly this time. Adam knew that she had been leading on to somewhere.

"Take a second attempt, just not at that particular contraption. In the outskirts of Graycott there is another such machine. This one is somewhat older than the one you spoke of. It seems to have a different means of making itself work."

Adam looked out over the countryside. Graycott was in Neeron. The country the army was rumored to be getting ready to march on.

"Graycott is both in Neeron and not necessarily near a section of the snake."

The queen nodded.

"True. But all things seem like problems until they're not. Once the army crosses south, and I squeeze my fist around Karacase, Graycott will belong to me, or to Ayr."

"Okay?"

"As for the machine's remoteness to the snake, I'm sure that all of your excellent mechanics can think of a solution to that problem. After all, your foundry works can make steel, can't they?"

Adam scratched his chin with a calloused, meaty hand.

"You want us to bring the snake back to life again?"

"Exactly. If it can be done, and I'm betting that it can, I would like you to do exactly that."

Adam pondered for a moment.

"We usually have a group of mechanics that assist the army. I would assume that they will be moving along with them as well. I can easily put together a second group to investigate your machine. However, such an endeavor won't be even remotely cheap."

The queen looked at Adam with a cold, all-business expression.

"Do I appear as one who can't afford to pay?"

"No, ma'am."

"Good. Make it happen."

Chapter Thirty-One

Tassos Kamber, elected ruler of the Mining Isles Mining Guild, and by proxy the island kingdom, sat quietly and contemplated the sunny, bright day presenting itself outside the palace. The weather in the island's capital city of Dyme had been excellent the past days. It had to be even nicer down by the beach than it appeared through the windows of the gathering room.

King Kamber, a solidly built man of about five-foot-ten-inches and fifteen stone, had the thick frame that made the islanders good fighters and good miners. Sun-darkened skin seemed natural against his long, black hair and beard, which were also staple features of his people. His dark brown eyes saw everything happening around him yet retained the twinkle of a generally good disposition. Numerous small scars were a collection from his life, some from fighting and some from mining. At thirty-eight years on from birth, he was considered an elder in the Guild, with a full breadth of knowledge and experience.

Tassos looked over at the secretary of the Guild. He was the person who documented all of the business conducted by the Guild in the gathering hall, and basically kept track of affairs. The secretary could sense Kamber's desire to be done for the day and casually held up three fingers. *Three more things that needed doing,* Tassos thought. *Three things will pass by quickly enough.*

He knew that two of them would be normal business affairs. The third one would most likely be business from the outside world. He had watched the ship glide into the port yesterday evening, bearing a house flag from the Kingdom of Ayr. The kingdom of Ayr hadn't been south to visit the Great Bank in a long time. King Gerald was a wise and resourceful man. He always looked out for the bottom line and made sure the crown didn't overspend. But then again, according to the spies employed by the Mining Guild, King Gerald was dead. That piece of news made the ship in the harbor a curiosity. A curiosity that Tassos was hoping wouldn't turn into a dilemma.

Tassos Kamber was an educated and experienced man. He didn't believe in omens or curses or the other superstitions of the common folk. Still, if he had to be honest, the ship floating into the harbor gave him a bad sensation.

The secretary cleared his throat and made a diplomatic gesture with his hands. Two Guild members who had been debating openly on the floor paused and took up their seats again. The secretary announced the next piece of business to be considered, and the idea's champion rose from his seat to begin speaking. Tassos listened to the issue with diligence and then agreed with the speaker. It was the same basic type of business that the Guild had been discussing all day. There was some minimal debate, but it was short-lived, and the original idea was moved along.

The next piece of business came and went with the pace of the one before it. The topics of the day were all straightforward and solved with minimal deliberation. Soon enough they had made their way through the docket and were to the one issue of note. Tassos liked to leave the potential problems for last. It helped to move the Guild members along, as messengers always made them curious. It also helped get the general business conducted, because the Guild members didn't have the messenger's message in their thoughts to distract them from the moment. Plus, making couriers wait for an audience was a not-so-subtle way of reinforcing the idea that they weren't in charge here. It was important to set that tone immediately when dealing with royal messengers.

The secretary looked up at the king, who simply nodded. The secretary looked over to the doorman-at-arms, who looked to the lads at the door. The lads pulled the high doors of the gathering hall open and retreated outside to fetch up the messenger. Stepping back inside with the man, the lads looked to the doorman-at-arms who announced the arrival of a royal messenger from the Kingdom of Ayr. The Guild members assembled for the day's business watched the messenger walk in behind the doorman-at-arms, moving with purpose to where the king was seated. Tassos Kamber took in the man's appearance, one of a person who was in every way unassuming. Someone that no one would take notice of in a crowd. Definitely a good choice in messengers.

"Greeting, King Kamber. I bring correspondence from the Queen of Ayr."

Tassos Kamber looked at the messenger quizzically.

"The Queen of Ayr? Not the King of Ayr?"

The messenger nodded to the affirmative.

"Yes, sire. The correspondence is that of the queen."

Tassos looked around the room. Many of the faces in the gathering hall held the same expression as he did.

"What is the correspondence regarding?"

The messenger pulled a parchment from a small pouch slung over his shoulder and oriented it so that King Kamber could see the silver ring and intact seal.

"I don't know the contents of the correspondence, sire. I was instructed to deliver it here and place it directly into your hands."

Tassos nodded to a man standing by the secretary, and the man stepped forward to collect the parchment. The man secured the parchment and stepped back to his original position.

"And now, good sir, you have fulfilled your charge. Will there be any other requests?"

The messenger looked confused.

"Will there be no response for the queen?"

King Tassos Kamber shrugged at the messenger nonchalantly, as if to say that it was all of little concern.

"I don't know yet. I haven't read the correspondence. Either way, your part in this affair is concluded. You said yourself that your only job was to deliver it, which you have accomplished. You should probably be getting back to your ship now. It's a long journey back to Ayr, and there are pirates about the seas these days."

Tassos nodded to the doorman-at-arms, and he walked the befuddled messenger back out of the gathering room. Everyone could see the look of confusion on the messenger's face as the large gathering room doors closed behind him.

Tassos rolled the idea of the parchment around in his mind a couple times before sighing audibly. He could sense that, if it was a bomb of some type, it would be going off soon.

Deciding that there was no better time than the present, he looked over to the man holding the scroll and stuck his hand out. The man promptly stepped forward and handed over the object. Tassos slid the silver ring off the role and tossed it to the secretary. Extending his hand, he pointed it to the doorman-at-arms, who collected it as requested. The new holder snapped the seal, unrolled the parchment in front of the assembled Guild members and cleared his throat to speak. Each representative in the gathering hall quieted himself to listen. Once all was quiet, the king nodded.

"King Tassos Kamber, and distinguished members of the Mining Guild, greetings. It is known that The Great Bank granted money to the Kingdom of Ubar to negotiate a trade arrangement with the Kingdom of Ayr some years ago. To date, The Great Bank has not received payment on the coin extended to Ubar. Ayr would ask that your institution request immediate repayment of the loan and any associated fees which it may possess. This act would go a long way in seeing Ayr's continued favor as it applies to the Mining Isles. Respectfully, Queen Anistasia Nosov, Queen of Ayr."

The doorman-at-arms stopped talking and the room immediately fell into an uncontrolled uproar. Tassos let the members go for several minutes before waving his hand to get their attention. As the noise level in the hall dropped, Tassos Kamber stood and began to pace about the open floor. A senior Guild member looked out at the king and asked the obvious question.

"Well, now what? How do we respond to this threat?"

The king paused his pacing and turned to address the man, though he was really addressing everyone in the room.

"Though the dispatch seems to be written in a friendly way, it does little to hide the threat it carries. That leads to several questions. The main one being, did this get sent before or after King Gerald died? I'm guessing before, or it wouldn't have made it here by now. That begs even more questions."

The hall broke into another round of animated exchanges between members. Tassos let them go until they exhausted themselves. Deciding they were done, for the moment, he continued speaking.

"I think that we should give her exactly what she asked for … in a way."

A group of shocked faces presented themselves throughout the large hall, but the king calmly looked past them all to an imposing guard standing along the back wall. The king nodded and the guard opened a heavy wooden door which led off into a small anteroom. One of several additional spaces, the room was used for special projects and private meetings. As the guard stepped clear of the doorway, a pirate named Toothless Tom, well-known to the members of the Guild as being Blue Bill Montgomery's spokesman, and a man named Saleh, Crown Prince Kamal Nazari's manservant, entered the room. King Kamber introduced the two men to the Guild members in the hall.

"These two men have also come to us this day with a proposition concerning the same matter. It would seem that the Kingdom of Ubar and the pirates have come up with a better way to satisfy the loan than what was proposed by the Kraeten queen. Seems that these two have struck a bargain, and the pirates are willing to repay the loan, on behalf of the kingdom."

A man stood in the back of the gathering hall.

"What terms have they come to?"

Toothless Tom looked over at Saleh and the manservant cleared his throat.

"Ubar will secure repayment of the loan by leasing a deep-water port on the kingdom's northern coast to the pirates for their use. The lease has an agreed upon timeframe commensurate with the value of the loan provided by your institution."

Another man stood to speak.

"And the pirates are good with this deal? It seems far too much for the value of the coin loaned to Ubar."

"Our leader has agreed to the offer presented by the Ubari prince, good sirs. It is an extravagant payment, but it also shows the truth of their offer."

An older Guild member seated closer to the floor stood and looked at Tassos directly.

"Our work here has always been the banking of coin. We don't deal in the politics of nations. If this is how Ubar wants to satisfy their loan, it is wholly agreeable with me."

Tassos nodded in agreement.

"I completely agree. Is there anyone present that is unhappy with the arrangement presented?"

No one spoke, so Tassos looked over to the secretary.

"We will consider the matter closed and the Kingdom of Ubar's loan fulfilled. Set the loan total against the pirate's balance sheet."

Tassos Kamber looked over at the unassuming desert man, Saleh.

"It would appear that your prince's timing is spot-on."

"There have been many rumors of unease, as of late. The prince wanted to eliminate any outside pressure on the kingdom, if that was possible."

"Pressure from the south?"

"Yes, your highness."

Tassos smiled warmly at Saleh. He seemed a good man.

"I'm an elected king, you don't actually have to address me in a regal fashion."

"Yes, sire."

"How is Ubar dealing with the news of King Gerald's death? The Mining Isles also have spies scattered about the lands. It would seem that this new queen is now mobilizing her army."

Saleh made a face that suggested he hadn't heard such news. Toothless Tom made the same expression.

"I'm sure that such news is a matter of deep concern for the kingdom, sire."

"I imagine it is also going to make for trouble on the seas," Toothless Tom added.

"I would think you both are probably correct. Now, let's do some paperwork and get this business of ours concluded."

Both of the travelers nodded and stepped off toward the secretary, each one carrying a new look of concern on his face.

Chapter Thirty-Two

Queen Anistasia Nosov snapped the last closure on the semi-rigid corset and shifted several times to get it where she wanted it to rest. After months in silk gowns the newfound back support made her smile. Her new attire was a dual-purpose item. Mostly it was for back support while she rode. But as important as the support that the wide, flat metal inserts gave, they also provided defense against knife and sword blows. The inserts wouldn't stop a heavy thrust from a battle sword, but they would stand up well against a glancing shot.

She slid her way into a thick, black linen riding dress and went about connecting all of the buttons and tie closures. It had been a considerable amount of time since she had been in anything but silk dresses or bed sheets. The rough feeling of the cloth took her mind back to earlier times. The difference in the thoughts between then and now made her smile again.

Standing before a large mirror, she had her long black hair collected down her back by the servant girl and tied tight by three black strips of cloth. When finished, the ties were all but invisible against her hair and the dress. They gave her hair more the look of a whip tail than a mane. Sitting, the servant girl added to her ensemble by sliding sturdy leather boots onto her one foot at a time, making sure to lace them tightly. The queen stood and checked their fit, feeling a good half-inch taller than her natural five feet nine inches.

Drawing a breath and bending down, the queen drew up the hemline of her riding dress to expose her leg. On her right ankle she strapped a half-sized version of the spike knife her guards used in the throne room. The four-sided blade was dipped in poison by her trusted friend Grgur. Deciding it was properly settled against her boot, Anistasia pivoted upright and exhaled. Inhaling deeply, she strapped a full-sized version of the knife around her waist with a leather belt.

Addressing herself in the mirror, she decided that she was ready to go. Anistasia reached out and lifted the crown for the Kingdom of Ayr off of the dressing table. Not her dainty crown, but Gerald's crown. She slid it onto her head and adjusted it to fit. Master Jonah had fashioned a small, padded band around its inside to take up the extra room. The purple band inside the golden crown fit snuggly on her smaller head. All-in-all she decided that she was ready. The first battle queen that the Kingdom of Ayr had seen in almost two full centuries. The land had been quiet for far too long. It was time for the axe and the pike. It was time for carnage.

Anistasia patted the servant girl on the head gently and pointed toward the leather bag on the floor. The girl picked the heavy mass up as best as she could and followed the queen out the door, knowing this new monarch saw her more like a pet than a person. Still, uttering anything would make her a dead pet, so she shuffled along with the bag behind her queen.

The queen strode through the hallways of the castle keep and out of a side entrance that opened into a cobbled carriage drive. The drive wrapped around the inside of the keep and opened onto the eastern side lower lawns, below the high wall, allowing exit out of the castle through a sturdy reinforced wooden gate. Waiting patiently in the drive was a stable keeper and Master Jonah. The stable keeper was holding the reins of a massive grey and black warhorse. Its normal saddle had been replaced with one more-sized for a female rider, and a sturdy hand-and-a-half sword hung in the scabbard where a broadsword would have normally hung. The queen pointed to the servant girl and the stable keeper collected the heavy leather saddlebag, securing it firmly to the flat behind the saddle's pelvic rim.

Anistasia stepped up onto a wooden step and then placed her foot into the stirrup. Throwing her leg over the horse in a pronounced show of superiority, she found the second stirrup and settled herself on the great beast. Taking the thick leather reins in gloved hands, she gave them a tug. The big warhorse between her thighs snorted at the gesture. Anistasia smiled.

Smiling boldly, Anistasia ribbed the big animal with a boot heel and it started off down the cobblestones toward the gate. The gate opened without command and the Queen of Ayr rode out of the keep into the lower lawns below the fortress wall.

Though still full-dark outside, several hours before the sun was due to rise in the east, the landscape laid out before her held an ominous yellow hue. Small campfires and ember piles stretched out past the limits of her vision. The army of Ayr was turning the night into day. She hadn't heard the final count on the troops, but from the view before her eyes she knew it must be a huge number.

Stationed just to the right of the gate entrance, the twenty-one men of her personal guard sat, mounted, formed and ready. The captain of her guard rode over and greeted her with an open-palmed metal glove. The traditional battlefield gesture of non-violence from days of old.

"Good morning, majesty."

Anistasia smiled. The captain of the guard seemed upbeat, considering that they were going to war. That was as good a sign as any. She inspected the man's chest plate. Emblazoned into the metal plate was the image of boar, tusks out for all to see. She smiled a second time. The boar was the sigil of the House of Savin. Ayr's standard sigil was that of an owl, the image of Gerald Nosov's house. A dead house. Or, soon dead, once she laid hands on his younger brother, Prince Jan.

"Are you ready to travel?"

The captain nodded once, definitively.

"Yes, ma'am."

The queen prodded the big horse and it stepped off.

"Good."

The queen's big mount moved instinctively. He knew the path to war, so she let him lead the way. The men of her personal guard fell in around her in the normal five-to-a-side formation.

The queen's party rode for what seemed like a day but was truthfully only hours. A full half of that riding time had been through the midst of the troops. There were countless groups deep on both sides of her path. There were so many men at arms to be seen that she thought there couldn't be anyone left to tend the crops. To her knowledge no kingdom had ever mobilized an entire kingdom of men during this age. Where had they all come from?

On the plains south of Kanash, in what she was guessing used to be several expansive wheat fields, Anistasia finally came to the point she was headed toward. With the sun contentedly edging its way into the sky far enough to produce a faint, pale daylight, she captured a glimpse of the man in charge of this massive gathering.

Standing with some older men in a loose, wide circle, around the embers of a fire which still emitted a strong smell of black coffee, Stas Bok held her gaze and watched her approach with a look that suggested she was going to war. To Anistasia's supreme surprise upon arriving at the fire pit, she found Stas Bok to be positively upbeat. She would have bet a good chunk of her wealth that he would be grumpy. Instead, everyone just waited patiently as the queen made her way over to the leadership circle. A man standing next to Stas waved his hand at a boy by the wagons and the boy scampered over to the queen with a wooden step so that she might dismount.

"Good morning, your majesty," the words animating Stas' bushy beard. "You come to see us off?"

The queen looked to the leader of Ayr's army with curiosity.

"No. I came to ask when we are going to be underway."

Several of the older men in the circle chuckled. Stas turned toward them and shook his head in the slightest way, as if to say, *if you want to keep your head on your shoulders, you'll shut up!* They all shut up. His control over his men was absolute. Anistasia knew that she would need to take that into account moving forward.

"Well, General Bok, while we wait, please give me a rundown of your preparations."

Stas made an inquisitive face.

"You mean captain, ma'am?"

The Queen of Ayr smiled.

"Captain of Kanash's defenses, yes. But armies are run by generals, or so I've read. So, General Bok."

Stas' eyes twinkled in the brightening light.

"Do I get a pay raise too?"

The queen smiled, not being able to help herself.

"If you win."

Stas Bok laughed heartedly.

"That's a given, ma'am. The winning, I mean."

"Please, tell me about this force that you've assembled."

Stas shifted his weight and his plate armor moved about slightly.

"You rode through a section of the infantry companies on your way here. Good lads, all. You have some sixty companies total."

The queen gave a shocked expression while doing the math in her head. Sixty companies would be some six thousand soldiers. Stas smiled.

"There are thirty companies of longbow archers, ten companies of mounted cavalry, and a full sixty companies of infantry, ma'am. That, plus two full companies of special operators; miners, saboteurs, and the like. There is one full company of timbermen, millwrights, stonemasons, and mechanics for assembly of siege engines once we arrive at the battle. Stuck in the middle of all that rabble there are twelve cannons, each drawn by a team of a half-dozen oxen and accompanied by a bunch of crazy chemists for making the black powder needed to fire them."

The queen smiled broadly. Stas Bok had well-exceeded her expectations.

"You've outdone yourself. You can forget about that *if-you-win* part from earlier."

Stas Bok bowed slightly. It was as far as he was going. Some movements you just didn't make in armor.

"Thank you, ma'am. The retirement plan just got a lot better."

Everyone laughed this time, the queen included.

"All jokes aside, majesty, this fine assembly you see stretched out before you is going to break the bank. The coin that has already been put out is sizeable."

The queen nodded. The Keeper of Accounts had been positively livid about the expenses he was being told to cover.

"The upfront costs have been considerable, yes. As far as the remainder goes, Neeron will be footing the bill for that."

The queen could tell that Stas had made a face under his bushy beard. If she had to guess, it was one of concern.

"That is all well and good, in theory. I don't know that it's going to work in practice though."

The queen was intrigued.

"Go on."

"We're obviously established to handle a force far greater than the one Neeron can muster, with or without the Watchtower assisting them. So, if we strip the lands as we go to feed this mobile city of soldiers, we leave starvation in our wake. That will make itself a problem when it's time to come home again."

Anistasia nodded without temperament. The general had solid points. One needed to plan for the entire campaign.

"Valid concerns, all. I tend to agree with all of your points. However, if we fare well in our endeavors, I don't plan on us returning by way of Neeron."

To everyone gathered in the leadership circle that meant turning east toward Udaass once they were finished with Oban to the south. Turning toward Udaass meant that she was bent on taking the entire continent. The queen let them think as they wanted. They didn't need the whole plan today. They just needed to fight when it was time to fight.

"Okay, a different question."

The queen nodded.

"There are five or six Watchtower garrisons on this continent. What are we doing about them if they decide to stand with our opposition?"

"If they stand with the opposition, they are the opposition," the queen said matter-of-factly.

Several men in the circle gave shocked expressions.

"Now, general, what time do we plan on being off?"

"When the queen commands it."

"The command is given. March."

Stas Bok turned to the men in the leadership circle and made a hand gesture that said, *get to it.* The men stepped off with purpose and without question.

Chapter Thirty-Three

The unassuming messenger from Ayr boarded his ship and set sail not long after meeting with the Mining Guild. He could sense that whatever the queen had wanted from them, she wasn't going to get. If that was the case, there was also no reason for him to hang around. Staying in an unwelcoming place always led to trouble.

The captain of the messenger's vessel had put out with the tide and ran them out of sight of the Mining Isles in very little time. Though liking to travel to foreign lands, as was the lot of a royal messenger, he was now happy to be on his way home once more. He stood against the rail and watched the dark blue water streak past. The sky was blue to match the sea and the sun was bright and warm. The messenger was sensing that it would be a good journey home again.

That sense of calm from the serene nature of the day lasted about a whole hour before the man up in the crow's nest broke the silence.

"Pirates! Captain, there's pirates off the stern."

Everyone above decks, the messenger included, ran to the rear of the ship to look out on the receding sea. The captain, an older man who had plied his trade on the sea most of his life, took out a spotting glass and extended the tube to its full length. Scanning the open water to the stern of the ship, it didn't take long to come upon the black sails of the pirate ship. Looking hard into the spotting glass, he found the flag marking the ship as one being from Pirate Bay, and exhaled.

"Pirates, right. Drop the remaining sails. Full sheets to the wind, men."

Without question, the entire entourage assembled on the rear deck turned and ran for their stations, each man knowing what needed to be done. The remaining sails were lowered into the wind and pulled tight allowing the ship to put on speed. Scanning the deck of his ship and then the deck of the pirate ship through the spotting glass, the captain considered his options.

"All men to the armory! Arm yourselves for the boarding."

Men peeled off of their stations in small groups and ran to a cabin in the rear of the ship. Returning back into the sunlight, the sailors reappeared waving an assortment of worn swords and axes. Some men had long pikes that could be used to stab at men as they attempted to climb over the sides. It took three cycles of men running about, but before long everyone was armed and ready. The messenger was given a large knife, just in case. He was sure that all of this was really just overreaction. No one bothered a royal messenger, not even pirates. Once they realized that he was onboard, they would go on about their business and leave the ship be. He had made many journeys by ship and had never been bothered.

The messenger looked up at the flag staff on the main mast. He could see the flag of Ayr and the flag of a messenger both stretched out in the air above him. Yes, the other ship would certainly break off soon.

Toothless Tom, for his part in the whole affair, had also left port shortly after meeting with the Mining Guild, having his own Ubari messenger in tow. Unlike the Ayr messenger, who had left the port of Dyme turning north around the eastern side of the island as the merchant trade tended to do, the pirates had departed from a secluded outlet to the west of the port and continued west, cutting north between two of the islands in the group.

The head start of the merchant ship was of little worry to Toothless Tom. The boxy design of the merchant ship meant that it pushed as much water as it moved through, making only four or five knots under normal way. The dhow-styled ship that Toothless Tom and his brothers operated had a sleek hull design and could slice through the sea at a good fourteen or fifteen knots when fully up and running. With the journey from the southern coast of Oban to the Mining Isles being a solid eight days for a standard merchant vessel, it had only taken the pirates a full day to bring them into view.

Toothless Tom looked out through his own spotting glass at the merchant ship they were fixed on, taking in the messenger flag stretched out in the wind. He definitely had the right ship in view. That was good. He didn't want to waste time on the wrong ship.

Saleh stood stoically next to the ship's main mast and watched everything unfold around him. The pirates knew exactly what they were doing. *That might come in handy later on*, he considered. *For now, they were getting the job done.* Toothless Tom looked back at the Ubari messenger and smiled.

"At our closing speed, we should be on her in about forty-five minutes."

Saleh nodded approvingly.

"There's no doubt that they will repel boarders."

The pirate smiled again; mouth closed.

"And that'd be right troublesome, if I planned on boarding them."

Saleh adjusted his gaze.

"Something more drastic?"

"This one is headed home to the bottom of the sea, and she's taking all her souls with her when she goes. Even pirates don't normally board a royal messenger's ship. It's bad practice."

Saleh considered the statement for a moment. It made good sense. If any sailors went back to a royal court and said that pirates had boarded a messenger's ship and killed the messenger, then they would be completely justified in mobilizing royal navies to hunt the pirates down. The pirates always did their best to avoid engagements with warships if they could. Having the whole messenger ship disappear at sea was just better. There were many reasons for a messenger ship to go down at sea, and pirates were toward the bottom of the list.

A second thing crossed Saleh's mind. Sinking the ship was infinitely more practical from a crew point of view. Merchant ships, almost exclusively, were unarmed vessels. It had been a concession when all of the kingdoms signed the Great Watchtower Pact back at the start of the age. Royal navies were allowed to be armed, but not average vessels. Most pirate ships mustered up at least one cannon. They didn't really care about the pact. They were pirates. Some pirate ships bristled with guns, such as the massive galleon *Seamus*, captained by Blue Bill Montgomery. Others had a tiny gun, as much for defense as attack. Each crew outfitted its ship with whatever it could lay its hands on. Normally, cannons were stolen from shore-based garrisons and then put into rolling cradles so that they could be fired aboard ship. Such was the case with the six long guns that Toothless Tom's dhow carried. They were located in stations that ran along the main hold and hidden behind doors which looked like the sides of the ship. They were only exposed when they needed to be fired.

"A broadside?"

Toothless Tom shrugged.

"Maybe, if the need arises. We'll start by putting three or four stones into her waterline. With her size and speed, the sea should do the rest."

Saleh nodded approvingly. The pirate seemed quite practical.

The pirate dhow tacked and ebbed, continuously advancing on the messenger's ship for a good hour before individuals on the deck could be properly identified through the spotting glass. Another good thirty minutes and the same thing could be done with the human eye. A call of "hands to the rail" came out and all the free deckhands mustered along the rail which was on the side of the vessel facing the merchant ship. Each of the men pulled out spotting glasses of their own and began scanning the target ship intensely. Each one made a careful study of the target and then reported their findings to Toothless Tom. He nodded his understanding and thanked each man in turn. Saleh gave the pirate a curious look.

"Just because merchant ships aren't supposed to be armed, that doesn't mean that they don't arm themselves anyway. Since the Watchtower Guild doesn't possess a navy, they don't enforce any of their seafaring rules. They tend to check vessels in port, but we've found that merchants are crafty at hiding both cannons and cannon doors. A lot of eyes inspecting the target ship means that, mostly, we only miss such things by accident. If we find that they can return fire, we tend to go about things differently."

Saleh considered everything the pirate laid out and agreed approvingly. He decided as the pirates went back to their work that he would need to be more wary of them, and Ubar should do the same. They were much more of a force than he had originally given them credit for. That could be a good thing, but it could also come back to haunt them later on. It all depended upon the mood of this seagoing horde.

Tom took a hard look through the glass. He could now see the handheld arms of the men standing on the opposing deck. They appeared to be ready to repel boarders. That was exactly what he was wanting to see.

"Alright men, man the port guns. Put four stones into her at the waterline. Helm, turn us into firing position."

The pirates scattered, with many a man disappearing below decks to man the cannons on the portside. The helmsman spun the giant wheel to turn the nimble pirate ship into the proper firing position. The main sail was trimmed to adjust the speed, pushing the gunship up next to their target. Toothless Tom waited patiently until his cannons were lined up directly perpendicular to the hull of the merchant ship. The cannon stones needed to strike the opposing hull squarely to punch through and make the required holes. At the speed that the target was moving through the water, if the stone struck a glancing blow it could bounce off of the solid wood, doing no real damage. That wasted both time and ammunition. It also allowed the opponent time to evade. In a worst-case scenario, stones had been known to bounce off the target vessel and come back hitting the shooting vessel or one nearby. It had all happened in the past and made pirates like Toothless Tom cautious.

Deciding the shot was as good as they were going to get, Toothless Tom leaned over a hole in the deck which let him yell down to the cannon floor below.

"Fire all guns!"

A cacophony of sounds and smoke came to life as the four cannons fired almost simultaneously. Four ten-inch cannon stones rocketed out of the pirate ship and slammed into the side of the merchant vessel, each stone producing a goodly sized hole in the target hull. Three of the four struck just along the waterline, shattering the boards of the hull and leaving holes two-foot in size or better. The fourth stone impacted just below the waterline. With the friction from the water slowing its velocity, that stone only made a hole of about a foot around, but its location fully below the waterline was like a shark on a sport fish. Water shot in with such pressure that soon enough there was a gash from rib to rib.

The pirate dhow shot out ahead of the merchant ship as the water resistance of sea tearing through its hull slowed its speed by half. Tom ordered the helm to come about and the guns to stand down. The gunports were closed and the sails loosened up to let out the wind. The pirate ship circled around and came to a pause on the sea, some hundreds of yards from the foundering merchant ship.

Pirates assembled quietly on the deck and watched as their target ship sank into the depths of the Halcyon Sea. The pirates were quiet, to a man. Many of the men making hand gestures or murmuring quotations of safe passage for the soon-to-be dead. Pirates were a superstitious lot and they knew that it could just as easily be them going to a watery grave. Someday it would be them.

As the messenger's ship slid out of sight below the surface, a random amount of flotsam could be seen in the water. It came from the loose items which had been about the deck. Toothless Tom scanned the debris field with his spotting glass looking for any kind of odd movement not produced by the sea. He found a pair still clinging to life, trying to hide as they swam amongst the debris.

"Lower the skiff. No one swims away from here."

Three men began pulling on ropes to drop a rowboat over the side as two other men jumped inside. Unhooking from the ropes, they rowed straight to the middle of the debris and churning water until they came upon the first man. The pirate in the bow slid a rapier through the swimming man's chest, causing a gasp of pain and surprise. The pirate punched two more holes into his chest before the unlucky sailor gave up his fight for life. The second man, though desperately trying not to meet the same fate as his companion, did so. The pirates made a slow pass through the debris looking for anyone else trying to hide in the chaos. Deciding no one was still clinging on, they returned to the pirate ship.

The skiff was retrieved, the pirate ship secured, and all men were accounted for. Deciding all was right on the sea, Toothless Tom looked up at the helmsman.

"Make heading for Doha Port."

The sails were fixed and the ship headed off to the northwest, leaving the debris to sink at its leisure and the sharks to claim the bodies.

Chapter Thirty-Four

The march of the army south from the sprawling fields of Kanash to the boundary city of Fatezh on the Neeron side of Ayr's southern border went smoother than old Stas Bok had planned on, even with the queen along for discomfort. The various companies of the force had collected smoothly into a train behind him as he and the queen had ridden off slowly. The different commanders moved their units on cue as it became their turn to join in with the marching. After only a couple hours, everyone was on the move south.

It took all but no time for the consistent pounding of armored boots and metal-reinforced hooves to turn the grass underfoot back to earth. Shortly after becoming earth, the marching trail turned to dust. The dust of the boots and hooves billowed up as the army continued on, raising a great cloud which could be seen many miles in the distance.

The queen had asked Stas if the dust cloud was going to be a detriment to them. He had explained to her that you didn't assemble this type of force without word spreading in advance. Neeron already knew they were coming south a week past. The answer seemed to placate the queen, and she went back to riding along quietly.

The pace of the complete army was slow, but steady. Little more than a week on and the edge of Ayr could be seen in the distance. Stas Bok rode quietly until he came to a spot situated along a low rise in the wheat fields. Looking out from the rise he could see the entirety of the Kalduhr Watchtower garrison stationed along the border. They were middled on the main roadway, with troops spreading out over the fields on both sides. A contingent of local troops were embedded with them. They were layered in a second wall behind the Watchtower troops. To Stas' practiced eye, they were a good two-hundred-and–fifty troops at best. Taking it in, he pulled back gently on the reins of his horse until it slowed to a stop. Patting the warhorse on its mane several times, he spoke to it in a calm and reassuring manner. With the beast in-check, he looked over at the two senior captains who were riding with him at the front of the column.

"Well, this looks like the spot. Let's rest the march and get some food. I could use one of those small hens nicely."

Stas, not waiting for the boy with the wooden step, flipped an armored leg up and hopped off the big horse like a man half his age. He'd probably pay for that later, but so be it. He scrubbed the horse's neck again to make it whinny. The queen dismounted more gracefully and gave the opposing force in the distance a curious look. Stas let her stew a moment.

"No worries, majesty. The sun has already tipped today. It's too late in the day for combat. The Watchtower captain knows this too."

Stas pointed out across to a figure standing in the middle of the main road.

"Captain Brittaney Fyr. She be the one standing in the middle of the road with a head of blonde hair and a battle axe in-hand. The one with the black and brown dog at her knee. She's smart and knows her defenses well. She, too, has been doing this her whole life. She knows that neither of us is doing anything important until morning comes."

"And when the morning comes?" the queen asked suspiciously.

"I'll walk over and have a chat with her. See what her plans are for the day."

A half-dozen boys came up alongside in a wagon. As the wagon stopped, the rider hopped off to join the walkers and they all began pulling off material, poles and ropes from its open back. Four of them went about preparing Stas Bok's tent and one began working on a fire. One came over to him with a sturdy chair which weighed almost as much as the boy carrying it. He placed the chair squarely on the ground next to the general and ran back to help the others. Stas sat down with a small groan and a large sense of satisfaction. The queen turned and wandered off toward her own group of boys and girls handling her own tent.

Evening came on to night and passed quietly, just as the old warrior had predicted it would. He was one of a few men in the collection old enough to remember open combat. His days had been to the east, by the border city of Neya. He had been young and had the vigor that all young troops have. Now, considerably older, he had the experience that few men earn with age.

He had spent a great deal of time on the march south considering the response of his adversary. Neeron did have troops. But none of those troops, as far as he knew, had earned their mettle. Were they really going to have the grit for the fight? For that matter, did the large portion of his own soldiers have it? It was hard to say.

Stas had assumed that they would align themselves with the Watchtower. It only made sense. The question was: What would the garrison really bring to the battlefield? Did they have the stomach to stand toe-to-toe? Stas was betting they had the stomach for the fight, but not the spirit of the warrior. The Watchtower Guild, for all of its storied glory, was not a military machine. They were, in every sense, a police force. Keeping city people in-check and putting down unrest was a different animal from open combat. Combat was loud, bloody, muddy, and ugly. The echoing screams of disemboweled men would break those individuals not seasoned for war. This had all consumed his thoughts during the many long hours on the road south. Now, he would soon have answers to his questions.

Stas had taken an hour or two to sit outside under the stars with the other captains and discuss the events of the coming day. The queen had come over, followed by the captain of her guard, to listen to the discussion. To everyone's surprise, neither of them spoke. They simply sat on the outside of the circle and listened.

Stas kept the mood light. There were as many stories about old times and misadventures as there were practical talks about battle planning. All of his captains knew what to do. They all knew how to lead men and how to conduct battles. There was no need for rousing speeches. Those would come later, when the horde was stretched out around them and they needed rallying. This night was about calm reassurance and a quiet glass of whiskey.

Early enough, all the captains departed back to their own fires and tents. A boy came over and offered Stas a bottle of whiskey to refill his glass. He thanked the boy for his thinking but decided he should probably have a clear head in the morning instead. He watched the queen and her captain make their way off into the darkness. As he watched them disappear into the night, he began to consider how this situation of convenience was going to play out.

The queen was, in a word, untrustworthy. She had proven such by her actions alone. Still, most nobles could only really be trusted to a point. Men ALWAYS did what was in their own best interest, and women were no different. At what point would she turn on him? When would he become a liability?

The fact that she had spoken very little during the march south, and not at all during the evening gathering, told Stas one important thing. Where she may be good at treachery and the landscape of the aristocracy, she didn't understand combat. She didn't know how to conduct war or lead troops. And from everything that the captain of her guard had shown, he didn't either. That was good for Stas. That meant that he had practical value to her. Like life in general, he would just have to see how this whole thing played itself out. For now, he had time on his side. Neeron, even with the reinforcement of the Watchtower, wasn't any concern. They were more of a good way of blooding his troops before the real war started. That certainly couldn't be said of the other kingdoms on the continent. Those kingdoms had armies and knew how to use them. He actually might not live to ride home from this affair due to them.

Stas stood and sat the whiskey glass in his chair. His life would end when it ended, just like everyone else's. He turned his head up and looked at the clear night sky. The sky was covered by a vast blanket of stars. He smiled at the scene and turned to head off toward his bed.

The rest was short but deep, and the leader of Ayr's army was again standing outside his tent looking around. This time he was looking at the opposition, even if the lack of day's light kept him from doing so clearly. At first it was just a series of yellowish-red spots scattered across the fields. As dawn finally broke, images of small tents and sentries emerged.

Two boys stumbled into view, still rubbing the sleep from their eyes. He looked at them and smiled. He remembered a time long ago when he was just a boy waiting on men-at-arms. It all seemed glorious back then. Now, he was just happy that he didn't know how it would all turn out back then, at the beginning. He told the boys to find themselves some food and then fetch him his armor. The two scampered off with immediacy.

Stas looked over toward where the queen's men had pitched her tent. He could see a light aglow inside. He was betting that she hadn't slept much, if at all. *She better not have,* Stas thought. *You don't get to start something like this and have a clear conscious, too.*

The boys returned. One with water and bread, the other with a steel breast plate and mail. He was almost fitted out when the queen appeared from inside her tent and walked over, sans her guard.

"Good morning, general."

Stas Bok nodded, as he was in the middle of fastening the buckles on his grieves.

"Good morning, majesty."

The queen looked at the scene laid out before them.

"It's just me, but it doesn't look so much."

Stas considered the statement for several seconds.

"It's not, ma'am. It's either a token resistance and the main troops are defensive around the capital, or … ?"

The queen looked at him quizzically.

"Or?"

"Or it's a feint, and the main body of their troops are staged just out of sight. I predict that it's the first one."

"Why?"

"Because Neeron can't field two armies, even with the Watchtower garrison. The king will protect the capital first."

It made sense to Anistasia, so she didn't continue the conversation. Stas flexed his armor at all the joints to make sure that it was properly placed. It was. He turned to one of the boys.

"Go find Captain Tyler and see if he's ready."

The boy ran off without question.

The leader of Ayr's army and the queen stood quietly and looked out over the opposition placed before them. Stas couldn't get to the place where he called them the enemy. They hadn't done anything to him, or Ayr, for that matter. Still, war was his job.

The boy returned and stated that the other captain was ready. Stas nodded at the lad and reached down into the chair to collect his helmet. Placing it on his head and tightening the leather strap that held it fast, he turned his head about several times before raising the faceplate and scratching his bushy beard. Looking over at the scene, he spoke to no one in particular.

"If the world is truly going to burn, someone has to strike the spark that sets it on fire."

Stas Bok looked over at the queen and nodded.

"Majesty."

And with that, Stas started marching toward the main road where Captain Fyr of the Watchtower Guild and her war dog stood guard at the border. He walked alone down to where she was standing, taking his time, as if he had nothing else to do with his day except look at the flowers in the field. The lone advancement stalled the opposition from acting. They surely thought that he wanted to talk. At the point when he was about two hundred yards from the opposition's line, Captain Fyr marched out to meet him. The point of intersection left the two of them detached from either formation line and out of earshot.

"Stas Bok, you've marched a long way, with a large host at your back."

Stas smiled.

"Captain Fyr, you seem in good temperament this fine morning."

She looked back at him with a neutral expression.

"Why is the army of Ayr on Neeron's doorstep? You should turn about and not bother with whatever melancholy has possessed you to come this way."

Stas considered her comments for a couple seconds, a jovial smile still visible beneath his bushy beard. Then, with the swiftness of a man half his years, he slid a heavy blade from the sheath on his belt and swiftly thrust the point of the blade up into the bottom of Brittaney Fry's unprotected jaw. The blade, made for pounding on armor, pushed straight through her throat, punching through the bottom of her skull before its hilt was stopped by her skin. Stas yanked it out and immediately fell upon her big black dog taking the wind from its lungs with his weight. Three quick thrusts of the blood-soaked blade and the dog was done, too.

Stas Bok couldn't hear the commands that came behind his initial knife blow. He didn't need to. He had put his life in the hands of his captains when he walked across the field. Now, he had to trust. Looking out the open helmet toward the enemy line, for they were definitely all enemies now, he found his trust well-placed. He had no more than gotten his vision up on the enemy when an entire fusillade of arrows began raining down on them. The enemy, still slightly unprepared, was scrambling about when the second fusillade hit them.

Stas came up to one knee and sheathed the bloody knife. Slapping the faceplate of his helmet into position, he pulled his two-handed sword free of its scabbard. Squeezing the handle rhythmically to make sure that he had a firm grip on the weapon, he came to his feet and began to advance. He had no more than hacked the first man down when he was joined by two full companies of his own troops wielding swords and pikes.

The controlled line of Ayr's men and women moving in step with one another advanced overtop of the scattered and dismayed coalition of troops from the Watchtower Guild and the Kingdom of Neeron. The carnage was immediate, and all but completely one-sided. It took a slight forty-five minutes for the Ayr fighters to work their way through the entire force set against them. Stas only lost a handful of soldiers in the clash. The companies spent another half-hour moving over the battlefield, dispatching anyone who hadn't managed to die in the fighting. They killed them all. Every opposition troop. All of the boys. All of the animals. Every living thing that was not of Ayr was slain and was left in the fields for the crows.

At just over two hours from leaving his tent, Stas Bok looked backward for the first time. They had officially crossed a bridge and burned it behind them. There was no stopping now. With the exception of the soldiers in his immediate charge, everyone within view had just stood there and watched it happen. Watched for a taste of the carnage to come. Even from the distance away that he was, he could see the smile on the face of the queen. To Stas, that smile seemed a bad omen for any chance he might have had left for a quiet retirement.

Stas Bok flipped his sword over in his hand, grabbing it by the blade. He waved the hilt and handle over his head. They were officially done. With the signal, a small army of boys and girls appeared out of the crowd and began to run toward the battlefield. The scavengers spread out across the blood-soaked fields and started collecting anything of value. Weapons, arrows, armor, money, food, and other things of note were collected into piles that other boys and girls loaded into carts so it could be drug back to the ranks.

The man who had started it all sat down on a large rock and flipped open the faceplate on his helmet. It had been some years since he smelled the smells that he now smelled. By nightfall, it would smell significantly worse. They probably should be on the march again soon. After all, the Neeron capital of Karacase wasn't going to take itself.

Chapter Thirty-Five

The day had been a long and boring affair. Of all the things in this world that Quinn truly despised, it was boredom. Inaction annoyed him at a deep level. It had done so ever since childhood. It was one of the only things that he and his father had come to coarse words over. He didn't know why he was the way he was; it was just part of his being.

He reached out and grabbed the turkey leg on the plate, trying to gnaw off a piece from the end that wasn't already all bone. Chewing, he looked over at Bernard. His best friend was perfectly content, no matter the boredom. Bernard had a deep-seated sense, or maybe need was a better word, for action and adventure. But if there was none to be done, he could sit and watch the sun set with the best of people.

The two of them had been sitting on the ramparts most of the afternoon. Bernard had found the little corner place, high up on the walls of the Asturias port surround. It was much more of a bar than a public house. Just a spot to get something to drink and eat. It was obviously popular with the local troops that patrolled the ramparts of the port wall and entrance. Its location saved them climbing all the way down to the city streets just to get something to eat. The old lady and her son that ran the place were nice, and catered to where their money came from. In such, the small space was decorated with numerous banners and sigils from the garrison companies stationed in and around Asturias. There was even a small banner from the Watchtower Garrison of Cadiz, directly across the big port opening from Asturias. Quinn could see the top of the fortified tower off in the distance, if he looked hard. He had looked at it several times over the course of the afternoon.

"What'd ya think, big guy? Have another pint or wander on toward some other stop?"

Bernard seemed completely at ease with himself, just happy to be alive and well on this day. Quinn wondered what it must be like to constantly have an outlook such as that. Bernard stepped inside the small place, returning almost instantly with two more pints. Sitting Quinn's drink down, he realized that the one sitting on the little wooden table was still about half full. Bernard made a face.

"Sorry. Normally when you don't respond, it means have another."

Quinn looked down at the cup, also not realizing it was still half full. His passing interest had been in the turkey leg.

"No, it's okay, B. I'm just slipping is all. Long day of doing nothing."

Bernard stretched, as if to imply that he had been lazy, too, and looked over the port to the east.

"Yup. Almost another day done. About time for the sunset. They have good sunsets out this way. Want to go over to that open staging area on the west wall? I think that there's a bar over there too."

Quinn soaked a hard crust of some black bread in the half full glass of beer and considered the question. Stuffing the dripping affair into his mouth and crunching, he shook his head.

"No. This place is as good as any for sitting and drinking."

Bernard picked up a bone from his own plate on the little table and inspected it. It was completely meat-free. Nothing to be gained from it, so he sat it back down.

"You getting bored? We can walk down to the local alderman and see what kind of bounty sheets are hanging up in this city. Or are you still thinking about the other business?"

Truth be told, he was still thinking about the other business. They had been chasing a bunch of pieces to some mystery. They had been put upon by paid brigands and Quinn was sure they had crossed paths with Shadowman. It all had to mean something.

He had been pondering the individual pieces of the puzzle all day.

They all seemed random enough, one by one. A collection of single events that could easily be disregarded as chance, and the fortunes presented by the Goddess of Good Luck. He understood the complete randomness of life better than most men.

Still, if you looked at each piece objectively, they all had one single point in common. In one way or another, they all had a connection to the Kingdom of Ayr. Some were faint, some were very direct, but they all had Ayr in common.

Now, they get rumors of conflict to the west. Rumors of Ayr amassing an army. The kingdom collecting itself for war. This on top of more rumors that King Gerald had died. The news of the king's death, not long after his wedding and the coronation of his new queen, had shot through the land. Quinn didn't know what it all meant, but it left him with deep concern.

"So?"

Quinn looked over at Bernard, who was sipping on his glass.

"So, what?" Quinn asked reflexively, figuring that he'd missed some new bit of idle conversation.

"So, are you bored? You want to run down a bounty to bust up the boredom, or is it that other business?"

"It's the other business. Besides, I think that we're set for a while bounty-wise."

Bernard nodded his head with a slight smile. They were definitely set. They had been amassing coin at an odd rate over the last weeks, whether it came from bounty sheets or dead bodies. They had a fairly good amount of coin, and a good deal of that coin was full-weight gold from the royal mint of Ayr. They were flush for the foreseeable future, no matter what came along.

"Okay, we seem to be at a bit of a dead end when it comes to that bit. The information from our crazy friend Raphael was no more helpful than that from the Master of the temple back in Fatezh. It would seem that if we want to continue, the road either leads to the Great Temple of Drakchi or someplace we haven't figured out yet. So, Rain-Shadow Islands? Not really my first choice, but whatever."

Quinn swirled the beer in his glass and watched the breadcrumbs turn small circles in the liquid. He knew the way to Drakchi and didn't want to walk it again. It was full of ghosts.

"I think there's an alternative."

Bernard looked over at his friend, genuinely intrigued.

"Go on."

"We could make our way west, to Oban."

Bernard now looked perplexed.

"How does going to Oban help us with our mysterious lock and keys?"

"It doesn't, directly."

"Go on."

"I've been thinking about all of these rumors of Ayr's king dying and the army gathering. I think it's the start of a legitimate war."

"The kingdoms don't go to war, Quinn. It costs too much. They have diplomats and trade politicians and regents for all that."

Quinn nodded and picked up his full beer.

"I completely agree, but hear me out for a minute."

Bernard nodded. This was the most Quinn had spoken in about two days.

"Is this a one beer or two beer story?"

Quinn held up one finger.

"Fire away, as the pirates say."

"If this business with the vault and keys is real, and not some fancy nonsense, then you need six scepters to make the lock work. If someone is batshit crazy enough to really want to open the vault, they will need all six keys to do that. Since no kingdom across the known lands is going to freely give up the object of its designated right to rule, the keys will need to be collected another way. That way, near as I can figure, is to take them by force. I think outright war is coming, and it will run across the lands specifically pursuing the collection of those keys."

Bernard scratched his chin. His expression said he wasn't fully on board.

"There's never been a war that I can remember. Some border conflicts, but not a real kingdom to kingdom war."

Quinn nodded his head.

"Exactly."

"So, why not head for Neeron?"

Quinn took a drink.

"Because we're a long way from there and won't make the trip in time. If this new queen is really after the keys, then her first true stop is in Oban. Neeron isn't an original kingdom, it's just on the way to one. Besides, you know that Ayr's army will walk through Neeron's defense force like the winter wind blowing the chaff from the wheat fields. It's going to be more of a blooding for Ayr's new troops than any kind of conflict. The real battle is going to come when they cross into Oban to take the next key."

Bernard sat quietly and thought through everything that Quinn had said. When he was finished, he did it a second time. Quinn was making sense. And that made sense, since Quinn was also a solid tactical thinker and a natural leader of men. Bernard was a skilled and gifted fighter, but his friend was a military leader who had led men in conflicts and understood warfare.

"Okay, let's say that I tentatively agree with what you're saying. Oh, and I do, by the way. Agree, I mean. How do we go about getting to Oban? From where we are, we need to go through Neeron to get to Oban."

Quinn made a face that said he knew that was coming.

"That's one of the things that I've been deep in thought about this afternoon. I figure that we can probably make Graycott without much bother from the Ayr army. There we cut south and take the pass over the mountains and down the coast to the border. Once over the border it's an easy journey back inland to Oban again. Once we are in Oban we just look around and figure out where the action is."

Bernard made a face.

"You mean to join the Oban army? Neither one of us is much for following orders. Do you think they pay mercenary rate?"

Quinn smiled broadly.

"You hit that one right on the head, old chum. And I would assume that they will have ranks of opportunists, such as ourselves. If it looks like something that we don't want to get involved with, then we leave."

Bernard smiled and chugged the rest of his glass.

"I like your plan. Let's do this. Besides, we've been here too long anyway. Time to be moving on."

They took the long way down off the port wall, as was their usual path, save this time they studied the view and took it all in. They casually counted the ships. They got a feel for the number of sailors and troops. They developed a sense for how ready Udaass was for going to war. Quinn knew that this information would be useful to the leadership in Oban.

The two had shaken off the doldrums of Asturias with the mere decision to be on their way. That's who they were. They weren't meant to be in one place for very long before moving on. It was an itch under their skin. Movement was life for men like Bernard and Quinn. Besides, staying in one place for too long drew attention. It was the type of attention that neither of them wanted.

Working their way back into the city following their standard route, Bernard said hello to several shopkeepers that they passed. The shopkeepers had seen the two men enough to lose their natural suspicion of strangers and greeted them warmly.

Stopping at the lodging that they had rented, they collected their travel bag and each man's collection of weapons from their room. Strapping on the tools of the trade, they readied themselves for the roadways of the land once again. Stepping out the door and into the street they were now on their way.

They had walked about two blocks toward the landside gate when Bernard's sense of ease left him. They walked about another block when Quinn's deep-seated sense of concern returned. Both men had situational awareness which was far better than that of the average man's, and they were both getting a bad vibe.

They turned a corner into a long, close alleyway and stepped into the smaller space several strides. Bernard made a small gesture with his sword hand and Quinn paused his hand close to his own weapon. He could feel something wasn't right, too. Someone was following them. Following or tracking; it was one or the other.

Quinn stepped off another couple strides, putting enough room between himself and Bernard so weapons could be swung without worry. Bernard began to walk at a practiced pace, and the two men continued on to the end of the alley. Moving out into the next street, Quinn reflexively twisted at the waist, bending almost halfway to the street in the attempt to avoid the sharp part of a one-handed sword blade. He pivoted back upright, boot knife in-hand, and blocked the retracting blow with the knife blade. Deciding not to directly engage the bigger man, the assailant pulled a small tube from his beltline and blew a dry white powder into Quinn's face. As Quinn wiped furiously at his eyes trying to regain his vision, the assailant jumped, turning over in the air above Quinn and landing on his feet in the entrance to the alley. He blocked an immediate series of blows from Bernard's short swords before kicking him squarely in the diaphragm and driving him backwards. Stepping in to close the distance, the assailant landed a series of stinging fist blows to Bernard's chest and side.

Not waiting for the assailant to land anything life threatening, Quinn was back on him without hesitation. The change of attacker allowed his friend time to regroup. He engaged the unknown assailant with his heavy boot knife in one hand, the large battle axe in the other, and about half his normal vision. It was even weight for the big warrior since he had arm-enough to swing the big battle axe like a training sword.

The assailant, covered in black from head to foot, checked an advancing blow from each of the other men. The blows went back and forth, with no man gaining an advantage. The exchanges of sword stroke, axe swings and knife thrusts continued at a furious pace, stinging clangs of metal on metal ringing out in the alleyway. In-between weapon strikes, random punches and kicks were thrown by one man or another. Some blows landing hard, others glancing off moving targets.

Bernard stepped in at an off angle, moving the assailant backward toward a small corner recess in the side of the alleyway's buildings. Sensing the enclosure coming, the assailant blocked the pushing blows from Bernard's short swords. Flipping the sword over in his hand to safety himself from Quinn, the assailant slammed Bernard's chest with another series of sharp, hard, rapid punches from a heavy leather-gloved hand. Bernard grunted hard, stepping back multiple steps. The opening allowed the assailant to move into his original position and attack and defend as before.

Sensing a growing symmetry in the exchanges, Quinn stepped back, drawing the black-clad assailant with him as he moved, pulling him off his center. The man tensed all of his muscles to adjust just as Quinn stepped back in quickly to strike, but the assailant slid the sharp end of his sword along the outside of Quinn's knife arm. Blood flew in a parabolic arc as Quinn sprang to separate himself from the attack.

Sensing the commitment of the assailant fixed on Quinn, Bernard checked the man's defensive weapon and planted his off-hand sword deep into the man's thigh. Pulling up and out at the same time, the extraction of the blade, combined with the movement of the two men, tore a good chunk of flesh from the assailant's upper leg. Their opponent collapsed to the ground and grunted an expletive that neither Bernard nor Quinn understood.

Not waiting for the man to get himself back together, Quinn spun the battle axe around in his grip and launched it at their attacker. The heavy axe sunk deep into the man's chest, setting itself firm. Quinn closed the distance and sank his boot knife into the man's neck several times, making sure the job was completely done.

Bernard looked down at the man and then over at Quinn, who was just fully realizing that he had been cut.

"Who the fuck is this guy!"

Quinn took a good long look at him and then down at his own arm. His blood was now running down his arm, off the end of his elbow, and making a puddle on the ground.

"He's the one from the public house in Fatezh. The one who paid your friends and searched our room."

Bernard looked down at the corpse with suspicion.

"This guy is Shadowman? Damn sure fights like one."

"That's a fact, but why is he here?"

Bernard threw Quinn a clean white strip of binding linen and a wrapping cloth to soak up the blood. The cloth had been soaked down with honey and would keep the wound from getting infected.

"Fix that before you lose too much blood. I'd say that he was here to kill us."

Quinn worked on securing the wrapping cloth with the linen and getting it tightly in place.

"I get that part, but why? The only person that knew we were headed here is the sorceress from Orba. She didn't strike me as the type that needed to employ people like Shadowman."

Bernard made a search of the assassin's person, coming up with a partial sleeve of full-weight Royal Ayr gold coins. He tossed them to Quinn, who was just completing his bandaging.

"Recognize those?"

Quinn rolled them over in his hand.

"Kingdom of Ayr, again."

Quinn stuck the coins in a pouch on his belt and looked back down at his arm. The wrapping was already soaked red, but the wound was starting to clot up nicely. He glanced around and then back down at Bernard, who had produced a whole host of items from the dead man. There were more small tubes of powder, a series of small blades meant for throwing, a handheld hook for climbing, and a length of some small but very strong rope. Quinn took it all in.

"Definitely Shadowman. Definitely an assassin. Grab the rope, leave the rest. Let's get out of this place."

Bernard did as instructed. The two men moved off without words, blending into the night of the city.

Chapter Thirty-Six

The trip away from Asturias under the cover of night turned out to be simpler than getting across the city with Shadowman in their way. After exiting the landside fortress gate, the two transited straight southwest into the gap between the mountains. Their path ran down the edge of a large flatland separating two mountain ridgelines on the south side of the wider range. The south ridgeline separated the two travelers from the ocean beyond. They moved with purpose, and as quietly as possible. It was unknown if Shadowman had any friends lurking about.

The two were a fair way into the flat when the sun broke in the east on the third day. The large, flat plain that they were on slowly declined to the west and the slightly downhill route helped them keep a quick pace. The path laid itself out in a snakelike motion between the base of the mountains and a goodly sized flat river which meandered through the plain's middle ground. The river moved with a steady flow but with few rapids or problem areas.

By the time midday had arrived the two were at the ferry portage where everyone going south caught the ferry boat downriver and through the great stone wall leading on to the border with Neeron. Both Bernard and Quinn had made the Neeron-Udaass crossing to the north, in the croplands, or up over the mountain pass, but neither man had ever been down through the great stone wall and out into the Bay of Tyna. They simply assumed that one border crossing would be the same as the next.

There was a small line for the ferry where it tied up on a short wooden dock. A jolly fat man stood at the head of the dock and collected the passage fee. Two large coppers seemed a reasonable price to pay for a ride downriver. Bernard gave the jolly man a small silver coin and he made change.

The open area where the dock had been built had slowly developed itself into a random collection of trader and merchant stalls selling everything from good luck talismans, to food, to weapons of every kind. There didn't seem to be any obvious rule or order of any kind in the place. It was more as if one seller stopped one day and another random person joined him the next day, until a general collection of sellers had assembled itself. The whole affair seemed to be self-regulating, with no armed presence in the area. It was a nice change of pace for both men.

Bernard picked up a loaf of white bread and a jug of water from a nearby lady, and the two ate quietly as they waited for the ferry boat to arrive. About an hour farther on, a small white sail could be seen tacking its way back upriver against the flow. The boat made its way through the water and pulled up into the dock with little effort, the ferryman having made the transition countless times. Two young boys ran over and helped the ferryman stow the sail and clean up inside the seating area so the half dozen new passengers could get in. The boat was a simple, wide, flat-bottomed affair with flat wooden plank seats for about fifteen.

The ferryman welcomed everyone onto the boat for the next journey, and asked two people to move one way or another to balance out the ride. Deciding things were acceptable, he pushed off the dock and allowed the current of the river to send the boat back the way it had come.

The ferry floated calmly down river straight toward the great wall. The massive monolith wall loomed before them in the distance, and only grew in size as the little ferry boat approached. Taking most of the afternoon to come within proper view, the sheer scale of the monolith became clear. The massive piece of stone was set at the end of the valley as a single wall. The wall was at least three-hundred feet tall. The shaped grey stone was smooth and formed into a single piece. Looking at the mountain edge it was obvious that the grey stone of the wall was a different stone than that of the mountain it had been set into.

The wall ran smooth along its top from both sides into the middle, where it had broken in two. A section a hundred feet or so in distance had either been smashed or ripped out of its middle. Now, the river everyone was floating down consumed all of that open space.

A large tower made out of the same piece of smooth grey stone stood on the inside of the wall and against the river's south edge. It was capped with a round, windowed observation area that the Udaass army had commandeered as a border crossing post. Quinn could see men looking down through the windowless openings as they grew closer.

"How did they get the stone smooth like that?" Bernard asked in approach of the wall. "There aren't any seam lines on it anywhere. It's like it's all one stone."

Quinn looked over at Bernard.

"I don't know. Last age technology, I guess."

Some other first-time passengers in the ferry marveled at the wall as well. It was impossible not to consider how it might have been constructed.

The ferryman continued on down the middle of the river that bisected the great wall. The pair of guards standing outside on the wall top waved down at everyone in the ferry as it finally reached the bottom of the wall. The ferryman and most everyone in the ferry waved back.

Bernard inspected the middle section of the massive stone wall. The grey stone seemed to be all one piece of rock, without joints or seams. At perfectly spaced intervals, rusty metal rods stuck out of the rock on both sides of the river and were all twisted away to the downstream side. It was as if the middle of the wall had been blown apart. Bernard couldn't fathom the number of cannons it would take to do such a thing.

"How do you think they put all those metal bars into the rock? It's like they were slid inside with sorcery or something."

Quinn shrugged.

"I don't know. Last age technology, I guess."

"For all of the volumes that you read, it would be nice if you could read one on how they make stuff."

Quinn looked over at his friend.

"So could you."

Bernard smiled.

"What's your point?"

"No point. Just stating the obvious," Quinn said, shaking his head slowly.

The ferryman continued on downriver with the current, letting the boat float along past the old-world curiosity. On the downstream side of the massive wall, several large structures could be seen at its base, made from the same grey stone. The symmetrical structures on both sides of the river had also been repurposed by the army and a variety of merchants. Quinn could sense that Bernard was about ready to ask a random question about the structures.

"I don't know how or what they did or how they were made."

"Why not?"

"Because, right this moment, I'm more interested with our friend from last night."

Bernard looked over at Quinn's expression.

"You think that whoever sent him will send someone else?"

Quinn nodded once with surety, now wondering how the mechanics of old actually did get the metal rods inside of the grey stone and what it all served. And why was the wall here, at the end of the valley with a river flowing through its busted middle?

"Well, considering that I didn't know there were still any more of them, I hope he's the last of his lot."

Quinn nodded, wondering to himself how people were able to make such massive things.

"It's odd, though, how everyone seems to have Ayr royal gold coins in their pockets."

Quinn snapped out of his thoughts and back to the ferry ride.

"True. Killing them is paying better than bounty sheets ever did, and they come to us."

Bernard smiled happily.

"That is true."

Some short distance beyond the great wall the ferryman maneuvered the flat-bottom boat into a rickety dock similar to the one they had embarked across earlier. After tying up, everyone disembarked the boat, as two different young ones waited to help the ferryman hoist the sail. A couple of passengers heading north climbed into the boat and found seats as the ferryman pushed off once more into the river.

Looking around, it was obvious that there was only one path heading south from the dock area, so Bernard and Quinn took it, continuing on in their planned direction. The walk south to the mouth of the river was short compared to their trek across the valley. They made it there in less than two days. At the river's mouth they found another menagerie of shops and stalls laid out around the edge of the bay, but nothing either man was interested in. Another ferry ride took them across the river to its north shore and a low area at the foot of the mountain range. Across the low area was the river Burle, and on its opposite bank, the border of Udaass and Neeron. The small mining and trading town of Tyna, once rumored to be a vast urban center of the last age, now all but submerged beneath the deep water of Tyna Bay, was a drop point for the mountain mines and a waystation for pirates. All things considered, it was just Bernard and Quinn's type of town.

Deciding not to make the move into and around Tyna at night, the two men pulled up in a stand of thick trees located in the middle of the low area and took a break. Quinn's feet were saying stop anyway. The night was warm and quiet and both men appreciated the solitude of nature.

Bernard and Quinn were both natural wanderers. They traveled from place to place as they chose, doing enough work to stay clothed and fed. However, since the night that they had found the man with the metal tube up in Ayr, they had been almost continuously on the march around the Kraeten continent. They had moved with purpose from one point to the next along a shadowy trail of clues that, so far, had only led to more clues.

The only thing that their journey had provided thus far was coin. Their collection of that coin seemed to have three important consequences attached to it. The first, and most important on a daily basis, was that someone obviously wanted them dead. Second, another major point of worry, was whoever that someone was, they were well-established in the Ayr court. And third, not to be forgotten in it all, killing all of the men which had been paid to kill them was paying them very well. They never carried as much coin as they were carrying now. The Kingdom of Ayr was paying for their travels in grand fashion. It was paying so well that Quinn considered picking up some horses in Tyna Town. It would make the trip more enjoyable.

Time was about an hour off from daylight when Bernard stirred to the point that it woke Quinn. The world around them was still locked in a deep twilight stage. It wasn't night, yet no light from a new day had managed to find its way out into the world. Bernard made a hand gesture forcing Quinn to sit up and look around.

"Where?" Quinn asked in a voice below a whisper.

"Moving along to our left. Not sure if its animal or mineral, but something's out there."

"Food?"

"Probably not."

Quinn reached down slowly and gripped the battle axe, flexing his hand a couple times to set the grip. Bernard was about to slide his short blades free of their scabbards when the movement at the edge of his vison solidified into a form. It was dark and upright, and slightly malevolent, but didn't have the smell of danger. Bernard made a second hand gesture and Quinn stayed neutral as the scene played out.

Step by step, like an old person worried over the placement of a wrong foot, the image came closer. It seemed to know instinctively that the two men were there in the wood and moved in their direction slowly.

Now with the image close enough in the failing darkness to see it obviously was an old woman dressed in a heavy black cloth dress, Bernard relaxed and stood. Quinn followed suit.

The old woman continued in until she was not two good paces from them, where she stopped. She inspected them both with a curiosity which suggested she was unconcerned by their weapons or purposefulness. She was old, too old to really be alone in the wood. Her dress and the throw over her shoulders were made of thick black linen or sackcloth. They had numerous holes and sew marks where they had been previously repaired. Inside the hood that the throw created, age lines upon age lines could be seen cut deep into blue-grey skin. Grey-black eyes looked out of the hood, conveying both knowledge and neutrality. Wispy strands of long, curly white hair framed an old woman's face.

Bernard quickly cycled through all of the stories he had ever been told as a youth and a deep shiver went down his spine. Quinn sensed the shiver but didn't know why his friend was keyed up.

"Hmm, two men who travel with names not their own, standing in a wood by a fallen city of old. There is a prophecy in a volume regarding such a thing."

Bernard stayed absolutely quiet. The old woman had the gift, as it was called. He released the grip on the sword and let it settle back into the scabbard. The old woman took in the gesture and smiled in a way that made both men uncomfortable.

"Sure, are you? Hmm, that's a good quality of both rogue and ruler. Which one are you, Bernard? Or are you both?"

Bernard made a face that suggested he had never met the old woman before. The old woman's smile became less suspect.

"I've known you both since the day that you came to life, and a thousand others just like you. If you're luckier than most, I won't know you when you move on to the next place."

Both men stayed unmoved by the comment, which made the old woman's smile grow, deepening the age lines in her face as it did so.

"Yes, surety. I tell you this as a gift. If you travel along the sea, you will come to the divide and a path that will lead you to war. But, if you turn north when you leave sad old Tyna Town, you will find both trouble and the next clue that you seek. A young princess is currently traveling there. If you go to help her, that action will lead you in directions that you, as of yet, have not planned to go."

Bernard looked at Quinn and made a face which questioned why they should listen to the old woman. Quinn had the same look. The two expressions were ones the old woman had seen a countless number of times, yet she smiled softly, nonetheless. She fixed her gaze on Bernard.

"Suspicion? A good quality for the continuation of living. South or north, you decide, Bernard. And yet, you don't have to think about it, do you? The decision has already been made by your friend, hasn't it?'

Bernard stayed neutral, but not as neutral as Quinn had been able to do.

"Hmm, make good choices and, maybe, I'll speak with you both again one day."

The old woman turned and wandered off in the direction which she had come, slowly placing one foot in front of the other, the way that old people do. Bernard and Quinn looked at each other in amazement and then back at the old woman in black. This time, she was gone, and the first light of day broke low and bright in her stead. The two looked back at each other again.

Chapter Thirty-Seven

The march south from the border had been straight and non-stop. The rhythmic clank of armor and the thudding of boots on dirt produced a natural cadence. The cadence of war.

The scene that they had left behind at the border was purposeful. It had needed to be done. It wasn't just or right for fighting men and women to be left for the crows, but the terror that it would produce in the opponents they were going to come up against in the near future was beyond price.

It had taken Stas Bok and the army of Ayr a slow four days to make the march from the border of Neeron to the small hill town of Tor Maginos, at the edge of the Karacase plateau. Stas hadn't picked the little town intentionally. It was the spot that the Neeron army had chosen to make their stand. It wasn't a bad spot, as spots went. It gave them control of the high ground, which could be useful. Being on the edge of the plateau also made flanking them inconvenient. No, for the size of the force that Neeron brought to the field, it was as good a place to choose as any. The spot did help them out somewhat.

Stas had his captains march the Ayr army into the open of the lower plain and spread horizontally to their natural width before setting up positions. His army completely filled the plain, blanking out the entire wheat producing area. With Neeron's little defense force looking down on the scene as they all marched in and set up their positions, obviously unconcerned by their opponent, both the presentation and the word of what had happened last had the intended effect. Stas could literally smell the apprehension floating downhill with the breeze. The smell of fear made him smile.

Stas Bok stepped over to a handful of lieutenants collected in the spot where his tent was being erected. They all looked excited and eager. *That look wouldn't survive their first real engagement,* Stas thought. *The sight of dying men was a wretched thing.*

The general nodded at the collection of junior leaders. They all gave a salute by raising their sword hand up at the elbow, palm out. It was the universal sign that they were coming unarmed.

"Spread out across your areas and inform your captains that we will have a war council after they have had time to rest and feed their troops. I don't see any conflicts coming today."

All of the junior officers ran off in varying directions, leaving Stas to look at the boys throwing up his tent. He pointed at the nearest one and the boy came running over.

"Go find where the queen stopped and is putting up her tent."

"Yes, general," the boy said, running away.

General? Stas really didn't take to the title. He was a captain. Captain of the Kanash Defenses, and Captain of the Ayr Army. He had earned captain with a lifetime of hard work. General, even if there really was such a thing, was just a title he had been given. There was no merit in something which hadn't been earned.

The boy came running back and pointed to the east. He said that the queen was in a tent about 100 paces to the east, by a large oak tree.

A pair of boys came up and handed him a jug of what smelled like dirty water and a nice fresh loaf of sourdough bread. He liked sourdough bread. And as long as it was fresh, he liked dirty water as much as the clean stuff. It didn't pay to be picky when you were on the march.

Stas sat down in the trampled wheat and looked straight up at the enemy while he ate his bread. He ate the entire loaf, unmoved by their observations. He even made them suffer the indignity of watching him take a little nap in the afternoon sunshine. He understood that the show of absolute control was a thing which could easily cause other men to fold under its presence. It didn't even matter if the control was real or not. It was the idea of it that meant something. The projection of power. He was in complete control of everything that would happen here, and now the entirety of the enemy force knew it.

Was he really? Probably so. Neeron's force wasn't overwhelming in any way, and all of his soldiers executed his commands without hesitation. He possessed more military experience than anyone he knew of in Neeron, which also played into his superiority. He probably was in full control of the battlefield. Still, that kind of optimistic thinking lost wars. Thinking you can't lose gives the enemy an advantage.

Stas rose, pausing from his thoughts for a moment, and took a turn around the center of his forces. The warm afternoon sun had recently been replaced by campfires and boisterous activity. Numerous troops called out to Stas and asked if they could lead the charge. Stas said yes to every one of them and threw out a salute. Who knew, maybe one of those companies would lead the charge. It was too early to tell such things. The sunrise would make that determination for him. He needed to see what the enemy was going to offer him for an attack first. Stas had been at the game of war for long enough to know that you never started out with just one plan. A good plan, no matter how well it was thought out, seldom survived the first clash of arms. It always paid to have options. His options for the morning were what he was considering as he walked among the troops.

Making it back to his tent, he found the captains all collected around a campfire. Standing to one side were the queen and her men. Well, the queen sat and the guards stood. Stas took up an open space between two captains and thanked them all for attending. Though they all knew attendance was mandatory there was no reason to lack decorum.

The commander spent the entirety of the gathering quizzing his captains on the status of their troops. Were they ready? Were they healthy? Were their specific arms adequate and properly maintained? He took in the information provided by each captain and filed it away in his brain for later use. He would need it all when the decisions were made.

Stas listened to the report from a captain of one of the infantry foot soldier ranks with special interest. Not because it was out of the ordinary, but because he liked the way that the captain spoke. Captain Emmily George, or Emma as her troops referred to her, spoke with both truth and conviction. Stas could tell that she loved her troops and that they loved her. He respected that bond. Stas considered that, if he was a much younger man, she would be just his kind of woman. He could just tell that she was fierce. He wondered as she gave her assessment if she had ever married. He hadn't. The idea never meshed with his life. Women were somewhat different in that regard.

Stas pushed the whole internal dialog to the back of his brain and returned to the matter at hand. It was time for fighting, not thinking about fancies.

A small amount of general conversation followed the captains' assessments, and then they broke and headed back the way that they had come. The queen stood and departed quietly, a pair of boys hustling her chair along behind her.

Stas stepped inside his tent and grabbed a sturdy wooden chair in a bear claw grip. He carried the chair outside and set it by the fire. Sliding his scabbard through the wide opening in the arm, he sat and adjusted himself to a level of semi-comfort. The chair, specifically designed for men wearing armor, didn't groan in the least under his weight. A boy came along to check on him. He asked the boy for a large pitcher of water, a small pitcher of ale, and some more wood for the fire.

Stas Bok sat in his chair by the fire most of the night looking out at the enemy. He put sticks of wood on the fire one at a time, creating just enough new light to allow him to see, but not enough brightness to ruin his night vision. The enemy seemed to be maintaining the formation they had shown Stas upon his arrival. *Sometimes,* Stas thought, sipping the ale, *consistency showed a lack of vison.*

He dozed off at about three in the morning to a non-consuming sleep. He woke again about dawn to a collection of boys awaiting direction, and with a very bad disposition. He was too old not to be sleeping in a bed.

Stas stood and stretched out as best as he could in his armor. As he stretched, he determined that it was past time he took a bath. He was starting to stink. Oh well, that, too, was a price of war. There would hopefully be time enough for comforts later in the day.

A lad came running up juggling a roasted leg from some large bird and a pile of carved meat on a plate. Stas applauded his efforts and stuffed the leg bone into his mouth, almost sucking the warm meat from the limb without biting.

While he chewed, he inspected the opposition. They were spread out across the ridge, taking up all the space from one edge to the other. It made them look to be a massive lot, but Stas knew that a rank that long couldn't also be very deep with soldiers. The force had been laid out to make it look bigger than it was. Not an unsound move. He had done similar things in the past. Still, the Neeron army was less than a quarter of the one he had at his back now. The serious question of the morning was could they fight. He was now going to bet lives on the idea that they couldn't fight as well as Ayr could fight.

The cagey old soldier had formulated an idea while sitting in his chair by the fire. Now, before he implemented it, he needed some direction of his own. Turning his gaze from that of the enemy, he marched the distance the boy had told him to where the queen's tent was. Her personal guard stood at the entrance to the tent. They didn't move as Stas appeared. He paused in front of the guarded door. The lead guard shook his head, as if to say go away. Stas reached down and jacked his sword free with his thumb. It rose up about two inches up out of its scabbard, letting the razor-sharp blade glint in the morning sun. The message was clear. Let him pass or die. There was one leader on a battlefield, and he was it.

The lead guard took the hint and spoke through the tent to the people inside. A girl came to the door flap, looked out at Stas in his battle armor, took in his expression, and waved him in directly. Stas stared down the lead guard for several seconds, locking the man's image into his mind, and then strode inside. That guard wasn't living through the entire campaign.

Inside the tent the queen sat wrapped in her nighttime robe, as if she had just been raised from her rest. Stas hoped her mood was better than his own.

"General Bok, how can I help you?"

Stas ground his teeth together slightly.

"In our various conversations the terms have been neither specific nor finite. Time has come to clarify a situation before we continue on."

The queen shuffled in her chair, obviously unimpressed with his tone.

"And what would that clarification be exactly?"

"I need a yes or no answer. Are we truly moving on to attack Oban after we're done here?"

The queen held his gaze.

"Yes."

Stas Bok considered the definitive nature of the answer.

"What is our termination point?"

This time the queen considered the question presented. She was about to give the warrior a telling off but stopped. He really did need to know what was expected and where they were going. It was a sound request.

"There are six scepters which represent the six original kingdoms of the age."

Stas nodded.

"Ayr, Oban, Udaass, Ubar and Meridian are the five surviving kingdoms."

The queen nodded with a smile.

"That's where we're going. We are collecting the six original scepters of the land back into one hand. The path that we take to get there is whichever one you think makes the most sense. But that is where we are going. That is your termination point."

Stas Bok was stoic for several long seconds and then nodded once, definitively.

"Majesty."

The leader of Ayr's army turned on his heels and strode from the tent. Returning to his own tent, he found a host of boys and junior officers standing, waiting for what word was to come. Stas looked at the first lieutenant and made a number two sign with his hand, and then a number three. The second number was followed by a finger pointing down at the ground. He turned to another lieutenant and made the same series of signs. Stas nodded and both men ran off. Stas took in the countenance of the remaining personnel. Looking at a man in the middle of the pack, he growled slightly.

"Tell infantry corps four and five to be ready to charge as soon as the archers have softened up the line. Both corps are going up the hill, and they are going to take the field."

The man turned and ran off at full pace. Stas turned and walked over to his chair, which was still sitting where he had gotten out of it. He had no more than leaned down to put his weight onto the chair's back when the first of the arrows from his longbow archers went screaming through the air overhead. A sea of arrows flew overhead and pounded into the enemy ranks at both outer edges. Ayr's archers launched flight after flight until there was almost enough wood in the air to act as clouds.

The initial thundering volley of arrows had the desired effect on the opposition. The archers' relentless pounding of the outside edges of the long line pushed the two edges toward the middle of the field. The archers continued pounding on the ends of the line and it continued to collapse into the middle.

A half-dozen infantry leaders appeared out of the pack and Stas nodded to them. He drew a quick series of designs in the dirt with a stick and then pointed at different individuals. All nodded a second time and disappeared the way they had come. A senior captain from the previous night's war council stayed and awaited the inevitable command.

The archers continued the bombardment until Neeron's line was half its original span. Deciding it was time to be about the real business of the day, Stas Bok turned to the captain waiting with him and nodded. The captain nodded to a pair of junior men, who then raised large red flags and waved them over their heads.

Some sixty percent of the infantry force which Stas had called out began to march straight up the middle of the field. The ranks moved at the best speed that they could make over ground without losing their formation. When they had covered more than half the open space in the battlefield, the red flags waved again and the remaining 40 percent began advancing up the outside edges of the battlefield, now cleared out by the archery bombardment.

Neeron launched arrows of their own, slowing Ayr's infantry advance. The arrows were followed by a flurry of crossbow bolts. The initial lines of infantry fell as arrows and bolts slammed into man after man. Having closed the distance across the open space of the battlefield before Neeron's forces could launch useful second or third volleys with their archers, the Ayr infantry engaged the opposition with a thundering clash of swords and pikes.

Holding the high ground, Neeron's forces initially pushed Ayr back down the hill into the debris of their dead comrades. The Ayr infantry, being more seasoned, planted feet and began the pushback just as the secondary forces coming up the outsides of the battlefield slammed into Neeron's flanks. Instantaneously engaged in a three-sided battle, Neeron folded. The Ayr infantry pushed in on all three sides, cutting down soldiers in waves. The press of the Ayr troops on the Neeron soldiers made them so congested that they couldn't maneuver their weapons or offer any sign of organized defense, as Ayr's troops hacked down men and women two dozen at a time.

Stas Bok rubbed his chin and considered the carnage. The enemy was officially broken. Both sides had lost good troops. It was probably enough. Stas looked over at the captain next to him and ran a pointed thumb across his throat. The captain turned and gestured to a group of men standing next to the flagmen. Loud bugles blew a repeating sound into the blood-soaked, arrow-filled, morning air. It took several minutes for the sound to be heard over the clashing of swords on plate and the raging howls of human voices, but the Ayr infantry finally pulled back several steps and paused.

Stas Bok slapped down the faceplate of his helmet and marched commandingly up through the mayhem of the battlefield to where the Neeron force remained. He stepped calmly through his ranks and took in the resulting numbers. A little more than a third of Neeron's original force still stood upright. It wasn't so much. *Probably should have stopped sooner,* Stas thought as he looked down at a disemboweled woman who had been trampled in the surging of the lines.

Neeron's remaining field commander, a junior infantry officer, stepped forward holding his sword in his non-fighting hand with a grip around the blade. Stas took the sign of submission as a good thing.

"It's as simple as this. You can fight for us and live or decide not to and die here and now. We won't make any of you fight your own, but you will fight nonetheless."

The junior officer thought it over for several seconds, weighing their remaining lives against their loyalty toward their soon to be fallen country.

"You have an arrangement."

Chapter Thirty-Eight

It was a straightforward affair to march unopposed from Tor Moginos to the rise holding the Fortress City of Karacase, capital of the Kingdom of Neeron. The word of the army's defeat had proceeded their march, as the entire area between the battlefield and the capital was devoid of either livestock or people. Stas Bok and all of his captains had expected this reaction from the locals. It was natural to run.

As the army closed the distance to the fortress city the scale and grandeur of the place became evident. The city was large. It was completely surrounded by a series of heavy stone walls that gave it layers of protection. First, the city sat on a rise, so an attacker had to advance uphill toward it from all approachable sides. The initial wall encountered was low and wide, made to stall both troops and cannon fire. Separated by a small troop area, the main wall was tall and mighty. Towers set into the wall at standard intervals gave archer protection and defensive measures to the men below guarding the outer wall. Extending out from the main wall were a series of secondary defensive walls and ravines cut into the earth, making it seriously dangerous for a force to move around the wall. One had to pick a spot in the defenses and attack it, making defensive protection much easier for the inhabitants of the fortress. For its great size, normally a defensive weakness for any city fortification, the place was as well-defended as one could make a city. Stas thought that Karacase would be a good test for what was to come.

Stas Bok had always been impressed by the city when it came into view. It was majestic, if that was the right word. A true royal city. He had seen the city many times in his life, having walked its ramparts more than once. It was left behind architecture of the best kind.

Since the day he had begun assembling the army, he had been contemplating this very point. He wanted to attack it and not do damage. He didn't want to ruin the city while he was taking it. Working out how he was actually going to accomplish that goal had taken considerable thinking. In the end he knew that, unless they planned to starve them out, which the queen didn't have the patience for, he would need to do some amount of damage to crack their well-established defenses. He knew that the best place to punch a hole in almost every fortress was at the gates. The point in the wall which wasn't earth and stone was always the weakest point. Because of this, it was also always the most heavily defended. In Karacase's specific instance, due to the way the fortress was oriented on the land, this wasn't necessarily the case.

There was a large gate to the south of the city proper which led into the great meeting hall, but that wasn't the best choice. Understanding this, Stas had directed the army to take a roundabout route and come at the city from the north. The traveling of the northern roads was the normal coming and going of the city's daily life. The initial path of attack was a little more uphill than the south, but the terrain flattened out when you approached the eastern gate. This flattening out allowed them to attack the weakest section of the wall on level-ish ground. It also helped them with blocking defensive attacks from Neeron's remaining forces. The eastside entrance also had several large-walled cemeteries along the roadway which could be used as impromptu defenses by the Ayr army.

The massive host came to and crossed the heavy stonework bridge that spanned the river Aude to the city's west and moved on toward the fortress without a break in step. Stas Bok, first man in the great train of men, women, and beasts, listened to the clanking sound of metal horse hooves on heavy stone and wondered how many times during the previous age the people of Karacase had looked down on a similar scene. He was sure that the city had been fought over many times since its founding.

Stas slowed his pace, sending a ripple backward through the army to slow their pace. The great train at his back acted instinctively, naturally adjusting to their leader's movements. The queen picked up her pace, moving forward through the column to where Stas was just casually riding along. Stas thought she seemed a little bit more cautious than she had been earlier on.

"You're slowing the march forward?"

Stas nodded to the question, keeping his eyes fixed uphill on the fortress.

"Yes, majesty."

Anistasia looked uphill at the great fortress and then back at Stas, who was still looking up the hill. She looked back up at the city a second time and smiled to herself.

"A strategic measure?"

Stas nodded definitively a second time.

"Yes, ma'am. The Old-World bridge we're using to cross the river is a natural choke point for our army, but the enemy is too far away to take advantage of it. They can, however, see it very clearly. It will take a good half-day for our full force just to cross the bridge. I want everyone up there on the ramparts to get a really good look at what's approaching."

"You're hoping to instill a little fear in them?"

"Yes, ma'am. This force setting itself up outside of Kanash would give you pause, wouldn't it?"

The queen smiled, unable to stop herself. The leader of her army was uncomfortably direct, but a brilliant tactician.

"I know you like to have a meeting upon the setup, but you already have a plan, don't you?"

Stas Bok looked over at the queen, taking his eyes momentarily off his target. He refixed them as quickly as he had separated them.

"Yes ma'am, I do. A siege will take a long sum of days for starvation to start doing its work. You're too new at this and don't have the patience for such things. A direct assault would lose too many men, most of them being knights, which we can't afford to lose this early in your campaign. The best plan, all things considered, is to blow a hole in the front gate with direct, aggressive, cannon fire."

The queen smiled to herself again.

"Violence of action?"

"Violent attacks make soldiers pause. Soldiers who pause in combat tend to die in combat. It's the natural state of things."

"It sounds like you have it well in-hand, so I'll let you get to it."

Anistasia was about to slow her horse when Stas Bok waved his hand at her to stay.

"We're still too far away for them to attempt any type of preemptive strike. You can stay at the head of the column if you choose ma'am."

The queen took the statement for what it was and kept her horse at pace. If she was ever to be seen as a leader by the army, she needed to put herself in a leadership position. Words didn't count in combat.

As the old soldier had predicted, it took a full half-day for the complete complement of Ayr's army to cross the heavy stone bridge over the river Aude. By the time the last infantry company was rounding the east side of the fortress at a safe distance, the captains had already set up their cannons for the attack. It was well past midday and Stas wanted to get this whole event rolling. He knew that they couldn't afford to sit idle overnight without inviting an attack from Neeron's city guard. That would cost soldiers he didn't want to lose.

Looking along the lower fortress wall, Stas surveyed the scene presented to him. Karacase had cannons stationed along the wall at even intervals. Each one of the units appeared to be fully manned with cannon men and an auxiliary pair of knights. The quick count showed every fifth man or woman to be an armored knight. Stas did the loose math in his head and concluded that the city guard was actually a bigger force than the one they had already put down. That would certainly need to be factored in moving forward.

Stas turned to a nearby lieutenant.

"Get the nearest archery captain and the head of the chemists."

It was an order, not a suggestion, and the young officer went sprinting off. The two requested parties came back with the officer at a brisk jog. Stas went for the captain first.

"I need a dozen of your best. The ones that don't get scared when they take fire."

The captain nodded and turned to depart, so Stas looked to the chemist.

"We're going to be pounding away with cannon fire for an hour or two straight. Are we prepared?"

"Yes," the chemist answered solidly.

"Good. Now, do you have any of the stinking smoke made? I want the archers to put enough up on those cannons so that they have to stop firing."

Stas pointed to the cannons on the low wall ahead. The chemist looked at the defenses quickly and then back to Stas Bok.

"Yes, we can make that happen. We have the stinking smoke. I'll just need to fit it into an arrowhead. The arrowheads will be heavy. The archers will need to be quite close to the wall."

"How close?"

The chemist paused.

"The base of the wall itself."

Stas nodded.

"Make it happen and do it quickly."

Stas looked at one of the boys who traveled with his wagon as the chemist departed.

"Boy, build me a fire."

The boy nodded and scampered off.

The queen, who had been standing silently next to Stas Bok the whole time, watched the sequence unfold while making mental notes about how he made his decisions.

It took a good half-hour for the plan to come together outside the walls of Karacase, but soon enough they were ready to attack. The chemist gave some five of the heavy arrows to each of the archery teams assembled. He explained that at least two of the bulky arrows had to find their target for there to be enough smoke to do the job. The archers collected their special projectiles and readied themselves. A group of infantrymen came up carrying big wooden screens woven out of wicker. It was planned to advance them toward the required firing positions while they protected the archers from their counterparts on the wall above them. They would be okay against other arrows but wouldn't help at all against cannon fire or other clever devices.

Deciding that it was time, Stas looked over at the cannon crew to the right of the gate and waved an arm.

"Fire!"

He repeated the command to the cannon crew on the opposite side. All twelve cannons roared to life and began firing non-stop. Six cannons a side, three cannons firing while three cannons were reloading. The concussion of sound from the thundering beasts shook both air and ground alike. Large stone cannonballs pounded the defensive wall and the area around each nearby opposition cannon with a continuous assault.

The soldiers of Karacase fired back as best as they could. The cannons on the walls of the capital city were smaller than Ayr's and lacked the range of their attackers. The defenders aimed ahead of the advancing troops and bounced their cannonballs across the expanse between the two forces and into the ranks of the troops that thought themselves at a safe distance. The first handful of volleys had the desired effect, before Ayr's army hastily moved out of range.

Ayr's teams of archers with their infantry cover moved forward with each cannon volley from their own side. The Karacase troops rained down defensive fire on them. Troops fell away and were replaced as the slow march forward was made. Finally, almost as if it would never actually happen, Ayr's archers and infantry advancing troops moved inside the shadow of the lower defensive wall. The height of the lower wall protected the advancing soldiers, as the defender archers could no longer see where they were. Stas looked on knowing the groups of attackers were by no means safe. The kill zone, as it was known, moved the men out of the archer's area and into the range of the crossbow men and stone throwers that stood directly above them on the wall. Defensive men would advance to the top edge of the lower wall and throw down buckets of thick oil which the crossbow men would light on fire with flaming crossbow bolts. The kill zone was nowhere Ayr's men wanted to stay, so they went to work.

The defenses to the right of the gatehouse were the first to pause action, with four of the five stinking smoke arrows finding their mark. The left defenses stopped shortly after, with three arrows breaking open in their space.

The chemicals in the flaming arrow heads mixed together when the heads broke open on impact, and the heat from the flames made a thick, white smoke with the heavy smell of rotten eggs. It was so unnatural to the senses that men who inhaled a good lungful of it would simply fall out and expire. It was a quick way to die, but not a very gallant one. Nor was it particularly painless.

With the pause of action from the troops on the wall, Stas reoriented four cannons and began pounding the main gate structure with direct fire. It took ten or fifteen rounds from the large cannons, but the port cullis shattered as planned. The way into the city was now wide-open.

Stas looked to a lieutenant and nodded. The junior officer raised a large red flag with a black stripe and waved it overhead. The knights moved forward into their attack groups.

"Time for the grapeshot!" Stas yelled to the cannon men as a weapon from each group began moving more in line with the opened gate.

As expected, the shattered eastern gate began to swell with defenses as troops filled the space. Swords, pikes, knights in armor, and crossbow men of all types filled the space to stop the advance of the enemy. They were of little bother to cannons filled with nails, spikes, bits of metal and little stones. The grapeshot ripped its way through the opening, tearing men apart and sweeping the area clean. The cannons continued firing into the opening until there were no more defensive troops willing to fill it.

Stas Bok nodded his head and the big red flag with the black stripe waved again. As it did, the first force began to advance on the city. Two companies of infantry troops followed, then more knights and more infantry. Archer corps moved forward and continued pounding the defensive walls of the great city, allowing the charge to move forward without undue opposition.

The Ayr army fanned out as it moved inside the walls of Karacase, ascending the wide steps and moving along the ramparts to put down the opposition with direct engagement. A main group of soldiers moved directly east-west across the city to the king's castle which stood inside the western defensive wall. The remaining royal guard protecting the castle gates offered little resistance to the force that advanced on them. Stas Bok and the queen moved with a company of knights and the queen's royal guard into the city, directly behind the advancing force. They entered the castle without issue.

A loud crack could be heard throughout every room and walkway inside the king's castle as the beams barring the throne room doors splintered and gave way. A host of armor-clad knights filed into the new space, attacking and dispatching the remnants of Karacase's royal guard. The last line of defense managed to fall several of Ayr's knights but quickly lost the war. The clanging of metal on stone could be heard in every inch of the emptied throne room as the sword of Karacase's last royal guardsman hit the floor.

Anistasia Nosov stepped over the dead bodies and made her way casually to the raised dais where King Jasper Lorimere and Queen Vivian sat in shock. Anistasia smiled at the old king in a way that made his blood drain.

"Jasper, I'll be taking your kingdom now."

Anistasia stepped forward and put out an open hand. The defeated old king handed over his scepter without resistance. The Queen of Ayr rolled her fingers around the object, feeling its weight when she took it from him. The weight of power.

Having the symbol of Neeron firmly in her hand, Anistasia stepped forward with a quick movement and planted her foot-long, four-sided, spike blade knife directly into the middle of Jasper Lorimere's heart. The old king fell to the floor, instantly dead. Young Queen Vivian screamed and leapt to the floor to grasp her dead husband.

Anistasia turned to Stas Bok.

"Tell the army to stop attacking. Neeron has fallen. If they encounter resistance, put it down hard and publicly. But stop killing those that stop fighting."

Stas nodded to the queen and yelled orders back out of the throne room door. Anistasia turned back to the dais area and looked down at young Vivian.

"Someone find some steel shackles for her. She's young and might prove a good bargaining chip later on."

Vivian looked up in horror as Anistasia Nosov turned and strolled back out of the blood-soaked throne room.

Chapter Thirty-Nine

Queen Bianca Rhodes stood and looked down a well shaft located in a quiet interior garden courtyard of Meridian Castle. She had stood and stared down into the well water for so long that her captain of the guard came round to make sure that she was stable. Apparently, all of the household staff had been possessed of the opinion that she might actually throw herself into its depths. To the relief of all concerned, the captain of the guard found the Queen of Meridian to be completely sane and steady. She was just deep in thought.

Bianca had been deep in thought for days now. Her sister, Princess Margerette, had been relaying news to her from the opposite continent. The news had gotten worse with each new notice. Meridian's deeply entrenched information network had been absolutely buzzing as of late. It had been buzzing to the point that Bianca no longer wanted to open the dispatches from her sister when they arrived. Margerette's attitude hadn't been helping things either. The leader of Meridian's army wanted to assemble her troops and make preparations. Bianca was against the idea. The large Central Sea had long been the buffer between her continent and the remainder of the world. She was sure that it would continue to be, at least for the immediate future.

Bianca pulled herself from the depths of the well and began to pace. She had to decide on what to do about what was going on over in Neeron. Did Meridian really need to do anything at all? Were they obligated to Neeron in any way? Did they need to send defenses or should they really be looking south to the lands of Oban instead? Oban had an army of numbers and a navy. They could stand on their own if need be.

From the news in Margerette's dispatches, it didn't sound like Oban and the Great House of de Santi had sent any forces to the aid of their northern neighbor. Bianca couldn't figure out why. Oban had a vested interest in the stability of Neeron, same as Neeron did looking south. There had to be something else at play, but what?

Bianca stopped pacing and looked down at the paving stones which made up the ground in her specific section of the courtyard. Her father had told her several times that ruling was easy, until it wasn't. When it wasn't, those were the times that decided if you were a good ruler or a poor one.

Bianca decided that her concern was going to be toward her people first, and the wider world after. Fortunately, even if the rest of the world burned, Meridian would still survive just fine on its own. Well, fine with the assistance of the Freelands Folk. Back in the beginning, when the entire continent was the Kingdom of Meridian, they had been autonomous, producing their own food, mining their own minerals and jewels, and producing their own coin. Even now, with the separation of northern and southern lands, the kingdom could make its way alone.

The near-term decision was aimed toward the stability of her continent. After that, she would consider what was going on across the sea. Her aunt had her own army and a stiff spine. Oban would fare okay. Bianca, Queen of Meridian, needed to see about the welfare of Meridian.

The first order of business was to see where everyone stood. What were the Freelands Folk and the pirates to the south thinking and planning? Her adopted sister to the north was a fighter. She would, most likely, stand with Meridian. The rogues to the south, across the great schism at Knightsbridge, were a different matter entirely. If Bianca could bring the pirate navy into her hands, if only temporarily, they would prove to be a powerful ally. The trouble with that idea was that pirates never did anything for nothing, and they didn't care much about right or wrong. To get Silas Khan onboard with her plan might cost her

her virtue this time. She had dodged or rebuffed his propositions for years now. She didn't know if she was willing to give in on such a grand scale, even for the cause of war. Bianca decided that she would make that decision when she was forced to make that decision.

Even if Silas was unwilling to play jacks with her, the great ravine that separated the pirate lands to the south from the Kingdom of Meridian was a mighty natural defense of its own. It would stall any advancing force admirably.

First business was to see about the defenses of the north lands. She needed to have a talk with her sister in Maiden's Tower.

Bianca made her way back into the castle and down its ornate hallways of white and gold to their opposite end. Stepping out into the inland side of the castle, Bianca entered the outer gardens. She walked with purpose along manicured walkways and purposefully trimmed hedges to a small round fountain inhabited by the local bird population.

Bianca sat on a little stone bench placed next to the birdbath and calmed her mind. She breathed in and out with rhythmic cadence until her mind was no longer on edge. Leaning over, she looked down into the still waters of the fountain and smiled. Reaching out, she tapped on the side of the stone fountain three times.

"Rosalyn. Rosalyn, can you hear me?"

Bianca waited several minutes, patiently looking down into the still waters with an expectant gaze. When they were girls, Rosalyn had taught Bianca how water could be used as a conduit to talk through. The two had spoken this way countless times as girls, and more times since as rulers. The water had to be calm and in a natural setting for the connection to be made from one plane to another. That was why Bianca always chose the stone vessel of the birdbath fountain. She tapped and called to the High Sorceress for a good forty-five minutes before the water beyond her eyes began to shimmer and Rosalyn's likeness appeared on its surface.

"Bianca, are you unwell? You look in a state of utter despair."

Bianca quickly ran a hand through her hair and smiled as best as she could.

"What do you know about what is going on over in Neeron?"

Rosalyn shrugged and made a conciliatory expression.

"I have the same sense of dread that I have had for some time. There is something bad in the ether and it will be afoot in the east first."

Bianca smiled at her sister. Rosalyn spent so much time with the ether that she could be prone to talking in abstractions.

"You can change will be to is. Ayr mustered its army and marched on Neeron. Ayr's new queen was at its head, seeing how the king is dead."

Rosalyn made a face and then reverted back to her neutral stoic expression.

"The king is dead?"

"Yes. Some days back. Soon after, the queen took command of the army."

Rosalyn's countenance turned dark.

"So, it's war between the Kraetons? That would explain the dread feelings coming from the east."

Bianca looked at her sister as though she wanted to choke her.

"You think?!"

Rosalyn made an apologetic expression and Bianca relented.

"Information from the continent says that Karacase is about to fall. It also seems like the force Ayr has assembled is far too large to just be after Neeron."

"So, you believe that the army will keep marching?"

"A large force only makes sense if you plan on engaging another large force. It seems straightforward enough that Ayr will keep marching south toward Oban."

"The southlands are well defended. Oban can look after itself."

Bianca made another face.

"If they can't? The next large force in the lands is here, in Meridian."

Rosalyn smiled at her little sister in a way that calmed Bianca to her core.

"Well, I wouldn't necessarily discount Udaass. They have a significant army and navy."

Bianca nodded but didn't respond.

"You think that if they prevail in Oban, they will cross the central sea?"

Rosalyn made a show of thinking before she continued.

"First, they would need to acquire a navy to get this far. They could take over Oban's, if it survives the initial battles. Or they could build transport ships. Even if they have the ships, they will need to pass through the pirate water to do it. I don't see the pirates letting them pass peacefully, no matter their size. Don't worry sister. If they come this way, then they come this way. There is nothing you can do about stopping what hasn't happened."

Bianca looked perplexed.

"I know that I can't stop them, but I just don't know the right path for my kingdom. Is it war? If it is war, do I do it alone?"

Rosalyn smiled softly.

"The Freelands Folk are a solid and dependable lot. If war finds its way to you, then it finds its way to us all. The north has a long and deep memory. It understands its roots. It will stand and fight."

Bianca smiled and exhaled a lungful of air that rippled the water and almost broke the connection between the two.

"Where do you stand with your neighbor to the south these days?"

Bianca gave a grim expression.

"The situation is the same as it has always been. They keep to themselves, and we do the same. The great ravine at Knightsbridge is the line in the lands which separates them from us."

"Would they come to your defense, if it were in their best interest?"

Bianca made another grim expression.

"To secure a deal like that I may have to give Silas Khan something that I'm not prepared to trade away."

Rosalyn looked at Bianca expectantly.

"What?"

"My virtue."

Rosalyn smiled softly, though she wanted to laugh. Her true-blood royal family had attachments to things that she saw as an accessory.

"Would that really be so bad, if it secured your kingdom? He's a man's man, and not unattractive."

Bianca sighed off to the side of the waters.

"Maybe. It's the one thing that has always been off the table in any deal, with anyone."

Rosalyn shrugged.

"He wants you, not your kingdom. Technically, he already has a kingdom of his own. And there are far more treacherous men in this land than Silas Khan."

"True. Still ..."

Rosalyn put up a hand to silence her sister.

"Talk to Margerette and look to your defenses. Be sure that the north will stand with you. As for the south, have Catherine go down and talk with Silas. Blue Bill has always treated her with princess-like respect. She'll be able to feel out his intentions without any bartering."

Bianca nodded. It all made sense, when someone else said it.

"That sounds like good advice."

"I generally give good advice. Now, if Neeron really is at war, what is the status of your exports?"

Bianca made another face.

"We have just started to collect up the larger amounts for export and they are sitting on the docks as we speak. The ships were coming and going from Neeron, and then just stopped."

"Do you have a plan for the immediate future?"

Bianca looked into the water and grinned.

"I do, and he lives in a nice desert kingdom to the north."

Rosalyn laughed this time, rippling the water at her end of the connection.

"Funny, but I was thinking the same thing. If The Freelands only trades for the salt, I will be happy to send it all that way."

"I had planned on sending Ubar everything that they could handle, and worry about the bartering later. I'm sure as shit not sending it to that usurper queen."

"If the Kraetons are forced to look internally, they have the grain fields to survive a mild winter. I wouldn't worry about Neeron eating, directly. Send your excess stores to Ubar and make friends with the desert prince. Talk to Margerette and have Catherine talk to Silas."

"More good advice."

"It is, sweet sister. Now relax and do those things that you can do. The rest is out of your hands."

Bianca thanked her sister as the image in the water shimmered out of existence. As the waters smoothed out and returned to calm, she looked around the gardens. Where was Catherine at?

Chapter Forty

Just like the old woman said, Bernard and Quinn turned north up the valley once they made their way past Tyna Town. The route north was not as well trod as the route south had been, but it was smooth-enough for two sturdy men. The distance had been covered without conversation. Both Bernard and Quinn had heard stories about the old woman in black. They both had always assumed that the stories were just tavern tales. It had been said that the old woman in black was a harbinger of doom. That her appearance signaled one's pending death or sticky bad end. She walked the world looking for those ready to leave and told them how to be about their task. Those were the stories, anyway.

Currently, Quinn was questioning most of them. The old woman was definitely a harbinger, but of doom? To him, her mutterings seemed pretty neutral. Her words did lead them to make decisions though. They would definitely not be heading north if they hadn't had run into her. But was she leading them to their inevitable end? Quinn suspected not. He had always had a good feeling for when death was present. The sensation swirled around him most days just like a warm breeze. Bernard had commented more than one time that he just knew when there was killing to be done. It was basically true. He could just look at people and know that the world would be a better place without them.

The two came to a medium-sized rise in the land which looked down into a pleasant green, bowl-shaped valley in the mountain pass.

Toward the valley's eastern edge, along the path which led through it, a tent could be seen along with some men and mounts. The tent was a heavy linen affair with a pole holding up its middle. Ivy vines were stitched into the cloth around the doorway, signifying both an entrance and wealth. An all but consumed fire reflected red embers as a group of men stood about in varying states of conversation. Bernard looked over at his big friend, who was pulling his longbow free from his shoulder.

"Princess?"

Quinn nodded as he notched the bow and checked the bowstring for a secure seating.

"Looks as though. From the ivy stitching on the tent, I'm betting she's Crown Princess de Santi, out of Oban."

"What's she doing in Neeron?"

"Good question. Probably have to ask her to get an answer."

Quinn pointed toward a spot to the west, slightly downhill of where the tent was located. A group of men were slowly advancing unseen on the tent.

"And right on time, there's the trouble the old woman said we'd find."

Bernard looked at the men, then looked at Quinn and sighed.

"Shit for luck these days. Intervene?"

Quinn nodded solidly.

"That's why we were sent here."

Bernard pulled his swords free and stepped off down the path as Quinn moved down the hill in a line more directly toward the opposition. Quinn ended up having to shift up to a jog to engage the men before they attacked the tent. Pausing at a good spot for view, he pulled two arrows free of the quiver and notched them so that the flights of the arrows were overlapping each other. Pulling the two wooden missiles back to launch position, he could feel every muscle in his back and shoulder strain against the great weight of the bow stave. It only took seconds of the sheer force to tear open the wound Shadowman had inflicted on his arm. Blood began to trickle down tightened skin. More knowing than aiming, he loosed the metal tipped projectiles into the late morning air and reached for two more. One, two, three, and four volleys were set loose in the time it would take a good archer to draw a solid breath behind the first. His arrow attack streaked through the air and slammed into the advancing men from above without warning. Three men dropped like stones and a fourth howled in pain as an arrow punched through his leg.

The howl from the downed man brought the inattentive royal guards into action. They managed to muster weapons before the advancing end of the remaining opposition came into direct contact. Bernard was running and shaking his head at the same time as he watched the royal guards get cut down one after another. The mercenary bounty man entered the fray with a sword in each hand, and the control of a master fighter. He ran the sharp edge of his short swords through two men when he noticed the long shadow of his friend Quinn's battle axe appear on the scene. He assumed while swinging that Quinn had shot arrows as fast as he could and then came in at full speed. He wasn't one to miss the business end of things. After all, there was a certain satisfaction about looking someone in the eye when you killed them.

Quinn took a long upward arching swing with the double-bitted weapon, separating the last attacker's head and right shoulder from his body and sending the parts rolling back down the incline like a child's toy. Pulling back on the handle to zero in on the next swing, he realized that he and Bernard were now standing alone in a sea of bodies. He paused and lowered the blade slightly. Giving the battlefield a full review, he noticed no more opposition, and more importantly, no female forms.

"I'm going back to get my bow and pull the good arrows. Why don't you dispatch this lot? I'm guessing that she's still hiding in her tent."

Quinn thumbed in the direction of the tent as he turned to head back in the direction he had run in from. When he returned, he found Bernard hovering over one of the royal guards. The man's wounds were mortal, and it seemed as though Bernard was giving him some sort of reassurance. Standing after a moment, he looked over at Quinn.

"Seems we're done with the first part. Probably need to find the princess now?"

Quinn reached out and dropped a big stack of full weight gold coins into Bernard's hands. As Bernard pulled his hands in to look at the items, Quinn smiled solemnly.

"Guess where our dead friends here came from?"

Bernard looked down at the gold coins. The things just kept piling up around them.

"The nice Queen of Ayr sent some men to say hello. Question of the day; were they sent for her or us?"

Quinn looked across the array of dead bodies on the ground and thought for a moment. They looked to be more hired muscle than soldier.

"I'm betting they were hired for us, and this whole mess was just a target of opportunity."

Bernard nodded in agreement.

"Boy, that smells right. Especially if Shadowman knew where we might be as well."

Quinn was about to say something stoic when a gasp came from the direction of the tent. The pair turned to see a woman with a ghastly expression on her face. Bernard looked over at Quinn and shrugged.

"There's our princess."

Quinn looked at Crown Princess Maria de Santi, heir to the house of Oban, and measured her countenance. Five-foot-eight and a willowy 8.2 stone, with long brown hair and what Quinn was guessing were grey eyes, she looked closer to Bernard's age than his own. To Quinn's trained eyes she appeared more pampered than powerful. That was okay, princesses tended to be that way.

"You sure she's the princess?"

Princess Maria looked around at the scattered presentation of dead men and began to shake and cry. She then looked at the only two left standing with an instantaneous look of fear.

"You killed all of my men! Why? What do you want of me?"

The princess began to cower back into the opening of her tent. Bernard looked at Quinn as if to say, *told you so.*

"Yup. Princess."

Quinn sighed.

"Shit."

Three long hours passed as they explained to the crying princess that the dead men had come to kill her guards, and they had happened along and killed the men. The two of them were as much as pawns in the game as she was. Once she started to calm down, the conversation became easier.

It turned out that the princess had been traveling home from diplomatic meetings in Udaass. They had stopped in this valley the evening before. The more she calmed, the better-spoken she became.

Bernard explained that war had come to Neeron, and she was no longer safe in the kingdom. The princess protested, saying that she was well-known to the Regent of Graycott and that no army would march against Neeron. Bernard spent some time educating the princess on the status of current events.

"Ayr marched south many days ago. War came to Neeron when Ayr invaded. The Ayr army killed everyone in the Watchtower of Kalduhr when they crossed the border. Everyone on the road has said that the Capital of Karacase has fallen and old King Lorimere is dead."

It took some time for the princess to absorb the potential problem she found herself in.

"What does Ayr want with Neeron?"

Bernard was about to respond when Quinn finally spoke. He had been standing silently in the tent's doorway the whole time, scanning the open area for more trouble.

"The queen doesn't want Neeron at all. It was a reason to assemble the army. She's just moving through it on her way to Oban."

The princess was shocked by the statement, but now calm enough to think clearly.

"Why would Ayr dare invade Oban? What is to be gained? Oban is well defended with a sizeable army."

Bernard looked up at Quinn.

"It's not Ayr, per se. It's the Queen of Ayr, specifically. She wants the scepter that your father carries as proof of rule."

"Why does she want to control Oban?"

Quinn could tell that his previous statement hadn't taken, so he let the whole conversation go.

"What difference does it make why? Why is irrelevant. Right now, you are in a warzone outside your own country and in need of solid protection."

Maria de Santi had assumed that the big one of the two was the muscle and the talking one was the brains of the pair, but now she wasn't so sure.

"All right, what would you suggest that I do? We were headed for the seaside road which leads south from Udaass along the mountain edge to the border with Oban. The mountains should still give me protection from the war, if I move fast toward home, don't you think?"

Quinn looked out at the tableau of dead men around the tent. The mountains might hide her, and they might not.

"The mountain pass may still be safe, but if it isn't you'll have nowhere to run to when you find out. We'll go with something a little more solid. We're headed back to Tyna Town. There, we'll hire a boat to sail us out and around to the capital of Castropol or the Watchtower of Bohumin. It will add a few days but be safer for you."

The princess looked at the big blond mercenary solidly. No single point of his plan was unsound. He was a thinker and tactical. He looked vaguely familiar, like someone in a painting she had seen once. She thought they might have met before somewhere. She met a lot of people in her travels, but not a lot of mercenaries.

"Have we ever met before?"

"Not that I know of, your highness. Now, we really should be on our way."

"Our way? Why are you going with me?"

"Call it providence," Bernard said happily.

The princess stood and straightened her dress.

"What about my things?"

"What about them?" Quinn said bluntly. "You can have your things or your life. It's your choice. Make it now."

"I won't be talked to in that manner. I'm the Crown Princess of Oban," Maria said with an uppity tone.

Quinn looked at Bernard and then back at Maria de Santi.

"I don't care if you're happy or sad. Let's get moving before anyone else comes along."

The princess collected a cloak from the back of a chair and stepped to the door. Pausing in the door, she took in the image of all the dead men.

"What about my men?"

"Sadly, the wolves need to eat just like you," Quinn said, not looking back or waiting.

Chapter Forty-One

Anistasia walked the stone hallways of Karacase's subterranean prison cells with a lightness in her step and a tune on her lips. Things in her world were going completely to task. Neeron had fallen like water from a high point, just as planned. Ayr's military losses had been minimal. Those losses had been somewhat compensated for by Neeron's converts. From a military point of view, her commander Stas Bok was proving to be a masterful leader. He was also proving to be a good teacher. She had already learned several lessons about leading troops. Those lessons would prove useful in the coming months.

She was making her way from the confinement cells to the work area of the dungeon. They had given ex-Queen Vivian a particularly uncomfortable cell to stay in while she waited to be transported north to the dungeons of Kanash. Anistasia wasn't going to leave her here, where she had loyalists and sympathizers to aid her. No, that type of resistance just would not do.

The body chains the new jailer had fashioned Vivian into, heavy iron chains collared at the neck and waist with shackles at her wrists and ankles, would be her new home until after she was sent north. Young Vivian was going to be dumped into a place where she had no power and left until a situation arose where Anistasia could trade her for something of value. She really was quite a prize to have. Many a man would give up a lot to have a queen of her caliber. Anistasia decided that she better send blunt word north with Vivian that she was not to be spoiled. The thought of Neeron's queen getting passed around between the jailers in Kanash until she lacked all value made Anistasia smile, just as the tears streaming down the young queen's face had done when she stopped to talk with her.

Stepping into the work area of the dungeon, the sight that greeted her made her smile grow broad. It was exactly the thing she had needed to put her day over the top.

Against the far wall of the large open area a heavy wooden apparatus stood leaning against the stone wall at a forty-five-degree angle. The raised wooden frame, with restraints at one end and a wooden roller at the other, came down from the hard men of the previous age. It was known as the rack.

Currently stretched out across it was a mid-aged woman with dark brown hair. Anistasia was guessing she went about five-foot five-inches tall and eight- and a half stone, if she was standing upright. With full lips and hazel eyes, she had an alluring appeal. Anistasia knew that any allure she possessed would be completely gone when this event was over.

The dungeon keeper was slowly turning the roller to its next notch to apply an increased pressure to the woman's joints. The roller clicked into its gear stop and the woman howled in pain, managing to push tears out of eyes long devoid of them. She had been slowly stretched almost to the breaking point. A handful of clicks more and her joints would start to tear free from her body.

The dungeon keeper turned slightly and took in the smiling visage of the queen. He paused and bowed.

"Your majesty. Good day to you."

The Queen of Ayr and Neeron softened her smile and nodded to her dungeon keeper-turned- torturer.

"Has she said anything useful yet?"

"No majesty, but we're right at the point where most give up. So, it shouldn't be long now," a scribe sitting nearby stated.

The scribe sitting on a comfortable stool next to the naked and tortured Mistress of Neeron looked neutral, as if taking dictation for a meeting of shopkeepers.

The queen walked over to the side of the rack where she could look at Neeron's mistress directly. The scribe might be right, Anistasia could tell that the woman's will was all but in tatters. Anistasia looked down over the woman's naked frame. The mistress's breasts were easily the size of her own, and her skin was smooth and well-kept for a woman of her years. Anistasia couldn't see any of the obvious signs of childbirth about her body and knew that it was too late for her to consider that now.

The queen nodded to the dungeon keeper, and he untied the red cloth from around her mouth. The headdress was the thing that denoted her as a mistress, and it was now the thing being used to silence her. The choice of the gag seemed a fantastic touch. Anistasia ran a hand over the woman's chest and abdomen softly and with a look of pleasure.

"Olivia, why do you resist? I know you were born in Oban and raised in a small town outside the Watchtower Fortress of Bohumin. You haven't been in Neeron so long, have you?"

Anistasia touched Olivia's cheek softly, with the touch of a lover.

"If you tell us what we want to know about Oban, all of this will end. I promise that it will stop immediately."

She waited for Olivia to gather what little bit of her wits she still possessed.

"I don't know what you want."

Anistasia nodded and the dungeon keeper turned the roller to its next stop without any forewarning. The click of the gear was instantaneously followed by a howling scream from the Mistress of Neeron. The piercing noise echoed down the stone hallways of the subterranean dungeon. Anistasia didn't as much as flinch when the mistress screamed directly next to her ears. Her self-control worried both of the men in the room greatly.

"Now, Olivia, I said it would stop if you talked. If you don't talk, it will get worse. Oh yes, dear mistress, it will get much, much worse."

Anistasia stepped back from the rack and nodded down at the mistress's red head covering. The torturer reinstalled the woman's gag tightly, making sure that the cloth didn't block her nose. She needed to breathe. Anistasia put her lighthearted smile back on and turned from Olivia toward the door.

"Why don't you heat up her skin a little? See if that has the desired effect on her tongue? She's a mistress and knows Oban's defenses. She grew up in Oban and studied there before going to the temple. I want to know when she cracks."

Olivia looked across the room in horror as her torturer lit a torch in the flames of the dungeon's fireplace. Anistasia walked to the door with a pronounced lightness in her step.

The new Queen of Neeron walked into the throne room and took in the assemblage of people. There were several regents from the old regime, a collection of aristocrats, and the royal guard. Anistasia looked about the room with a lack of concern. No guild masters were in the room, no members of the mint, nor anyone who spoke for the running of the land. Stas Bok wasn't there either. She was guessing that he was still busy with other affairs.

Anistasia Nosov, Queen of Neeron, walked to the dais. Stepping up onto the raised platform which held the empty king and queen's throne, she looked down at the two crowns sitting gently on the seat cushions and smiled broadly. She scooped up both crowns before sitting down in the king's throne in a luxurious fashion. Adjusting herself in old man Jasper's seat, she found it less comfortable than she would have expected from a man of his advanced years. Smiling over at the head of her royal guard, she nodded her head in such a way that suggested he approach.

"Be a dear and put these with the scepter. Nobody in Neeron will be needing them anytime soon."

"Yes, majesty," the guard pronounced with authority, collecting the two royal crowns. He turned and handed the crowns off to a more junior man, taking in the broken looks of the well-to-do people in the room.

"Now," the queen said in a more-business tone, "where is Sanson Zear at?"

A large, imposing figure pushed off a side wall and strode to the receiving spot before the dais. The queen looked him over a second time, for surety. She had chosen him out of her group because he possessed all the hallmarks of good middle management. He was imposing, stern, had good vision, wasn't for tolerating disobedience, and was prone to violence. Anistasia's second look at the man showed she was right with her first assessment.

"Sanson Zear."

The man nodded and bowed before his ruler.

"I name you caretaker, and lead regent for the principality of Neeron. Anyone in your land that disagrees with your stewardship of this principality, whether they be barons or bondsman, shall be put to the headsman. Afterward, their lands and property will be given over to the crown, by order of the queen."

"I will do my duty, majesty."

"Yes, and your duty is to keep Neeron's food crops and mines humming along, the same as they were last week."

"It will be done, majesty."

Anistasia could hear the power in the man's voice. Change required a strong hand. His hand would be strong.

"You will need to rebuild your defense forces. Choose wisely as I'll accept no dissension, understand?"

The big man nodded once, authoritatively, and then bowed.

"It will be done, majesty."

"Good," the Queen of Neeron and Ayr said, standing. There was a quick shuffle as everyone in the room bowed, out of a deep concern for a long life. "You have a great amount of work to do. I'll let you get to it."

Sanson Zear was just taking the dais when Anistasia made the throne room door. Half of the royal guard moved with her this time; the remainder stayed fast in the throne room as a show of force. All-in-all, she was having a really good day. She decided that next she would track down Stas Bok and check on his mood. They would need to be heading south soon.

Chapter Forty-Two

It had taken several days to quell the major resistance in the city and get the aristocracy onboard with the queen's way of thinking. In truth, several days was faster than anyone in a gambling den would have wagered coin on. The queen's choice in caretaker for the new vassal principality of Neeron, Sanson Zear, proved himself to the wealthy class as an even-handed man. That alone went most of the way toward getting the City of Karacase in line.

The huge number of bodies now occupying the area around the capital city was having a distinctly different effect on the morale of the populous. The Ayr army was drinking, eating, and brawling the city into starvation. The situation wasn't sustainable for much longer, and Anistasia Nosov knew it.

Walking up the wide stone steps which lead from the interior of Karacase's castle fortress onto the ramparts of its interior surround, the queen saw the armor-plated back of the very person she came looking for. Standing square on the wide fighting line of the interior ramparts, looking out into the surrounding city, Stas Bok scanned the streets and buildings for any sign of unrest.

Even with his being the captain of the city defenses in Kanash, the queen knew that peacekeeping wasn't what Stas was made for. He maintained peace well enough, but he was made for war. He was continuing to prove himself very, very good at war. The queen moved up beside him slowly, leaving all of her guard back down in the courtyard.

As protection went, they were quite good. But they weren't tacticians, or decidedly wise in any specific way. That second part seemed to annoy Stas.

"Good morning, majesty."

Stas didn't divert his vision to the queen, but kept it out over the city streets. This wasn't court, it was work.

"Good morning. What do you make of the city?"

Stas turned his head so that he might look down a long side street which led along the bottom of the interior fortifications. An older man was moving a cart along. He appeared to be one of the City People. The group held a well-respected place in Karacase society. The old man stopped at a building midway down the street and opened a hatch cover at the base of a multistory building. With a bucket on a rope fastened inside the hatch, the man began emptying out the waste from inside the pit and placing it in the cart. Stas watched for a moment and shrugged.

"Everything seems to have settled down adequately. For the moment, anyway."

The queen smiled, looking out over her new conquest.

"What do you make of the army's status?"

Stas made a face as to suggest that he had been thinking about that very thing.

"I think that it's time to put whatever long term plan you have for this place into action and be moving on. The army is eating and drinking this place dry and empty. Letting them do so will only cause unwanted unrest with the local population."

Anistasia smiled a noncommittal smile, as if to say that she thought the same thing.

"I do appreciate your directness. Most people here don't have the spine for that."

Stas shrugged again.

"It is what it is. I make decisions based upon the present, not what someone wants the present to be."

Anistasia nodded in agreement.

"Prudent. That's why I ask you these questions, not the entourage in the throne room."

Stas was about ready to ask her what she really climbed the rampart steps for when Adam, the Grandmaster of the Mechanics Guild, appeared in the courtyard below. Anistasia waved a hand to summon him up the steps to the surround and he began climbing the steps.

"Majesty, General." Adam greeted the pair with a brisk nod of the head which substituted for a bow in the current circumstances.

"Guild Master, how is your morning?"

The burly man smiled broadly.

"Timing aside, majesty, quite grand. I was in the middle of securing my breakfast when the herald appeared with your invitation."

Both Anistasia and Stas smiled, as if to say that it was going around.

"I'm sorry to hear that. I'll do my best not to keep you from it unduly."

"How may the Guild be of service, ma'am?"

Business first. Anistasia liked that about him.

"I have a project for you and your Guild."

"Yes, ma'am. I had assumed that you didn't invite me along on this grand adventure just to keep your dozen cannons working and your armor fixed. Is this the project we spoke of earlier?"

The queen smiled broadly. She had two men with a spine in her company of thousands.

"No, Adam, but that project should get underway as soon as things are quiet."

Adam made a neutral expression.

"Yes, ma'am."

"Now, south on the way to Orba, taking the fork that leads to the mountain mines, Neeron has a set of foundries."

The Guild Master nodded.

"Yes. At the base of the mountains, in a little hamlet. I know the place you mean."

"Good. I would like you to travel there. I would like you and your brothers to make me some new cannons."

Adam and Stas both turned inward toward the queen, who was standing between them.

"Do you have any specific requirements or are you just adding to your current arsenal?'

The queen looked down at the stone under her feet for a couple of long seconds.

"I would like you to keep the maneuverability of the ones that we possess, and the power, but double the range."

"Double the range of the same sized cannonball?'

The queen looked at the Guild Master squarely.

"You can all but guarantee that if we make our way through Oban and reach the capital city at Land's End, they are going to destroy the bridges leading onto the capital island in a defensive measure."

Both men nodded in agreement.

"Once there, we are committed. And, once there, we don't have cannon enough to span the gap between the mainland and the island. I will need something with the range to hit the island. That means that we either build massive catapults, which will take time, or we bring bigger cannons."

Both men nodded in agreement a second time.

"Once we get to the capital, with our face to the sea, we cannot stop and camp for the time that it will take to construct catapults. That would invite an attack from our back. An attack from our back would leave us pinned into a position where we can't fight or run."

Stas Bok smiled slightly this time. The Guild Master simply nodded.

"When would you like your new cannons, ma'am?"

Anistasia looked over to Stas Bok, who made a contemplative face.

"Hmm, a good five days or so to march south to the Oban border and pound their initial force into submission. A full week's march south on to Castropol, where we will no doubt deal with the main army of Oban and reinforcements from the Watchtower at Bohumin. Regroup at the crossing and look out onto the island. Say, 17 days?"

The Grand Master of the Mechanics Guild swallowed hard.

"It will take almost that many days just to figure out how to do the casting; not to mention the time needed to design, build, and test them."

Stas looked at the queen and then back at Adam.

"I guess you're wasting time standing here then?"

The big man nodded to the queen respectfully and turned to head back down the stairs.

The queen turned her head to speak to Adam as he made his way down the stairs.

"Send the bill to Sanson Zear. The new caretaker of Neeron."

Stas looked back down the long street to where the man from the City People had been doing his work. The hatch by the building was now closed. He had apparently finished his work and moved on, the same as Stas was about to do. Looking over at the queen, he produced a neutral expression.

"You learn fast. I might get to retire after all."

The queen smiled knowingly at her commander.

"Not quite yet."

They both looked out at the city for several minutes without talking. If one didn't know better, they might be led to believe that it was an ordinary day in Neeron's capital city.

"What's your plan for after?"

Stas didn't look over. His voice was quiet, almost distant somehow.

"What do you mean?"

"I mean when it's all over and done, whatever this is? After you've taken the kingdoms of the continent, or the world, I mean whenever you plan to stop. After you've won whatever it is that you want to win, then what? The known land will have been turned upside down. You'll have one country with a queen, as opposed to six or seven kingdoms with leaders. What's your plan? Is it all going to become one kingdom? Will you let vassal kings and queens rule minor lands? Or are you just out to let it all burn?"

Anistasia was growing to like Stas Bok more every day. He was the only one of them who had the balls to ask the hard questions. To speak to her as if she were a person. He made pointed comments. And what she liked most was that he knew how to do it. He only spoke level with her when they were alone, and when they were on equal footing with one another. He was much more of a politician than she had given him credit for.

"In the end, it will probably all end up in flames. But until then, the idea of vassal kings and queens resonates pretty well. Keeping the basic structure intact will make the transition of power easier for the people as a whole. It will probably present the opportunity for fewer uprisings."

"That sounds about right. In that case, we probably want to be on our way sooner rather than later. The army is eating these people out of house and home. Summer is not long from becoming autumn. Hungry and cold people are the very stuff of uprisings."

The queen made a telling face as she looked out over the roof tops of Karacase. Her general was spot-on in his assessment. It was definitely time to be going.

"Let's take a walk, general."

The two turned inward, and the queen led Stas down the wide stone steps back into the interior courtyard of the castle fortress. They moved on at a casual pace, the queen's royal guard falling into formation around them as they passed by.

The queen moved slowly but with purpose. After all, movement was a display of power to those watching from the shadows. In the castle, men-at-arms, servants, and laypeople of all stations scattered as the group moved from one room to another. Making the entrance to the throne room, the lead guard opened the doors to the large chamber, visually dismissing the old king's herald in the process. The queen made a mental note to have her guard back down their bias. She had no intentions of ever becoming benevolent, but pacifying the gentry helped quell uprisings.

Sanson Zear abruptly stopped the conversation he was engaged in with a local aristocrat and stood upon seeing the queen enter. Everyone in the throne room paused, and bowed or curtsied, as if their lives depended upon their performance, which they did. The action made the queen smile. They better understand who was running the place now. She paused her stroll in front of the dais and leveled a neutral gaze at Sanson Zear.

"How are the affairs of state?"

Zear adjusted his countenance to a much more subdued one that he had been employing a moment earlier.

"Majesty, things in the kingdom are coming back to the middle fairly quickly."

"Principality."

Zear nodded respectfully.

"Yes, principality, majesty."

The queen considered the original statement for a second or two.

"Good, I'm glad to hear that. Do you have a good grip on things?"

Zear nodded respectfully, like a child at schooling.

"Yes, majesty. There are still a few pockets of resistance and some issues to be sorted, but yes."

The queen made a quizzical face and then turned to Stas Bok.

"Can we afford to leave a company of infantry here to bolster his cause?"

Stas quickly considered his options.

"Yes, majesty. That shouldn't be an issue."

"Good. Pick one of the more loyal ones, would you?"

Stas Bok nodded appropriately and the queen turned back to Zear.

"The army will be readying to march south today. That should alleviate some of your immediate problems. We will be taking enough food to get us on our way. You should look to Neeron's trade deals and see what outgoing stores you can retain to compensate the people for the oncome of winter."

Sanson Zear visibly relaxed. Apparently, what the people were going to eat was one of his main agenda items.

"Yes, majesty. We will make proper preparations."

"Excellent. Now, get to it."

The queen turned and started back for the door she had just come in through. Stas Bok looked to Sanson Zear and shrugged, as if to say that he was on his own now, and turned to follow the queen.

Chapter Forty-Three

The horse had been on the move for the entire afternoon without complaint. The large beast barely noticed the added weight of its passenger as it moved along the queen's road heading into the fortified garrison town of Knightsbridge. The rider, cloaked in black, rode on all but unnoticed to the local townsfolk. The rider on the big warhorse had been seen on this road many times over the years. People generally knew to let her pass unbothered.

The rider and her steed moved on at a continued pace out the south side of Knightsbridge. The big warhorse advancing as if on autopilot, east toward the Y in the roadway which allowed travelers to properly turn south onto the only road leading that way.

The moon was up and dim, heading toward a dark night, when the rider came to the single bridge to span the great chasm. Stretching out of sight from the ocean to the east until the mountains in the west of the continent, the great chasm in the earth cut the western continent in two like a jet-black river painted upon the nighttime dim. Hovering above the chasm directly ahead of the rider was the only crossing of any kind. A wide, heavily built stone bridge known as the Knight's Bridge stood ahead of her in the darkness like an aberration. She had seen the sight many times in her life. Each of those times, whether day or night, the sight still shocked her.

The great chasm was a scar which cut directly across the continent and physically separated the lower lands from the Kingdom of Meridian, which controlled the entire middle of the continent. Though not terribly wide, the gash in the land dropped out of sight into the stone belly of the planet and was said to be without a bottom. Though it ran into the mountains on the west side of the land and didn't cut the land truly in two, the mountains running down the western spine of the continent were all but completely impassable. Piles of jagged rock so high that they were continuously covered by ice and snow, from the capital city of Meridian to the flatlands at the south end of the landmass. Other than costly, rough roads for the opening of Meridian's mines, the mountains were unbothered by people, and formed the secure western anchor that the great ravine disappeared into.

Folklore said that the chasm had been caused by the ending of the last age, when the great battles of men shook the world till it ripped itself in two. Those same battles were said to have produced the vast Central Sea that now separated the two major landmasses of the world. The stories were just that, stories. What was true was that the massive crossing known as the Knight's Bridge, which was the only thing allowing land passage from north to south, was created at the very start of the current age. A heavy span of cut stone, it had been fashioned by men left over from the previous age, before they shuffled off to the next place.

As would be expected of such a thing, in an age such as the current one, the garrison town of Knightsbridge was the domain of the Watchtower Guild. The Guild controlled the crossing via the Watchtower fortress of Knightsbridge to the south of the crossing. They kept the peace between the settled lands to the north and the less law-abiding lands to the south.

The rider in black rode up to the bridge guard, stopping an appropriate distance away so that she was visible in the darkness. Sliding the cloak's hood off of her head in a practiced move produced a mane of blonde hair and a delicate expression. The guard, a sturdy and capable soldier, inspected his visitor. A small creature sitting atop a large warhorse. She was covered by a cloak as black as the night around her. The cloak all but covered a wine-red dress of high quality. From a spot just above where her heart would be, a reddish glow pushed its way through the cloth of the cloak. She moved to better cover the subtle glow. Of course, the red glow and the head of blonde hair was all that the soldier required to positively identify her in the darkness. He turned his head to yell over to the crossing guards who moved the barriers at either end of the bridge.

"Princess Catherine Rhodes has arrived to cross the bridge. Open the gates and stand aside."

"You're very kind, sir," Catherine returned in her quiet manner.

Catherine replaced the hood of the cloak to obscure her features and begged the horse forward. Her mount stepped off toward the bridge, not completely comfortable with the looming darkness about to be under its hooves.

Getting to where the guard was standing, Catherine tossed the man a small leather bag full of coins. The normal price of crossing was two copper coins, same as would be expected for a pint back in town. The coins the bag held were enough for a small army to make the crossing. In truth, it was a token from the Kingdom to the Guild. The guard caught the bag and shook his head under its weight.

"The lady is too kind."

"The Watchtower is ever our ally."

Princess Catherine continued on without pausing, the horse producing a pronounced thud as its shoed hooves slapped down on the stone surface of the bridge. The big beast quickly found its footing on the new surface, and with a gentle pat from its rider, moved across the span with a smooth cadence.

Every soldier in the bridge detail moved to give the princess a wide berth as she crossed. Where it was universally agreed upon that Princess Catherine Rhodes was the most genuine and nicest of the royal sisters, out in the rural and quiet parts of the land some said she was a witch. The pendant she wore allowing her to fly in the sky like birds, and make thunder and lightning come down from the clouds. Like the stories of how the great ravine had come to be, they were just stories. It was unheard of, however, for a member of the royal family, especially one of her station, to travel the lands without an armed escort. That surely could only be put down to the magic pendant around her neck. The one said to defend her against evil or attack. The one, that it was said, no person could remove from her body. The stories didn't genuinely matter to folk. Not really. Witch or princess, she was universally loved just for being kind.

Once on the far side of the chasm, Princess Catherine put in at the Watchtower fortress for the remainder of the evening. At the end of a hard three-week ride, the commander ushered her inside and into a comfortable room without ceremony. Her steed was given a good stable and two men to look after it with food and brushing. The travel had been long, and Catherine slept soundly until nearly midday. Deciding not to start the trip into the lax lands of the south at such an hour, she enquired if it was possible to stay another night. As the commander was in no position to say no, he said yes, and Catherine passed the day on the surround with the garrison watch looking out over the seemingly quiet lands to the south.

The sun had no more than cracked the edge of the world when rider and mount were off once more. This time the big warhorse was at full gallop and the dainty rider atop it was holding on for purchase. Catherine wasn't really worried about falling off, as the two of them were well-practiced at this section of the journey. She also wasn't so much in a hurry, but it just didn't pay to linger and present an opportunity for thieves in the lawless lands of the south. Truth be known, none of the lawless in this lawless section of the continent were going to risk crossing the Watchtower, the Kingdom of Meridian's army, or, more importantly, crossing Captain Blue Bill Montgomery. To do such would surely get them done in. Still, Catherine knew that it paid to be prudent.

The big horse ran at stride for most of the morning hours. Catherine pulled him up to rest and drink at a cool stream with some trees. Waiting until she was sure that he wouldn't lather, she jumped back on and they were off again.

The princess put in at two houses which she knew to be safe along the way. The farmers were always happy to see the princess and her coin, as times in the lax lands could be unpredictable. She was safe and slept well at both locations. The farmers had capable men in their employ. Catherine would stay the night and be off with the sunrise.

The afternoon of the third day in the lax lands was broken into sequences of ride hard and rest before the afternoon sun tipped over the west side of the world and the outer edge of Bay Side came into view. Catherine slowed to a trot and rode into the capital of the pirate kingdom, if there was such a thing, with a manner befitting its owner. She made her way down quiet streets, greeted openly by several of the locals, moving inward toward the bay. Turning a corner in the street, the deep-water port of Bay Side came into view. It was almost completely full of ships. She made a face at the scene. The ridiculously independent privateers, ruffians, scoundrels, and cutthroats of the pirate ranks didn't normally convene to discuss matters. They almost always deferred, usually under threat of cannon fire, to Blue Bill's ideas, as he was the decided-upon leader of the gang. Otherwise, they did as they pleased.

Catherine moved quietly to an imposing three-story building, with columns and wide steps, which fronted the focal point of the harbor. Looking at it she smiled. Blue Bill Montgomery's residence was loud and raucous. All the noise meant that he was at home. That was good. Catherine continued on and made her way around the back of the building to a stable on the backstreet. She dismounted and deposited her horse with the stable man. He smiled brightly when the coin hit his palm.

"I'll take better care of him than I do my wife, Princess."

Catherine smiled in her tired and melancholy way.

"That makes me feel sad for your wife, but thank you."

The stable man laughed and began unbuckling the woman's riding saddle as Catherine made her way out of the stable, across the street, and into the back door of the once-opulent building that was now Pirate Central.

The young Princess of Meridian didn't need to speak as she moved through the building. People parted a path for her on sight. No one questioned her presence or purpose. They simply moved from her path and bowed their heads for good measure.

Silas Khan, aka Blue Bill Montgomery, aka Pirate King, stood at the top of a wide stairway leading up out of the grand lower ballroom area. The house was absolutely full and he had needed to migrate up to the second-floor landing for a place quiet enough to talk with the two ship captains standing by him. The designated leader of the pirates felt the silence sweep into the room beneath him and turned to see what had prompted the change in sound level. Looking down from his vantage point, he locked his gaze onto the outline of the princess and smiled broadly, yet suspiciously.

"Is that the Princess of Meridian?" One of the captains asked to no one in particular, almost sounding shocked.

"That it is," Blue Bill said with surety.

Catherine located Silas in the throng of people and continued at her steady cadence through the crowd and up the wide staircase. Pausing at the top step of the grandly carved affair, one step below where Silas Khan and the two captains were standing, Catherine slid the cloak hood back onto her shoulders, exposing her radiant sun-blonde hair and soft features. She put her hands together and bowed her head slightly, the normal first greeting of one royal to another.

"Is there safe port for a stranger in a strange land?"

Silas Khan smiled at the gesture as if his cheeks would break, and then dropped to one knee, forcing the other captains and everyone in the ballroom below to follow suit.

"A safe harbor and a warm hearth, m'lady, for you are not a stranger, but a welcome guest."

Catherine smiled softly.

"Thank you, Silas."

The three captains stood in a small wave as Catherine stepped up onto the landing.

"Highness, you must have ridden like the wind itself. I've heard nothing about you heading this way."

Much like her sister, Princess Margerette, the pirate lord had a well-established gossip network spread out around the various kingdoms of the planet. Silas Khan normally knew anything of note that was worth knowing.

"I made fine time. The roads across the land were quiet."

The princess and the pirate captain talked with an open comfort that no one else in the room would dare attempt with royalty. It reinforced his status as the most powerful of the pirate captains.

"I'm happy that you've come. Your assistance with the book men will be fully welcome. They have been busy as of late. Still, your timing seems odd. What brings you south?"

Unlike everyone else of affluence in the settled lands, Princess Catherine found a welcome comfort and a kind of joy in the pirates of Bay Side. In return for their hospitality, she offered her learning to help the book men balance their tally sheets. Even with a band of heathen cutthroats, the balance of the books needed to be checked and exact. As a schooled member of a royal house, no one questioned when Catherine did the sums and stated that the figures were one way or another. Her honesty and neutrality had gained her full acceptance in many places where sturdy men would hesitate to tread.

"I would be happy to assist the book men while I'm here, but that's not the reason for riding south. I'm here on business."

Silas made a face. Princess Catherine Rhodes never once had come to Bay Side on business. She came here to avoid it.

"What kind of business?"

"The Kingdom of Meridian and the Pirates of the World kind. Or Guild, I guess? If you chose to call yourselves one."

Silas Khan made a dire face and waved a hand out to one side, clearing a path for the princess turned envoy. Catherine stepped off without making a sound, the Pirate King one step behind her. The door to a large sitting area closed directly behind Silas, removing everyone else from the conversation.

Catherine removed her cloak and rolled her shoulders around to loosen up the knots in her back from the ride. She flipped her tousled hair from one side to the other to free the blonde locks from the wad the cloak had mashed them into. Finding herself set, she sat in a comfortable chair with a practiced elegance and smiled to her host as he handed over a large goblet of wine.

"So, all of this talk about war is true then?"

Silas sat in another chair, a proper distance from Catherine's.

"Yes. Rumor says that Neeron has fallen to the army of Ayr. Apparently, the army also killed every soldier in the Watchtower of Kalduhr on the way south."

"Kalduhr is located in Oban."

"Yes, but the garrison went to the defense of Neeron. To keep the peace, for all the good that it did."

Silas Khan took a drink. He knew what was coming next.

"And?"

Catherine collected herself and looked the big pirate straight in the eye. It made him instantly uncomfortable, which had never happened before.

"And, the House of Rhodes wants to know what the stance of the pirates is going to be in this whole affair. Are you going to be out profiting off the chaos? Are you going to be running wide and avoiding combat? Or are you going to stand firm, here in the south, when it all inevitably reaches our shores?"

Silas Khan shifted in his chair. He had conversed with Catherine countless times and had never known her to be this direct. Or, royal, maybe?

"Do you really think that it's coming here as well?'

Catherine looked down at her wrist. A small golden locket on a heavy chain hung gently against the edge of her palm. She slid the piece back up inside the collected cuff of her dress and thought. Silas watched the moment pass without words. He had seen the locket several times. Catherine wore it always, but never opened the clasp. He had always wondered what was inside it.

"It is inevitable. If the army of Ayr is going to march through all of the kingdoms of the central continent, and the Kraetons are all new subjects of Ayr, they certainly can't stop. All trust between the kingdoms is gone now."

Silas stood and began to pace.

"Are you implying that they are going to build a navy?"

Catherine shrugged.

"Ships are easy to build. You know that. It's even easier when you have a large subjugated workforce."

"And you want to know if we're your southern defense?"

Catherine fixed Silas with that look that made him uncomfortable again.

"No offense to your own formidable naval force moored in the harbor, but pirates are notoriously unreliable. That's part of what makes you all pirates. That bit of information makes the south end of the continent the softest spot in which to enter, when war inevitably comes. So, to be direct, are you going to disappear as they appear? Are you going to defend this space which you've all carved out for yourselves, or are you just another enemy that we'll need to deal with later?"

Silas Khan spun on his boot heels as if he'd been slapped in the face. Catherine's expression was unwavering, and all business. It was an older and wiser countenance somehow than the young lady she actually was. She put up a hand to keep him from saying anything ridiculous.

"We're all coming upon the days when people are as good as their word, or they're not. If Meridian is going to stand alone, say so now, and be done with it."

Silas Khan went back to pacing. He walked back and forth for a minute or more. When he stopped pacing, he looked sure. Catherine made a face that suggested he proceed.

"I have two statements to make, your royal highness."

Catherine considered the way that he used her reference as royalty and knew that she had pushed him too hard.

"First, I cannot speak for the Guild, as you put it. We are a loose collective and do as each of us sees fit to do. That being said, the ships in my command have NEVER run from a fight. EVER. We won't be running from this one, if it actually happens to come. I don't know, nor would I consider to say that we are your ally, but we are certainly not your enemy. The truce of the gorge is the truce."

Catherine considered the uneasy truce that had been watched over by the Watchtower for a century, the great chasm separating the lawless pirate lands to the south from the Kingdom of Meridian and the Freelands Folk to the north. It had been pushed to frayed edges upon occasion, but the truce was the truce.

"And your second statement?"

Silas sat back down in his chair and grabbed the pitcher.

"No offense to your sister, since I'm no battle commander, but I think her tactics are wrong. As a man who understands naval combat, I'm not landing my force down here in the south. That forces my entire army to bottleneck crossing Knights Bridge. Stas Bok doesn't make mistakes of that nature. If I was he, I would slam my force head-long into the Great Watchtower of Thorne."

Catherine was interested in his opinion. She was always interested when Silas spoke with the surety that he was speaking with now.

"Why?"

"Thorne has a deep-water port that will hold the better part of a naval fleet. The Watchtower itself is mighty, but it's only slightly defended, and susceptible to a good, sustained naval bombardment. It's built too close to water. And the Watchtower sits at the end of a good, wide road, which runs straight to the capital."

Everything the pirate said was sound.

"Why not travel around the southern tip and attack from the western shore? The march to the capital from the western shore is nothing at all."

"Because large land armies aren't good naval soldiers, and a man like Stas Bok knows that. He will take the most direct route from dry land to dry land, if he decides to come this way."

Catherine rolled it all around in her head a couple times. She wasn't the daughter raised to be a military leader. She didn't know about combat tactics or understand naval strategy, but what the pirate leader was saying rang true in her ears. She nodded, as if to say that they were done conversing, and stood, setting the untouched wine down on a small table.

"I appreciate your candor, Silas. And I apologize for my directness. But, as I said, we're coming up on a time when one is as good as their word, or they're not. If your book men would like me to look in on their work, I would be happy to do so. Otherwise, I'm headed back to the capital."

"Please, stay the night. It's too late to be on the roads anyway. I'll have your room prepared. Tomorrow, when the sun has risen, you can be on your way north again. Now that business has been concluded, let us be slightly more civil."

Catherine's soft, melancholy smile returned.

"Thank you, Silas. I'll go see the book men then."

Chapter Forty-Four

The deep brown eyes of King Marco de Santi burned as he read the dispatches from the outer lands of the kingdom. The garrison from the Watchtower of Kalduhr had been killed to a man. That meant that there was no defense in the entire upper third of the kingdom, from the border of Neeron all the way through the wastelands to Lugo. That, in and of itself, probably wasn't the real issue of the day. No one in their right mind was going to travel through the wastelands of the last age without reason. It was lawless country, full of misdeed and mystery. No, since the Ayr army had marched basically straight south from Kanash to Karacase, they would likely march straight south out of Karacase again. *If that was the case,* Marco thought, *Castropol would be ready for them.*

The dispatch from Woetown, the settlement closest to the Neeron border, stated that every able-bodied man, strong boy, and sturdy woman had been armed and readied for combat. The dispatch from Orba, the city closest to the mountain passes, said that they had assembled almost as much of the army as they were going to commit there. They were waiting for the remainder of the miners and mountain folk to come down out of the hills and join them. Still, they should be at full strength before they needed to fight.

The dispatch from Lugo was the most promising of the bad news he had seen. Their entire force had been assembled and Count Luca Perin had them all marching east toward Orba. Perin was a seasoned warrior.

He had won more battles in his life than he had lost. The army would be in good hands until the commander from the capital arrived. Perin also knew the lay of the land. He had been born and raised in Neeron, so he would know how to use the terrain going north.

Marco rubbed his eyes. They were dry from all of the reading. He straightened up in his chair and arched his back to take the stiffness out of his muscles. Setting the stack of letters down on the table, he stood and began to pace about his study room. The view out of his open window showed the sea and the mountains on the mainland to the north. Everything about that view was quiet. That was the way with things like war. They were quiet, and then instantly, they were not.

Marco pounded a fist on the stone window ledge. There would really be war in his time. He was the third in his line to be king of Oban. With the exception of the years directly following the start of the age, which had been led by a different line, the years of the de Santi reign had been quiet and successful. There had been many battles along the way, but a legitimate war had never been fought.

The door to the study opened behind him and he turned to see the queen enter with Watchtower Captain Rolant Thiralle, commander of the nearby Bohumin Fortress. Marco looked at Rolant squarely. A large man, all of six-foot three inches and a muscled fifteen- and one-half stone. The armored knight looked the part of a Watchtower captain. The broken nose, penetrating brown eyes and scar on his forehead only half-hidden by the mail hood, made his look one of being unafraid. That was also good.

"Captain Thiralle, it is good to see you here with us."

Marco de Santi tried to sound upbeat. It didn't work.

"Your majesty, the Watchtower stands prepared and ready to assist the kingdom in whatever role you require of us."

Marco looked over at his wife. Queen Valentina de Santi looked royal and resolute. *Nothing less could be expected from the House of Rhodes,* Marco mused to himself. That was one of the countless reasons that he loved her. She had spirit. But she also had children.

"Captain, I appreciate that, as does the kingdom. Before we get into your role, I was wondering if you might offer the crown a personal favor."

Thiralle cocked his head to the side. The king had no need of asking a Watchtower captain for anything. He could simply command it.

"What is the service, sire?"

Marco smiled. The man was always business.

"Our daughter, Maria, is traveling. She was conducting some business in Udaass. She should be on her way home, currently in the approximate area of the border mountain pass running down into Tyna Town. She has an armed escort with her, but might my wife and I impose upon you to send some Watchtower men to find and retrieve her? Your men will move with more ease than our soldiers."

Thiralle looked over at the queen with an equally resolute expression.

"Consider it done. They will leave before midday."

The queen smiled softly.

"You are too kind, sir."

Thiralle nodded but said nothing. Marco decided to get to the business end of things.

"So, what news do you have of the battle in Neeron?"

"The army of Ayr, led by the queen but commanded by Stas Bok, their real military leader, marched straight south to Karacase. They didn't work on securing the countryside, they moved straight to the capital. After Karacase fell, and the king was dead, did they look to securing the countryside. That directly implies that this is not a war of just cause or resolution. This is about taking kingdoms."

Marco nodded in affirmation.

"I completely agree."

The big Watchtower captain slid the mail cover off of his head, letting it lay on his shoulders.

"The question, sire, is why?"

Marco looked at Captain Thiralle with a wise and fatherly expression. He walked several paces to a desk and reached over a stack of correspondences to pick up his scepter – the ornately carved rod which was the sign of his sovereign right to rule.

"She's coming for this, captain."

Valentina gave Marco a knowing look that the Watchtower captain didn't understand.

"If she plans on taking over your kingdom, then yes, that would make sense."

Marco smiled as one would at a small child.

"No, she wants this, specifically. That's why she didn't waste any time in Neeron. They just had the misfortune of being in the way of her getting here."

Rolant Thiralle didn't understand, but he hadn't been raised on the stories that Marco had been raised on.

"I don't understand, sire."

"I know. It's a story, folklore really, that takes time to explain. There will be plenty of time for such things in the coming days."

Rolant was about ready to press the king for a better answer when the door opened. One of the many regents of the capital stepped in slowly and gained the attention of the king.

"Your war council is assembled in the map room, sire."

Marco de Santi nodded once and looked at Captain Thiralle squarely.

"Time to go to work then."

The king of Oban turned and headed for the door, followed by the queen and the Watchtower captain. He walked soundly down the stone hallways, turning one corner and then another until coming to a large set of double doors stationed at the end of a hallway. Opening both doors at the same time, the king stepped into his castle war room with the surety of a man who was in charge.

Large windows on three sides, which looked out over the serene northern waters of the Halcyon Sea, filled the room with a warm light. On all open wall space, maps were hung showing the various sections of the kingdom in detail. In the center of the room a large table was stationed holding a scaled replica of the Kingdom of Oban. All of its cities and natural features were reproduced faithfully, making it Marco's preferred planning tool. Around the table, three military generals from Oban's army and two naval admirals stood confidently. The king walked to his usual spot and the Watchtower captain moved to a space at the far end of the table. The queen walked to a sunlit corner and stationed herself comfortably in a high back lounging chair. Though arguably the single most powerful person in all of the lands, defending a kingdom was a king's job, so the queen sat quietly and deferred to her husband.

The king looked around the table and collected the looks of his field leaders. They all seemed confident enough.

"Okay, men, let's hear the plan."

Looking over at his lead general, as if to say that the floor was his, the king nodded once soundly. The man pointed to a spot between the city of Orba and the edge of the kingdom to the north of it.

"Ayr's army marches due south from Karacase, pointing them to a border crossing near Orba. We will meet them there. The army will set up on the high ridge outside of the city, which runs straight with the border for some thirty miles or more. The opposition will not be able to easily maneuver around our defenses. The high ground gives us the tactical advantage in terrain, as well as adding distance to both our archers and our cannons."

The king nodded with a definitive bob of the head. The plan made sense to him.

"Good. Go on."

The lead military man looked to the man next to him, who took up the presentation.

"With the men and women which have mobilized from the northern reaches of the kingdom and the mountain folk, we will put approximately 12,000 soldiers in front of them when they arrive. It is a larger force than the estimated 10,000 troops that Ayr has collected. It is also more than we really need to fill the high ground ahead of them. We will be more than a match for Ayr when it arrives."

The king stepped in and looked at the spot on the map surrounding the city of Orba. He looked at the mountain passes which ran to the city from both the mountain mines and the highlands of Neeron. Looking back up at the second man, he nodded for him to continue.

"Sire, the southern forces and the Watchtower garrison will stand in the open lands north of Stone Cliff and defend the entrance onto the capital should the northern forces fail. If a follow-on engagement becomes necessary, the city guard will secure the capital itself."

The man speaking turned to look at the naval admiral standing beside him. The naval commander nodded and took over the briefing.

"The navy has been recalled and is being refitted for combat as we speak. We have enough functioning vessels to secure the waters around both the causeway bridge and the capital island."

"Does Ayr have a naval force to be concerned about?"

The king was looking over at a map of Ayr and its defined coastline.

"Not to speak of, sire. They have never required one, save for defending ports against pirates. It is unknown, however, where the Kingdom of Udaass will factor itself into the battles. They have been assembling their naval force ever since Ayr began assembling its army. King Diego de Paz has made no intentions regarding where he appears to stand in all of this. That, along with the opportunistic nature of pirates, makes it prudent to have the navy at full strength."

Marco scratched his beard and looked over at his wife.

"If the navy does fail us, the capital is on an island for a reason. We can always use other ways."

Valentina nodded emphatically but stayed quiet. It was obvious from the looks of the others in the room that they did not understand. That was fine with Marco.

"So, do we prevail?" Marco asked, looking back at the man who had started the briefing.

"We do, sire."

The remaining members of the war council nodded in agreement.

"And, saying you're wrong, how are we provisioned?"

"The capital can stand alone for at least five solid months, sire."

Five months, Marco thought. He had read of sieges in the previous age lasting five years or more. Still, no war had ever happened in this age. Who knew what would really happen?

"Very good. Let us be about the remaining tasks and preparations."

The queen stood, which was the sign that everyone could now leave, whether they wanted to or not. They did so without further questions or comments.

Chapter Forty-Five

Quinn pulled himself up onto the sandy shore of the island and rolled over to sit. Debris from their ship could be seen halfway down the shoreline. A whole line of objects could also be seen still bobbing around outside of the tideline, trying to work their way toward dry land.

Looking out at the flotsam and jetsam in the water, Quinn decided that everything which had taken place since they had spoken with the old woman was a disaster of one type or another. He and Bernard had been able to make their way back to Tyna Town with the princess in tow. That part hadn't gone so badly. The rest of it had been downhill.

The news of war had been fully established in the gossip stream of the town upon their return. All of the locals were fearful. With Tyna Town sitting just inside the Neeron border, it was possible that they could see fighting. Strangers, all strangers, were now looked on with suspicion. Considering the town was a waystation of travelers, suspicion hung heavy in the air.

Bernard and Quinn did their level best to barter passage south to Castropol, the capital city of Oban, but no ships were going south. Getting the princess back to her home seemed a nonstarter with the sailors of the port.

Quinn considered heading north back to Asturias, but that, too, seemed problematic. If Shadowman had found them there, others would as well. That would put the princess in danger. It was probably a bad idea.

Plan three came in the form of pirates. Pirates weren't to be trusted, but they also weren't afraid of much. Quinn knew that Oban kept excellent relations with the Mining Isles to the direct south. The Mining Isles could be a good place to deposit the princess for a short time. She could wait there until she could be returned to her home. The Mining Guild would certainly look after the crown princess of their nearest neighbor. And the Great Bank was neutral in the affairs between kingdoms. Neutral ground was a great place to deposit their charge.

Finding a pirate captain that would take the eight-day sail south across the Halcyon Sea was another matter. There were four pirate ships in port when they arrived, and they ended up talking to all of the captains before finding one who was amenable. Considering the times that were upon them and weather currently out at sea, the price had been steeper than Bernard had wanted to pay, but in the end, pay they did.

The first five days out of Tyna Town had been without worry. The ship had made good time. Bernard and Quinn sat on deck and passed the time by staying out of the way. The princess sat in a small cabin which the captain had provided, and sulked. She had been pouting ever since the battle in the pass. *But that was what spoiled children did*, Quinn considered. So, he let her pout.

On day six, the seas turned decidedly bad. Winds picked up to the point that the sails had to be halved. Waves lashed to ship repeatedly, each hit shaking the ship to its core. Somewhere in the middle of day seven, the mast snapped from the strain. The pirates attempted to cut it free and save the ship, but the weight of the beam in the swells pulled the hull over on her side and she flooded.

With their transport officially going to the bottom, and no sign of calm seas appearing in the immediate future, it was time for every man to be for themselves, princesses included. Quinn collected their charge and Bernard found a good chunk of floating ship debris to ride on. The three of them, plus a pair of pirates who seemed the good sort, clambered up on the chunk of ship and used it as a lifeboat. The section of deck was big enough to hold all five of them, even with the angry ocean swells.

Midway through day eight the storm blew itself out and the famous blue skies of the Halcyon Sea returned. The softer trade winds were still pushing south and the group rode the current in whatever direction that it wanted them to go. Sometime in the middle of day ten, land was sighted. The pirates conferred and decided decisively that it was the island of Dyme, Capital Island of the Mining Isles. The good news lifted everyone's spirits.

The slab of ship being used as a lifeboat made its way on the current to a spot about a half-mile from shore and turned in a pronounced arc to the right. With the turn, it began running parallel to shore, along the outside of the island's coral shelf. Deciding that the easy part of the journey was over, both pirates dove in and began swimming for shore. Quinn collected his wrapped-up cloak and bow, left the heavy axe, and did the same. Bernard pushed the princess into the water and dove in after her, not waiting for the kicking and screaming to begin.

Sitting on the beach, Quinn looked up the shoreline to see the two pirates now walking in his direction. They seemed as pleased with themselves as they would be on any other day. *Being a pirate was a strange life*, Quinn thought, *but maybe not so removed from his own*?

Looking back out at the surf line, Bernard could be seen dragging the waterlogged princess along. Neither of them looked to be having an especially good time in the surf. But they would both be onshore soon enough. That was all that really mattered.

At the standing point, Bernard separated himself from angry princess and began marching toward shore. Getting dry sand under his boots, he walked to where Quinn was sitting and plopped down beside him.

"No. More. Princesses."

Quinn looked at his unamused friend.

"I hate ships."

Maria de Santi, Crown Princess of Oban, crawled up out of the surf looking every bit a drowned rat, and began coughing the seawater out of her lungs. The pair of pirates, now within proper range, waved hello. Bernard waved back. Quinn looked at the debris in the surf line and cursed quietly.

The pirates wandered up to where the threesome had collected and stood in an open space of the loosely forming circle. They looked at the group, trying not to laugh at the princess who was still expelling saltwater.

"Strange. Most people living along the coast of Oban learn to swim quite well," one pirate said to the other.

"Perhaps she's from the interior? Orba or Lugo, maybe?"

Bernard decided that he couldn't hold back any longer and began to laugh. The princess put on a decidedly unhappy expression, which made one pirate nod to the other.

"Yup, looks like the interior."

"I will have you know that I reside in the Castle of Castropol, on the island of Land's End, thank you very much!"

Bernard was happy to exact a small bit of emotional revenge for the sustained beating he had taken in the surf.

"Living on an island and still can't swim?"

"I haven't gotten to it yet," Maria de Santi said in a huff.

Bernard considered the princess a second time. Sitting in the sunshine of the beach, soaking wet, her hair all matted against her face, she had a remotely pleasant quality. Well, if she wasn't the solid pain in the ass that she was.

Quinn had finally regained his calm and found his former frame of mind by the time the jesting was over.

"Seems to be a consensus that this island is Dyme. If it is, where does the civilization hide?"

Pirate one looked at pirate two, and both of them pointed over their shoulder at the island's interior.

"The capital city sits in a protected harbor on the south side of the island. Pretty much straight south from here. The mines are set along the mid-island range and flow down into an interior valley. We will want to go around that area. The sentries and guards that watch over the mines don't take to outsiders."

Quinn thought about it for a moment.

"So, along the beach then?"

Pirate two shook his head.

"That's the long way round. Dyme is pretty big, for an island. It would take a number of days to walk around the outside. Probably best to move down the beach a ways and then take the inland roads along the lowlands."

Bernard was looking past the group, at the lush tropical jungle and considering that their two pirate friends knew an awful lot about the island, when he spotted movement in the treeline.

"We have company."

Everyone in the group turned to look at the treeline up at the beachhead behind them as a dozen armed men appeared. They were all similarly attired and appeared to Quinn as to be militia from the capital guard that the pirates had spoken of.

Pirate one looked at pirate two.

"That didn't take long, did it?"

"Nope," the other commented, "faster than I would have thought. They must have already been over this way."

Bernard was about to ask a question when the guards advanced and readied arms for combat. The leader of the men took in the collection and made a face.

"Pirates?"

Pirates one and two both shrugged and raised their hands.

"We're pirates."

The guard commander looked at them and nodded in return.

"None of your lot here, right now, but you'll soon find a ship in the capital. Probably going to want to head that way."

The pirates thanked the commander and smiled as the armed man redirected his gaze onto the others.

"And what's the story with you three?"

"I'm Quinn. He's Bernard. She's Crown Princess Maria de Santi from Oban. We were traveling with the pirates on our way to Dyme City. There's war on its way to Oban. We were heading here to drop the princess someplace safe," Quinn let out in a huffy tone that the commander didn't take to.

"Maybe you are. Maybe you're not. Either way, we'll sort it out in Dyme. Now, surrender your arms or bleed out here on the beach."

Bernard looked to Quinn for the go sign.

"There's only a dozen of them, and they seem the common variety."

Quinn pushed the cloak wrapped longbow away from his body with his boot and tossed the big boot knife on top of the pile.

"I don't have it in me, right now. Let's just go to the capital."

Bernard shrugged his shoulders and pulled his swords free in a non-threatening manner as the commander looked on with a smug expression.

Again, the old woman's generosity continued to pay dividends for Bernard and Quinn. The forced march across the middle of the island took the majority of two full days. Upon getting to the capital city, they were searched and questioned. Their reputation as men of mystery and intrigue didn't help them in their current situation. Their weapons, and the large stack of Ayr gold they were still carrying, painted them as agents of the queen and not do-gooders out to help a random princess. They were separated from their belongings and dumped in a central cell of the Dyme dungeon. The princess, for her part, was recognized by regents of the Mining Guild and promptly escorted to a guest room in the castle proper.

Quinn sat on the floor of the cell with his back against the rock wall and looked through the heavy steel bars of the cell door down a sunlit hallway. Bernard paced about casually, taking in all of the idiosyncrasies of their new home.

"Well, I guess one thing's as true as time," Bernard said, a basically happy tone in his voice.

"Hmm."

"No good deed goes unpunished."

Quinn nodded.

"That's a fact. No more good deeds for a while."

Bernard laughed and continued looking around.

"So, we're stuck in a dungeon, in a strange land, unbelieved, with no weapons, and awaiting an uncertain fate. Conclusion?"

Quinn shrugged, rubbing his shoulder against a protrusion in the stone wall behind him.

"Must be a full moon or something."

Bernard laughed again as a dungeon guard came along and wrapped a large wooden war club on the bars, signaling them to shut up. Bernard looked at the guard and then back at Quinn.

"You're an optimist, old chum."

Quinn closed his eyes and sighed.

"I hate ships."

Chapter Forty-Six

Cosimo Agosti rode out of Orba with purpose. The normal traffic of the area had been replaced by the war machine of Oban. A not-so-tall but thickly built man, Cosimo tipped in at five-feet-seven-inches, with a heavy mass just shy of sixteen stone, all of it layered muscle. Short, dark brown hair and a trimmed beard showed the youthful face of a pit fighter, and the deep brown eyes showed someone who knew more than they spoke about.

The unquestioned leader of the Oban army, Cosimo Agosti headed straight for the battle line. Leaders led from the front. They inspired the men and women in their ranks by not asking anyone to do anything that they weren't already doing. Cosimo understood the effect of good leadership on troops. He understood the rallying effect it possessed to overcome the fear of battle. He had tested himself in battle. He was unafraid. Many of his troops, however, had not been tested. They understood that if others were standing up, that they should as well. His show of strength out front would help them to continue to be strong and to charge when needed.

The powerful soldier rode up to the ridge overlooking the slope down in terrain which led to the border with Neeron. Inspecting the scene, he could see men putting in the layered defenses of tipped poles and trenches meant to hobble Ayr's cavalry troops attempting to cross the battlefield. The defenses would also have the initial effect of funneling the advancing infantry troops, as the front facing soldiers would take the easiest path into battle that they could find.

Walking up the inclined plain which led to the ridgeline, Cosimo could see Count Luca Perin, the Regent of Lugo, walking with Sara Zanon, the Countess of Orba. They appeared to be discussing the defenses. The slim and trim beauty looked out of place in the wild scene of hard knocks men and women. At five-feet-ten-inches tall and just the pleasing side of ten stone, with a mane of blonde hair running to the small of her back, and blue eyes one could swim in, the countess was a touch too young to have acquired her station without being royalty or aristocracy. Truth be told, she had been given the regency of Orba because she possessed a large information gathering network which kept her ahead of everyone else. With that information she seemed to possess the natural ability to find and maintain neutrality. The last bit alone had made her well-liked with the royal set. Every time Cosimo looked at her, he was sure that she was plotting something, which she usually was.

For a woman of her station, beauty and youth, she should have been coupled long ago, yet Sara Zanon was unwed. There were rumors that she kept many lovers scattered about, and that they were the backbone of her information gathering system. That type of tactic didn't bother Cosimo in the least. At least she paid for her information up front.

The leader of Oban's army dismounted his horse and flexed the muscles under his mail and plate to get rid of the kinks. He untied the stays that held his long cloak in place and let it slide off his back. Turning it into a loose roll, he placed it over his saddle, letting the heavy wolf's fur shoulder covering hang off the far side of the horse. The cloak, a holdover from his mountain heritage, kept the heat inside his metal armor. Down in the capital it was a touch warm but acceptable. Here, on the wheat covered plains of the north, it was far too warm to be comfortable.

Seeing Oban's combat leader on the field, Count Luca Perin motioned up the hill in his direction and began walking. The countess followed his lead and they made their way to the top of the ridgeline within minutes.

"Lady Zanon, Lord Perin, I'm pleased to see you engaged in preparations. Where do we stand?"

Agosti's question was directed, and obviously aimed at Perin, though he left it open to the pair.

"We are all but ready to assemble the main force. We were making a check of the battlefield obstacles before collecting up all of the craftsmen and women."

"Status of the opposition?"

This question was definitely oriented toward the countess.

"Information says that the main army of Ayr had left Karacase five days back and is marching due south toward our location. The front of the column should arrive around sunset, two days hence. It will take most of that night for the entire army to arrive."

General Agosti looked around and nodded approvingly. The road south wasn't over-wide, so Ayr would have a long column of soldiers and equipment. A long time for Ayr to fully assemble could be good and bad for Oban. It allowed Agosti time to instill fear and doubt by a show of force. It also allowed Ayr time to calculate before the battle began. Oh well, it couldn't really be helped.

"What does your initial layout consist of?"

Luca Perin scratched his chin. This was the sticking point. He had won more battles than he had lost and was a good military planner. He, like Agosti, was also unafraid to be the first one into the fray. That being said, the two men thought differently. They saw the battlespace differently. The general would either like his plan or not. Which one? Luca had no idea.

"The ridgeline is a broad, basically straight affair, allowing us to show a large presence of troops. We have sixty companies of infantry which will be laid out two-deep in a double course of thirty. That will be backed up with a full ten companies of heavy cavalry. Archers behind the cavalry for support, and some forty companies of bowmen and women."

General Agosti nodded, listening and thinking as he scanned the wheat field-turned-battle-zone.

"Since the ridgeline has a small amount of fall off on both sides, we have cannons and archers at both ends. They will be used to push the Ayr forces back toward the middle, should they decide to try and flank."

"How many cannons?"

"Eight per side, with two companies of archers for support."

Agosti smiled and Perin exhaled.

"It sounds like we are as ready as we can be. Let the workers finish their work and then we can assemble all of the commanders for a council."

"Yes, General Agosti, right away."

Where Luca Perin and Sara Zanon were regents and controlled the land, they were completely outranked by the leader of the army. From the moment that General Agosti arrived, he was in charge.

Cosimo looked out over the descending slope a second time. He had met Stas Bok in the past. He was as good as they came. Would a man with Bok's tactical ability really march his army into place, in column formation, potentially during the dark of night? Cosimo certainly wouldn't. The defense had every advantage in that situation. So, what would Bok do, and when would he do it?

Out on the southern plains of Neeron, Stas Bok had been wondering the exact same thing. He had been riding his horse at a moderate pace, not wanting to unduly work either his mount or the men and women marching behind him. The current day had been nice for a march. Sunny and warm with a breeze that moved the fragrance of the fields and woods around with it. Stas had enjoyed the ride south. As the heat of their engagements had increased, his joy of his natural surroundings had also increased. Hard to say exactly why. Maybe he was just old and now had a greater appreciation for such things? Maybe life became sweeter as it became more fragile? He wasn't a Master and didn't know about such things. He just knew that he enjoyed what he enjoyed.

Riding through a small narrow in the treeline that separated one track of farmlands from another, Stas came out into a wide-open area which held the border of Neeron and Oban. As suspected, it was completely empty of people. That made good sense to Stas. He wouldn't have picked this spot either.

Spearing his mount mildly in the ribs, he trotted out ahead of the rest to a spot in the middle of the open expanse, just on the Neeron side of the line. He made a wide sweeping arm movement in a big circle and then swept his hand down, pointing to the ground. It was the army's stop here sign, and the column of following troops did just that.

Stas waved to one of the senior leaders and the man rode over to join him. The queen, coming into the opening with the column, did the same. The senior man rode up next to Stas Bok and paused for instructions.

"Pass the word. We are stopping, not camping. Don't unpack anything. No more fires than necessary. Bread and cheese over meat and ale. I want every soldier formed and ready to continue well before the sun comes up again. Understand?"

The man nodded authoritatively.

"Good. Make it happen."

Stas' wagon appeared and a boy came trudging over with a wooden step so he might dismount. Stas pointed the boy toward the queen and he instantly turned his direction. After the monarch was lowered, Stas climbed down and bent himself in several directions to loosen the tight muscles under his armor.

"Why pause here?" the queen asked inquisitively. "Why not continue on into Oban?"

Stas Bok pulled his helmet off and ran a hand through a matted mess of hair.

"Did you spend any amount of time in Old King Jasper's war room?"

The queen nodded slowly, in an unsure manner.

"The old fellow had a very good map of his kingdom and surrounding lands laid out across his war table. See, if we cross the border here, we will quickly move onto road that narrows, so we can only move in column formation. That column will be about ten-men wide or so, which will turn your army into a great big snake crawling its way along through the woods."

The queen nodded again, understanding that she needed to keep up with her military education.

"When you exit the snake section, the road opens into a wide plain which quickly runs uphill to a pronounced ridgeline. The ridgeline is a very defensible point, and most definitely where Oban's army will choose to meet us."

"Go on," the queen said in a more respectful voice than normal. This was a lesson and she wanted to absorb it.

"At the pace the army is currently moving, we will get to the open battlefield below the ridgeline sometime into the dark of night, which means that the army will be the entire night moving out of the snake and into its basic formation. Doing such a thing, in the pitch black of night in the woods, is good for them and bad for us. It allows them to attack us under the cover of darkness, on ground that they know and can travel without torchlight. It also means that we enter the main battle being marched and unrested. So, we stop here for the evening. Then we move into position in the light of the morning, when we can get a better sense for things. Understand, majesty?"

"I do. When you say it, it makes perfect sense. Do you think that they see it the same way?"

Stas Bok nodded.

"Their leader is a younger man named Cosimo Agosti. Mountain bred and mean as an old brown bear. He's very, very good at war. He would do the same thing if in our position."

The queen nodded.

"Okay, no fires. No meat tonight."

"Get some good rest, majesty. Tomorrow will be a long and decisive day for you."

Stas turned and waved to the boys waiting by the wagon. Some ran over and immediately began unsaddling the horse. Another wrestled over his heavy chair so that he might sit down. The old general sat down and watched on as the army continued to funnel into the open area around him.

The night that followed was short and warm. Stas was thankful that it was warm. He picked himself up from the spot he had chosen on the ground next to a wagon wheel and began the task of loosening sore muscles. It was going to be a long day ahead. The boys had been at it even earlier than he. They had already packed up his chair and left him a loaf of bread next to a pitcher of water. They were currently saddling his big warhorse, and dusk was just breaking on the edge of the world. Several of his captains approached; Each one looking like they had enjoyed the same rest as he.

"Good morning. You lot look like I feel."

All of them laughed. It was the way of military men to put off problems with levity. Stas smiled at them knowingly.

"It's probably time to get this show on the road, as they say. As soon as everyone is standing and formed, we march."

A round of various affirmative comments came from the captains who moved off toward the troops immediately. Stas called one of the men back. The captain of an infantry company turned back, ready to do whatever his leader asked of him.

"Let your lieutenants form up your soldiers this time. Grab two or three of your quietest and most cunning and head out ahead of us. I want you to sneak out to the edge of the battlefield clearing and get a good look at it. I want to know where they put their cannons and their archers. Understand?"

The man gave a single affirmative reply.

"Good. Now, be quick and quiet, and get moving."

The man ran off toward the way he had originally come. Stas blinked a couple times in the easing dim and reached for the bread with a sigh.

It took about an hour, but quickly enough Stas was back on his horse and moving slowly into the Kingdom of Oban. Stas looked down at the ground as he rode across the border. There was no turning back now. All of the pretenses of previous days were officially done. Now, it was open warfare between kingdoms. This was the reshaping of the map. Invading Neeron could be explained away by the regents. Invading Oban was a wholly different matter.

Stas had intentionally placed the queen and her fancy-boy private guard behind two companies of heavy cavalry for protection during the final leg of the march. It was the smart thing to do. Who knew he might have it all figured wrong?

Sure enough, right where the map had predicted, the terrain became woodland and the roadway narrowed to a cart path. They were at the mouth of the snake. Stas continued on at his even pace. Stopping here wasn't going to solve anything. Deciding better on it, he drew up the reins and paused. He waved back for a junior officer. A cavalry lieutenant came up at a trot, looking ready.

"Send word back down the column. I want a company of infantry to move through the woods on each side of the road, as side cover. They may have ambush troops in the woods."

The lieutenant turned without a word and galloped off. Stas stood steady for some thirty minutes, giving the infantry time to get where he wanted them to be. Deciding they were good, he started on again. The going was slow and the trees helped to hide the rising sun.

He had moved about halfway through the congestion of the woodlands when his infantry captain-turned-scout reappeared on the edge of the path by a tree. Stas paused as the man came up and spoke in a low tone. Stas started the report with an exasperated look but turned to a wry smile by the end. He exchanged some hand gestures with the captain and started riding forward again.

About four good hours after full light, Stas Bok rode out of the snake and into the edge of the wide-open space of the battlefield ahead. It was exactly as he would have done it. He could see the layer of spiked poles and trenches set to hobble the cavalry and funnel the infantry. Sweeping his head from side to side, he could just take in the cannons at the far end of the ridgeline. They were obviously there to stop a potential flanking action. That was a smart move on Cosimo's part. Or maybe that was Luca Perin's touch? He was a fine military commander as well.

The Ayr army funneled in behind Stas and moved in an automated fashion to their normal formation places. The commander of the invading force sat in his saddle and summed up the defensive force ahead of them. It was a huge force. Deep with infantry and heavy cavalry. He couldn't see any archers, but he was absolutely sure that they were there, and en masse. Two things became immediately evident to Stas. First, the man standing defiantly out in front of the forces on the ridgeline was General Cosimo Agosti. He was directly to the left of Count Luca Perin. Oban had obviously assembled the main army to come out and meet him. The second thing that became obvious quite immediately was that they were probably outnumbered. If Oban's army was comprised anywhere close to his own, then the army on the ridgeline was definitely larger than Ayr's. They also possessed a terrain advantage, and they knew the land better than he did.

Stas Bok looked up at Cosimo Agosti and sighed contentedly. He probably was never going to get that retirement.

The queen rode up next to him and paused. Her eyes were slightly wide, taking in the size of the opposition. The two sat quietly on their mounts, looking at the opposition, as their own forces slowly moved into position behind them.

Not being able to take the silence of impending doom any longer, Anastasia looked over at Stas Bok. He was as calm as any person she had ever seen. How could he be so calm?

"Well, general? What do you think?"

Stas looked down at the ground beneath him, understanding that once the carnage started, that ground would quickly turn from grass to a mix of mud and blood.

"Well, those big cannons you were wanting? You probably won't be needing those as soon as you thought."

Printed in the United States
by Baker & Taylor Publisher Services